UNDYING

Books by V.K. Forrest

Eternal
Undying

Published by Kensington Publishing Corporation

Undying

V.K. Forrest

KENSINGTON BOOKS
http://www.kensingtonbooks.com

KENSINGTON BOOKS are published by

Kensington Publishing Corp.
850 Third Avenue
New York, NY 10022

All Kensington titles, imprints, and distributed lines are available at special quantity discounts for bulk purchases for sales promotion, premiums, fund-raising, educational, or institutional use.

Special book excerpts or customized printings can also be created to fit specific needs. For details, write or phone the office of the Kensington Special Sales Manager: Attn.: Special Sales Department. Kensington Publishing Corp., 850 Third Avenue, New York, NY 10022. Phone: 1-800-221-2647.

Kensington and the K logo Reg. U.S. Pat. & TM Off.

ISBN-13: 978-0-7582-1717-2
ISBN-10: 0-7582-1717-X

First Printing: December 2008
10 9 8 7 6 5 4 3 2 1

Chapter 1

He stood beneath the lengthening shadows of the Acropolis, high on the hilltop over the city of Athens, and watched as the last rays of sunlight faded. With the coming of darkness, he could feel the evil of the night slither in on its belly, much like the quarry he sought tonight.

Arlan walked quickly through the Agora, keeping his head down, leaving behind the noisy tourists boarding their tour buses.

Two weeks ago, thousands of miles away in the little U.S. town of Clare Point, the vote had gone against a human by the name of Robert Romano. With the plunging of twelve daggers into an ancient oak table, the man's fate had been sealed. For more than a decade, the pedophile, a monster who dealt in the underground sale of child sex slaves, had been pursued across several continents by law enforcement. Robert Romano, known by multiple aliases, had recently made the FBI's most wanted list after the abduction of a five-year-old from a grocery store in the suburbs of Detroit. At the present time, the FBI did not know his whereabouts. Romano was careful, and he was clever.

Not clever enough.

In twenty minutes, forty-six-year-old Romano would be waiting at a designated spot on the southern end of the Agora, a spot that came to life after dark, both with ghosts of the past and the haunts of the present. The human would be there to accept a cash payment for the delivery of two male children, ages six and nine, who were currently being held in an apartment two blocks away. Delivery of the children was to be made once Romano received his cash in small currency euros. The unfortunate buyer would not receive his merchandise because Arlan would be waiting. A clean-up crew would rescue the children and see that the buyer was arrested by local police. Romano would no longer be the authorities' concern.

Now almost dark, the warm evening air had grown thick with the sounds and scents of the ancient city. It was funny how cities all smelled the same, sounded the same, when Arlan closed his eyes. This could have been any street in any city in the world in the last thousand years.

He inhaled deeply, lifting his chin, flaring his nostrils. Someone was roasting meat in one of the nearby restaurants that catered to the tourists . . . lamb. Elsewhere, sewage overflowed. He caught the hint of a woman's cheap perfume on the air, although he walked alone in the twilight. Embedded in the night air was also the sour scent of human body odor. The fetid bouquet of fleas feasting on rodents.

In the distance, beyond the ruins, Arlan heard doors opening and closing. Footsteps, both heavy and light, echoed through the gathering fog. Over time, the sputter of car and motorbike engines had replaced the rhythm of wooden cart and carriage wheels, but in his mind, they were still somehow the same.

These were the sounds and smells of humanity. For better. For worse. Despite the ugliness of much of it, Arlan longed to be a part of this world. He was jealous of the man roasting lamb for gyros on the street corner, the woman slamming the window to muffle the harsh words she flung at her cheating lover. Arlan would never know the mundane life of a mortal.

At the sound of shrill laughter, he tensed. Despite the cover of darkness, standing here in human form, he was vulnerable. He gazed intently in the direction of the noisier, busier Plaka, blocks away, where tourists flooded the streets eager to sample the moussaka and ouzo. Eager to buy their trinkets to mark their journey, they had no idea of the evil that lurked in the shadows or the salvation about to descend on two helpless children.

Arlan's partner was late. He checked his cell phone, noting the time. No call and Regan was twenty minutes late.

Arlan worked his jaw in indecision.

The plan had been for Regan, pretending to be the "customer," to meet Romano at the Areopagus. Arlan would serve as the lookout. Regan was to lure Romano into a secluded area amid the ruins and there, the execution would be carried out as ordered by the High Council. Arlan and Regan would carry it out together. Two daggers. Two were required by primordial sept law.

But Regan wasn't here and time was running out. If Romano slipped out of their hands, there was no way to say when the planets and moons would align again. There was no way to know when the opportunity to catch him would offer itself again, or how many more children would lose their innocence in the intervening time.

The coarse laughter of the woman grew louder, closer. Arlan heard a second woman's voice. They were speaking Greek. Both were drunk, or high, or both. He caught a flash of short skirt and long bare legs. Prostitutes. After dark, when the museums closed and tour groups were led to the safe streets of the Plaka, the Athens underworld came to life here. From the shadowy Areopagus situated beneath the lights of the Acropolis, one could see the whole city. In this place, one could buy drugs, sex . . . and even children.

Arlan made the decision. There was no time to call the council. No time to await further instructions. The sept had been watching this bastard for eighteen months. They couldn't afford to let him go. The Kahill sept's duty to God would not allow it.

One moment Arlan was a thirty-something guy in jeans and a black leather jacket and the next he transformed into a hundred-pound canine with a mangy spotted coat and yellow eyes. The physical morph came easily to him, like slipping on a worn leather glove.

The moment the morph was complete, Arlan felt the change in his psyche. Judgment grew hazier. In this animal body, he lived for the moment. Surrounded by the scent of dangers, he had to force his man-brain to remain in control of the beast. He could feel that control stretched taut, thin and tight as a wire.

Arlan slinked behind a rock and darted across the footpath, behind the women, his tail brushing a skirt. One of the prostitutes cursed him, first in Greek, then Italian, but they continued walking. Hundreds of packs of wild dogs roamed the streets of Athens. The locals gave them no notice. Arlan knew he could blend in with the others.

Knowing he had a few minutes before Romano would appear, Arlan had time to assess the area and determine how he could fulfill the mission alone. He wondered if it would be safer to appear as a man or as he was now, a four-footed predator. He trotted lightly up a slight, rocky incline, skirting the silvery light cast from the Acropolis, blending into the shadows of the olive trees.

It was fully dark now and while Arlan was not a superstitious man, mentally, he crossed himself. At night, in ancient places like these, the haunts came out. A man or beast could do his best to ignore them, but there was no denying their presence. The coarse yellow hair along his spine bristled and he caught a whiff of something that was not living, but not quite dead. Out of the corner of one rheumy eye he saw a misty human form floating just above the pathway.

Some said ghosts held no real presence, that they were only impressions left from the past. Arlan didn't know what they were; he only knew that he did not like this feeling of being watched. He had experienced similar encounters in several places in recent months; the Coliseum in Rome, Stonehenge in England, and the blood-soaked battlefield of Culloden in the Highlands of Scotland.

Bypassing the wispy spook, Arlan kept his head down, letting his long tongue loll. His yellow eyes took in his surroundings. With his long muzzle and enhanced sense of smell, he observed as only God's four-footed creatures could observe.

Stones pinched the pads of his feet as he followed a path tread heavily by tourists in the daytime. The Agora had once been a marketplace, a public area that served as an integral part of the ancient Greek city-state. It had not only offered a place to trade, but it also served as a forum to its citizens. Here, men once gathered to buy and sell commodities and also to discuss business, politics, and current events. Here was where Greek democracy first came to light, setting an example to other great cities in the ancient world.

At the far end, the rocky hill overlooking the Agora was where Arlan would meet Romano. The area of the Agora known as the Areopagus had been the sacred meeting place of the Greek prime council, which had once combined judicial and legislative functions in the fifth and sixth centuries BC. Much later, the apostle Paul was said to have stood on the same rocky hill and preached to early Christians.

A holy place. A haunted place.

Arlan caught the scent of another dog on the night air and thrust out his muzzle. He twitched his black nose. Two dogs, three. More. A pack.

The muscles in Arlan's rear haunches tightened as the dogs approached. Arlan could become any of God's creatures, although he was better at some manifestations than others, and some were much more difficult to keep in check. Despite his experience, there was always a moment of panic when he encountered a creature of the species he'd manifested into. There was the chance they would know him for the charlatan that he was and attack him. It would be impossible for them to kill him because he had to be beheaded to die, but dog bites could lay a man up for weeks.

A whine and then a growl halted him. Out of a grove of stunted olive trees came three, four, five dogs, all his size or larger. A big gray with the pelt of a wolf led the pack of three females and a sullen young male. Animals did not speak, but they communicated. Members of the Kahill clan had some form of extrasensory perception; they could all, on some level, communicate with each other without speaking. Arlan's accompanying gift was the ability to communicate with animals.

The dogs' thoughts floated around him. They were simple. Primal.

Fear. Distrust. Hunger.

But there was also an inquisitiveness, particularly from the young male who hung back, guarding the rear.

The big gray parted from the pack, leaving the others behind to wait for his command. If he so ordered it, they would all attack at once. Arlan would not have the opportunity to morph back into a man before he was seriously injured.

The gray approached.

Arlan's hackles rose. He froze, eyes downcast. His breath came in short pants as he attempted to stifle the twinge of fear he felt deep in his canine bones.

One of the others, a black bitch with a torn ear, whined. She seemed to be the first to understand he meant them no harm. That he had no intention of usurping the pack leader's authority or taking his females.

The gray bared his teeth but made no sound. He wondered what Arlan was doing there. He recognized the stranger as one of them . . . and yet not one of them.

Arlan communicated that the pack had nothing to fear from him. That he was merely a traveler. He attempted to seem casual although he wasn't quite sure how that translated in dog language.

The gray met Arlan muzzle to muzzle and sniffed. Arlan kept his gaze downcast. To look into the leader's eyes would be a direct challenge.

I mean no harm, Arlan communicated firmly. While he had to make it clear he had no intention of taking the gray's place, he could not cower. To cower would show weakness, and the way of God's creatures is to kill the weakest. A form of natural selection, he supposed. *I simply wish to pass.*

Our territory. Why are you here? What do you want? Barely enough food for us.

On a journey. A mission. Passing through. I do not take what is not mine.

The gray looked Arlan directly in the face. Arlan slowly lifted his gaze. The powerful male's nose twitched. He was still attempting to assess Arlan, but he seemed to sense that Arlan was no threat to his pack.

I only wish to pass, Arlan repeated, lifting his gaze slightly. He still wasn't making direct eye contact, but now he was studying the gray in the same way that the dog was studying him.

The alpha male continued to stare, reminding Arlan of a game he used to play with other boys in the sept during mass or at a particularly boring family dinner. A version of Chicken. They would stare at each other until someone broke the spell; the first to look away was the loser and would later be subjected to juvenile name-calling and a healthy dose of shoving.

Pass, but continue on your way, the gray warned. *I see*

you again and I'll rip your throat out. My bitches will eat your innards.

Ouch. Arlan choked down the growl that rose in his throat and remained where he stood until the pack leader walked away. The other dogs slowly turned and loped after him.

Arlan exhaled heavily, his hot breath stinking in his nostrils. He could feel his heart pounding in his chest. He waited until he saw the last swish of tail disappear into the olive grove and then continued in the direction he had originally set out. His tongue lolled, testing the night air.

He only had time to circumnavigate the meeting place once before he had to get into place prior to Romano's arrival. As he peered over a rock, taking care with his footing, he silently cursed Regan. His partner had not been himself for the last year. This was not the first time he had not shown up at an appointed time and place on sept business. Arlan had been trying to cover for him longer than he knew he should because he was Fia's brother.

Thoughts of Fia made him smile. At least on the inside. He didn't think dogs could really smile.

Arlan loved Fia Kahill. He had been in love with her for at least a thousand years, but it was unrequited love. Or so she said. Right now she had a boyfriend. A *human* boyfriend. She told Arlan that although she and Arlan were occasionally lovers, she wasn't interested in a relationship with him. With any man in the sept. But Arlan was sure he was slowly working a chink in her iron resolve, had been for at least a century. Fia loved him. She just didn't know it yet.

So . . . to protect her, he protected her kid brother. As did Fia's other brother, Fin. As did other young men in the sept.

Arlan wondered now if he had been remiss in not calling Regan's shortcomings to the attention of the council. His irresponsible behavior was not only affecting him now, it was affecting others. It was affecting the sept's ability to do its job efficiently. They could not afford to have one of their own so far out of step.

Maybe it was time Arlan talked to the council, or at least Fia. It was time he stopped trying to talk to Regan. The warnings had obviously gone unheeded.

Arlan shifted his weight on his haunches and eyed the place where Romano would come for his money. It was a good spot for a man dealing in the human slave trade to make a transaction. The cover of darkness. No police around. Few people present and those who were would turn the other way if they saw anything suspicious. There would be no good citizens loitering in the shadows of the Areopagus, waiting to give their statement to the authorities.

Arlan smelled the human before he heard the footfalls. The stench of his evil flesh pierced the air even sharper than the intense, smoky aroma of his cigarette.

This was, indeed, an excellent place to commit a crime. But it was also a dangerous place for a man being hunted by a dog.

Or a vampire.

Chapter 2

Macy stood at the picture window and stared into the darkness. Into the nothingness. It was a little after midnight. She had a prestigious assignment for *Home & Garden* tomorrow. She should be asleep. But she couldn't sleep.

Not tonight. Not when she knew he was out there, restless. Agitated. She could feel his anxiety building and knew that when it reached its peak he would act.

She hugged herself. In the dark, there was barely a glimmer of her own reflection in the glass. A soft, humid breeze drifted through the pines, filtering through the open windowpanes.

She lived alone. The nearest house was half a mile away. She did not lock her doors at night or close her windows.

A death wish?

Macy studied the magnolia tree in her front yard. Her mother had always liked magnolias.

There had been a branch of magnolia blossoms on her mother's white coffin. No lilies or gardenias or the usual funeral flowers. Only magnolias.

Daisies on Mariah's.

Peonies on little Minnie's.

No flowers on her father's coffin. He hadn't been a flower kind of guy.

Macy walked away from the window that had never had the drapes pulled on it since she rented the cottage outside Charlottesville, Virginia, more than a year ago. She had nothing to hide. Her soul had been bared to the bitter world a long time ago.

She walked barefoot, in nothing but a pair of panties and a men's ribbed sleeveless T-shirt, through the dark house. It was only June but June was hot in Virginia.

The rooms were quiet except for the sound of her footsteps. She had no cat or dog to keep her company. She hadn't had a pet since she was fourteen.

Fritz had been sent to the pound. No one ever knew what happened to Snowcap, her sister's white Persian cat. Lost in the confusion of the police cars and emergency vehicles, Macy supposed.

Macy exhaled, fighting the dark cloud settling over her. As much as she hated herself for it, she couldn't stop thinking about Teddy.

She guessed he was thinking about her. That was why she couldn't sleep. There was this crazy, weird connection between them. Had been for as long as she could remember. And she couldn't escape it. It was like cancer, a cavernous, black hole eating her from the inside out.

She wandered through the living room into the office. When she had rented the home, the landlady had said the cozy room would make an excellent spare bedroom for family or friends. Macy had no family left. No friends.

The Apple logo on her open laptop glowed, but the room was as dark as the others in the house. The open window as naked.

From here, she could hear an owl hooting.

She sat down in her chair and flipped on the lamp. Soft light glowed in a circle on the old oak desk she had found at a yard sale. She hadn't bothered to refinish it, just removed the center drawer and added a keyboard drawer.

When she was here at the cottage, which wasn't all that frequently, she liked to use a full keyboard, sometimes even an additional monitor connected to her laptop. It gave her a better sense of proportions in the pictures she shot.

She touched the drawer and it glided out. She tapped the mouse beside the wireless keyboard and the laptop screen lit up. She had an instant message.

He had been waiting for her.

Her stomach tightened. He always seemed to know when she was awake in the middle of the night. Worse, she knew when he was.

You there?

The cursor pulsed.

She could feel him waiting.

She glanced at the dark window. He said he watched her. She had never known if he meant literally. Was tonight the night he was out there? Would tonight be the night he took her life and ended the last fourteen years of agonized waiting?

She looked back at the laptop screen.

Maybe tonight would be the night she took a stand. Maybe tonight she would ignore him. Maybe she'd even threaten that if he contacted her again, she would call the police.

It was an empty threat, of course. It would be nearly impossible to track him to a computer, to a location. He traveled for his work, too. He IM'd from Internet cafes, hotel business offices. Even truck stops had Internet access for their customers now. And when he contacted her from home, he said he used different laptops that he bought and sold regularly on the Internet. The stark truth was that even if she could convince the FBI that he was the nutcase they were looking for, it would be nearly impossible for them to track him down through his Internet use. The police would never find him. He knew it. She knew it.

The curser pulsed. Marceline? Teddy probed.

He always called her by her given name, as her father had. When Macy had complained as a child about being burdened by such a name, her father had promised she would, one day, grow into it in the same way that Minnie would grow into Minerva. Minnie hadn't lived long enough to grow into it.

Macy sat back in her chair, drawing her legs up, hugging her knees to her chest. She stared at the screen. Her hand ached to close the laptop. If she could just walk away . . . But she couldn't.

And he knew it.

Knees still drawn to her chest, she typed with one finger. Why won't you leave me alone?

Because I can't, he replied.

Why don't you just kill me, then?

I don't want to kill you. I want to love you.

She drew her hand back and stared at the words. This was love? Killing her family? Stalking her for more than a decade?

Bastard. Her index finger flew over the keys and then she pulled her hand back.

Whore.

She stared at the screen again. Thought for a minute and then typed. Why can't you sleep?

I hear her.

Is she speaking loudly tonight?

So loud I can hear nothing else.

Macy's lower lip trembled. What he was saying didn't make sense. The full moon had come and gone. What is she saying? she asked.

You know. The usual. She's upsetting me. She's making me upset. You know what happens when she upsets me. . . .

Teddy, please don't, Macy begged, a lump forming in her throat as her fingers tapped the keyboard.

I have to.

Macy stared at the pulsing cursor for a long moment before she found the courage to reach out and close the laptop. She switched off the light and walked out of the office, through the dark living room, into her bedroom.

She lay down on her unmade bed. It smelled of the man she had slept with the night before. Derrick.

Or had last night been Thomas?

She wondered where he was. What he was doing. Not Thomas or Derrick. *Teddy.*

Would a family die tonight? It seemed too soon after the last. Only seven months. But weren't they always too soon?

She rolled over on her side and stared through the open window, waiting for tears. They didn't come.

They never did.

Arlan had, for some reason, expected Romano to be a bigger man. He had no idea why. He knew from experience that evil came packaged in a variety of ways, from bright, bubbly female, to dark and brooding male, and everything in between.

Romano was short, no more than five foot five, with a slight build. His hair was sandy colored with a receding hairline. He was wearing tan pants, a polo shirt, and a navy sports jacket with a silly little handkerchief peeking from the breast pocket. On his shoulder, like most European men, he carried a small brown leather bag. He did not look like a pedophile. He looked like a father, a friend, a grocery store clerk.

But when Arlan lifted his muzzle and sniffed the night air, he was quickly able to sort out the scents; a chewing gum wrapper on the ground, still minty fresh, the roasting lamb, the whore's perfume, the dogs. Somewhere in the midst of the scents, he smelled Romano's malevolence. Undetectable to him was the stench left on his hands by the things he had done. The filthy money that had changed hands. The touch of what should never be touched.

Arlan's stomach twitched and bile rose in his throat. Anger buzzed in his ears. His first impulse was to leap out of the darkness and take Romano by the throat. He wanted to rip his jugular and lap up the blood that would spurt from it.

Arlan felt his entire canine body tremble with the eager thought of it. This man did not deserve to die so easily. He deserved to be tortured before he was murdered. He deserved to watch a dog eat out his entrails.

But that was not Arlan's mission, the human side of his brain reminded him. This execution had been entrusted to him by the High Council, by his beloved sept.

His pulse throbbed in his throat. His heart pounded in his head.

Arlan could not allow the beast in him to take over. The execution had to be carried out as planned, in the manner in which it had been ordered. Or, in this case, considering his lack of a partner, to the best of his ability.

Something itched behind his ear and Arlan lifted his rear paw to scratch it. It was a good morph. It had come complete with fleas.

Romano drew a hand-rolled cigarette from his pocket and pushed it between his lips. He tapped his trouser pockets, coming up with nothing.

He had forgotten or misplaced his lighter. It was the perfect opportunity.

Arlan had to concentrate to shift inside his present morph in order to use his human voice. "Light?" he asked in Greek.

Romano turned toward the thick stump of weeds growing up between the rocky ruins of the Areopagus. If archeologists dug for the next ten years, they would not uncover all the ancient treasure buried by rock, human trash, and the natural sediment that came from time and battle.

Arlan narrowed his yellow dog eyes, every muscle in his powerful body poised to strike as the ordinary-looking monster turned toward the darkness.

"*Ne,*" Romano said in affirmation, his cigarette bobbing, his eyes squinting to see the stranger in the dark.

Arlan glanced left and then right and sprang off his powerful haunches. Standing upright, he was nearly as tall as Romano.

Arlan sank his needle-sharp canines into the man's throat, locking his jaw. The cigarette flew from Romano's mouth, his brown eyes widening in shock.

Arlan dragged Romano into bushes so no one would accidentally come upon them. Romano flailed, calling out, and stumbled to his feet again.

For a split second, Arlan feared he had made a mistake. In his eagerness to see the task done, had he jeopardized the assignment?

The sound of a growl emanating from the bushes startled Arlan so badly that he nearly let go of Romano.

Out of the darkness, a shadow leaped. Arlan cried out in surprise, a deep rumble of a growl.

The gray dog hit Romano in the side, forcing him down on the ground again. The young male from the pack leaped next. The victim cried out once, but his voice was muffled by the growling and snapping of the dogs. The bitches came down on the child-seller from all sides and for an instant, they all bathed in the fury of the bloody flesh.

Teeth still deep in Romano's neck, Arlan felt dizzy from the taste of the human blood. For some, it was merely nutrition and even distasteful, but for Arlan it was a heady drug. The man convulsed beneath them. With the aid of the pack of wild dogs, Romano would be dismembered in a matter of minutes.

Not like this, the human inside Arlan's dog brain warned. This must be done correctly. *There can be no mistakes. You cannot let your fury take over your common sense.*

It was all Arlan could do to relax his jaw. He tore his mouth away, his teeth shredding through delicate human flesh.

Two daggers were required by law for the execution, but one would have to suffice. Arlan would answer to the High Council later.

With a blink of the dying man's eye, Arlan morphed back into a man. "Go," he ordered the dogs that had come to his aid.

Shocked by the transformation, the big gray fell back on the ground, eyes rolling in his head.

"Go on! Get out of here," Arlan grunted in Greek.

The gray took off, followed by his pack, whining and yelping as they made their frightened retreat.

Thank you, Arlan telepathed after them. *You did a good deed tonight, my canine friends.*

The metallic taste of human blood in his mouth, Arlan slipped the ancient dagger from his leather jacket and leaned over Romano. *"For the little children"*, he said softly, in ancient Irish Gaelic.

Arlan plunged the dagger into Romano's heart and the light behind his eyes flickered. By the time Arlan was drawing back the steel, the light had already gone out.

A pity he did not suffer longer.

Arlan stared for a moment at the dead man, then glanced up. He could hear voices in the distance. A drug buy. But no one had seen him kill Romano. No one would see him go.

He plucked the silly handkerchief from the man's bloody suit jacket pocket. First, he wiped his mouth, then he wrapped the handkerchief around the blade. He slid the dagger into his leather jacket, stepped over the dead body and walked out into the dim light cast by the Acropolis high on the hill behind him.

"Looking for a party?" one of the whores called to him

as he headed west, back toward the pulse of the city and the restaurant where the rest of the team would meet him later for a glass of wine.

"Nah," Arlan answered in perfect Greek, Romano's blood still on his breath. "Already had one tonight, sister."

Chapter 3

A rlan was on his second glass of wine by the time Jimmy
and Sean arrived at God's Restaurant on Makrygianni
Street. Both men took seats at the sidewalk table. Jimmy
poured two glasses of wine and refilled Arlan's.

"Task complete?" Jimmy lifted the tumbler to his lips to
drink the bloodred house wine.

"Complete."

Jimmy glanced at the fourth glass, still empty. "Regan?"
He looked around.

Arlan swirled his wine, watching the way it climbed up
the side of the glass before spinning in the center in a
whirlpool. "A no-show."

"Ah, Jezus," Sean cursed under his breath. Like his father, he was a big man, and also like his father, the chief of
police in their hometown, he still carried a slight Irish accent,
even after all these centuries. It became especially pronounced
for both father and son when they became emotional. "Yer
shittin' me."

Arlan didn't meet either of his companions' gazes. He lifted
the tumbler to his lips, sipped, and glanced up at the Acropolis, lit up and gleaming in the darkness. As the wine
touched the tip of his tongue, he realized he could still taste
Romano's blood.

"And you went through with it anyway?" Jimmy's voice was taut. Jimmy was the worrier of the team. Jimmy worried, Arlan teased, so that the others didn't have to. "That's not protocol. You should have aborted."

"You get the kids?" Arlan asked. He was in a dark mood. Had been since his encounter with the dogs and Romano. Tonight he had almost lost control, almost given in to the animal inside him, and he didn't like it. It scared him. After all these years he thought he had learned temperance. He thought he had become a better person. More human. Had he been kidding himself? He glanced at Jimmy. *"Did we get them?"* he repeated. "The kids?"

"Yeah, we got them. Both were still alive, seemed to be scared but . . . *unharmed,*" Jimmy said delicately.

Unmolested was what he meant. Jimmy was a tenderhearted man. Emotional. Always had been, even after the fall from grace that had hardened many of the Kahills.

"And I got Romano, so all's well that ends well."

"We saw that play. Shakespeare." Sean pointed at Arlan. "Like seventeen forty in London. Goodman's Fields . . . or was it Drury Lane? You remember? The orange girls—"

Jimmy dropped his empty glass on the table. "Sean."

"Sorry." Sean reached for the carafe of wine and poured the last of it into his glass. He lifted the carafe to a waiter who was serving a table of tourists.

Jimmy looked back at Arlan. "You're missing the point. Again. You don't go it alone. You're supposed to follow protocol. It's what keeps you safe," Jimmy said.

"What was I supposed to do?" Arlan turned his dark gaze on Jimmy. "Let that pervert, that murderer, walk?"

"Protocol is what keeps us *all* safe," Jimmy insisted firmly. "This isn't just about you. Or even us." He drew his glass in a circle, indicating their tight knit group.

Arlan set his glass down and ran his fingers through his dark hair, still not making eye contact. "All right," he said quietly. "You're right. Next time, I follow protocol."

"Sure you will." Sean chuckled under his breath.

The men were silent as the waiter approached, bringing another carafe of wine. He took the empty one with him.

"So what do we do about Regan? He call in?" Jimmy asked when the waiter had gone.

Arlan plucked his cell phone from the pocket of his leather jacket and checked the screen. "He never called."

Sean poured more wine for everyone. "We know where he is?"

Arlan shook his head. "Haven't heard from him since the meeting in the airport two nights ago." He shrugged. "Of course I didn't expect to see him until tonight unless there was a problem."

"Well, we've got to find him." Jimmy wrapped his fingers around his glass. "He could be in trouble."

"Oh, I'm sure he is." Sean plucked an olive from a tray on the table and sucked on it noisily.

"I'm serious." Jimmy looked to Sean, then back at Arlan. "We have to find him."

Arlan didn't pick up his glass. Suddenly he no longer wanted wine. Or the company of his friends. The situation with Regan had been out of hand for some time. What if Regan really was in trouble this time and not just off binge drinking, whoring, and gambling—simply losing track of time, which was usually his excuse? It would be Arlan's fault if something happened to Regan. Arlan was the one who had insisted that the rest of the team keep Regan's nefarious activities to themselves.

"How you think we're going to find him, Jimmy? We're in a city of what, three million? Four?" He lifted his hand and let it fall. "Besides, protocol requires that we return to Clare Point. Immediately."

Jimmy was quiet for a minute. Sean spat his olive pit into his hand and dropped it on a plate in front of him.

"You're right," Jimmy conceded. "It's best if we go home. Regan will find his way. He always does."

Arlan rose, tossing some euros on the table. "See you back at the ranch, partners." He walked down the sidewalk, away from the lights of the restaurant, into the dark, feeling very alone.

Macy woke hot and sweaty, overwhelmed by a heavy sense of dread. As she showered and went through her morning ablutions, she tried not to think about the meaning of it, or the IM's last night. How many times had she been through this? There was nothing she could do. Nothing last night. Nothing this morning. Except maybe make that dreaded call.

The call would make it real.

She dressed and poured a cup of black coffee in a travel mug. Her appointment today was just a pre-meet, but the assignment was a big one; five full-color pages of the exterior of a house and its garden, northeast of Richmond. She collected her laptop, some files and photographs from her desk, and the canvas backpack she always kept packed in her closet. She did not lock the door when she left.

Late morning, Macy met the homeowners, walked through their garden and made suggestions as to what could be done to improve the property aesthetically before it was photographed. Often, she took her own photos, but for this assignment, the magazine would be using their own photographer. Then, while waiting on the photographer assigned to her, Macy excused herself to check phone messages.

Instead of checking her voice mail, which was a pretty involved process, she made the call, punching in the extension she knew from memory.

"Special Agent Kahill."

Macy hesitated. She always did at this point. Why did she torture herself this way? The FBI was no closer to finding him than they had been fourteen years ago. Why did she make the calls?

Because she had to.

Because it was her penance.

"Special Agent Kahill," the female voice repeated.

"Fia, it's me. Maggie." Macy had picked the name. No last name, just Maggie for Magnolia. For her mother.

There was a pause. "How are you, Maggie?"

"Anything more on the McNaughton case?" Macy said softly. The McNaughton family had been the last to die.

A blue Toyota pulled into the driveway. The photographer. Macy would have to go.

"Not really, Maggie. I check on it from time to time. The agents are keeping the investigation active, but no significant changes."

Macy ran her fingers through her fine, long blond hair. It was hot. She needed a band to pull it back into a ponytail.

"What can I do for you, Maggie?"

Macy exhaled. "He . . ." Her throat constricted. She stopped and started again. "You need to check the morning reports. Today. The next couple of days."

She didn't have to say any more. She and Special Agent Fia Kahill had an interesting relationship. The agent accepted Macy for what she could offer, what she would offer and what she would not. Other law enforcement agents might have pushed her until Macy completely disengaged and stopped calling. But Fia seemed to understand how brittle her informant was.

"Sweet Mary, Mother of God," the FBI agent whispered. "So soon after the last? This is unexpected."

"Maybe I'm wrong," Macy murmured. But the silence between them that followed made it evident that neither thought so. Not in their bones. Fia understood *knowing something in your bones.*

The photographer had climbed out of her car. She had her hatchback up and was pulling bags from the trunk.

Macy turned her back to the car. "I . . . I'm at work so I

can't really talk. I don't know anything, Fia, except that Teddy's out there. He's on the move. He's going to do it again . . . if he hasn't already."

Fia sighed. Macy imagined her running her hand over her pretty face. They had never met in person, but Macy had seen Fia's photograph in the news last year when she'd solved a string of murders in her own hometown. It was after that that Macy had contacted. They talked about once a month but this would be the second time she made this kind of call. Last time, Macy had been right on the money. Upstate New York. Mother. Father. Two little girls and an infant boy.

"Where do you think he is?"

The photographer headed up the driveway toward the house, cameras swinging on both her shoulders. She waved to Macy, smiling. Macy waved back and turned away again, gripping the cell tighter in her hand.

"Listen, I have to go. Check it out. There was nothing on the news this morning, but you know how it goes. Sometimes it takes a few hours to find them." *Once it had taken four days.*

"Can I call you back, Maggie? After I look into it?"

Macy hesitated. She usually didn't do things that way, but the cell only had a few minutes left on it. Then she would toss it. She already had a new one on the floor of the back of her car. She'd bought it at a Piggly Wiggly two days ago. "Sure, you can call me."

"What's the number?" Fia played it cool.

Macy almost smiled. She liked Fia Kahill. In another life, they might even have been friends. "Don't get your panties in a twist, Special Agent Kahill. You're not going to find me. It's a disposable, as always. I'm tossing it tonight whether I hear from you or not."

"You're good, Maggie-With-No-Last-Name."

Macy gave her the number and hung up. She met the

photographer at the wrought iron gate covered in crepe myrtle and shifted into work mode, setting Special Agent Kahill and Teddy aside for a few hours.

Arlan turned on his cell phone as the seat belt light on the overhead cabin went out. He checked the last missed calls. There was only one he cared about.

"Fee," he said when she picked up the phone.

"Arlan." She sounded stressed. "You're home?" She was making a point to sound professional, maybe for the sake of someone near, but Arlan knew her, maybe better than she knew herself. She was upset.

"Just landed. Still on the tarmac." Although the plane was still moving, passengers were beginning to get up and mill around in search of carry-ons and lost shoes.

"Your trip successful?"

"Yup."

"This was a big one, Arlan." She didn't hide the pride in her voice.

"They all are, Fee. What's going on?" She never called just to chat. She showed up on his porch in the middle of the night for that.

"Want to take a ride with me?"

The plane nosed into the terminal and passengers began moving toward the door. "Sure. Where we going?" He tried to sound light, but he sensed this wasn't a pleasure trip. Neither he nor Fia were very good at telepathing long distance, but he knew from the tone of her voice that this was business. Ugly business, if he had to guess.

"Northeast Virginia. On the peninsula. I need—"she was quiet for a breath—"I need your perspective."

"This an official case?"

"Does it matter?"

He smiled. "No."

"I'm already on my way."

He heard an elevator ding.

"Pick you up outside of baggage," she said.

"I don't have any baggage."

"Yeah," she chuckled. "Right."

Macy was done by midafternoon and made arrangements with the homeowners to return in a week. By then, she would have had time to look at the photographer's prelim shots and have a better idea of exactly what she wanted her to take for the spread.

Ordinarily, Macy would have gone home. Home to read. Home to work. Instead, she drove east, not knowing where she was going or why. She wasn't surprised when the disposable cell phone on the car seat beside her rang.

"Special Agent Kahill," Macy said into the phone.

"You were expecting me."

"I don't give my number out to many people," she said glibly.

"You gave me your permanent number, this would be a whole lot easier."

"But it wouldn't be as much fun, would it, Special Agent Kahill? You wouldn't be able to spend all those hours contemplating who I am and why I picked you."

"Good point," Fia agreed.

They were both stalling. Macy could feel the dread again, creeping up with long, black claws. In the moment of silence, she knew Fia felt it, too.

"You were right," the FBI agent said on the other end of the phone. There was no emotion in her voice.

"Where?"

"Outside a little town called Accomack on the eastern shore of Virginia."

Macy knew the area. She knew the whole country. She'd been to almost every state in the Union. Driven through most. Running. Always running.

"Maggie?" Fia said after a moment.

"I'm still here."

"I want you to think about meeting me. There," she said.

"There?" Macy shook her head. She signaled, glanced over her shoulder and passed an SUV pulling a pop-up camper. She tried not to look at the happy faces of the family inside as she cruised by. "Oh, no. I'm not going there. I don't want to see them."

"No. You don't have to," Fia said quickly. "It wouldn't be allowed, anyway. Let me go to the scene, then we could meet. Maybe you could help me out. Help us catch this guy."

"I can't help you," Macy said incredulously. "This was a bad idea. I should never have called you. I'm going to hang up now."

"No, no. Don't hang up. Maggie?"

Macy signaled and edged back into the right lane.

"Maggie, listen to me. I don't know what your connection is to the guy, but I know it's got to be personal. I know you want me to catch him."

Macy didn't say anything.

"If you didn't want to help catch him, you wouldn't keep calling me. You wouldn't keep checking on the cases. You wouldn't keep making sure we were doing our job."

"I . . . I just call because I want him caught. He . . . he's a monster."

"It's more than that. We've got plenty of monsters out there, Maggie. This is personal, somehow, between you and him. You want to help me. You need to."

Was that true? Did Macy want to *help* the FBI catch him? The idea was ridiculous. She couldn't help. What could she do? She was helpless. She had always been helpless when it came to him.

"Maggie?"

"I . . . I don't know if I can do it," Macy said, her voice shaky.

"I think you can."

Macy gripped the wheel, staring straight ahead. She was going in the right direction. She had been for more than an hour. It was as if she had known, subconsciously, where the murders had taken place. It was as if she had known she would go this time. She could be there in a couple of hours.

"Maggie?"

"I'll think about it." The phone beeped in her ear. "Look, my time's about to run out on this phone. I'm going to have to go. Sorry."

"Maggie—"

Macy hit the End Call button and tossed the phone on the car seat beside her. She wanted to turn the car around and head back to her cottage.

She didn't.

Couldn't.

Chapter 4

Arlan watched Fia set her cell phone on the console between them. He glanced out the window at the scenery
flying by. Green grass. Trees. She was driving a good fifteen
miles over the speed limit on Delaware Route 1 South. She
always drove this car too fast. She'd had the old BMW for
years, a six speed. Arlan owned a pickup truck. He didn't
understand Fia's need for speed. Being immortal, they had
forever.

"Weird call," he commented when she said nothing
about the conversation he'd just overheard.

She kept both hands on the wheel, ten and two o'clock.
They had learned to drive together around 1910. The two
of them had spun circles in a cornfield for hours. Fia had
laughed, hanging out the open window, letting the wind
blow her then short-cropped red hair. It had been a Model T
pickup belonging to one of the old guys in town. Arlan
wished he still had that Model T. He wished he could see
Fia laugh the way she had laughed that day. But they had
been young. Seen less. Killed fewer.

"What's she got to do with this?" He pointed his index
finger in the direction of the cell phone.

"I don't know exactly."

Arlan watched Fia. He couldn't see her eyes because of

her black Ray-Ban sunglasses. They looked as good on her as they did on Tommy Lee Jones and Will Smith. Better. Very clandestine and *FBIish*. "You don't know what she's got to do with the case? Is she an informant?"

She lifted one shoulder and let it fall. "Sort of. It's an unusual situation."

She had removed her navy suit jacket and was wearing a tight, silky sleeveless shirt that showed off her muscular shoulders. She was hot, for an FBI agent. Way hotter than Will Smith.

"But she was the one who tipped you off to this case before anyone else did?"

"She called me for the first time about a year ago." Fia glanced at him, and then back at the road. "She saw me on TV after the beheadings. She asked me to look over the Buried Alive killings. I didn't get any further than anyone else in the bureau, but I kept up with the cases. She checks in periodically. Now he's killed again."

"How many does this make, if it's the same perp?"

"Oh, it's the same one."

"How do you know? You haven't been to the scene yet."

"Just wait until you see them. You won't be sleeping tonight."

He glanced out the window again, fighting the shiver that crept up his spine. This was part of his job, seeing the horrendous atrocities humans could commit. Witnessing so that he could justify their deaths. So why didn't it get any easier? "How many times has he killed?"

"This makes ten families in eleven years."

Arlan was always amazed by how calm and removed she could be from what she did. It came so easily to her, setting aside her emotions. He wished he could be more like her. In a morphed state, the way he usually conducted sept business, he was always emotionally raw. Always on the edge. He felt as if he carried that into his personal life.

His niece Kaleigh always said he wore his heart on his sleeve.

"Could he have killed more? Cases not yet connected? It happens with serial killers."

"I don't think so," Fia said slowly. "Maggie would know."

"How would she know?"

She shook her head. "I don't know her connection to this guy, but she knows him. Knows what he's doing, but can't stop him. It's a brother, a father, maybe a boyfriend. Women get trapped in the middle of this sort of thing all the time. You know that. Pretty common."

"Pretty freakin' weird. Doesn't that make her an accessory? Shouldn't you arrest her?"

"I've never met her. She uses disposable cell phones to call me. It's always from a different number and untraceable. Once in a while, I get an e-mail from her, but she somehow manages to hack into other people's e-mail accounts. She's made sure I can't track her down."

"Sounds like she definitely has something to hide." He adjusted his sunglasses. "How do you know she's not helping the killer? And calling you to appease her guilt? Hell, how do you know she isn't the killer? Sounds guilty as hell to me."

"I don't think so. I don't know how to explain it except to say that she's scared of him. But more than scared." She glanced at Arlan and then back at the road again. "This is even more complicated than I understand, yet. I just get that feeling. You know?"

"Is there anything about your life that isn't more complicated than either of us understands?" He kept his tone good-natured.

She smiled, which was what he was hoping for.

"So, how's the HM?" he asked.

"I hate it when you call him that." Now she was frowning.

"What?" Arlan open his arms innocently. "He is, isn't he?"

"Glen is fine. *We're* fine."

He glanced at her. "Pretty quick to throw that detail in." He made a clicking sound between his teeth. "Doesn't sound good, Fee. Doesn't sound good at all. Bloom wearing off the rose? Getting tired of stealing into the kitchen after he's asleep, waiting on the blood to thaw in the microwave and then having to sneak into the bathroom with it?"

He was just teasing her. They all did it at some point. It was part of the price of living among mortals. Trying to fit in. But the look on her face made him want to take it back. There *was* something wrong. She and her human *were* having problems.

"Can we talk about something else?" she asked.

"Like when you're going to marry me and have my babies?" It was an old joke with them. Sept members could only marry their own spouses, lifetime after lifetime, and reproduction was impossible. One of God's blessings.

"Something else," she said.

"Nice weather we're having."

Macy parked her car alongside the road behind an older model BMW and sat in the driver's seat for a moment. She debated whether or not she should drag out the press badge she kept in her glove compartment. The seven or eight vehicles parked on both sides of the street faced in the same direction.

A loose stone driveway led east off the paved road, through neat rows of maple trees, disappearing over a hill. The Virginia Peninsula was narrow here, and even though she couldn't see the bay or ocean surrounding the point of land, she could smell it. The family had lived on the bay side, a couple of miles south and west of town. The property had been easy to find. She had followed the emergency vehicles that she knew would be racing up and down the highways and byways for the next twenty-four hours. A case like this took time to process.

She could see only the rooftop of the family's farmhouse from the road. And the red and blue flashing lights of the emergency vehicles . . .

In the end, she decided to tuck her press badge into the pocket of her jean jacket. There were TV and radio news vans parked on the road, but she doubted they were being permitted to actually gain access. The police never let the news hounds too close to a scene this grim. There was too great a chance some fool looking for a viewer-ratings increase would run a clip no one should have to see.

Macy left her keys in the ignition, her backpack with her wallet on the floor of the car. There was no ID in it. Nothing to steal. No credit cards and little money. She kept her credit cards and various IDs locked in the trunk in the wheel well. Mostly she operated in cash, but sometimes prepaid credit cards that could now be purchased in mini-marts. She did take the new cell phone she'd pried out of its package while stopped at a gas station. She didn't know yet if she would call Fia. She wouldn't know what she was going to do until she reached the farmhouse down the hill.

Macy followed the driveway, passing several state and local cops. She kept her head down and strode purposely, as if she belonged there. She had been amazed, over the years, as to how well the tactic worked for her.

The pebbles under the soles of her shoes were rough. Bumpy. The early evening air was warm, and even above the sound of the rocks crunching underfoot, she could hear frogs croaking. Insects chirping. The air smelled of the Chesapeake Bay, and of the faintest scent of honeysuckle, which grew along the woods line to the north of the property. As she walked around the bend in the driveway, her feet feeling leaden, the farmhouse came into view. It was white clapboard, two story, typical for the turn of the century in the area. She'd done a piece on a similar house in Maryland the year before. The lawn had recently been mowed and clusters of bright orange flowers bloomed at the posts of the split rail fence that encircled the yard. Daylilies.

A serene setting for a mass murder.

Chapter 5

"This might take a little finagling," Fia warned Arlan. They approached a strip of crime scene tape stretched between two peach trees and the three Virginia State Police troopers guarding it. "I'm not authorized to be here."

"Never stopped you before," Arlan pointed out under his breath.

"You either," she murmured. Her hand brushed his sleeve. "Be careful."

It wasn't necessary for either of them to telepath the other. Fia knew what he was going to do. At times like this, their relationship seemed to go deeper even than those they held with their friends and relatives in the sept. Which was *precisely* why Arlan thought they were perfect for each other.

He walked away from her, hands in his jean pockets. It wasn't hard to blend in among so many people: uniformed police, detectives in suits, emergency medical technicians, media personnel, neighbors, relatives, probably extended family members.

The parking area next to the white farmhouse was utter chaos. The Buried Alive Killer, as the news media was calling him, had struck again. Everyone was talking. There were tears. Sobs of disbelief. The emergency responders were taking care to keep their voices low and unemotional, but not always accomplishing their goal. A young male EMT stood on the far side of the yellow tape, hands pressed to his knees, head hanging, as an older woman in an identical uniform leaned over him, talking quietly. Coaxing him.

News teams with cameras and microphones had set up camp in the driveway between a red minivan and a Chevy pickup. A police officer was trying to move them away from the vehicles, which Arlan guessed might have belonged to the family. Who knew what kind of evidence could have been left behind?

Arlan's gaze strayed to the soccer ball decal in the rear of the van window. It read "Go Shore Cats." A kids' local soccer team.

He walked away, a lump rising in his throat. He could hear Fia talking to one of the state troopers, although he couldn't quite make out what she was saying. FBI agents out of Baltimore would be here soon, if they weren't already on the scene. This was really out of Fia's jurisdiction and it wasn't her case, but unlike in TV dramas, in real life, officers of the law often found common ground, overlooking the rules at times like these.

Arlan heard a soft mew and looked up at the back porch. A tabby cat wearing a blue collar with a bell hanging from it sat on the edge, observing the commotion of the backyard. A living witness to the murders?

Arlan walked over and sat down on the top step of the stairs leading to the porch. Someone had recently added a new coat of white paint. He could smell its freshness.

Arlan reached out to the cat and it curled under his hand. He stroked its back. Scratched its ears. *Can you tell me what happened here, little buddy?* Arlan crooned telepathically. *You know anything about this mess?*

The cat looked up with big green eyes. Blinked. He seemed to know Arlan was trying to communicate with him, but the message was coming through scrambled. It was difficult for Arlan to telepath to animals from a human state.

See anything? Arlan pressed. *Anything you want to tell me?*

Arlan sensed a heavy sadness.

"Poor boy," Arlan soothed, stroking the cat's back.

The cat arched beneath his hand, tail stiff in the air, and then leaped from the porch and took off across the grass. He went through a flower bed of purple impatiens, around a kid's red plastic wheelbarrow, and past the peach tree. He flew unhindered under the line of yellow tape. On the far side of the tape, he stopped and turned back.

Arlan glanced around. No one was paying attention to the cat, of course. Not the police, not the blonde with the microphone from WBOC, not even Fia.

The cat waited.

Arlan knew an invitation when he saw one.

He glanced in the direction of the crowd being herded to the end of the driveway away from the family vehicles, then at Fia and the state troopers still in dialogue. He doubted anyone would notice him disappear around the rear of the house. Even less attention was given to the second cat that appeared a moment later.

Arlan walked lightly over the freshly mowed grass, lifting his kitty paws high. He preferred big cat morphs over the common house cat variety, but a panther would have appeared out of place here, even in this uproar.

Helicopter blades cut through the air as Arlan ran, tail in the air like a flagpole, under the police tape barricade. One of Fia's newfound friends backed into an open area in the grass and waved away the helicopter.

Arlan glanced ahead. The tabby was waiting for him, keeping one eye suspiciously on the helicopter. He didn't seem as surprised by Arlan's morph as he was by the news cam in the sky. The cat took off and Arlan trotted after him.

The tabby was barely more than a teenager. Arlan sensed that he was scared. The cat didn't know what was going on, but he knew it was bad. The bell on his collar tinkled as he ran through the grass.

They circumnavigated two ambulances and a white van marked "COUNTY CORONER" in big block letters. The tabby couldn't read, didn't know what the van was, but Arlan did. Seeing those vehicles always bothered him. He couldn't imagine how a person could do that job day in day out—investigating deaths, performing autopsies.

Of course the coroner probably wouldn't have understood Arlan's job any better. Vampires righting the wrongs of the world by selective execution were highly misunderstood. Pretty weird in its own way.

Where are we going? Arlan conveyed to the cat as they ran through the legs of several uniformed police officers.

Bad, the tabby said. *Bad.*

They raced across a patch of grass toward a huddle of men and women under a picturesque silver maple tree that was so perfectly shaped that it appeared as if it had been drawn by a kid's crayon.

Arlan noticed at once that the humans standing under the tree, speaking in hushed voices, were all wearing latex gloves. He felt the hair rise along his spine. His tail bristled. The air was suddenly thick with the smell of dead flesh.

Human flesh.

A part of Arlan wanted to turn around and run back to the freshly painted white porch. That part of him wanted to sniff around the outbuildings behind the farmhouse and look for a tasty mole or mouse. He wanted to morph into an ostrich and stick his head in the sand . . . metaphorically speaking. He didn't do ostriches.

But Fia needed his opinion. Fia needed *him* and he could never tell her no. Not ever. So he followed his tabby friend, who had slowed to a trot. They went around the men and women in gloves talking in hushed tones.

Fia had tried to warn him to prepare himself before seeing the victims. Ambulances had arrived to take the bodies away, but the dead had not yet been moved. Photos and evidence were still being taken by the crime scene investigative team.

Arlan thought he was prepared as he walked under the tree, a step behind his feline friend. He had seen plenty of dead people before. Made quite a few of his own.

He was not prepared.

For a moment, Arlan just stood there, blinking his slanted kitty eyes. The scene that stretched out before him under the pictorial tree appeared to be something out of a bad slasher movie. It didn't seem real. Their faces were waxen. Their open eyes gelatinous. Their arms artificially limblike.

The tabby gave a strangled meow and Arlan took a stumbling. Not in fear. He wasn't afraid of dead people. He was far more afraid of the living ones. But he was so shocked, so taken back with surprise. He thought he had seen the worst of mankind.

He apparently had not.

Five heads.

Five sets of arms stretched over the heads.

Dead humans.

All buried to their chins.

Buried alive, Fia had warned. Then suffocated, one by one.

The closer Macy drew to the farmhouse, the worse she felt. He wasn't here, but he had *been* here. She could sense the remnants of his presence. She could almost smell him on the warm, early evening air. He was taunting her.

Macy thought she would be scared to come here today. She always was. She always went to the crime scenes, sometimes hours later, or days or weeks, but she always went as if pulled by an invisible thread. And she was always scared. Something was different tonight.

The closer she moved to the congested crowd of TV crews, cops, medical personnel, and everyday rubbernecks, the more tied in knots she became. But there was something about this feeling that was different than before. Different than all the other times she had approached one of his gruesome vistas, in their aftermath. As she walked, contemplating her state, Macy found herself surprised to realize this wasn't fear that balled in the pit of her stomach and threatened to constrict her airway. It wasn't terror that made her mouth go dry and her ears hum. It was anger, pure and simple.

Anger at him. At herself.

As she met the edge of the mingling crowd, and felt their fear, she become conscious of the idea that she was tired of being fearful. She was tired of running. Tired of hiding. Tired of renting cottages, buying disposable cell phone minutes, and tired of living out of the trunk of her car. She was angry with him for doing this to her and even angrier with herself for letting him.

The emotion that washed over her was so overwhelming that she halted for a moment to catch her breath. No one seemed to notice her. It was as if she was invisible.

She stared up at the helicopter that circled high above the farmhouse and then sped north, as if to escape the horror Macy knew waited somewhere beyond the lines of yellow crime scene tape.

How had she let her life become this? How had she let him do this to her? She'd have been better off letting him kill her years ago.

Was that the point? Was he letting her live to torture her this way?

Macy skirted the crowd, avoiding the cameras and microphones. She didn't like pictures taken of herself ; you never knew where they might pop up later.

Macy didn't know what she was looking for here. She certainly didn't want to see the dead family. She guessed it wasn't *what* she was looking for here, but whom.

She spotted her, on the far side of the yellow tape strung

between peach trees, walking between two guys in suits. Macy only caught her profile, but she knew it was her.

Special Agent Fia Kahill was prettier in person than she had been on TV and in the news magazines and newspaper photos. She was hauntingly beautiful, with dark red hair that fell silky over her shoulders, lily pale skin, and dark, luminous eyes. And she was tall. At least six inches taller than Macy. She had to be six feet. An Amazon.

Why hadn't the camera angles reflected that?

Macy, like most of America, had been glued to the TV news programs when the beheadings began to take place in the sleepy little seashore town on the Delaware coast. But after the first murder, the story had seemed to take a back burner to other news: the fighting in the Middle East, a passenger train wreck in Spokane, an earthquake in South America. Then suddenly, at summer's end, the story broke again. All at once, Special Agent Fia Kahill's face was everywhere. She was making statements and doing interviews on *Larry King Live*. She was a celebrity. She solved the mystery of the beheading murders, and three young men were currently serving multiple consecutive life sentences for their crimes. Agent Kahill was a hero.

Macy had read the news articles. She had listened to Fia's statement on *Fox News Live*. It wasn't the beheadings that had fascinated Macy, or the fact that the clever female agent had been able to solve the mystery. It was something much more basic about Fia that had intrigued Macy. There was something about the agent that set her apart from others. Something that made her different. Macy had seen it reflected in her dark, incandescent eyes.

Macy slipped her hand into her coat pocket and wandered away from the crowd. There was a quaint back porch that smelled as if it had been recently painted. She sat down on the steps leading up to the porch and dialed the phone number.

She watched as Fia responded to the vibration in her

pocket. Special Agent Kahill was too professional to leave her phone on ring at a crime scene.

From across the lawn, through the branches and leaves of the peach trees, Macy saw Fia glance at her phone in her palm, note the incoming call number, then speak to one of the FBI agents in suits. She stopped, letting the men continue walking. Fia couldn't have known the number because the cell was new, but Macy knew Fia knew it was her.

"Special Agent Kahill."

Macy continued to watch her. "Hey," she said, suddenly feeling almost shy. What was she doing calling her, right here where he had been? "It's me."

"Hey, me." Fia spoke lightly. "You thought about what I said?"

"Thinking about it." Macy watched her turn and look in the direction of the two agents walking away. They had to be going to the actual burial site, beyond the lean-to barn.

"I'd really like to talk to you, Maggie. I'd like to see you. Meet face to face. I think it's time."

Her elbow resting on her knee, Macy lowered her head until her forehead touched the heel of her hand. Her blond hair fell over face as she cradled the phone to her ear. Hearing Fia's voice on the end of the line made Macy realize how lonely she was. It was good just to hear Fia's voice. How pathetic was that?

"Will you come?" Fia prodded.

Macy lifted her head, throwing her hair back. "I'm here," she whispered.

"You are? You're *here*? At the scene?"

Macy watched the agent turn around, studying the crowd. She started walking back toward the yellow line of tape, her long legs taking long strides. Fia Kahill didn't look past the crowd, beyond the commotion, to the lonely back porch. To the lonely, invisible blond sitting on the step.

Macy had made a career of remaining invisible.

Except to him, of course.

She felt the anger bubble in her chest again.

"I want to talk to you," Macy heard herself say. "Face to face."

Fia stopped walking, but she was still scanning the crowd. More uniformed police had arrived. Macy would have to join the crowd if she was going to stay any longer. Otherwise, someone was going to spot her. Macy made it a point to never stand out in a crowd. Never be singled out for anything if she could help it. She didn't even like to be the only one in line in a grocery store.

"But not here," Macy added quickly. "I can't talk to you here. Besides, you have to go see them. You have to . . . bear witness," she said.

Fia removed her dark sunglasses. "Okay. I'm headed there now."

"There's a . . . a beach not far from here," Macy said, still watching her. "A state park." She'd been there before. Eighteen months ago or so. She'd gone walking on the beach after a photo shoot of a cottage in Chincoteague. "You want to meet me there about eleven tonight?" That would give Macy time to check in to a hotel. Think about what she wanted to say to Fia. Even think about whether or not she just wanted to get in her car and drive back to Virginia.

"I can certainly be out of here by then, but it'll be kind of dark for a walk on the beach. Maybe a coffee shop or something?"

Macy watched Fia check her wristwatch. Macy never wore a watch. She wasn't all that caught up in what time it was. She always felt as if she had plenty of time to kill. A lifetime. "There's a big waning moon," she said into the phone. "The beach is pretty in the moonlight."

"Okay. Sure." Fia slipped her hand into her pants pocket under her jacket. She turned away, seeming to give up on trying to spot Macy. "I can meet you at eleven."

Macy gave her the directions.

"Got it." Fia Kahill hesitated. "How will I know you?"

Macy almost chuckled. "You're quite the crack agent, Fia. I thought you guys could spot your man a mile away." Somehow she managed to find a wry smile. "I'll be the only one, other than you, crazy enough to be sitting on the beach in an empty state park that late at night."

Chapter 6

Fia held her cell phone and glanced over her shoulder, looking toward the farmhouse. She scanned the crowd, which was beginning to look like a mob. Where was Maggie? Was she really here?

Fia sensed she was. Sensed Maggie was watching her. She was an intriguing woman, this informant of hers. There was something about her that tugged at Fia's heartstrings.

And here she thought she didn't have any. . . .

More uniforms had arrived to serve as crowd control and the multitude seemed to be getting bigger by the moment. How could so many people have found out about the murders so quickly, in such a remote area? she wondered. How could they have all gotten here so quickly? Didn't they have jobs? Families? Dinner to put on the table? It was morbid, humans' fascination with the dead. Somehow she didn't think they would be quite so enthralled if they were one of the living dead.

Fia's gaze shifted from one face to the next, but she didn't see Maggie. Or at least she didn't *think* she saw her. Fia had an idea in her head, from the voice, what the woman looked like, but she had no real idea. It had been her experience that bodies sometimes matched voices, but not always.

The crowd was beginning to work into a frenzy the way a crowd could. The TV news reporters' voices were getting shriller, even the men's. The helicopter, waved away once, was apparently attempting to make another fly-by over the property in the hopes of getting a couple of gruesome head shots.

Fia groaned to herself at the bad pun. She'd been doing this too long. Next life, she was going to be a gardener, or maybe a basket weaver. Unfortunately, she didn't have a green thumb, nor was she artistic. This was what she did well—the dead. Some days she considered it a gift from God used to serve mankind and help right the wrongs committed by her sept. Other days, it was another one of His sick jokes. A curse.

Tucking her phone into her pocket, she started down the path leading through the orchard. Agents Richter and Evans, from the Baltimore field office, said the bodies were just past the lean-to toolshed, over the little crest. They were buried under a tree. From here, Fia could see the branches and leaves. It was a big maple. Hundreds of years old. She liked old trees. They made her feel . . . less old.

Fia met Arlan on the path beside the toolshed. He was just walking along, hands in his pocket as if he belonged there. "You been to the scene?" she stopped and asked.

He nodded.

She noted he was a little pale. And still as devastatingly handsome as ever. He was always getting offers in big cities to try his hand at modeling. With a face and a body like his, he could sell a ton of tight black BVDs from a billboard in Times Square or Tokyo.

"You just walked over and had a look at a dead family of five, buried to their chins, and no one stopped you?"

"No one stopped two pitiful cats checking out their owners' remains."

She knew Arlan had the ability to morph into any animal. She'd once seen him morph into a nine-foot-tall polar bear in her mother's backyard. But he usually kept it to applicable animals. Animals native to the area. The whole idea was to be able to blend in. And while he could be feline, bovine, or canine, he couldn't split himself into two animals. Not even two measly five-pound cats. That was beyond his gift. "Two of you?"

"Found a friend. He's over there." He pointed behind him. "Other side of the shed. Family cat. He didn't see anything. He was out chasing rabbits in a field somewhere when it happened. He came upon them after they were dead."

"He call it in?" she quipped.

It was a poor attempt at humor. Neither of them smiled.

"Hey, my girl called," she said, giving Arlan a tap on the arm. He was still wearing his sunglasses. The color seemed to be coming back to his suntanned cheeks. Who would have thought a vampire would tan so well? "She says she's here, though I didn't see her. Don't *think* I saw her, anyway. There's so many people. It's crazy." She gestured in the direction of the driveway commotion.

"What'd she want?"

"Believe it or not, she's agreed to meet me."

He made a face, demonstrating he was impressed with Fia's skill as an agent.

"She won't meet me here, though. Later tonight. On a deserted beach, of all places."

"You think it's safe?"

It was Fia's turn to make a face. "For me? *She's* the one who ought to be scared of *me* in the dark."

"Yeah, I know." He smiled. Their gazes met. His smile slipped. His focus drifted with his thoughts. "I saw them, Fee. It's pretty awful."

"I'm sure it is. I saw the last family." She put her sunglasses back on. It was really too dark for sunglasses now.

Neither needed to wear them. But they were both hiding behind them. Hiding the emotions they both knew had no place here. No place in doing their job.

"So what did you think?" she asked, pushing past the tightness in her chest that ached as much for Arlan as it did for the family and for those who had to see them this way. Arlan had always been what their resident wise-woman called *a gentle soul*. "Tell me your gut reaction."

"One crazy son of a bitch." He shook his head. "I mean kids? Grandma?"

She grimaced. "I know."

"How is he getting them in the holes? How long is it taking him to dig the holes?" He became more manic. Talking faster. "How's he physically managing it, Fee? How's he subdue a whole family? How does he get in and out without anyone, including the family cat, seeing him?"

"All the autopsies, so far, showed the use of an injectable drug in each of the victims' bloodstreams. The actual drug varies, but it's enough to knock them out for a short time. Sometimes he digs the holes hours before he imprisons the family. That was the case on the last one, the only one I actually saw. But once, before I was following his cases, I read in the files that he made a father dig the holes for his family before rendering him unconscious. We could tell from the blisters on his hands and the blood on the shovel. In all the incidents, we think the killer buries them while they're drugged, then allows them to come to."

"So they have to watch each other be strangled?" Arlan asked incredulously. "Unfucking believable." He wiped his mouth with the back of his hand as if to attempt to wipe the foul taste of the killer's sin from his mouth. "I want this guy."

"I want him, too," she said.

"No, I mean when we get him, I'm going to be on the

kill team. My dagger goes into his black heart first." He made an angry stabbing motion.

"I wouldn't mind being there with you," she said gently, trying to temper his emotion. She hesitated. "Look, I gotta go. I've got those agents from the Baltimore office waiting for me." She walked past him, patting him on the arm as she went by. "Catch up with you at the car later? We'll find a place to stay, grab something quick to eat before I make the meet."

"We talking double bed or singles?" He lifted a brow suggestively.

"I'm monogamous, Arlan. I have a boyfriend. I've told you that, what? Like a hundred times in the last year."

"You never know when the answer will be different." He turned around to watch her go, hands stuffed in his pockets. "Catch you later."

"What are you going to do?"

"I don't know. See if I can talk to my kitty buddy. Maybe find some cat chow."

Fia smiled to herself as she walked away, wishing she could fall in love with Arlan.

Arlan chatted with the tabby again, gave a half-hearted chase after a mouse in the toolshed with him and then wished the cat good luck. As Arlan walked, in the dark, back toward Fia's car parked up on the main road, he wondered what would become of the dead family's feline. Would a distant relative or neighbor think to take him home, or would he be forgotten and left to live on his own? Arlan found it sad, but there were animals all over the world left behind like Tabby. Arlan couldn't save them all. There were days when he could barely save himself.

There were cat rescue centers, though. Maybe, once he got home, he would give the local rescue organization a call. Surely they could find a good home for Tabby.

Arlan was leaning against the hood of the car, wishing he had a cigarette, even though he rarely smoked, when he heard Fia's voice. She was approaching the road from the driveway, talking on her cell.

"Ma, listen to me. You have to calm down. I can't understand what you're saying."

Fia paused, then responded. "No, no, don't put him on the phone. Dad's less communicative calm than you are hysterical. Isn't anyone else there? One of the boys?" Another pause. Fia was on the street, walking directly toward Arlan. Her high-heeled loafers tapped hollowly on the pavement. "No, not Aunt Mary. She'll have had her sherry by now. Isn't there anyone else there? Where's Fin, Ma?" She looked up at Arlan. "Regan called home," she told him. "He never made it back from Greece. He's in some kind of trouble." She looked down, speaking into the phone. "Ma, either you have to calm down or you're going to have to call me back."

She looked up at Arlan again. "I don't know what to do with her. I can't understand what she's saying."

"She say where he was calling from?" Arlan felt an instant pang of guilt. He shouldn't have left Athens without Regan. Procedure or not. Fia's brother had been headed for trouble for months. Arlan should have known this was coming. "She know where he is?" he asked.

Fia shook her head. "Ma, I can't come home tonight. I have an appointment I can't—Ma, please stop crying." Fia ran her hand over her silky hair, obviously at a loss. "Ma . . ."

"You want me to go home?" Arlan offered. "Let me talk to her. I can get a rental car and be there in less than three hours."

"Ma . . . Ma, how about if Arlan comes over? You tell him what Regan said and—" She was quiet for a second; then she looked at Arlan. "She wants me," she said, seeming nearly defeated. "I can't deal with this," she told him, her hand on the mouthpiece of the phone. "I can't deal with her right now and this case. I need to go home, but—"

"Why don't you let me meet your Maggie tonight?"

"She'll never agree to it." Fia lifted her hand off the mouthpiece. "Ma, just a minute. I'm trying to figure something out." She lowered the phone to her side.

Arlan could hear Mary Kay Kahill sobbing hysterically. "So we won't tell her I'm coming. I'll go to the meeting place, morph, check out the situation and then decide whether or not to attempt the meeting or not. If I don't think it's a safe bet, I'll call you, you call her and tell her something came up." He shrugged.

"I don't know," Fia hemmed. "She . . . she's obviously scared. Brittle, I think. She has to be handled carefully."

"Who better than me to handle an HF with kid gloves?" He raised his hands to her, fluttering his fingers, giving her his sexiest smile.

Fia spoke into the phone again. "Ma, I want you to go to the kitchen and make some muffins. Ma . . . yes, blueberry would be fine. Then cranberry nut. By the time you've got the second batch done, I should be almost home."

Arlan opened the car door for Fia and she climbed in, cell phone still to her ear. "We'll find him, Ma. I'll go get him myself if I have to." Another pause. "Ma, you know how he is. He exaggerates. I'm sure he's just drunk. I'm sure he'll call back tomorrow saying he's fine and on his way home."

Arlan got in the passenger's side of the BMW. Both of his parents were dead and even after all these centuries, he still missed them. Sometimes he didn't think Fia realized how lucky she was to have her parents, even if her father was a distant, self-absorbed alcoholic and her mother half crazy.

"I'm hanging up now, Ma. Hanging up," Fia sang as she started the car, racing its engine. "See you in a couple of hours. Blueberry and cranberry." She hung up.

"You're a good daughter," Arlan said.

She tore away from the side of the road, leaving rubber on the pavement, and the dead bodies being loaded into ambulances behind.

Macy left her car, unlocked, windows down, in the gravel parking lot of the state park. During the day, she imagined it was filled with minivans and SUVs; families on vacation or just celebrating a day in the sun. Unlike further north in Ocean City or Rehoboth Beach, there were no concessions, no stores lining the beach, on the Virginia Peninsula. Here were just miles of sand and ocean, for the most part, unblemished by condos, restaurants, and arcades. It was the perfect place for picnics, frolicking in surf or simply reading a book to the rhythmic sound of the incoming waves.

But this late at night, with the park officially closed, there were no minivans, no families on vacation. The parking lot was empty except for two red porta-potties and a couple of overflowing trash cans.

Macy grabbed a hooded sweatshirt off the floor of her car, pulled it on, lifted the hood, and traipsed up the sandy dune crossing, over the crest of the man-made dunes. She had discovered this beach one day while driving south, after an assignment. Although it was on the ocean side of the highway, there was a scraggly woods line not far off the beach. Somehow, over millions of years, plants and trees had managed to evolve enough to live in the sandy soil, just a couple of hundred feet from the salty body of water. She admired those trees with their prickly needles, and the low-lying bushes with the spindly branches. They had managed to survive in adverse conditions. They had adapted.

Much in the same way Macy had adapted.

On the far side of the grassy dune, the beach stretched out to the north and to the south. As she had promised

Fia, the moon was glowing bright over the ocean. But it was no longer full. Teddy had missed his walk. She crossed the clean beach, walking toward the water. She was early. It would be a few minutes before the FBI agent arrived.

Macy had checked into a motel and sat on the edge of the bed with a yellow bedspread and contemplated what she would say to Fia. She had no real information to provide. All she had was this feeling of being on a high-speed train, rushing forward. A train with no brakes. A train about to derail. So why was she here? Did she really think she could stop the train?

Could she and Fia do it together?

Macy had an idea that Fia understood something about Teddy. She had picked up on the fact that this was too soon for the killer to strike again. Not enough months had passed. She seemed to sense that some sort of urgency was building in Teddy.

Macy stopped at the water's edge and contemplated taking off her shoes to feel the wet sand between her toes. She stared down at the frothy water washing up on the shore, then at the waves, then beyond the breakers to the rippling expanse of the Atlantic seeming to move as if it were alive.

She walked south, keeping an eye on the parking lot. She had not heard Fia's car yet, or seen the headlights. It had to be near time for their meeting.

She'd be here. Macy knew she would come.

Just as Macy was about to turn around and head north again, movement caught her eye at the woods line. She stopped and stared into the darkness. A pair of glowing eyes—light reflected from the moonlight—stared back.

She felt her mouth turn up at one corner in a half smile. It was a gray fox. A rare treat. Gray foxes were native to North America as was not the case with the more often seen red fox, which was brought to the continent by colonists wanting to hunt them. Macy stood still, staring at the fox. The fox, poised to run, every muscle in his sinewy body tense, stared back. Should she move, she knew he would startle and lope off into the darkness.

Macy, at once, felt a kinship to the woodland creature. She understood perfectly his flight instinct. It had been her modus operandi for the last fourteen years.

Chapter 7

Arlan stood beneath the prickly low-hanging pine bough as he stared at the woman on the lonely stretch of beach. She was small in stature, slender, almost boylike in shape. She wore jeans and a dark sweatshirt with the hood pulled up. From beneath the hood, golden strands of hair were visible. Her eyes were luminous in the moonlight.

Arlan swung his long tail one way and then the other, unable to tear his gaze from hers. He had morphed into a large male *Urocyon cinereoargenteus* so that he could get a better look at Fia's Maggie. He'd arrived ahead of her and had been watching her since she walked out on the beach. When she spotted him, he should have darted into the brush, as any fox with sense would have done, but there was something about this woman that held him spellbound.

When she saw him, she had gone completely still, but it appeared she had done so to prevent frightening him. She was not afraid. In fact, from the intensity of her gaze, he sensed that she was as momentarily fascinated by him as he was of her.

This petite woman with green eyes and spun gold hair was not what Arlan had expected. He had worked with informants before, male and female. They were often drug abusers or alcoholics. They were humans down on their luck, willing to accept money for information. They were skinny, malnourished, and hollow eyed. They had a look about them that was often pathetic. Maggie had never asked Fia for money, for anything actually, and in no way did she appear pathetic. This woman was healthy and she was on her game. Whatever game that was. He could smell that much on the salty night air. Yet, she also seemed sad. Lonely.

When their gazes locked, he felt some kind of instant connection with her. An understanding. Arlan could not read the minds of humans, but he sensed a vulnerability about her that made him want to reach out. To touch her. To take her in his arms.

And her neck was so lovely, so pale and slender. . . .

Arlan shook his head, trying to dislodge the forbidden thoughts from it.

She didn't flinch. Instead, she surprised him by taking a tentative step toward him.

He wondered what she would do if he bolted toward her. Nothing, he decided. She wouldn't be afraid of him, wouldn't fear he was rabid. She would stand there and let him trot up to her.

Arlan had to force himself to turn away. He loped into the brush, running back toward the rental car he'd parked on the road south of the parking lot. He didn't morph until he reached the car. Then he hopped in and drove the quarter of a mile to the lot. He parked beside her car and walked up over the dune.

She was waiting for him in the moonlight.

"Maggie?" he called, as he crossed the dunes and walked down the sandy slope toward her.

Now she was the one poised to lope off into the darkness. She still wore the hood up on her sweatshirt. All he could see was her hair and her eyes. Nothing of her face.

"Who are you?" she demanded.

Arlan was suddenly desperate to see her face. "My name is Arlan Kahill. Fia sent me."

"She didn't say anything about sending someone else. Fia would have called me and told me if she couldn't make it."

"She had a family emergency and she asked me to come in her place. Had she called to tell you, you wouldn't have shown up, Maggie."

She watched him with guarded eyes. "You FBI, too?"

"No." He stood still, trying not to spook her, much the same way she had done when she had approached him further down the beach a few minutes ago. "I . . . I'm an old friend. I help her out with tough cases sometimes."

"That doesn't sound legal."

He smiled to himself. She was pointing out that what they were now doing probably wasn't legal, but she was making no attempt to walk away. "Fia really wanted to be here, but—"

"Right, the family thing."

"The family thing," he repeated.

Both regarded each other for a moment.

"You said you were friends, but you have the same last name."

"We come from the same town. A lot of us have the same surname."

She nodded. "I don't really know anything more than she knows," she said softly after a moment. "I'm not sure what the point of this meeting was."

"But you came anyway," he pointed out.

She remained quiet.

Arlan slipped his hands into the pockets of his leather jacket. "Fia was . . . *we* were wondering what your connection is. To him," he said carefully. "How do you know him?"

"I don't *know* him," she said, her tone prickly.

He waited.

"Teddy contacts me sometimes. Tells me things. Awful things," she half whispered.

There it was again, that vulnerability he had sensed earlier, so strong now that he could almost taste it on the tip of his tongue. "Teddy?"

"I'm sure it's not his real name. It's what he calls himself."

"And how does he contact you?" He took a step closer. He had suggested to Fia that she might be the killer, or at least be involved in the murders, but now that he'd actually seen her, had a chance to sense her being, it didn't feel that way to him.

She watched him, but did not move. "Over the Internet. We've never spoken."

"So . . . he's stalking you?"

"I suppose you could call it that."

"Why you?"

She looked down at the sand, breaking eye contact for the first time since he'd approached her. "I don't know," she murmured.

"And how long has he been contacting you?"

She shrugged her slender shoulders. "I don't know. A year or two, maybe."

She was lying. Anyone who had a murderer stalking them would know exactly when it started, down to the very date and time. His gaze narrowed. "And you have no idea how or why he chose you?"

She shook her head, not speaking. She was watching him again, almost beseechingly.

Arlan wanted to believe her. Logic told him he shouldn't, but he wanted to. He tried a different tack. "Does he ask you to participate in the murders?"

She slid her hands into the pockets of her sweatshirt. The wind off the ocean had grown cool. "No."

"Does he threaten you?"

She was slow to answer, as if contemplating the question. "Not really."

"I don't mean to be insensitive, Maggie, but I find this all pretty hard to believe. Men like this . . . this monster are very purposeful in everything they do. Everything they say. Every decision they make. You're not telling me the whole truth here."

"You calling me a liar?" Her head cocked at the slightest angle.

"Maybe."

Moonlight bathed her nose and lower jaw when her chin jutted forward. "Would you blame me if I was lying? At least about certain *details*?"

She had a fair point. If she was telling the truth, if the Buried Alive Killer was contacting her, she should be cautious. And she should certainly be afraid. He took another step closer, hoping to get a better look at her. She smelled good, like a new rain. "Why didn't you just go to the police? What are you afraid of, Maggie?"

Her response was incredulous. "He says he'll kill others. Many. And it will be my fault."

He looked over her shoulder to the waves crashing in, the foam sweeping the sand clean and smooth. He remembered the night of the shipwreck. Swimming to shore at Clare Point. A new beginning for him and for the sept.

Arlan shifted his gaze to her again. She was watching him intently. He took a chance and slowly reached out and pushed her hood down. An abundance of blond hair tumbled down her back, smooth and straight and long, and he remembered another woman's hair the very same color. Same texture.

Arlan closed his eyes for a moment and in his head, time shifted and he saw her as clearly as if she were standing in front of him. *Lizzy,* his sweet, pretty Lizzy. And then he saw the blood.

Maggie cleared her throat. "Arlan?"

He opened his eyes. Blinked. The memories were like this sometimes, washing over him with the force of strong ocean waves. He was helpless against them. He could not stop them.

Maggie was so like Lizzy and yet different. Lizzy had been so confident, so bold and strong and full of life. This young woman before him, she was barely a shadow in comparison. He would not have been surprised if he had reached for her and grasped nothing but air.

"I'm okay," Arlan said.

"You thinking about someone? Someone gone. Dead?" she asked, her voice as light and innocent as a child's. Almost ethereal.

He wondered how she knew. Humans were generally so insensitive to feelings. Everything always had to be written, spoken, explained clearly for them to understand. And even then, they didn't always get it.

"You want to sit down?" Arlan asked, gesturing toward the water's edge.

"No. I'm not going to talk to you about this. I want to talk to Fia."

"And she wants to talk to you."

"So I guess we'll both have to wait."

Clouds drifted, settling in over the peninsula, blocking most of the moonlight, and the night suddenly grew darker. They both glanced up at the dark sky.

"Is there a way Fia can contact you?" he asked. "A phone number?"

"I'll call her."

It was obvious the meeting was over, yet Maggie continued to stand there.

"You lonely, Arlan?"

The question stunned him. He wasn't sure how to respond.

"Because I am," she continued. "And what lonely people are best at spotting"—she took a step forward and boldly took his hand in hers—"is other lonely people." She raised his hand and drew it across her cheek.

Arlan literally felt his legs go weak. He'd heard a lot of come-ons in his lifetimes. There was no doubt that the ladies liked him, human and otherwise. And he liked them. But he'd sworn off HFs a long time ago. Vampires and humans just didn't mix well in the sack. It was too risky. He had learned that lesson over a century ago. At least he thought he'd learned. . . .

"A beautiful woman like you," he said, trying to lighten the tone of the conversation. "No husband? No boyfriend? Don't you have family?"

"I have no one," she told him quietly and matter-of-fact. "No one to know if I live or die. It's just me. So come back to my hotel room with me." She tipped up her chin to look at him.

A most amazing neck . . .

Arlan was intoxicated by her nearness, by her touch, by her voice.

He knew he shouldn't do it and yet he leaned over and brushed his lips against hers. A tentative kiss. Just a taste.

Her lips were soft. Sweet and begging to be kissed again. Harder.

"Come on," she whispered. She started to walk away, tugging his hand. "You take your car, I'll take mine. You don't have to stay the night."

She released his hand. "Just follow me."

And bless his mother's sweet, tortured soul, he did.

*   *   *

"Kiss me," Maggie whispered, stopping inside the doorway of the motel room dimly lit by lamps on either side of the bed. She pulled her sweatshirt off and tossed it on a chair. Her pale green T-shirt was tight, showing off her hardened nipples. She wore no bra. "Kiss me. Make it all go away. Just for a few minutes."

He slid his hand around her neck and fingered her soft nape beneath her hair. She stood in front of him, not touching him with her hands or any part of her body, but she touched him with her gaze. Connecting so deeply with him, so profoundly, that he feared she would see him for what he truly was. As lonely as he really was, as much as he needed to connect with someone, it also scared him. He closed his eyes to hide the truth and found her mouth with his.

Maggie slid both of her palms upward over his chest, pressing against him with the same pressure she used with her mouth. Both her touch and her kiss were hungry.

"Make it go away," she begged as she parted her lips.

He delved deep with his tongue, the recesses of her mouth cool. He tasted her desire, her fear, and as he drew back, breathless, he tasted the ever-so-subtle taste of weariness. Arlan understood weariness. He had been alive since the fifteenth century. Any man or woman that old understood weariness, but what had happened to this young woman, this human who appeared to be only in her late twenties, to make her such an old soul? Had the killer done this to her?

"Can you do that? Can you make it go away?" she asked, grasping his T-shirt in handfuls.

Arlan pushed her inside the door and kicked it closed. "Do what I can," he whispered, drawing his mouth from her ear, across her cheekbone to her lips again. He reached behind him and turned the deadbolt. He found her mouth again.

They stumbled to the bed, which looked like every other hotel bed in the United States. They fell on the yellow quilted bedspread. HF or not, it just felt right to him to be here. To make love to her. *She* felt right.

Still mouth to mouth, she pushed his leather jacket off and threw it on the floor. He rolled her onto her back and flattened his body over hers. She was so petite, seemed so fragile, that he tried to be careful. But her kisses were fierce. Her body's response to his touch was ferocious. The woman was an amazing enigma. She had been so soft-spoken, so unsure of herself on the beach, but here in bed, in his arms, she knew just what she wanted and how to get it from him.

He kissed her cheek, her chin, her pale throat.

He did not allow himself to think of the sweet blood pulsing there. Could not. This was the reason HFs were so dangerous. Even a man with his willpower had a difficult time not sampling blood when it was offered so willingly.

He moved his mouth over the hollow of her throat, lower. Her small breasts pressed against his face. He pushed up the hem of her T-shirt and kissed his way up from the flat of her belly to a peaked nipple. He massaged her other breast with his hand. She had small breasts, but big, dark areolas that strained against the thin fabric of her T-shirt. She was perfection.

Maggie threaded her fingers through Arlan's hair and moaned softly. He sucked one nipple, then the other, dampening the cotton. She grabbed the hem of her shirt and wiggled upward, the fabric skimming over her belly, her breasts, her head.

Lamplight fell from the bedside tables, bathing her in a soft glow. "You're so beautiful," he whispered.

"You don't have to say that." She yanked his shirt over his head and tossed it.

"But you are."

She did not meet his gaze. Instead, reached down to grab the waistband of his jeans. She tugged on the button, popping it open on the first try.

"Hey, hey, slow down," he murmured, gently taking her hand away from his throbbing groin. "You have somewhere you need to be?"

"Life's short," she reasoned.

He kissed her again, chuckling. "Not for everyone."

"You talk too much."

He smiled down at her and kissed her. He'd met plenty of women like Maggie before. Hell, he was just like her. Quick sex. Eyes closed. No talking. Get your rocks off and go.

But Arlan kept his eyes open, gazing down at her incredible face as he stroked her rib cage and the taut muscles running the length of her belly.

Maggie wiggled out of her jeans and lay completely naked beside him, except for the tiny scrap of black lace she wore as panties. Arlan drew his fingertips lightly over her waist, her hips, down her thigh. She shifted her body and rolled onto her side, facing him. As he caressed her slender but muscular body, he gazed down at her, studying the pale fringe of lashes that framed her brown eyes and the tiny freckles on the tip of her nose.

She stroked his biceps, his pecs. Her touch was well-practiced. Exquisite, actually, as she thumbed his nipple, sending a hard tremor of pleasure through him, and he tried to think about something other than her naked body pressed against his. She was so adept with her attention to him that he was concerned that while he was telling her not to rush, his body would rush to the finish line.

He thought about the broken leg of his kitchen table he needed to repair.

And her perfect, hard nipples.

And the milk that had probably soured in his refrigerator while he was in Greece.

And the patch of golden hair he knew was just beneath the black fabric of her panties . . .

He rolled her onto her back and lowered his body over hers. He kissed her breasts, the flat of her belly, then just above the waistband of her panties. Then he tugged on the stretch fabric with his index finger.

She sucked in a breath, sliding her fingers into his hair.

Arlan took his time with his kisses. Maggie moaned, lifting her hips, writhing beneath him. She seemed so sweet, so lost, that he wanted to draw out her pleasure as long as he possibly could.

The minutes that ticked endlessly by in his life came to a standstill for a short time. Twice she called out, her body arching in ultimate satisfaction before he slipped out of his jeans. She kept her eyes closed, he kept his open as he pushed inside her.

He moved slowly at first, watching her face. Studying the pout of her mouth, the gentle flair of her nostrils, her small hands clenching his shoulders.

She wrapped her legs around him and lifted her hips to meet his. Arlan tried to hold back, but he couldn't. It seemed as if all his emotion had suddenly built up in his chest to the point where he could no longer breathe. The only way to catch his breath was to push inside her, again and again.

As Arlan had feared, it was over all too quickly. But the way he was feeling right now, even if he had been able to last all night, it would have ended too soon. Every muscle in Maggie's body tightened and she sank her nails into his back as she arched against him in another orgasm.

He managed only two more strokes before he surrendered.

Afterward, she said nothing, just curled herself against

him, her back pressed to his chest, and he drew his hand over her narrow waist. She fell asleep almost immediately, wrapped in his arms, but Arlan lay awake for a long time. And for once, it wasn't because he couldn't sleep, but because he didn't want to.

Chapter 8

Slightly disoriented, Arlan woke at dawn to the rattle of the air-conditioning unit. A woman's bare bottom pressed firmly against the flat of his stomach. Maggie. Maggie the Mysterious. Maggie, Fia's informant. Possibly Maggie the killer.

The first rays of sunup filtered through the thin drapes and he studied her bare shoulder peeking from beneath the sheet they'd pulled over them sometime in the middle of the night, after they'd had sex a second time.

His gaze shifted to her long, slender neck. The back of her head. Her tousled blond hair. Back to her neck again. She had certainly satisfied him sexually, but there was still an inkling of need deep inside him.

He gazed down at her. *It would be so easy to sample her blood.*

It had been a long time since he'd tasted a human, really *tasted* one as he longed to. Like most Kahills, he kept up his nutritional needs by using deer on the game preserve outside their town. They were well cared for and the animals provided enough blood for all who needed it, without having to sacrifice their lives. When he traveled for long periods of time, bloodletting became a little trickier, but because he only needed blood once or twice a month, it was a minor inconvenience.

Drinking human blood, as they had done in the old days, was now forbidden by the sept. They were *beyond* such primitive behavior. Or so they liked to think.

Back in the beginning, when the family had been cursed for fighting against St. Patrick, for refusing to give up their pagan worship, they had been turned into vampires by God. After that, they had scourged the hills and valleys of their homeland and taken blood, uninvited and indiscriminately, no matter the cost to life, human or otherwise. They had told themselves they did it to survive. Some had killed, others had recklessly made humans into vampires. They had hated themselves for what they had become. Animalistic was too tame a word to describe their behavior.

But that was all behind the Kahills now. In the seventeenth century, they had fled Ireland and the unrelenting vampire slayers to find refuge in the New World. Shipwrecked in a storm, the surviving members of the sept washed up on the shore of the Delaware Bay. Spared, they believed they had been given a second chance. In a plea for redemption, members dedicated themselves to the one true God and vowed to rid the human race of its foulest members. They would hunt down serial killers and pedophiles the human race could not capture and convict, and execute them. And with the elimination of each criminal, they prayed that they were a step closer to falling into God's favor once again. With the eradication of each deadly criminal, they prayed that they became a little more human. Each man and woman in the sept hoped he or she was a little closer to mortality and an end to the everlasting, damned life they suffered.

Arlan looked at the sleeping woman in his arms again. Despite his true belief that his life's work *did* put him on the road to redemption, a part of him still craved human blood. That primal part of him did not seem to change with the passage of time. He still dreamed of human blood. Studying her in the pale morning light, he still tasted it.

There were ways to drink one's fill and truly satiate. Ways to kill without turning a human into a vampire. She said herself she had no family, no lover. He doubted anyone would ever look for her. Ever know she was gone from this earth. If she did have something to do with the Buried Alive Killer, this would be a simple way to end her involvement. It would certainly save the taxpayers a heap of money.

Arlan lowered his mouth to her neck and pressed his lips to her warm skin. He licked her with the slow, deliberate stroke of a lover. As he did, the crucifix he always wore around his neck fell on her bare shoulder. She sighed in her sleep. *A part of her wanted it, too . . .*

No. He pulled away from her, carefully untangling himself from her and the bed sheets without waking her.

Disgusted with himself, with his sick, dark, evil thoughts, Arlan grabbed his jeans and T-shirt and quickly dressed. As he sat on the edge of a chair slipping on his shoes, he looked up at her. She lay asleep, curled on her side, utterly unaware of who she'd picked up on that beach last night.

Leather jacket thrown over his shoulder, Arlan stopped in the open doorway to glance at her one last time. He felt guilty for leaving her without saying good-bye, but right now, he didn't trust himself. He needed to get home. Home where he would be surrounded by people like him. People who understood his base desires. There, he would be safe.

And so would Maggie.

Macy opened her eyes and blinked against the bright light that poured through the cracks between the parted hotel drapes. She could still smell Arlan on her skin. Taste him on her tongue. She could still feel him inside her.

But she was alone.

Of course she was. It was better this way, really.

The clock beside the bed said ten after ten.

She stared at the water-stained ceiling tiles, realizing he'd probably been gone for hours. Good for him. He was one of the brighter ones. He understood his purpose, understood when he'd worn out his welcome. Macy hated it when she had to push men out the door.

She got up and walked naked to the bathroom. As she passed the sink on her way to the john, she saw that there was coffee in the coffee maker. She touched her hand to the glass carafe. It was still warm. He had made her coffee? Then she saw the pack of powdered sugar donuts—they looked like they'd come from the vending machine in the hotel lobby.

He left her coffee and donuts? The thought made her smile.

Then, just as she turned to step into the bathroom, she saw a plastic cup. Filled with water, it held a single scraggly daisy.

Flowers, too. Who was this nutcase?

Macy lifted the flower from the cup of water and touched it to her cheek, wishing she still knew how to cry.

"Mary Kay." Arlan walked into the airy dining room and kissed the top of Fia's mother's graying head.

"Arlan, thank Sweet Mother Mary you're here. You're a savior." She beamed up at him. "Let me get you something to eat. You must be starved."

"Don't get up," he said as she started to rise from her chair. "Sit right where you are." He touched her shoulder lightly, easing her back into her chair. "Eat your lunch. I'll get something myself."

"Fia's in the kitchen," she called after him. "But I'm so glad you're here. I told Fia you needed to come home. I knew you would know what to do."

"No word from Regan?"

She shook her head, reaching for her glass of homemade iced tea with a sprig of mint in it. "Chicken salad in the ice box. Made with grapes and walnuts, just the way you like it."

"Bless you. I'll be right back. You relax." He pushed through the swinging door that led from the bed and breakfast's dining room to the gourmet kitchen.

Fia's parents, Mary Kay and Tom, had been running some form or another of a hotel ever since they arrived in the New World hundreds of years ago. First it was just a coach stop, but later, an inn, then a boarding house and finally, in the seventies they remade themselves once again. With bed and breakfasts so popular with vacationing Americans, the couple made a healthy living in the seaside town of Clare Point as modern day innkeepers. Each day, Mary Kay baked and cooked and cleaned and played hostess, and Thomas sat on the back porch, smoking one cigarette after another, waiting until it was time to walk up to the pub for his daily dose of stout.

Arlan found Fia standing at the kitchen's center island, scooping chicken salad onto a bed of lettuce on a plate. "Hey," she called as he walked in. She didn't look up. She didn't have to. She knew it was him.

"Hey," he called.

"Chicken salad?"

"You makin'? Sure." He watched her take another plate from the cupboard. "Your mom said you haven't heard from Regan. Fin heard from him?"

Fin was the oldest of her siblings, after her. Besides Fin and Regan, there were actually three more boys, currently teens, who she also considered her brothers. The younger boys had been left orphans after the massacre in Ireland and Mary Kay had taken them in as her own children.

"I haven't talked to Fin. He's on assignment, but I left him a message on his voice mail."

Arlan watched her tear lettuce from a head of Romaine

and arrange it on the second plate. "Hey, I want a croissant."

She scooped chicken salad onto the lettuce. "Too bad.
Too many carbs." She offered him the plate.

He looked down at the small serving of chicken salad
on the lettuce. "But Mary Kay always makes me chicken
salad on a croissant," he protested.

"Suck it up." She walked past him, smacking him in the
stomach with the palm of her hand as she went by. "Literally. You're getting soft, my friend."

He pressed his free hand to his abdomen. He worked out
regularly. He had great abs. What was she talking about?
"I am *not* getting soft. Try me again. I wasn't ready." He
thrust out his chest, sucking in his stomach.

She returned the gigantic aluminum bowl of chicken
salad to the restaurant-sized refrigerator. "You sure
Regan didn't say anything about going somewhere after
Athens?"

"Hey, we're not done with the jelly belly discussion yet."

"We're done." Skirting him, she sidled up to a drawer
and pulled out two forks. "Ma's already got iced tea in the
dining room."

He followed her through the swinging door. "He didn't
say anything about going somewhere else." Upon his arrival in Athens, Arlan had met with Regan and the others
briefly; that was the last time he had seen her brother.

When Arlan spoke, he left out the name of the city where
they had convened. Fia knew where the men had been because she was presently a member of the High Council,
but Mary Kay wasn't privy to that information. Thirteen
sept members served the High Council at a time. To protect
the town, certain facts regarding the criminals they stalked
remained confidential. Mary Kay rarely knew where the
sept sent her sons. The individual investigations were secret,
as were the executions.

Arlan took a seat at the massive antique oak dining table with seating for twelve, across from Mary Kay and beside Fia.

"I'm sure Regan's fine, Mary Kay." Arlan took a bite of the chicken salad. It was good, but would have been better on one of her buttery homemade croissants. "You know Regan." He kept his tone light. "He's never where he's supposed to be when he's supposed to be there."

Fia's mother refused to be comforted. "When he called, he said he was in deep trouble. We got disconnected before he could say anything else." She poured two more glasses of iced tea from a pink carnival glass pitcher. "I thought for sure he would have called back by now," she worried.

The front door opened and a balding, forty-something man in plaid shorts walked through the foyer and into the dining room. He was carrying a teary-eyed toddler in his arms. A human guest staying at the B and B.

"Gosh, you have company. I'm sorry, Mary Kay. I was wondering if you could help us out." He jostled the child. "Seems Todd got stung by a bee. I was wondering if you had some tweezers or something to get the stinger?"

Mary Kay was already out of her chair, wiping her mouth with a pressed yellow cotton napkin. "Of course, Bradley. This is just my daughter and nephew." She waved him toward the kitchen, ever the good hostess, even in the middle of a possible crisis with one of her children. She'd been through a few over the centuries. "Come right this way. I've got a first-aid kit in the kitchen."

Arlan watched the door swing closed behind them before he turned to Fia. He lowered his voice. "You think Regan's really in hot water?"

She shrugged. "I don't know. You know Regan. He exaggerates. I came home for Ma, not Regan."

She was eating cubes of Mary Kay's delectable chicken

with bites of lettuce. Arlan was trying his damnedest not to contaminate perfectly good chicken salad with the rabbit food.

"You want to tell me about Maggie?" She put the last forkful of salad into her mouth and rose, grabbing her iced tea as she left the table. "Come on. Outside. Away from nosy tourists."

Arlan grabbed his glass. Left his lettuce. He joined Fia on the front porch, where she'd settled on the swing.

"What did Maggie have to say?" Fia asked.

"She wasn't happy about you not being there." He dug his heels into the floorboards and they glided backward.

"But she talked to you?"

"Eh." He shrugged, sipping his tea. "Sort of."

She looked him. "So she *did* talk to you or she didn't?" She watched him for another second and then punched him hard in the shoulder. "You jerk! You slept with my informant?"

"Ouch!" He rubbed his arm and then ran his hand over his T-shirt where he had spilled iced tea. "Fee, that hurts."

"So you're saying you didn't sleep with her?"

When he didn't answer, she slapped the arm of the wooden swing. "Damn it to bloody hell, Arlan. Why is it always like this? Why can't you keep your dick in your pants?"

"You used to like it when I didn't keep my dick in my pants."

She groaned and looked away. "So, you get anything out of my informant, *before* you slept with her? *After,* maybe?"

"I have to tell you, she's not much of an informant, Fee." He was trying to tease her, but she obviously wasn't in the mood.

"So that's a no." Fia still wouldn't look at him.

"Actually, I think she knows something, but I'm not sure how easy it's going to be to get it out of her."

"And you know this how, Mr. Man-whore?"

He smiled. "You're jealous."

She looked straight ahead. "I'm not jealous, Arlan. I'm annoyed with you. I have a potential witness to multiple homicides and you're screwing around with her. Literally and emotionally. I expected better out of you. I thought you could handle this. That you could do it for me."

"But I did do it." By the time the words were out of his mouth, he realized he'd made one joke too many.

Fia glared.

"I tried, okay? I was upfront with why I was there, Fee. She wanted to talk to *you*, not me. Remember, if it wasn't for this issue with Regan, you could have been there yourself," he chastised gently.

The swing came to a halt. Neither pushed it again.

"So she didn't want to talk to you about the murders, but she wanted to sleep with you?"

He hesitated, setting his empty glass on the floor beside the swing. She was right of course. Fia was right. She always was. "Yeah. She wanted to sleep with me. She's the one who came on to me."

Fia looked at him doubtfully.

"She did," he defended. "I swear on my mother's grave."

Fia scowled, putting her own glass down. "You do anything else to her?"

"Anything else?" he asked innocently.

She was referring to bloodletting. It was against sept law, they all knew it. And they all, on occasion, broke the law. Even Fia. He knew that for a fact. Fia had a little problem with stalking men in bars and feeding on them, an act doubly forbidden by the sept. At least she had before her current boyfriend.

"No. No, of course not," he said, trying to sound offended, feeling guilty at the same time for the dark thoughts that *had* crept through his mind this morning while Maggie lay asleep in his arms. "I just had sex with her. Plain old intercourse. Just the ol' in and out. Nothing else."

"I suppose that's something." Fia exhaled. She gazed out at the nicely trimmed green lawn in front of the rambling Victorian house. "I don't suppose she gave you a way for me to contact her? A phone number? An e-mail address?"

"No. But she said she'd call you."

"So you just left her. Screwed her and left her?"

"Fee, what was I supposed to do?"

She shook her head. "You could have *not* screwed her. What if you scared her off? What if she doesn't call me? This is five more murders. This guy is a bad one and the human authorities are no closer to catching him than they were last year. I can tell you that right now." She rose from the swing and walked over to the porch rail.

Arlan followed her, unable to explain to Fia the connection he'd felt to Maggie last night. She would never understand, even if he tried to explain it. But then how could she when he didn't understand himself? "I really am sorry. I screwed up."

"You're right. You did." She put her hands on the rail and leaned forward.

"But she's going to call you. I know she is. She wants to talk to you. She wants to help catch this freak."

"And you know this how?" She looked up at him.

He reached over and rubbed her back gently. "I don't know. I just have a feeling about her. You'll hear from her again."

"I sure hope you're right." She shifted her gaze from him to the lawn again.

He leaned on the rail next to her. "So what do you think we should do about Regan?"

"Nothing we can do. I think I convinced Ma of that last night. We just have to wait. You know him. He'll pop up."

Arlan realized this was the perfect opportunity to tell Fia that Regan had probably gone AWOL *prior* to the kill. But still, it seemed like tattling. It wasn't the first time Regan hadn't showed. And in every previous instance, he'd been off playing when he should have been working. Regan was just immature. He'd work his way into the job.

But what about the call home?

It wouldn't be the first time Regan had called someone drunk, babbling some overblown story.

But he didn't usually call his mother.

"You . . . you want me to see if I can find out when his flight was supposed to leave?" Arlan asked. "See where he was going? I'm not even sure he was coming back to the states. We've still got several active investigations going on in that part of the world."

"I can do it," she said.

"No. You're busy. You've got this case." He lowered his hand. "Other cases," he added, remembering she wasn't officially on the Buried Alive case.

"Yeah, I talked to the Baltimore guys about letting me in on the investigation. Just as a consultant. Of course their bosses have to talk to my bosses. It might work out. Might not."

"Having Maggie would get you in."

"Probably."

"She'll call."

Fia's cell rang and she slid it out of her jeans pocket. She checked the caller ID and looked at him.

"Lover boy?" he asked.

"Excuse me," she said curtly, and walked away. "Glen," she said into the phone.

Arlan watched her move to the far side of the porch,

talking quietly to her boyfriend. Her *human* boyfriend. He stuffed his hands into his pockets and went down the porch steps, fighting the urge to look back. Fia didn't need to be jealous over him sleeping with a human. Arlan had enough jealousy bottled up inside him for both of them.

Chapter 9

Women. They always were his downfall. Arlan knew that. If he could just swear them off for good, he'd be better off. Arlan kept himself busy the rest of the day so as to not think about Fia or Maggie, but he didn't have much success.

He loved women. He loved them in all shapes and sizes and colors. Young women to old women; it made little difference to him. And in all fairness, they liked him.

A carpenter by trade, when he wasn't on sept business, he did light construction work in town. After giving an estimate to repair a deck and construct a built-in entertainment center, Arlan stopped at the market and bought a steak, a bag of potatoes, and some frozen green beans. He passed on the sour cream he wanted for his baked potato. He knew Fia was just teasing; he was certainly not growing a paunch. But it was never too soon to start a healthier lifestyle.

At home, he emptied out his refrigerator of containers with unidentifiable foods, put a potato in the oven, and washed the crusty dishes he'd left in the sink when he went to Greece. With the kitchen in order and the stinky garbage in the outside bin, Arlan went out on his back deck to light a fire in his barbeque grill. Most people had gone to gas grills, but he was a purist at heart. He loved the smell of charcoal burning and the smoky taste of his rare steak, flavored by the embers.

Arlan carefully stacked the briquettes he removed from the bag and then pulled his trusty lighter from his back pocket. Charcoal fires got a bum rap because they took so long to prepare. However, match-light charcoal was a miraculous innovation. In twenty minutes he'd have a perfect bed of coals to cook that perfect steak.

He flicked the lighter and nothing happened. He flicked it again. Then he realized the safety switch was on. He slid the switch and flicked the trigger again. He was rewarded with a small blue flame. He could smell his baked potato roasting in the oven and could imagine the taste of the T-bone, bloody rare and barely warm in the center.

The blue flame on the end of the lighter went out. He looked closer. The briquette hadn't lit. He flicked the lighter, impatiently. It took three flicks to get a flame again. The fluid inside had to be running low. "Come on," he muttered. He was getting hungry. "Light."

The cold black tower seemed to mock him.

"Damn it," he muttered. He'd been fine all day after being chastised by Fia for sleeping with Maggie. He'd been fine. He could deal with disappointing Fia. But what he could not deal with tonight was charcoal that wouldn't light. He flicked the lighter again and again.

"Bloody bastard."

The latch on the gate in his backyard clicked and the heavy gate swung open. "Arlan, that you?"

He recognized the woman's voice. After living with the same people for centuries, everyone knew everyone else's voice, their smell, the sound of the way they walked. "Hey, Peigi." He poked one of the charcoal briquettes with the end of the lighter and flicked the trigger repeatedly, his irritation rising. *Click, click.*

"I rang the doorbell."

"Broken." He flicked the trigger. *Click, click.* "It's on my to-do list." Had been for at least two years. It was a long list, but when life went on forever, two years was barely a drop in a very big bucket.

Peigi was a short, lumpy woman of about sixty. Her gray hair was styled in a bowl cut and she wore baggy shorts, a striped T-shirt, and sensible shoes. She looked like a middle-aged model for L.L. Bean. Peigi Ross was a *sensible* woman. "Having trouble lighting that?" She pointed to the round charcoal grill.

"Nah." He clicked the lighter. "What can I do for you?"

"We have a favor to ask."

Along with being sensible, Peigi was also direct.

"We?" He didn't like the sound of that. *We* meant the sept. *We* usually meant something dangerous like killing a notorious vampire slayer or cat-sitting for Miss Lucy's five cats.

"I'm listening." *Click, click. Click, click.* "Damn it. I wonder if the charcoal got damp. It's a new bag. I used charcoal from it the day before I left." *Click, click. Click, click.* Now the lighter wasn't lighting at all.

"As you know, Johnny Hill's gout is acting up again."

"I'm sorry. I hadn't heard that."

"Both feet now," Peigi said. "It's too long a walk for him from his house to the museum for High Council."

Arlan looked up. His thumb was beginning to cramp. "He can't take his car?"

"We don't drive to meetings. We walk. We've always walked, you know that." She watched him push the briquettes around with the end of the lighter. "Would you like me to do that?"

"I can get it." He shook the lighter, listening to see if he heard any fluid sloshing around, and tried again. "So what does Johnny want? He need me to take him to meetings?"

Click, click. "I can drive him. Why didn't he ask me himself?"

"We don't drive and we don't ride. What he needs is some time off." She placed her hands on her sensible, middle-aged hips. "He wants you to take his place on the High Council."

"I absolutely am not—"

"Temporarily," she interrupted.

"Peigi." Arlan stepped back from the grill, as frustrated by the conversation as he was by the fact that he couldn't get the damned charcoal to light. "You know me. I'm not High Council material. I'm grunt work material."

"Nonsense," she fussed. "You'd be an excellent High Council member. You're already on our short list, should a permanent position become open."

"Peigi," Arlan groaned. "I can't make those kinds of decisions. Trying to decide who should live and who should die. Who's evil and who's just bad." He clicked the lighter halfheartedly over the grill, shaking his head adamantly. "You know how I am. I like being told where to go, what to do."

"Step back," she ordered sharply.

When Peigi Ross told you to step back, you stepped back.

There was a sudden whoosh of air as if all the oxygen in the space in front of him had been depleted. Flames leaped from the barbeque, twenty feet into the air. Arlan took another quick step back, swearing he could feel his eyebrows singeing. He raised his hand to deflect the heat from his face. "I think that'll do it, Peigi."

All sept members shared some inhuman abilities: their sense of smell was amazing, they were able to speak telepathically to each other, and then of course there was the bit about living eternally. But they each also had unique gifts that contributed to the common welfare of the sept. Peigi's gift happened to be pyrokinetics. Simply by setting her mind to it, she could light a cigarette or make a ten-story apartment building burst into flames so hot that the place would burn to the ground in a matter of minutes. She was like the Drew Barrymore character in the movie, only all grown up and gray-haired.

"Think you could have warned me?" Arlan muttered, still holding his hand up to block the heat.

"So you'll be there tomorrow night?" Peigi was already on the deck steps, on her way out.

"I didn't say that, Peigi."

"Come by. See how you like it."

"You give me a black hooded cloak and a fifteen-hundred-year-old dagger and you ask me to *try it out*?" He followed her to the edge of the deck. The boards needed staining and resealing. "You're kidding me, right?"

"I'll tell Gair he can expect you," she sang, giving a one-handed wave as she stopped to open the back gate. "Enjoy your steak. Glad to have you home."

Arlan turned around. There was no sense arguing with her any further. If Peigi Ross told him to do something, he was going to do it. No matter how loudly he protested or who he complained to, sooner or later, he would do it. She knew that. He liked her the way he liked all women and she took unfair advantage of that. It was one more aspect of Peigi's personality that made her so sensible.

Sensible Peigi, in her sensible shoes, who could set a freighter on fire in the middle of the Atlantic Ocean. In a rainstorm.

Macy sat in her car with her hands white-knuckled on the wheel, her forehead pressed to the center. She'd already inadvertently beeped the horn once.

The parking lot of the rinky-dink motel where she'd spent the night was empty. Traffic passing by the place was almost nonexistent. It was like she was frozen. Couldn't think. Couldn't drive. All she could do was sit here. It was as if she was having some sort of silent panic attack.

She'd already been to the bathroom in the lobby twice. The clerk had watched her closely when she'd purchased a bottle of green tea and a pack of crackers from the vending machine. He'd asked her if anything was wrong. And she'd mumbled something about waiting for her cousin.

Macy lifted her head, taking in a deep breath. The sun was low in the sky. When she'd left the room, it had been directly overhead. Had she really been sitting here that long? She had to go before the clerk got really suspicious and called the cops.

Macy didn't talk to cops. Not if she could help it. Just Fia, and she didn't really count, did she? No, there was something different about Fia than other cops. Something that made Macy trust her, made Macy believe she understood secrets. She suspected Fia had secrets of her own.

Macy released the wheel one finger at a time. Her hands were hot and sweaty and sticky.

She thought about Arlan. He'd been smart to run. He knew what kind of woman to run from.

Then she thought about the coffee and donuts he had left her. And the flower. She'd pressed the flower in a book she was reading. How girlishly silly was that?

No sillier than the idea that she might be able to help Fia Kahill catch the killer. Catch the man who had ruined her life. Would continue to ruin lives.

Macy exhaled.

It was time to go. Time to go back to the cottage. She started the car. Pulled out of the parking lot.

But instead of turning right, heading south toward the Bay Bridge Tunnel, she turned left. North.

What was north? Who was north? What was drawing her this way? Was it Teddy? Was this it? Would he finally kill her? Was he on a *hot streak* as the cops liked to call it? Was she the only thing that would end his hot streak? Would her death cool his jets?

Her life seemed like a small sacrifice to her to save the lives of others.

But she knew it wasn't that simple.

Arlan was just flipping his steak on the grill when he heard the back gate creak open again. He couldn't believe Peigi'd had the audacity to return after she'd bullied him like that. But when he looked up, ready to give her hell, he saw his niece, Kaleigh, closing the gate behind her.

"Hey," she called. "You're back."

He hung the cooking tongs on a hook on the grill and closed the lid. He opened his arms. "I'm back."

"I thought you were supposed to be home last night." She walked into his arms.

After a hug, he sat down in a chair and pushed another toward her with his foot. "I ran an errand with Fia. Stayed the night in Virginia and drove home this morning."

She plopped down in the chair, crossing her arms over her chest. To look at her, she appeared to be like any other teenager across America. Her red hair was long, pulled straight back in a ponytail. She wore denim shorts so short that her mother probably called them obscene and her double-layered tank tops appeared to be spray-painted onto her torso. She wore big hoop earrings and cherry lip gloss.

But Kaleigh was by no means a typical teenager. She wasn't even typical for a teenage vampire. Kaleigh was the sept's wisewoman who, when she grew completely into her own again, would be the most powerfully psychic member of the sept.

With each death and rebirth, Kaleigh seemed to grow stronger, more perceptive and more commanding. As an adult, she would have all the sept's powers rolled into one. She was the person everyone relied on when making decisions, not just for the entire sept, but personal, as well. However, like every one else in Clare Point, she had to die, be reborn as a teen and grow into herself once again. It had been less than two years since the girl's last rebirth, so she was still maturing.

A kid or not, Arlan certainly wouldn't challenge Kaleigh to any kind of psychic duel. When she got wound up, she could be scary. She scared them all, which was probably what generated such a healthy respect for her, even in this state.

"You want a beer?" He picked the bottle up from where he'd set it on the deck when he got up to flip his steak.

"I'm underage, remember?" She snatched the bottle from him, took a drink—an obviously *experienced* drinker—and handed back the bottle. "I don't drink." She smirked.

He grinned and tipped the bottle, finishing it off. "You need something or you just looking for free beer?"

She shrugged, perfectly imitating a human teenager. "Mostly free beer." She sat back in her chair, slipped a tube of lip gloss out of her pocket and began to apply it. "I'm working at the Dairy Queen."

"Like it?"

She frowned. "Hate it. But Mom and Dad said I had to find a job this summer. You know, work my way slowly up the corporate ladder; cashier this year, wisewoman next year." She rolled her eyes, still smearing on the lip gloss. He could smell the cherry flavoring. "They seem to think wearing the paper hat will keep me out of trouble."

She was referring to the beheadings that had taken place the summer before. She had inadvertently gotten wrapped up in a relationship with a human who thought himself a vampire slayer. He killed three members of the sept before he was stopped. Had it not been for Fia, Kaleigh and two other teenage girls might have lost their lives, their souls damned forever in a fiery limbo created solely for vampires. Not dead, because vampires couldn't die. But not alive. Not of this earth any longer.

"A job's a good way to spend the summer. You get to talk to all the cute human guys who come for ice cream."

She frowned, holding up the clear tube of lip gloss. "I'm done with humans, I swear, Sweet Mother Mary and Joseph. I'll be happy if I never see another human again in the next ten lifetimes."

He chuckled at her naiveté. Part of God's curse was living among humans but always having to keep your guard up, not ever being able to quite fit in. The sept couldn't break the curse if they didn't work to save mankind and they couldn't save mankind if they didn't live among them.

"So if I come by the DQ, do I get free milk shakes?"

Again, the frown. "No. If I'm going to risk getting caught giving away free milk shakes, it's going to be to cute guys *my* age."

He laughed, opening the grill to check his steak. "So everything else okay? Your mom and dad? Your brother?"

"Same old, same old," she groaned, doing a great imitation of a bored human teenager. "Connor's a dick already."

Her brother had recently been reborn, so he was back in her parents' house, and Arlan had heard that the siblings were into fighting like teenagers again. The week before, the two became embroiled in a contest, hurling French fries while at the local diner. The owner had threatened to call the police when Kaleigh hit a tourist in the back of the head with a ketchup-drenched steak fry.

Arlan lifted his steak with a fork and, satisfied, dropped it on a plate he'd brought out earlier from the house. "Want some dinner? I've got plenty of steak to share." He showed her the hunk of meat on the plate.

She wrinkled her freckled nose, reminding him of Fia in

her teenage years. Cousins, they looked a lot alike. "I don't eat meat. It's gross. I'm a vegetarian. Thinking about becoming a vegan."

He raised a brow. "But you still drink blood?"

"Of course." She said it as if he was a complete idiot. "No steak, but I'll have some of those green beans." She sniffed the air. "They smell good. Olive oil?"

Arlan came back out of the house a few minutes later carrying two plates and forks. He handed Kaleigh the plate with just green beans on it and sat down to eat his steak, potato with butter, and green beans.

"So what's up with you?" Drawing her knees up in the chair, Kaleigh stabbed at a bean with her fork. "You and Fia figure things out?"

"I've got things figured out perfectly. She just isn't with the plan yet."

"I don't like that human FBI dude. I don't care if he does look just like her true love"—she rolled her eyes—"who betrayed her a gazillion years ago. I think she ought to dump him for you."

He sampled a piece of steak. It was perfect, warm and bloody. "You tell her so?"

"Every chance I get." Kaleigh stabbed another bean. "So what about this other chick? What's her name? Maggie?"

"Hey. You're not supposed to be reading people's minds without being invited." He poked his fork in her direction. She was good. He hadn't even felt her probe his mind. "You know better than that, missy."

"Guess I must have done it by accident." She smiled in a way that made him think she knew perfectly well what she was doing.

"Maggie's nothing. No one."

"Another one-night stand, huh? You know, you're going to get tired of those eventually," she chastised, waving her fork at him.

"Ah, now I'm taking romantic advice from a woman who dates psychopathic vampire slayers."

She hurled the bean off her fork in his direction. He ducked and it sailed over the back of his chair.

"I didn't know he was nuts," Kaleigh continued matter-of-factly. "That wasn't my fault. I was temporarily . . . I don't know. You know." She munched on another mouthful of beans. "I don't want to talk about him. Never again."

"So who do you want to talk about?" Arlan and Kaleigh always got along but it wasn't like her to just stop by. Not at this point in her life. She was too busy doing teenage things. Growing into herself.

She set her plate at her feet and her fork clattered. "Ummm. You know Rob Hill died, right?"

"Ah," he said, having a feeling he knew where this conversation was headed. "Sure. Burial's Tuesday night. I'll be there."

"So . . . ummm, he'll be around by the weekend.

Reborn as a teenager. As a male, he'd enter life again at around the human equivalent of sixteen or seventeen.

"Right."

"So . . . you think I should go, you know, over to his house? Say hello?"

Arlan smiled inwardly, but he knew better than to trivialize the situation. While permitted to sleep with other sept members, from the beginning, they had ruled that they must remain with their original mates forever. Again and again, Kaleigh would marry the man who had been her husband the day they became vampires. What was difficult was that each time they were reborn, they had to re-remember. They had to get reacquainted and even go through the same awkward romantic phases humans went through.

Rob Hill would one day be Kaleigh's husband again.

"I think that would be nice if you went by. Said hi. Maybe offered him a free shake at the DQ." Arlan cut off a piece of potato and pushed it into his mouth. The soft, buttery saltiness was good, but not as good as the steak.

"You think that would be okay?" She squirmed in her chair. "I mean . . . I know he won't remember." She gazed out into his backyard. It was beginning to grow dark and lightening bugs sparked in the dusky half-light. "I mean, I barely remember."

"It'll come back to you," he assured her.

She got up. "Guess I better go. I told Maria I'd meet her at Katy's. We might go to a movie or something." At the top of the deck steps she turned back to him. "So, um, I guess I'll see you around."

He smiled at her. "See you around."

Arlan finished his dinner alone in pleasant silence on his deck and then went inside with the intention of washing his dishes. Instead he set them in the sink and ran water over them. He checked his cell phone to be sure he hadn't missed a call from Fin or Regan. He'd called them both several times throughout the day and left messages. Seeing that neither had phoned, he headed out the front door. It was eight o'clock and for many in the town, first call of the night at the pub.

Chapter 10

The Hill, as it was known in town, was the second oldest continuously operated bar in the United States,
right after the White Horse up in Newport, Rhode Island.
If it hadn't been for the eighteenth-century hurricanes, it
would have been the oldest. Originally built down near
the water on top of a sand dune by one of Arlan's distant
relatives, they had finally surrendered to the power of the
elements and rebuilt inland on higher ground. The town
had sprung up helter-skelter around the pub, and year-
round, the public room was the heart of the Kahill sept.

Arlan had to duck under the hand-hewn beam to enter
through the building's archway. Inside, he was immediately
assaulted by the sights, sounds, and smells that had been
ingrained in him for centuries. The resonance was overwhelming, not just of audible voices, but also the voices in
his head. When alone and free from humans, the Kahills
talked aloud while also speaking telepathically on a different subject. At the same time.

On occasion, especially in the summer months, humans
wandered through the door of The Hill, but they didn't
stay long and they almost never came back. There was another pub up the street, O'Cahall's, which was more suitable
for tourists, and with some instinctual sense of self-

preservation, they were easily guided in that direction. Tonight, there wasn't a single human in the pub and there was a buzz of excitement, even relief among the locals because of it. Sometimes, even vampires needed to let their guard down.

As Arlan crossed the rough floorboards, headed for the bar, he was bombarded with thoughts and words.

"Bar tab's too high again, Mungo. Pay up."

'Bout time dead, he was . . .

You know, the blue with the ruffle . . . Wore it last Easter Sunday.

". . . Say it again, Jimmy, and I'll walk out, I will. . . ."

A shame.

A pitiful, sorry shame.

Arlan took the only empty stool between brothers Mungo and Sean Kahill, Fia's uncles. Sean Sr. was the chief of police and Arlan's buddy Sean's father.

"Evening, gentlemen."

"Evening." Mungo tipped an imaginary cap. The man went four hundred pounds if he went an ounce. *Tavia tapped a new keg of stout. We should celebrate your recent accomplishment, we should,* he telepathed for anyone within listening distance. "Eva, a stout for my handsome friend," he called to the barmaid.

"We're proud of you, son, we are," Sean said soberly.

He had always been a jolly man, but after the murders the previous year, he had never quite seemed like himself. Arlan knew that on some level, Sean held himself responsible for the deaths of Bobby McCathal, Mahon Kahill and Shannon Smith, even though everyone agreed there was nothing he could have done. His behavior was subtle, but Arlan had seen the change. He'd lost so much weight that his jowls sagged, and he drank too much.

Vampire beheadings would do that to you. Once beheaded, a vampire could never be reborn. He could never really die, unsaved by God, as he was, so he was left to linger in some burning limbo far worse than any human's hell. Only vampire slayers knew a head must be separated from the body to kill a vampire. All that other nonsense— garlic, silver bullets, sunlight, spit from a virgin—it was all baloney created in books and movies.

"You're back," Eva said, leaning on the bar to bare more than a little of her ample cleavage.

Arlan glanced at her breasts and smiled with amusement. Eva swore she was a lesbian, but he wondered, sometimes, if she wasn't bisexual. Why else would she always be showing men her boobs?

"I'm back."

She wiped the wooden bar top salvaged from the original seaside pub. Before that, the boards had served as the keel of the ship they'd come to America aboard. "Everyone else safe and accounted for?" Eva asked.

He glanced up at her. *You've talked to Fia?*

Mungo and Sean were busy watching the TV mounted in the corner of the room. The Phillies were up by one over the Orioles. Both men were shouting as a player in orange rounded second. They weren't listening to Arlan and Eva, but he tried to put up a mental barrier anyway.

Eva did the same. *Ran into Mary Kay at the produce stand. So Regan really is MIA?*

He shrugged. *Hard to say with him.* He looked up, meeting her gaze. She was pretty in a punk kind of way, with spiky hair and wild, dark blue eye shadow.

Eva caught his drift. Arlan didn't know how much she knew about Regan's previous screw-ups, but he guessed it was more than Mungo and Sean knew. Eva was the same generation as Arlan and Regan. They all hung out together whenever they were in town.

You talk to Fin? She reached for a clean pint glass and pulled a stout for him.

Not yet, but he had sept business in Europe. He may have made a stop on his way home, Arlan said, still telepathing. He pulled a bill from his front pocket and tucked it into Eva's cleavage as she slid the ale across the bar toward him. "A round for the three of us and you."

She chuckled. "You're such a gentleman, Arlan. If you were a woman—" She waggled her finger at him.

He grinned, picking up his glass and tasting it. "You seen Fia tonight?" He tried to sound casual.

"I think she went back to Philadelphia. Mary Kay said she was working on that big Buried Alive case. Said she was heading up the investigation."

The stout went down smooth and hardy. It had a honey oak taste that was a particular favorite of his. The master brewer and pub owner, Tavia, knew her stout, that was for sure. "Fia is not heading up the case. And she finds out Mary Kay is telling tourists that, she's going to have her mother's head."

"Just telling you what Mary Kay told me over the new potato bin." She raised both hands in innocence.

Arlan looked around, sipping his stout. He knew every face. Some sept members he liked better than others, some he knew better. But they were all family and he felt an intense loyalty to them. It was for these men and women, for their souls, that he risked his life in the shadows of places like Athens, Greece, and Akron, Ohio.

"Eva!" Johnny Hill called from a table. "Can a man dyin' of thirst get a pint here?"

Eva rolled her eyes and tapped the bar top with her palm before walking away. "Catch you later, handsome." She winked at him. "I'll put a good word in for you with Fia, if I see her."

Maryann Hill caught Arlan's eye and waved cheerfully. *You'll be there for the burial?* she telepathed. It would have been too noisy for him to have heard her at this distance.

She was referring to her son's funeral. At times like this, their whole life cycle got a little weird. Maryann was in her midforties. Her son, Rob, had died at the age of eighty-two. He would be reborn three days after his burial, as a teenager.

Arlan raised his glass to her. *I'll be there.*

And that cute niece of yours? Kaleigh?

I imagine she'll be there, too. He turned on the barstool, away from her. He was not playing matchmaker. If Kaleigh and Rob were going to get together, it would have to be by their own efforts. Couples were expected to eventually live together because it helped keep up appearances to the outside world. Sept rules, however, did not demand that each couple live each lifetime as exclusive bed partners. They had realized early on that it was hard enough for a couple to live forty years in marital bliss. Four hundred years would be impossible. Sept members were permitted, once they reached the age of eighteen, to have sex with any other consenting vampire adults so long as they continued to live with their permanent partner. It was a strange form of monogamy, but it seemed to work well enough. The downside was that men and women like Arlan and Fia, who were not married at the time of the *mallachd,* the curse, could never marry.

At the crack of a bat on the TV, Sean shouted, raising a fist in the air. "I told you they'd come back, I did!"

His brother turned away, disgusted by his team's error in the field. Sean eased off his stool, slapping Arlan on the back. "Thanks for the ale, kid. Tell my brother he pays for the next round, he does."

Arlan watched as Sean weaved his way between tables where patrons were eating supper, back-slapping as he went.

As Arlan slid his empty pint glass across the bar top, there was an audible change in the atmosphere of the room. Voices died down considerably and telepathed thoughts flew around the room faster. The ball game on the TV suddenly seemed to get louder.

Who's that?
Who the hell does she think she is?
One night of peace and quiet is all I ask.

Arlan didn't look up. It was just a tourist who had wandered too far afoot. Someone would steer her the right way. She'd probably gotten confused and was supposed to be meeting her girlfriends down the street.

"Another?" Eva asked Arlan. She wasn't interested in HF tourists either.

"One more." He slid his glass toward her. If Fia didn't show up by the time he'd finished his pint, he'd head home. Now that he was here, he realized he wasn't all that interested in socializing tonight. He had too many things on his mind.

Where the hell was Regan? Why hadn't Fin returned his calls?

Had Fia gone back to Philadelphia to the human boyfriend? She didn't normally tell him every time she came or went in town but after the trip to Virginia they'd shared, he thought maybe . . .

"Here you go, big boy." Eva slid a fresh pint across the bar top.

"Hey, big boy." Someone sat down on the barstool beside him.

Her voice startled him. He looked over.

"Could I have what he's having?" Maggie asked Eva.

Eva looked to Arlan. He nodded slightly.

"One honey stout coming up."

"What are you—" Arlan closed his fingers over the cool glass, looking away from her. How was it possible that she could be here? he wondered. He hadn't told her what town he lived in and he certainly hadn't told her about the seedy pub where he liked to take a pint of ale a couple of nights a week. This was a little eerie. He tracked men and women for a living. People didn't track him. "How did you find me?"

She waited for her pint, took a sip and wiped the foam off her upper lip in what was an amazingly sensual gesture. "I'm good at hiding," she said in that disquieting way of hers. "I'm also good at finding who I'm looking for."

Fia sped north on Route 1. If she didn't hit any serious traffic on 95, she'd be in Philly in an hour. She felt bad leaving Clare Point without talking to Arlan, but not bad enough to call him. She didn't want to talk to him. Not tonight. He had a way of reading between the lines.

She told her mother she had to get back to work, which was true. She told Mary Kay that Regan would turn up and that was *probably* true. She'd told Glen she was staying with her mother another night. *A flat-out lie.*

But she just couldn't go home to her apartment and her cat tonight. She was too keyed up, so keyed up that she felt as if she was busting at the seams.

It had been months since Fia had been out on the prowl, and it was killing her. A taste of human blood was all she needed. Just a taste.

Nothing in her life was going the way she had thought it would. After solving the big case in Clare Point last year, she had thought she would be promoted in the bureau. That hadn't happened. She had started dating Glen and she had thought that would make her happy. It hadn't, and lately it seemed as if she wasn't making him happy, either.

And it just got better. Regan was now possibly missing, possibly in some kind of serious trouble. And the Buried Alive killings were starting to get under her skin. Maggie was starting to get under her skin and she didn't often let that happen with a case. She couldn't afford to, not and do her job right.

Fia was annoyed that Arlan hadn't gotten more out of the chick. She'd expected better out of him. He was so good with women, really good with H.F's, although it pissed him off when she said so.

Now, with no way to contact Maggie, Fia would just have to sit tight and wait for the woman to call her. If she did call again. What if Arlan had scared her off? Fia couldn't believe he had slept with her informant. Arlan was such a slut.

She smiled to herself, looking down at the short black leather skirt, fishnet stockings, and four-inch heeled boots she'd changed into at the rest stop. Her black T-shirt was so tight, she could see the rings of her areolas through it.

Nothing like calling the kettle black.

"Why are you here, Maggie?" Arlan asked.

He had never expected to see her again and now that she was sitting here beside him, looking so small and unassuming, he felt guilty all over again for his thoughts back at the hotel. How could he have even considered biting her and drinking her blood? What kind of man on the road to redemption was he? There were plenty of willing female vampires here in town, and elsewhere in the world. Attractive, smart, fun vampires in Ireland and France and Germany. Why a human? Why *this* one?

Arlan was annoyed that Maggie had brought out the worst in him and that she was now here to remind him of it. He knew he shouldn't have gone back into the room and left the flower and donuts.

"I asked you a question," he said stiffly.

"I'm not a stalker."

Her tone was dry. Almost amused. She was an interesting person, this HF. She came off so vulnerable, so skittish, and yet she had a backbone.

"I didn't tell you where I lived."

"I was hoping to find Fia." She sipped from her glass, casually glancing around the low-lit pub room.

So she hadn't come looking for him. Arlan was relieved. Maybe just a little disappointed. "Fia had to go back to the office in Philadelphia. She's expecting your phone call."

"I just thought face to face might be better."

He turned toward her on his barstool and her knees brushed his shins. "You have information for her?"

"I just want to talk to her."

He looked down at her. "You're a strange woman, Maggie."

"You're pretty odd yourself, Arlan," she came back.

That made him tilt his head back and laugh. *And* a sense of humor. He loved women with a sense of humor.

"Can I buy you another?" He pointed to her glass.

They each had two more pints and then Arlan decided it was time he called it a night. If he didn't, he feared he'd end up asking her to come home with him and that was definitely on the top of the list of *very bad ideas*. He stood up and paid the bar tab.

The Hill was already beginning to thin out. Disgruntled sept members had gone home. Arlan was sure he would hear of their displeasure tomorrow, what with him bringing a human into their sanctuary—even though he hadn't invited her.

"You staying in town tonight?" he asked.

"Motel down the street." Maggie picked her bag up off the floor under her barstool. "Guess I got lucky. The old lady at the desk said she was usually booked most of the summer."

"Ah, Mrs. Cahall. She's older than the hills. Hard of hearing, too." He cupped his hand to his ear. "What's that, missy? You want a *broom* for the night?"

Maggie chuckled, but her laughter was a little sad, much like her demeanor. Arlan wondered if she would ask him back to her room. He shouldn't say yes, of course, but what if she did? That certainly wasn't the same as having her back to *his* house.

They walked together toward the exit. By the time he opened the door for her, he had decided that he would say no if she invited him back. He was already in hot water with Fia; he didn't need to push it to the boiling point.

"Thanks for the beer," she said out on the sidewalk. "Good night."

Arlan stood in the dark for a moment, stunned. She hadn't asked him back to her room. And he was so sure she was going to. She'd just had that look on her face that he knew so well. Lonely and horny.

He walked home alone in the dark, hands stuffed in his pockets, unsure if he was insulted or just plain hurt.

Chapter 11

Fia pressed her back to the brick wall in the alley and slowly slid down until she was sitting on the ground, her knees pulled up to her chest. She was cold despite the heat of the steamy June night. Last call in the bars had been at least half an hour ago. She needed to get home, get cleaned up and catch a couple of hours of sleep before she had to go to work.

First she needed to do something with *him*.

She glanced at the unconscious man sitting across from her. He was handcuffed to a drainpipe with one of the disposable plastic ties that she, like most law enforcement agents, always carried with her. He was wearing a gray pinstripe suit. He *had* been wearing a red power tie until he slipped it over Fia's neck and tried to choke her.

Big mistake on the suit's part. Wrong miniskirt to cross.

It was a good thing she'd artfully disposed of the drinks he'd ordered for her. At least one of them had been laced with some kind of date rape drug; she had seen him pour the powder from the envelope into her glass when she was on the dance floor. Dumping the martinis in the potted plant had been easy. How stupid had the jerk thought she was?

But there were plenty of women out there naive enough

to accept drinks from a good-looking stranger in a five-hundred-dollar suit, and that didn't mean they deserved to be drugged and sexually assaulted. No one did.

She slipped her hand into her bag and pulled out her cell phone. She dialed from memory. As she listened to it ring, she was surprised by the lump that rose in her throat and the way her chest tightened. *Cry?* She was going to *cry* over something so stupid as a man who had tried to take advantage of her?

The phone continued to ring. He didn't always keep his cell next to his bed. Maybe it was charging in the kitchen.

Fia was just about to hang up when she heard a click on the other line, then a sleepy male voice.

" 'Llo?"

She thought about hanging up. Of course he would know it was her. He'd check his Received Messages and know she had called at 2:35 A.M. He'd wonder where she was and what she was doing. He would *know* she was somewhere she shouldn't be. They'd been together too long.

"Fee?"

She pressed the heel of her hand to her forehead, drawing into a tighter ball. Somehow she'd torn her stockings. "I screwed up," she said.

"Where are you?"

She closed her eyes. "I don't know. An alley behind some bar in north Philly. I've got an unconscious guy handcuffed to a drainpipe." She looked up. Even in the dark, her vision was good. Superhuman. There was a large, red egg rising on his temple.

"He alive?"

She watched him for a second. His chest rose and fell. "Oh, yeah. Sure," she said cheerfully.

"Did you—"

He didn't have to finish his sentence. She could see the

two red bite marks and the glisten of blood, even in the dark. "A little."

"Fee, you can't do that!" He groaned on the other end of the phone. "You have to let him go. You have to remove the handcuffs and get the hell out of there before he wakes up."

"But the bastard tried to slip rhohipnol into my drink. He wanted to play some kind of crazy erotic asphyxiation game with me in the alley. He didn't even have the good manners to take me back to his apartment or a hotel."

"Fee, if he wakes up and sees you, you might have to feed again. It could kill him."

The drinking of blood had a crazy side effect on most humans. They lost their short term memory and never knew what hit them. The suit might vaguely remember meeting Fia in the bar, but he was drunk enough and her blood-taking was hypnotizing enough that he would never remember that she had bit his neck and sucked his blood. However, if he woke up and saw her, he might be able to put the pieces together. If she drank his blood again, so close to the last feeding, it might kill him.

"Fee, you have to let him go. *Now.*"

She closed her eyes, focusing only on his voice. "I was thinking about calling the police."

"And telling them what? That you tried to pick him up in a bar so you could drink his blood and he played one-up-manship with you?"

"That's not how it went down! And look who's hand-cuffed to a drain-pipe. Not me."

"Fee, you know better." His tone was judgmental.

"Arlan . . ." Her voice nearly cracked with emotion. What was wrong with her? She was losing it. She was losing her professional edge. She was losing her vampire edge. She was becoming so damned . . . human.

He was quiet for a second. "Do you want me to come get you?"

"No." She snapped her eyes open. "Of course not. Don't be ridiculous. You're hours away."

"Where's your HM?"

"Asleep in his bed in his own apartment where he ought to be."

"He doesn't know you're missing?"

"I kept my place," she admitted. "We just play sleep-over. Besides, he thinks I'm still in Clare Point."

"You're lying to the boyfriend now?"

The sound of his voice made her cringe. "It's complicated, Arlan. You know that."

He sighed on the other end of the phone. "Listen to me, Fia. You cannot call the police. You need to remove the handcuffs and get the hell out of there, do you hear me? Go home before you get into trouble you can't easily get yourself out of."

The threat was ominous. There were a lot of ways this could go down if anyone saw her. None would be good for her. At the very least she would be investigated by her own office. Worst, she could be investigated and then punished by the sept. Human blood-feeding was forbidden. Human stalking was absolutely taboo.

"Right." She rose to her feet. "I'll just cut the cuffs. He'll wake up hungover wondering how the hell he got here." She slipped the red tie off her neck and dropped it over his head so that he wore it like some kind of weird bandana, dangling over one ear. He looked stupid and he deserved it. If she had the time she'd have written something clever on his forehead with her lipstick to make him look like an even bigger idiot.

"Where's your car?" Arlan asked.

"A few blocks away."

"Walk straight to it. Speak to no one," Arlan instructed. "No bums, no one."

"No bums. No one," she repeated as she cut the plastic handcuff tie with a pocketknife she always carried in her handbag.

The suit's hands fell to his lap. His head lolled a little, but the tie stayed in place. Fia walked toward the street-lights at the end of the alley, a tunnel in the darkness.

"I cut the creep free. I'm walking out now," she told Arlan. She stopped when she reached the sidewalk. The air was cleaner here. Cooler. She felt more like herself again.

"You okay?" Arlan asked.

"I'm okay." She nodded, even though she knew very well he couldn't see her.

"Good. Now you call me later and we'll talk."

"I don't want to talk about this, Arlan. We're just going to pretend it didn't happen. We're going to pretend I never called you."

"Okay," he said, even though she could tell he wasn't really going for the idea. "How about Maggie? You want to talk about *her* later?"

"What do you mean?" She walked under a streetlight. She could see her car on the next block. "She call you? I thought she was going to call *me*."

"She's here, Fee."

"There? There where? In your bed?"

"No," he scoffed, seemingly offended. "Of course she's not in my bed. She's in town. Apparently you told her where you *live*."

"I *live* in Philadelphia, Arlan. She knew about Clare Point because she found me through the beheadings. It was all over the news, remember?" Fia pulled her keys from her bag and unlocked her BMW. "So exactly where is she?"

"She said she was staying at the Lighthouse Inn."

"And you sure she's there?"

"No, I'm not *sure she's there*. I'm not the cop, you are. She wants to talk to you, face to face," Arlan said.

"I don't want to lose her again. Tell her to call me." Fia got into her car.

"I don't even know that I'll see her."

"Go to the hotel in the morning and tell her to stay put." She started the engine. "Better yet, get her to move to Ma's place. You can keep a better eye on her there."

"I'm not even sure I can find her, Fee."

"Just do it," Fia said. She hung up before she started getting all mushy and thanking Arlan for being there when she needed him.

Arlan fell back on his pillow, cell phone still in his hand, and stared at the ceiling. The paddle fan turned slowly, but it didn't seem to be cooling off the room.

What the hell was wrong with Fia? He thought she'd put an end to the stalking after she started dating her human. Hadn't she been working on this with her shrink for years?

Arlan tossed his phone on the nightstand and threw back the sheet. He needed something cold to drink. Water. Better yet, a beer.

He walked nude out of the bedroom and down the hall. In the kitchen, he opened the refrigerator and light fell on the tile floor. He stared as if something would magically leap out at him.

A sound in the front of the house caught his attention. He had no cat. No dog. His current position in the sept took him away too often to have pets. He grabbed a bottle of Mexican beer and let the refrigerator door swing shut. He walked out into the living room and studied the furniture cloaked in shadows cast by the streetlamp out front. Everything was as he had left it when he went to bed. Books were piled beside his leather recliner. Clean clothes were piled on the couch, waiting to be folded or at least tossed in a dresser drawer.

His shifted his gaze to the open windows that looked out over the front porch. He'd installed central air in the house, but he hated to turn it on. He liked to smell the ocean when he slept. It reminded him of the shores of his homeland of Ireland. It reminded him of when he had once been human.

Twisting the cap on the beer, he padded barefoot to the window. The curtain drifted in the faint breeze. Nothing stirred outside. Everything was so quiet, so still, that he didn't see her at first. Just the porch rail. The steps. The overgrown forsythia bush. He didn't see her, but he smelled her. It was a combination of his enhanced senses and her erotic scent that he couldn't quite get out of his mind.

He walked to the front door and yanked it open.

She rose off the step as if she had been expecting him. She walked past him, into the house, taking his beer as she walked by.

Without a word, she walked through the living room, down the hall.

Arlan followed her in silence.

She dropped her purse just beyond the living room. She stepped out of her jeans, carefully balancing the beer, at the doorway to the spare room. As she walked into his bedroom, her thin T-shirt drifted off her fingertips. She sat down on the end of his bed, her bare skin glistening in the soft moonlight as she took a sip of the beer.

"What are you doing here?" he finally asked.

"What do you think?" She touched the rim of the bottle with the tip of her tongue.

He frowned, remaining a safe distance from her. "I'm serious, Maggie. How did you find me? Did you follow me home?"

"Didn't have to. In a small town like this, everyone

knows everyone's business. Mrs. Cahall's nephew has the night desk at the hotel. He was more than happy to give me directions." She offered the bottle. "Beer?"

He crossed the room, snatching it out of her hand. "What do you want from me?"

She looked up, her pale, beautiful face so earnest. "Do you want me to leave? I can leave if you want."

He eased down beside her. She smelled amazing. "I just want to know what you want. I'm not used to women following me." He took a long drink of the cold beer.

"You mean, like, do I want a *relationship*? Marriage, a picket fence, and kids?" Her caustic laugh didn't seem to match the softness in her face. "Not hardly." She rested her hand on his bare knee. "I just want to be with you, Arlan. Don't you want to be with me?"

Her words were over-the-top sexual, but the tone of her voice, the softness in her face, took away the tawdriness of it. From her mouth, the proposition seemed almost chaste.

"You're scaring me a little, Maggie." He took another drink. "You sure you're not a stalker?"

She took the bottle from his hand and climbed across his lap, straddling him. She looked into his eyes, unblinking. "A stalker is the last thing on this earth I would be," she whispered.

Her mouth lingered just over his, not touching, just hovering. His for the taking.

He thought about Fia. Hadn't he just ten minutes before told her Maggie wasn't in his bed? Hadn't he just chastised her for making poor choices? And now here Maggie was. Here they were naked, already hot for each other.

He knew he should send her away. He knew all the reasons why, but he couldn't do it. He covered her mouth with his. *He just couldn't.*

She tasted of the beer they shared, but something more. Something deeper. Darker.

Macy slid her hand over Arlan's amazing shoulder, allowing her fingertips to explore the firmness of his sculpted muscles. She opened her mouth to his. She didn't know what she was doing in his house. She wasn't even entirely sure how she had gotten here. Yes, she had asked the night clerk where he lived, but she didn't remember walking here. She didn't remember how long she sat on his porch steps before he opened the door. It was as if she'd, again, been inexorably drawn to him.

There was something strange about this town. Something strange about Arlan. He was dangerous; she knew it in every fiber of her being. But she couldn't stay away from him. Moth to a flame?

Arlan shifted beneath her and she felt his erection between her legs. Desire. It was something she could always count on. The one thing that would carry her away, up and out of the darkness in which she existed. If only for a while.

Just a quickie, she told herself. *Then back to the hotel.*

If she had any sense, that's where she'd be right now.

But she was tired of lonely hotel rooms. Tired of her empty bed in her empty cottage. She wanted this darkness to be over. One way or another. So what if Arlan was a crazy ax murderer, a monster just like the man she'd been running from all these years? So what if she was murdered in a stranger's bed, midcoitus? At least it would be over.

Arlan ran his fingers through her hair and her scalp tingled pleasantly. He kissed her mouth, her cheek. He was a gentle, attentive lover. He knew how to make her feel alive, if only for a few fleeting minutes.

She lifted her chin, encouraging him to kiss the sensitive place on her neck just below her earlobe.

He was a great kisser. An amazing neck-nuzzler.

He took the beer bottle from her and finished off the last of it before rolling it across the carpet. Then he enveloped her in his arms again and she moved rhythmically on his lap, grinding hip to hip as his kiss deepened again.

Macy threaded her fingers through his and leaned back so that he could take one of her nipples between his lips. He licked, teasing her until she laughed and then groaned with pleasure. Then he took it between his teeth and tugged ever so gently.

Her groan grew huskier.

She was already wet and soft for him. She could smell the heat of their desire wafting upward between them. She lifted up, pushing her toes into the soft carpet, grasped his phallus in her hand, and slid down over it.

His heavy lidded eyes opened and she smiled up at him sadly. She liked this man. She liked how he talked. How he made love. How gentle a soul he seemed to be.

Even if he was an ax murderer.

She groaned inwardly. What was she doing here, not just in Arlan's bed but in Clare Point? She didn't really think Arlan could offer her any comfort, did she? She didn't think she could help Fia find the killer. She didn't really think the waking nightmare of her life would be over. Not really. Did she?

Macy closed her eyes, letting her thoughts drift out of her head to linger somewhere above where she couldn't reach them. She wrapped her arms around his neck, savoring the weight of his male hands on her waist. She lifted upward and he moaned. She hesitated and then lowered herself over him and was rewarded with another moan.

She could feel her own pleasure building. First it was just a spark in the pit of her stomach . . . the smallest sensation of pleasure. But it quickly blossomed. Ripples of pleasure grew from the epicenter outward until every nerve in her body was alive with sensation.

Perspiration beaded above her upper lip. It was warm in

the room despite the turn of the ceiling fan whirling overhead.

"Maggie," he whispered in her ear. "Sweet Maggie."

Remorse swelled in her chest and she lifted herself up
again, coming down hard on his lap to chase away the
guilt. She'd lied about her name too many times to too
many men. Sometimes she couldn't remember who she
was pretending to be.

But this was Arlan.

She panted. She knew this one. The guilt that plagued
her faded.

She remembered him. She had thought about him after
he was gone from her bed. The fear that seemed to be her
constant companion ebbed when she was with him.

Arlan began to move faster beneath her. Her breath came
in short little gasps. She tried to hold back. She tried to
make the ripples of pleasure that had become rivers last a
little longer, last into forever.

But she couldn't stop it. She never could. She tipped her
head back and cried out as every muscle in her body tensed,
released and tensed again. He got up off the bed, lifting
her with him, pushing hard into her as his fingers sank into
the soft flesh of her buttocks. She clung to him.

"Arlan," she whispered, squeezing her eyes shut.

"Maggie."

And then it was over. One more groan and he climaxed.
He collapsed backward onto his bed, taking her with him.
She rolled off him, onto her back, her legs hanging over
the edge of the bed. She looked up, watching the fan blade
turn, listening to the low hum of the motor as she caught
her breath. Orgasms always made her light-headed, made
her feel as if she were floating. Better than any drug on the
market.

"I have to go," she said softly.

"Now, Maggie?" he panted.

She made herself get up. She picked up her shirt in the doorway and pulled it over her head, over the thin sheen of perspiration covering her body. "It's Macy," she said as she walked down the hall in the dark. "My name is Macy."

Chapter 12

"Hey, where are you?" Arlan said into his cell.

"Getting coffee at the Starbucks near my office, as if it's any of your business."

Fia was her old self, as self-assured and haughty as ever. Her dark moment had passed.

"Ah, so that's how we're going to play it this morning, are we?"

"That's how we're going to play it. Vente latte light," she quipped.

"Coming right up, ma'am." Arlan stepped off the sidewalk to get around a family headed for the beach. The father was pulling a wagon filled with a cooler, chairs, and half a metric ton of plastic beach toys. A boy and girl trotted behind the wagon. Mom, in a too-tight tube top and terry cloth shorts, trailed after them. "So, you okay this morning?" he asked Fia, his appreciative gaze locked on the young mother's jiggling ass as he passed. "Cops didn't come for you?"

"Thanks. Have a good day."

He guessed that was addressed to the barista rather than him.

"No one came for me. I apologize for calling you. It was foolish. End of discussion. More discussion than necessary."

"What was foolish was what you did, Fee." He stepped back onto the sidewalk in front of the wagon train.

"You going to chew me out? Because if you are, I haven't the time right now. I've got a stack of case files on my desk and a conference call with the agents on the Buried Alive Killings in two hours. If I want in on this, I have to have my shit together."

He softened his tone. "I didn't call you to chew you out. I plan to do that in person next time I see you. I called about Maggie."

"Jesus, Mary, and Joseph, don't tell me she's left town already."

"No. Well, I don't think so. I'm on my way to the hotel now, but I wanted to give you a heads-up. She's lying about her name."

Fia didn't answer right away. He heard the blast of a car horn. Traffic sounds. Voices. She was apparently on the street and headed toward her office now.

"You hear what I said? She lied to us."

"Not that big a deal," she said into the phone.

"No?"

"No, actually that might be a good thing. She must really somehow be involved with this bastard."

"You think so?" Bonnie Hill drove by in her new blue Miata and waved. He lifted his hand in greeting.

"Sure. This is getting way too complicated to be some kind of sicko hoax. She's not getting her rocks off leading me along. She knows something and she wants to tell us."

"You think she's in on it?" he asked.

"What do you think?"

Arlan hesitated. He wanted to say that of course she wasn't involved. Not sweet Maggie. *Macy,* he mentally corrected himself.

But she *had* lied to him. And she *was* practically a stalker.

"I'm at the hotel. If I can find her, I'll tell her she needs to call you. I'll see what her plans are as far as staying in town. If she intends on being here a few days, I'll get her moved over to the B and B."

"Great. Sounds like a plan. Hey, how did you know she lied about her name?"

"Mrs. Cahall, good morning. How are you?" Arlan spoke loudly.

"Arlan?" Fia said on the other end of the line. "How did you—"

"Gotta go. Talk to you later." Arlan slid his phone into one of the pockets of his cargo shorts. "I said, *how are you* this morning?" he repeated even louder.

"Alive, I am. That's always a good thing." The elderly woman rubbed a bony elbow. "But my tennis elbow's acting up. Must be gonna rain." She was wearing a short, white, pleated skirt, sneakers, and a sleeveless blue polo with a tennis racket embroidered over one saggy breast. To Arlan's knowledge, she had never played tennis a day in the last seventy-some years, but she did read *The Great Gatsby* annually. Gin rummy was her game. And gin, oddly enough, was her drink. She could beat the pants off anyone Arlan knew playing gin rummy or drinking gin and tonics.

"I was wondering if you could tell me the number of Maggie Smith's room."

"Who's coming soon?"

"No. No, *room,*" he said patiently. "One of your guests. I need to know where Maggie Smith is staying."

"You know we don't give out information like that." Mrs. Cahall sipped coffee from a cup, leaving a pink lip imprint on the rim. "You going to Rob Hill's wake tomorrow night? Mary Kay is making blueberry cobbler for after." She smacked her lips together. "I love a blueberry cobbler, don't you?"

"Mrs. Cahall, I wouldn't ask if this wasn't important. Actually, it was Fia who asked that I contact Miss Smith on her behalf. I think it's FBI business." He looked across the Formica counter at her meaningfully.

"Why didn't you speak up, then, son?" She practically shouted at him. "Room twenty-two."

He turned away. "Thanks. I'll see you tomorrow night. Be sure Mary Kay saves me some of that cobbler."

"You can go up if you like. She's in twenty-two, but she's not there," the old lady called after him.

"She checked out?" He turned back.

"Too early for stout." She frowned as she rubbed her elbow, looking as if he had lost his mind. "Pub's not open yet. She walked over to the diner for some breakfast. I told her Mary Ann had a mean buttermilk pancake. I like the strawberry syrup myself."

"She say how long she was staying?"

The woman cast him an odd look. "No, she wasn't swaying." She drew herself up indignantly. "Not that drinking is a crime."

"How long's she *staying*?" He had changed directions and was now headed for the opposite lobby door.

"A few days. She writes for magazines, you know. *House and Garden. Southern Living.* She couldn't keep a job like that if she was a drinker. She makes a very good living. She's going to feature some of the cottages here in Clare Point," she said proudly.

"Is she now?" Arlan muttered under his breath. He waved as he went out the door. "Thank you, Mrs. Cahall."

"You let that girl have a beer if she wants one," the old woman shouted after him.

At the diner, Arlan walked past the PLEASE WAIT TO BE SEATED sign. He found Macy all the way in the back, in the corner booth, facing the doorway. Arlan always picked the same table in public places. It was the best way to keep an eye on who was coming and going. The best way to stay alive.

He slid in beside her on the Naugahyde bench.

"You thinking pancakes or waffles?" she said, not even looking up, as if she had been expecting him to join her at any minute. "Mrs. Cahall recommends the pancakes, but I'm feeling like a waffle this morning."

Arlan leaned back as Mary Ann, head waitress and owner of the diner, held a stainless steel coffee pot over his cup, waiting for the go-ahead. Vampires weren't big on stimulants, but he was feeling the need this morning. He nodded.

"Back to get your order shortly, cutie pie," she said.

"Why did you lie to me about your name?" Arlan asked the minute Mary Ann was out of earshot.

"Why do think? You always tell your one-night stands your real name?" She set down her menu. "I doubt it."

He met her gaze. Her green eyes were the most incredible shade, somewhere between moss and falling autumn leaves at that point when they were no longer green, but not yet brown. Even when he closed his eyes, he saw hers. "That's not a very good answer. You lied to Fia. Why are you lying to FBI agents, Macy? If that's even your name."

"It's what my parents called me," she said, suddenly going from cynical to sad in a single heartbeat.

And here it was again, the guilt. Thick, heavy. Encumbering. He'd been unkind and there was no reason for unkindness. The world generated too much of that on its own for him to add to it.

"You lied to protect yourself? From what?"

She frowned. She was drinking orange juice. Her coffee cup was turned upside down on the table. Apparently his Macy didn't need any additional stimulants, either.

"Why do you think? Don't you get it? He buries them up to their necks, waits for them to wake up and then he suffocates them," she whispered harshly under her breath. "He gets off by watching the fear in their eyes. Their fear not just for themselves, but for each other when they realize what's happening. When they realize they can't do a damned thing about it."

"You seem to understand a lot about the way the man ticks."

She frowned, not biting on his insinuation. "Pretty simple psychoanalysis, don't you think?"

He changed his tactics, knowing the bad guy wasn't going to work in the good guy/bad guy game. "Has he threatened to do the same to you, Macy? Because if he has, the FBI can protect you."

"Yeah, right." She laughed, but her tone was without humor.

"Mrs. Cahall said you were staying a few days. That you were doing research for your job. Fia's mom has a B and B here in town. We think you should move over there where we know you'll be safe."

"You mean where you can keep an eye on me."

"I'm just passing on a message from Fia." He hesitated. "You can talk to me. You can trust me, Macy."

She sipped her orange juice, staring straight ahead at the ball cap on the man's head in the next booth. "It's not about trust. It's not about wanting to speak up, finally." She exhaled. "I tell you anything and you're at risk, too."

"What about Fia? You think giving her information won't put her at risk?"

"I thought about that, but she's a cop. She does this sort of thing all the time. She caught those kids who were beheading people, didn't she?" A hint of a smile turned the corner of her sensual lips. "She's kind of a superhero, in my book."

Superhero? Arlan wondered what Macy would think of Fia if she knew what Fia really was, if she knew of Fia's constant hunger for human blood. Then he couldn't help but wonder what Macy would think of him if she knew what he did for a living when he wasn't installing gutters. He wondered what she would think if she saw the centuries of human blood on his hands.

"No," Macy said firmly. "I want to talk to Fia. I just want to sleep with you."

He ignored the sex part and tried to concentrate on what Fia needed from him. "So call her." He pulled his cell phone from his pocket and slid it across the table. "Call her now."

"Breakfast, now. Call later." She looked up at Mary Ann, who had reappeared at the tableside in the magical, perfectly timed way only seasoned waitresses could. "We'll have the Belgian waffles."

"At least tell me you'll think about moving over to the B and B," Arlan said. They were standing on the sidewalk outside the diner. It was a beautiful, sunny day and Macy was sure the temperature had already hit eighty degrees.

"I have thought about it. I like the Lighthouse Inn. I like Mrs. Cahall. I like her tennis skirt and her bony knees. I like her cheesy bedspreads and the ceramic seagulls on the wall."

He frowned, adjusting his wraparound surfer sunglasses. "Look, I have to get to work."

She wondered what he did, but she didn't ask. She rarely asked questions. It made it easier not to answer any. Subsequently, she had become good at deduction. Good at reading people.

He worked for himself the way he came and went freely on a weekday morning. Something with his hands, she guessed. An artist? Did he make ceramic flowerpots and vases to sell to tourists in this obviously touristy town? Or did he do something more manly like sculpt bronze statues? He'd look hot in a leather apron and goggles in more ways than one. She imagined sweat trickling down his pecs, down the flat of his belly, and she smiled.

"What?" he asked, suspicion tingeing his tone.

"Nothing. Thanks for breakfast," she said, looking up at him. "And last night," she offered more softly. "I didn't mean to creep you out. I just didn't . . ." Her gaze searched his but she couldn't see his eyes behind the dark sunglasses. "I didn't want to be alone."

Silence stretched a moment or two longer than was comfortable.

"Okay, well . . ." He started to back away from her, sliding a hand into his pocket.

Obviously he didn't quite know what to make of the fact that she made no attempt to avoid the subject of their physical intimacy. Most men were that way. They were all about getting in your panties so long as you didn't mention it later.

"I'm going to get to work and you're good with Fia, right?" he asked, giving her a thumbs-up.

"I'll call her."

"You need anything else? I mean, what are you going to do the rest of the day?"

She slid her sunglasses on. "Not everything is about you, Arlan Kahill. I really am researching a piece. Victorian beach cottages." She smiled at him, thinking that there was something about this man that genuinely made her smile. It wasn't forced or fake as it was so often. "See you around."

Leaving Arlan standing on the sidewalk in front of the diner, Macy walked east, toward the ocean. In the hotel lobby, she'd picked up one of those tourist maps with colorful parking signs and ice cream cones printed on it, but she preferred to get a feel for a new town on her own. She'd been through Delaware numerous times, staying in

Rehoboth Beach and in the New Castle area, but she'd never been to Clare Point. Mrs. Cahall had suggested that she go east and then north. That's where the prettiest cottages were, the old woman had insisted.

So Macy walked east and then a block off the bay, turned north. As promised, the street was lined with neat, quaint cottages that appeared to have been built at the turn of the century or earlier. Not a single house was less than a hundred years old for what looked like a two- to three-block radius. Like the houses in Cape May, New Jersey, though smaller, they were painted pastel Victorian colors: pink, yellow, robin's egg blue, making for a picturesque scene.

Delighted by her find, Macy slipped her camera from the canvas bag slung over her shoulder and began to take random shots. Tonight, back in the hotel, she would look at them more closely. Once she chose a couple houses she was interested in, she'd chat with someone in the local Chamber of Commerce office. It had been Macy's experience that the chambers of small towns were always eager to help her find homes to photograph when they thought there might be some free publicity for them in the deal.

Macy was halfway down the second block when she spotted an attractive woman watering zinnias that flanked both sides of her quaint entryway. The woman appeared to be in her late twenties and had short, spiky hair that was almost a fluorescent red. Not the person one expected to see watering flowers in her front yard. The young woman smiled.

Macy smiled back, reading *invitation*. "Good morning," she called.

"'Morning." The woman held the spray trigger on the hose and a soft rain fell over her brightly colored flowers.

"Beautiful houses on this street." Macy looked up at the pale peach porch trimmed in white. "This your place or a rental? It's amazing."

"It's been in my family for generations," the woman said, taking Macy in casually.

Macy slung her camera over her shoulder and reached into her knapsack, coming up with a business card. "Macy Smith. I work for *House Beautiful* and a couple of other home and garden magazines. I'm always scouting for unusual homes and gardens to feature."

Directing the hose away from Macy, the woman accepted the card, read it and looked up. "Pretty cool. Would you like to have a look around?" She gestured with the hose nozzle. "Out back, I have rosebushes from Ireland that are more than two hundred years old. The blooms are incredible." She smiled almost shyly. "Eva Hill." She shrugged. "I have this thing for roses and other thorny things."

Macy smiled back, offering her hand. Eva didn't look like the typical rose gardener with her wild hair and dark makeup. Macy liked it when people surprised her. "Nice to meet you, Eva."

The redhead turned the valve on the sprayer off and dropped the hose, taking Macy's hand. She had a warm, confident grip.

"Nice to meet you. Come around back. Want some iced tea? It's going to be another scorcher today."

That night, unable to sleep, Macy sat at the dinette table in her room at the Lighthouse and flipped through the photos she had taken of Eva's house and others on the same street. She sipped an iced herbal tea. It was after midnight. She was tired. She should have been able to sleep, but she couldn't, so she worked. Other than sex with strangers, work was her only balm when she was restless like this.

After a tour of Eva's amazing rose garden, Macy had ended up touring the inside of the house, too. They had hit it off so well that Eva not only offered her home to Macy to feature in a magazine article, but suggested she might be able to persuade some other homeowners on the street to do the same. Macy was thinking of a serious feature article. Ten-, maybe twelve-page spread. A feature piece would take a lot of time and effort, but she was sure more than one of the publishers she freelanced for would be interested. These houses on the shore were so unusual, true gems tucked away in Smalltownville, East Coast, USA. It might turn out to be her most profitable sale to date.

At three this afternoon, she had spoken to Fia on the phone, telling her she would be in town for a few days. They agreed to meet Friday night. Fia hadn't been crazy with the idea of being put off any longer, but she was savvy enough to realize that Macy had the upper hand here. Macy was relieved to be able to put the encounter off a few more days. It would give her time to think about what she was going to say. How much she was going to tell. It would also give her the opportunity to chicken out and hightail-it back to Virginia if she so chose.

Walking away without saying good-bye to Arlan might prove more difficult than usual. There was something about him that was different from other men she had known. Something about him that made her wish she was different. But who was she kidding? He wasn't different. He wasn't special. None of the men she ever met were. No one could save her. Of course she could walk away. She'd done it countless times before.

After looking over the photos and sending out several e-mails to editors at various magazines, Macy logged online using the wireless Internet code Mrs. Cahall had provided her earlier in the evening. Somehow, Macy wasn't surprised that the spry old woman was Internet-connected.

Macy was halfway through the mail when the IM box popped up with a *ding*. It was Teddy, of course.

I've been waiting for you. Where have you been?

She stared at the flashing cursor.

Did you see the papers? The news. She's quiet tonight, very quiet.

He was talking about the voice. The voice that he said made him kill. A mixture of fear and anger tightened her stomach. She wanted to close the dialogue window. Shut him up. But if she was serious about helping the FBI, she needed to remain in contact with him and stay in his good graces.

I saw. She hit the Enter key, then added, How could you?

I don't like your tone, he responded. Her fingers flew over her keyboard. You're a liar. You lie to me. You lie to yourself.

Orphan.

"Ah, so we're going to play that game tonight, are we?" she said aloud. "What, we're twelve?" She hesitated before she typed. I wish you had talked to me. I wish you hadn't done it.

If wishes were horses, Teddy answered.

I'm serious. Macy didn't know what was making her so bold. We should talk.

But we do talk, dear Marceline. You're my best friend in the whole world. We talk all the time.

The idea of being this monster's friend made her want to throw up. The idea that he *thought* they could be friends after what he had done was somehow even worse.

Her fingers hovered over the keyboard as she considered what she should say. If she was going to talk to Fia Friday night, she should have something to take to her. Some sort of proof she wasn't a nut job. Some sort of information that really could help.

I noticed the moon that night. It wasn't right, Teddy. You missed the full moon. You hesitated. Then you did it anyway.

His words popped up almost instantly. The moon? How do you know about the moon????

She sensed she'd struck a nerve. I know all about the moon.

Teddy didn't answer. She waited. She sipped her tea. As the seconds stretched to a minute, two, she began to feel empowered. All these years she had just sat here afraid. Afraid to talk to him, afraid not to. Now maybe he was afraid.

Just when she was ready to shut down her computer and go watch something mindless on TV, another line of text appeared.

No one knows about the moon . . .

She thought before she typed. No one but you and me. Because we're friends, right?

Another hesitation before she read, Friends.

So why did you do it when the moon wasn't right?

I . . . I don't know, he answered. *I thought I could wait but I couldn't.*

Does someone tell you to do it? she probed.

No, no one tells me. No one is the boss of me!

No one is the boss of me? The surprising outburst made Macy sit back in her chair and stare at the computer screen. He seemed to have regressed further. Now, he sounded like a five-year-old. She thought about all the pictures he had cut out of magazines and sent her years ago when he still did that sort thing. The reccurring theme had been little boys. At one time, she had wondered if he was some kind of sexual predator, too, but now she wondered if all the little boys were him. Were Teddy.

So you do it on your own. Why? she typed.

He hesitated. I have to go.

This was the first time in all these years that she recalled him signing off first. The first time she had ever felt in control of the situation.

Good night, she typed. Then she closed her laptop and got up from the table before he could respond.

At the window, she looked out on the street that ran along the front of the motel. It was quiet and deserted. This was a family resort town. No bars, no arcades. All the restaurants and shops closed at ten P.M, which really was a little odd. Even the local watering hole where Macy had found Arlan the previous night sported a CLOSED sign this time of night, although she would have sworn she had seen light seeping from behind its pulled shades.

The entire town was quiet. Dark.

A large black Labrador trotted along the sidewalk. Seeming to sense she was watching him, he stopped and turned toward her, ears pricked.

She studied him. He studied her.

She took a step closer to the window, placing her hand on the cool glass. Suddenly she had this crazy impulse to go to the dog. To lead him inside. He didn't seem injured or hungry. In fact, he was muscular, his coat sleek, his eyes glimmering. But she sensed he needed her.

How weird was that?

Chapter 13

Arlan had to force himself to continue walking along the street in the direction of the museum. He hadn't expected to see Macy tonight. Hadn't expected her to be *waiting* for him.

Had she really been waiting for him?

He'd just been trotting down the sidewalk, minding his own business in the form of a Labrador retriever. When he passed the Lighthouse, he had glanced in the direction of room 22. No reason.

And there she was at the window. *Waiting for him.*

It was a ridiculous thought, of course. She didn't know it was him. All she had seen was a big black dog that had wandered from its yard. She didn't know he could morph into a Lab any more than she knew he could morph into a fox. It was pure coincidence that she had been standing at her open window after midnight, just at the time that he passed, headed for a meeting where he might vote on whether or not to execute a serial killer or a pedophile.

Down a couple more streets, Arlan turned off the sidewalk into an alley, and nearly ran into a pair of long female legs.

"Hey!"

Arlan barked, falling into step at her side.

"What are you doing here?" Fia asked, looking down at him. "Nice collar."

Arlan morphed from the canine form to his human one. "What am *I* doing here?" He scratched behind his ear. "What are *you* doing here? It's the middle of the night. You're supposed to be in Philly. Lover boy is going to catch you one of these nights and then you're going to have some explaining to do."

She frowned. "High Council meeting. You show up unless you're dead."

"Not much chance of that," he joked.

"Exactly." Reaching the rear of the museum building, she pushed a series of numbers on the key pad and the door opened. "So Peigi convinced you to sit in for Johnny Hill?"

"More like muscled me into it."

"If it's any consolation, I think the council is right. You belong here." She pointed to a closed door, her voice taking on a solemn tone, almost as if they were inside a church. "Men change in there." She indicated a closed door with a jerk of head. "Women here. I'll see you at the table."

Arlan watched Fia disappear into the room, closing the door behind her. Instead of going where he had been directed, he walked to the end of the long hall and stepped into the main room of the museum. The lights were off, but he had no difficulty making out the furnishings. He could have navigated the room with his eyes closed.

The present building, built over an older foundation, had been constructed in the late sixties to encourage the town's burgeoning tourist trade. Portraying Clare Point as a pirate's den in early colonial days, the museum mixed fact with fiction, displaying many objects that had actually been on the ship the sept had traveled aboard from Ireland three centuries ago. When the vessel had wrecked on a reef in a storm and they were all washed ashore, they had collected the objects as well as the scrap wood from the beach and the splintered hull. They had built their first homes with those warped planks; portholes had become windows and the simple white bone china, now displayed in glass cases, had been used on dining tables for decades.

There had been a small colony of wreckers living in lean-tos on the beach when the Kahills washed ashore, but once the sept's leader, Gair, declared that the family had reached their final destination, the Kahill women had drawn their fangs, the men had raised their swords, and being realists, the pirates had moved south to Virginia to safer ground.

The display cases in the rinky-dink museum, identified by printed signs and sometimes with humorous sketches, were filled with pieces of china, brass candlesticks, and other assorted junk, mostly brought from the ship, although some of it was bounty the wreckers had left behind in their eagerness to escape a colony of vampires. There was also a small exhibit of arrowheads and spear points from the area's earlier history, when Native Americans had hunted and fished the land now located inside the town limits. Some of the items were often displayed on the round table that had come from the ship captain's cabin.

His gaze settled there and he fought an ominous shiver. Now cleared of the knickknacks, he knew this was where the High Council took the *aontas*. Tonight, he might be expected to vote, to thrust his dagger into the scarred tabletop and sentence a man or woman to death. Or, withhold his *aonta,* and demand further evidence of the guilt of the human in question. The responsibility seemed overwhelming for a handyman.

He shifted his gaze.

During the museum's operating hours, a five-minute movie was shown in one corner of the room and there was a small gift shop off the hall, near the restrooms. There, plastic swords, eye patches, fake coins, tomahawks, and other assorted souvenirs were sold. On rainy days, in the summer months, the museum made a surprisingly tidy profit.

Now the shadowy room was filled with an eerie energy. *All those years of life and death decisions,* Arlan thought. They couldn't help but leave an indelible impression in the air.

The central air-conditioning unit clicked on, startling him, and he turned back as cool air blew in his face. Arlan dreaded going into the small room and donning the council robe. He dreaded the memories it would churn up. He hadn't served on the High Council since the midnineteenth century. Not since he had voted to execute his lover's brother.

It was after three A.M. when Arlan hung his cloak, returned his on-loan ceremonial dagger to Gair, and walked out into the hot, humid night air. Lost in their own thoughts after the night's proceedings, no one spoke as council members filed one by one out the rear door. The contemplative silence seemed appropriate, a sort of reverence to the momentous decisions made behind those closed doors.

The group splintered, headed home to catch a few hours of sleep before they would have to wake and greet and serve tourists and pretend to be human again. Arlan walked Fia to her car, she apparently being the one exception to the *no one drives to High Council* rule Peigi had been so adamant about.

"You okay?" Fia asked softly as he opened her door for her.

"Sure. Why wouldn't I be?" They stood face to face with the car door between them.

"You get used to it." She rested her folded arms on the top of the door, leaning toward him. "You learn to pick and pull through the information. You get a gut feeling about these people. You know when it's right."

Arlan had been greatly relieved that no vote was required of him tonight. Fortunately, it had been a meeting where information was exchanged and orders were sent out to teams for further investigation. All he had to do was stand at the table and listen, in a hooded cloak some member of his family had worn for more that two hundred years. Fia had offered up the Buried Alive Killer, making it an authorized sept case. Whether the FBI officially put her on the case or not, as far as the sept was concerned, she was, and it was a top priority.

For a moment, Fia and Arlan stood there in the dark. The waning moon was already beginning to fall below the horizon. Night insects chirped. A frog croaked from a nearby drainage ditch. They were comforting sounds to him; sounds that were always the same, no matter in what century or on what continent he lived.

"You look tired." She reached out and stroked his beard-stubbled cheek.

He closed his eyes, savoring her touch. He had ached for Fia for so long that sometimes he forgot about the pain and then suddenly, there it was again, so tight in his chest that he could barely speak. He wanted her so badly, not just in his bed, but in his arms. In his heart.

But she belonged to another man. Her choice. Her life.

"Long day," he admitted. "I repaired the cracks in Johnny's tomb and installed some track lighting in Mary Hill's new media room."

She chuckled. "Pretty exciting life you lead."

He opened his eyes. "I think so." He looked down at the white line of the parking space in the museum's lot. "So you talked to Macy?"

Fia pushed back a lock of red hair. She was letting it grow out. The longer locks made her look younger, less severe.

"She says she's going to stick around a few days. Some kind of freelance magazine job. I'm going to look into her work, see what kind of dirt I can dig up on her. We're going to meet Friday."

"You coming back for Johnny's funeral?"

She shook her head. "Gotta bunk with the boyfriend once in a while."

"Ah," he acknowledged. "Don't want him to get suspicious. Otherwise you might have to suck all the blood from his body, speak the magic incantation, and turn him into one of the living dead."

"That's not funny." She cuffed him on the ear.

"Ouch." He stepped back, rubbing the offended appendage.

" 'Night," Fia called, slipping into her car and pulling closed the door.

"Night."

He walked home in human form, taking his time, his hands stuffed in his pockets, his sunglasses propped on his nose. He liked the way the dark lenses changed the light cast from the silver moon. Maybe it was the polarized technology. Maybe it was the magic of the night. Like it or not, he was now a member of the High Council and the responsibility the position possessed was once again on his shoulders. He'd forgotten just how heavy a burden it was.

Arlan was not surprised to find Macy on his porch steps. Maybe he should have been, but he wasn't. He was glad to see her. In silence, he walked past her, up the steps, and turned the doorknob.

"You don't lock your doors," she pointed out, seeming more a spirit of the night than a human. "Me neither," she said with a sigh.

In his bedroom, they slowly undressed each other as if they had done it a thousand times. They stood naked, face to face, surrounded by a puddle of clothing. Arlan threaded his fingers through hers and held her hands tightly, gazing into her eyes. He was sad. Sad for himself because he could not have Fia. Sad for Fia because she couldn't break her addiction to human men. Sad for Macy because . . . he wasn't even sure why. But he wanted to know. He wanted to know her story.

"Tell me how you know him," Arlan said, lowering his head to kiss her bare shoulder. He breathed deeply, taking in her feminine, human scent. "The killer."

"It doesn't matter." She rested her palm on his cheek and guided him down to her. She brushed her lips against his, butterfly-light and teasing. Painfully sensual.

"I want to understand," he whispered against her mouth. "I want to feel your pain."

"No, you don't," she breathed, flicking out her tongue to taste his lips. "Believe me, you don't want to feel this. I don't want to feel this."

He kissed her more roughly. "I can help."

She grasped his head with both hands, pulling him down to her, meeting him with an equal, building urgency. Her breath was already quick, her voice raspy. Almost desperate. "You can't. No one can help. No one can save me." And then she reached down and clasped his already burgeoning erection in her warm hand.

"You cheat," he half whispered, half groaned.

She stroked the length of him, maintaining eye contact with him. There was something about the way that she looked at him as she caressed him that sent a shock wave through his body. He grabbed her up in his arms and carried her to his bed, flinging her down on the unmade sheets that still smelled of last night's lovemaking.

Macy gave a little cry of surprise at his sudden roughness, but she didn't protest. She reached up to him, pulling him down on top of her, meeting his greedy kiss.

Arlan didn't know what had gotten into him. Maybe the power and magnitude of the evening. Tonight, he didn't just want to make love to Macy; he wanted to possess her.

He squeezed her breasts and ran his hands down her slender torso, kissing her hard, thrusting his tongue into her mouth. He pushed his groin against hers, and grabbed her bare legs, forcing them around his back. They kissed and stroked in a seeming frenzy, their desire for each other rising with each panting breath they took.

"Arlan," she gasped. "Now. I need you *now*."

But he did not take her. Instead, he pressed his mouth to her neck and tasted her salty skin with the tip of his tongue. He even went so far as to draw back his lips.

No. He would not bite her. He would not take her blood, although he thought she probably wouldn't even care. She seemed, at this moment, to be as out of control as he was.

Instead of biting her, he spread her legs wide and sank hard into her. She cried out with pleasure and he did not relent. He pushed again and again, their movement so violent that they slid across the bed, taking sheets and the coverlet with them. Macy clung to him, making little whimpering sounds of passion.

They climaxed, Macy first, then Arlan, both closing their eyes and gasping in satisfaction. Breathing hard, he lowered himself over her, propping himself up so that he wasn't too heavy on top of her. He brushed away the golden hair that had stuck to her damp cheek, kissed her closed eyelids.

She put both her palms on his chest and pushed. He rolled over onto his back and for a moment they just lay there in the dark, the ceiling fan ticking overhead, listening to each others' labored breathing.

Arlan was suddenly so tired, so spent, that he felt himself drifting. She moved on the bed beside him and he reached for her, opening his eyes. "Where are you going?" he asked, groggy.

She brushed her fingertips across the palm of his hand and climbed out of the bed. "Back to the hotel."

"You can stay the night." He never invited anyone to stay after sex. No one but Fia had that privilege, but as the un-expected words came out of his mouth, he realized he wanted Macy here. He wanted her to sleep in his bed beside him.

"I don't stay the night," she said, picking through the clothing on the floor, trying to identify what was hers.

He closed his eyes. Just for a minute. Just to decide what he should say to make her stay. When he opened them again, it was daylight, the clock read 9:10, and he was late to repair Eva's pantry shelves.

"You invited her *here*?" Arlan's words were garbled by a mouthful of nails.

"She might feature the house in a magazine," Eva said enthusiastically. "I don't get anything for that but the fame, but she says that sometimes advertising money comes out of it. You know, people see photos of the house and they want to shoot their toothpaste or hemorrhoid cream ads in my rose garden."

He plucked the nails one by one from between his lips and laid them on the counter that ran under the shelves on one end of the eight-by-six room. Arlan had specifically built the room back in the nineteenth century to store dry goods. "This is going to take more than nails. I'm going to have to pull down some of these shelves, rebrace them and then put them up again. I've been telling you for years that you needed some maintenance work in here." He turned to her. "Eva, you can't invite Macy here. You can't get all friendly with her. She's an HF."

"And you've never had humans in your house?" Eva stood in the doorway between the kitchen and pantry, a perfectly plucked black eyebrow raised. "Puh-lease."

"She's here to talk to Fia about the Buried Alive Killings."

"She's Fia's snitch?"

He frowned, not liking Eva's choice of nouns. Not liking the connotation of the word. "No, she's not a *snitch*. She might have some information that could help the FBI on the case, that's all." Arlan wasn't sure how much he should say. He didn't know what Fia would want him to say. What Macy would want him to say. He suspected he'd already blabbed more than he should. How did he always get into situations like this? Trapped among women.

"Okay, so she's possibly got some info for Fia. I don't see how that concerns me." She lifted her elfin nose haughtily. "She's a photographer. She takes great pictures. Arlan, she *understands* my rosebushes."

He rolled his eyes. "She's not a lesbian, Eva." He removed his measuring tape from his leather tool belt and began to take down numbers on a scrap of paper. "You're barking up the wrong tree if you're looking for love."

"How do you know what her sexual orientation is?" Eva was quiet for a second and then she gasped. "Don't tell me you slept with her?" She slapped her muscular thigh. "Saint Mary, Mother of God's bones! You screwed Fia's snitch!"

"She is *not* Fia's snitch!" He grabbed his scratch paper and strode past her, into the kitchen. He was aggravated. Aggravated with Eva for being too friendly with Macy. Aggravated with Macy for snooping around where she had no business snooping. Eva could be a dangerous woman; hell, he could be dangerous. He was even aggravated with Fia for *her* relationship with Macy. He was pissed at them all.

"I'm going to the lumber store. I might be back today. Might not."

Eva followed him to the foyer, nonplussed. "You think she might be bi?"

"Stay away from her, Eva." He yanked the front door open. "I'm warning you. And I don't want her invited to any of your damned *feasta oiche* parties at your mom's place."

Eva was well-known for her bloodfest parties where all her friends dressed up in costumes to look like what humans thought vampires looked like. They invited human freaks who thought *they* were vampires. Everyone ended up in orgies or blood feasts or both. The *feasta oiche* had been banned from Clare Point years ago, but Eva had never been one to follow rules.

"Come on. I've seen you at my parties," she teased.

He walked out the door, pointing at her with his carpenter's pencil. "I'm not kidding, Eva. Not this time. I'm serious. I don't want Macy caught up in your nonsense."

She followed him onto the porch and leaned on the railing, calling down to him as he climbed into his pickup. "Arlan's got a human girlfriend," she teased. "Arlan's in love."

As he slipped on his sunglasses, he caught a glimpse of himself in the rearview mirror. Was that what was going on here? Was he *falling in love* with Macy?

The idea scared him to the very core of his black soul. If he was in love with Macy, could he still love Fia?

Chapter 14

Fia cradled her cell phone between her shoulder and her chin as she searched for quarters in the bottom of her handbag. So far she'd only come up with pens, a roll of mints, and unidentifiable lint. Frustrated, she dug deeper, feeling along the seams.

She was beginning to think that this had been a bad idea.

She had chosen the Rehoboth Beach boardwalk to meet Macy, primarily because it *wasn't* Clare Point. In just a few days' time, the young woman had apparently made quite an impression on the town. Arlan was sleeping with her. Eva *wished* she was sleeping with her, and Mrs. Cahall wanted to adopt her. Everyone was talking about Macy Smith, about her success as a freelance writer, about how beautiful she was, how mysterious. Fia didn't have time for that kind of crap. She cared for her family. She felt a deep responsibility for them, but they were definitely full of crap sometimes and they could never keep it to themselves. They were always in each other's business. Always in *her* business.

Here in Rehoboth Beach, Fia could get away from all her nosy relatives and conduct her interview out of earshot of telepathic eavesdroppers. A public place, it was a good location to meet an informant who was skittish. There were plenty of humans around, lots of activity, commotion. Fia was hoping Macy would feel safe here.

What she hadn't counted on was just how busy the board-walk was on a Friday night in June. She'd had to park blocks from Rehoboth Avenue, the main street in town. She'd have to hustle if she was going to meet Macy on time at the Dolly's Popcorn stand.

"Fia, are you still there?" came the voice on the other end of her cell.

Damn. She'd almost forgotten Glen. "Yeah, yeah, I'm here." Her fingers finally grasped several coins in the bottom of her bag and she pulled them out. "Sorry. Trying to do ten things at once. It's been crazy . . . today."

"I just wanted to let you know that I can't make dinner tonight." He sounded uncomfortable. Not like himself. "I . . . there's probably no sense in you stopping by later, either. I'll probably be late."

"Oh, okay." She tried to sound disappointed. She had completely forgotten that it was Friday. Well, she *knew* it was Friday, but she'd been so caught up with trying to make some headway in the Buried Alive Killings that she had forgotten about her and Glen's standing Friday night date for dinner and sex. They usually met at some restaurant and then went back to his place.

"I really am sorry," he said.

What she was, was relieved. When she got around to re-membering, she would have called and canceled; something she was doing often lately. And she *would* have remembered. Eventually.

Fia fed the parking meter three quarters and a pepper-mint. It didn't take the peppermint.

"No, it's okay," she said. "I'm out, anyway. Not sure when I'll be done here." She didn't know why she hadn't told Glen she was back in Delaware working on the case. No reason not to tell him. Except that he got funny about her going to Clare Point too often. He didn't like Arlan. He didn't like the relationship she had with him. He didn't understand. Sometimes she liked the idea that he might be jealous. This week, she just didn't have the time.

She strolled away from the parking meter, headed toward the boardwalk and the sound of the waves washing up on the beach. She smelled popcorn, cotton candy, and fried clams, with just the faintest hint of human blood in the air.

"So . . ." Glen said. "I'll talk to you tomorrow?"

Their conversation sounded so stiff. When had things gotten awkward? "Sure." She tried to sound cheerful. "Tomorrow. Maybe we can do something. A movie, maybe?"

"Maybe a movie."

At the Boardwalk Plaza Hotel, Fia turned right and headed south. As she hurried, she scanned the crowd of families with strollers, couples holding hands, and singles cruising. She kept her eye out for Macy. Or at least for the woman Arlan had described to her in detail. The girl was illusive. Fia didn't want her getting away, not at this point. She was tired of playing phone tag. Tired of playing games. She wanted to know what Macy knew.

It wasn't until after Fia hung up that she realized Glen hadn't said what he was doing tonight that prevented him from meeting her. If she'd had the time, she might have been annoyed.

Fia ended up arriving five minutes late, but she beat Macy by ten. They met in the center of the boardwalk, between the avenue and the Atlantic Ocean. Fia held two small boxes of Dolly's famous caramel corn in her hands, one for each of them. A peace offering.

"Macy Smith." The strikingly beautiful woman offered her hand.

"Nice to meet you at last. This is for you." Fia handed her the box, taking her in through the dark lenses of her sunglasses.

"Thanks."

They juggled the boxes and shook hands. Macy's grip was firm.

"I was afraid you weren't going to show." Fia nodded in the direction of an empty bench facing the wide expanse of the ocean. "You want to sit down?"

"Sure."

The young woman, late twenties, Fia guessed, was dressed for an evening at the beach in a graphic T-shirt, shorts, and flip-flops. Fia felt painfully conspicuous in her dress pants and sleeveless silk blouse. Even without the jacket, her ensemble screamed *cop*.

The two women sat down on the wooden bench close enough to each other to keep their conversation private from the people on the benches that flanked theirs, but not so close as to be in each other's personal space. "Heard you've had a busy week in Clare Point."

"Have you?" Macy spoke quietly, making eye contact with her intense green eyes. She held the box of caramel corn in both hands. "Where'd you hear that?"

Fia smiled, looking away as she untwisted the tie on the bag that held her box of caramel popcorn. Macy's voice was soft, shy, but she sensed a spine of steel beneath the timidity, the model good looks and golden locks. "The whole town is full of gossips. And Arlan is probably one of the biggest."

Macy turned her head and gazed straight ahead. She set her box down beside her. "He doesn't strike me as the gossipy kind. He's a good man."

Fia popped a piece of caramel popcorn into her mouth to cover her moment of discomfort. Where had that bitchy comment of hers come from? "Arlan is that. So, uh . . . what's your relationship with him?"

"Why do you ask?" Macy continued to look out beyond the sand dunes at the panoramic view of the incoming tide.

"Okay, I'm sorry." Fia crunched her popcorn. "Don't be offended."

Of course Macy was offended; Fia had just maligned the man Macy was sleeping with. But Fia needed to establish their relationship here. She needed Macy to know she was in charge and she wasn't above bullying a little to do so.

Macy opened her box of popcorn and sampled a piece. "I don't like personal questions."

"You don't want personal questions, but you want me to believe you when you tell me you know something about this case? You want me to trust you merely on your word?"

Macy delicately popped another piece of popcorn into her mouth. "I talked to him the other night."

"He calls you?"

She shook her head, taking her time as she chewed. "That's why I always use the rechargeable phones—you know, they're disposable. Not registered. No, he IM's me."

"And he IM'd you the other night?"

"Monday night around midnight."

"You were up at midnight at your computer?"

"I suffer from insomnia." She turned to Fia, thoughtfully. "You do, too, don't you? I bet you get restless just like I do. When I get restless, I have sex with men I don't know. Or . . . I work." She put another kernel of popcorn in her mouth. "What do you do?"

Fia did suffer from insomnia. Had for lifetimes. But how did Macy know that? Fia had to fight the urge to bring her fingertips beneath her eye. Bags? As for what she did to ease her *restlessness* . . . She thought about her embarrassing call to Arlan in the middle of the night. The man she had picked up and handcuffed to a drainpipe.

Not a pretty picture. Not something she was proud of. Certainly not anything she wanted to share.

"I'm asking the questions here." What she really wanted to ask was about Macy's men. She wondered if they were like hers—easily forgettable and practically disposable. But that would be totally unprofessional. "I'm the FBI agent trying to gather information on this case," she pointed out.

"Okay, Special Agent Kahill." Macy gestured with a piece of popcorn. "But tell me something first. Is everyone in your town related to each other? There's an awful lot of Kahills," she said thoughtfully. "And come to think of it, all the surnames I've encountered sound similar. Kahill with a K. Cahill with a C, Cahall, Hill . . ."

"I thought we agreed that I was the one asking the questions." Fia dug into her box of popcorn. She normally prided herself on how well she controlled interviews. Something told her she was *not* in control of this one right now. "Back to this man who contacts you. You think he's the killer?"

"I know he is." She rubbed her hands together, brushing the sticky crumbs from them.

"How do you know?"

"He tells me he is, but even if he hadn't told me, I would know."

Her words seemed mysterious but they came from her mouth sounding very matter-of-fact. Deep down, Fia knew Macy was telling the truth. She *knew* this was her connection to the killer.

"And you're sure he's a he?"

"He's able to physically control entire families. He digs holes deep enough to bury people up to their chins." She eyed Fia. "There aren't too many women who could do that, except maybe a woman built like you. Besides, most serial killers aren't women."

Fia ignored the personal comment. At nearly six feet tall, she probably did seem big to petite, slender Macy. "How do you know most serial killers are male?"

"Male, white, middle class. Thirty to fifty years old. I watch TLC and the Discovery Channel. Someone's always got a show on about serial killers. They're very in, apparently. Ever since the BTK killer."

Fia smiled to herself. She didn't know that she liked this young woman; it wasn't her job to like her. In fact, liking her could get in the way of her job. But she could see why Arlan would like Macy. Beside the obvious reason—the fact that she carried the X chromosome.

"So you're sure it's him. How does he know you?"

"I don't know."

"What's your connection to him?"

"I don't know."

"He just randomly picked you and started e-mailing you? A year ago when you called me? Two?"

"Something like that."

Fia looked directly at her. Fia was wearing sunglasses; Macy was not. Fia could see the dark specks of brown in her green eyes. She could also see the slight dilation of her pupils. "I'm not sure I believe you."

"I'm not sure I care."

Fia exhaled and gazed over the sand dune that had been constructed after a nor'easter a few years ago. It had been built to hold back Mother Nature, to retain expensive beachfront property and protect landmarks such as the popcorn stand. Nonetheless, the strip of sand between the boardwalk and the ocean narrowed each year. A century ago, it had extended more than a hundred yards from this spot. Sadly, she knew that it was only a matter of time until the boardwalk, the bench she was sitting on, and Dolly's would disappear under the relentless, crashing waves.

"Macy, you've been calling me for a year. You obviously want to help me catch this monster. So, let's stop dancing around each other. Just tell me what you know."

Macy clasped her hands in her lap. "I don't want to talk about myself." She spoke so quietly that Fia had to move closer. A child in a stroller at the next bench over was screaming for another bite of corn dog.

"He's been stalking me for years," Macy continued. "It used to be that he only told me after he killed people. He would tell me to pick up a newspaper, check the evening news, something like that. About a year ago, though, he started hinting at when he would kill. This . . . this last time . . . in Virginia. He basically came right out and he told me he was going to do it before he acted."

"But he didn't tell you where or when, or who?"

She shook her head. "He's too smart for that."

Fia looked directly at her. "How long has he *really* been contacting you?"

"Since the Downings in Chattanooga in 97."

"Since the very first case? Mary, Mother of God." Fia shifted on the bench. "How old were you?"

"Eighteen. He sent me their obituaries from the newspaper. I moved. He found me again about a year and a half later."

"The Shorans in Pennsylvania."

"So I moved again," Macy said. "After that, I just kept moving. When he found me on the Internet, I decided that that was relatively safe. He seemed satisfied to be able to talk to me that way."

"Does he ask you to participate?"

"No."

"Why do you think he tells you about the killings? Do you think he wants to impress you?"

"No."

Macy stared at the sand on the far side of the dune. From up above, on the boardwalk, she had an excellent view. A family walked toward the water, mother, father and three children, all in a row like ducks. This was harder than she had thought it would be . . . talking to Fia. She thought she could remain detached. She thought she could keep herself from thinking about her own family. She never recalled walking on the beach with her mother and father and little sister, but they had lived in Missouri. Not a lot of oceanfront in the Midwest.

"Macy?"

Macy looked at Fia, realizing she'd missed a question.

"Why do you think he contacts you?"

Macy slipped out of her flip-flops and drew her knees up to her chest, resting her bare feet on the bench. "He wants to terrorize me, I suppose."

"Why *you*?" Fia pressed again.

Macy stared straight ahead, hugging her knees. "He said something the other night. I don't know what it means, but I think it's important."

"What's that?"

"The moon." Macy looked at Fia. "Check your records. The murders have always taken place on a full moon, only he was a day late this time."

"A full moon?"

Fia sounded intrigued. So it *was* a clue.

Macy nodded. "I asked him if someone told him to do it. You know, I was thinking crazy voices in his head or something. He sort of went off on me when I asked. He said *no one's the boss of me*. Those exact words."

"No one's the boss of me?" Fia repeated. "Sounds like something a kid throwing a fit would say."

"Exactly what I was thinking."

"So let's see. Usually a full moon or close to it, I guess. But no one tells him to do it. No one is in charge of him.

No one controls him," Fia said, thinking out loud. "Interesting."

"You think so?" She almost felt a twinge of hope. "It doesn't sound like much to me, but I think this was the most revealing conversation I've ever had with him. Usually he just . . . taunts me."

"This could definitely mean something." Fia held the plastic bag at the top and spun the box of popcorn to seal it. She looked back at Macy. "He taunts you?"

"He calls me names," she whispered. "Mostly in reference to my promiscuity. I think he must follow me. Somehow he always ends up knowing where I am. Who I'm with. But only in generalities. It's very odd."

"Does he contact the men you've been with?"

"I don't think so."

"Bizarre," Fia remarked, looking away.

She didn't seem to care that Macy had practically admitted to being a whore. Well, not a *whore* because there was never any financial transaction, she thought wryly. *Tramp* was probably a more suitable word.

"And you don't know what he looks like?"

Macy could see that the wheels of Fia's FBI agent mind were still turning.

"You've never seen him?" Fia asked.

"I try to always keep my eye out for familiar faces, you know, at the grocery store, in a crowd. If I've seen him, I don't know it. He's made no attempt to contact me in person. Not ever."

They sat in silence for a moment.

Macy breathed deeply. Her pulse had slowed to a normal rate again. It had been scary actually speaking aloud about him, but it been emotionally freeing, as well. She could almost feel some of the ties that had bound her to Teddy for all these years breaking away.

"That's all I have," Macy said finally.

"I doubt that. But it's a good start." Fia stood. "Tell me you're going to stick around a few more days, Macy Smith. Give me some time to look over all the cases again. I think we could be on to something with this moon thing."

"I'm in no hurry to leave Clare Point. I like your hometown. It's a little weird." She managed a shy smile. "But I like it. And, as I'm sure you heard through the grapevine, I may be writing a piece about some of the seaside cottages. Could mean a couple of weeks' worth of work."

"If you decide to move on, I just hope you'll let me know." Fia watched her carefully, through the dark lenses of her sunglasses. "You have a way of slipping through my fingers, Macy Smith."

Macy gave her a half smile. "I'm not moving into your mother's B and B. I like the hotel. But if I decide to go, you'll be the first to know. I do have to go back to Virginia to finish a photo shoot, but that'll just be a day trip."

"I think I'll head back. Stop by and see my parents. I guess you've heard that my brother seems to have gotten himself into a little trouble. We're not entirely sure where he is. You going back?" Fia hooked a thumb north.

"Nah. I think I'll sit here a while longer." Macy settled on the bench again. "Maybe get some pizza. I hear Grottos is pretty famous for their pizza pie."

"More popcorn?" Fia offered the box.

"No thanks. It was good, but I'm not much for sweets."

"Well, thanks again for your help. I would ask for your new phone number but I suppose it'll be different by the end of the week."

"You can leave a message for me at the hotel."

"Right. Well, give me some time to look over all the case files, any witnesses, and I'll see if I can dig up Moon Boy. I'll get back to you. Midweek probably."

"Thanks for listening." As Macy watched Fia walk

away, she felt the strangest sensation. It had been so long since she felt it—since she was a kid probably—that she almost couldn't identify it. And then she realized with a smile what that was.

Hope.

Chapter 15

At the sound of the front door opening, Arlan turned from his perch on the step ladder. Seeing Fia walk in the door, he returned his attention to his phone call. "You're sure you don't need me to come?"

It's Fin on the phone. Regan called him, too, Arlan telepathed to Fia. *He wants him to meet him in Florence.*

Inside the door, she set a box of caramel popcorn on a chair stacked with newspapers, bundled for recycling.

"Is Regan all right?" Fia crossed the living room.

Fin thinks so. He's in some kind of trouble, but he was able to call. Apparently he thinks he can get out of Greece and into Italy.

"You don't need to come. I think this is another one of my brother's adventures," Fin said to Arlan. "A highly exaggerated event meant to impress the ladies later."

"You're sure?" Arlan climbed down the ladder, leaving his putty knife behind. He'd been trying to patch some cracks in the ceiling in preparation for painting it. "Because I can be there by morning. Afternoon at the latest."

"He tell Fin what was wrong? What kind of trouble he was in? He's sure he's okay?" Fia fired.

"Fin thinks he's fine," Arlan said to Fia; then to Fin, "Your sister's here. You want to talk to her?"

"Can't. Boarding a plane. Give her a kiss for me. Tell her I'll bring our pain-in-the-ass brother home. Tell her to tell Ma to stop worrying."

Arlan heard voices in the background. A flight attendant welcoming passengers in German, then English, then Italian.

"Coach," Fin groaned. "I'm going to kill my brother. This short of notice, I couldn't find a first-class seat. He knows I hate flying coach. Gotta go. Stay safe."

"You, too, buddy." Arlan ended the call and tossed the phone on his leather recliner. "He says for you and your mom not to worry. He says he's going to kill Regan when he catches up with him for forcing him to fly coach to Italy."

"He's going to kill him and take that pleasure from me?" Her tone was thick with sarcasm, but relief as well. "So Fin really thinks he's all right?" she repeated.

Arlan shrugged. "Sounds just like what we thought— another one of Regan's merry jaunts."

"So why haven't we been able to get hold of Fin, either?"

"Sept business. He was in Prague. Had cell phone issues." Arlan headed for the kitchen. "Beer?"

She frowned. "No, thanks."

She leaned against the doorjamb between the eat-in kitchen and living room. She looked pretty tonight in an FBI bad-ass kind of way. Her dress slacks hugged her firm buttocks and they made her already long legs appear as if they went on forever. The pale blue silk top was clingy, but not hoochie. She had a nice rack for a woman a couple of centuries old.

Arlan grabbed a beer from the refrigerator. Dogfish Head, brewed locally. He twisted the cap, wondering vaguely why Fia had stopped by out of the blue like this. It wasn't that he wasn't happy to see her; before the boyfriend she'd come by regularly. Sometimes for sex. Sometimes to talk. Other times just to share each other's silent companionship. He sensed she was here for a reason, but she had a solid wall up blocking her thoughts. Arlan attempted psychically to knock, but she refused to open the door.

Sometimes he had to just rely on good old-fashioned human methods of communication. "So . . . how did the interview with Macy go?"

"Good. Um . . . she might actually have something that can help us find this monster."

"Really? You want to go sit on the deck? Mosquitoes aren't bad yet."

"Sure."

He started for the door. "Sure I can't get you something? Water? Blood?"

"I'm fine."

"How about a wedding band?" He pushed open the screen door and stepped out onto the deck. Summer darkness, which never seemed as dark to him as winter darkness, was settling over the town. He took one of the Adirondack chairs that faced the fenced-in backyard. She sat in the chair beside him.

"Will you never let that go?" she asked.

"What?"

"You know what. The marriage thing. The . . . the you and me thing."

"Eventually." He glanced at her, giving her his best ladykiller smile. "Another century or two." He took a sip of beer and then gestured with the bottle. "But I sense some weakness in you. Maybe a little jealousy?"

"Of Macy?" She laughed, breaking eye contact with him. "Since when have I ever been jealous of any of your women?"

"There was Lizzy."

She leaned back in the wooden plank chair he had built

with his own hands and painted a whimsical teal color. He was sitting in the mauve one. "Okay, maybe I was a little jealous of Lizzy, but she was a possessive wench. And she was crazy," she added.

He smiled sadly. Fia had been jealous of Lizzy because he had loved Lizzy. Not the same way he loved Fia, but still, he had loved her. Which led him to the question, *was* he falling in love with Macy and did Fia sense that?

"Okay, so we're discussing old haunts. How's that ex of yours, the one you couldn't quite shake? What was his name? Jasper? Joshua? Dickhead?"

"You're not all that funny, Arlan. His name was Joseph and I believe he's settled in Las Vegas."

"I *am* funny. Can be, at least, and you know it. *You* think I'm funny."

She exhaled. "I should go."

"No, no, don't go." He tapped the arm of her chair. "Tell me about Macy. About the investigation."

"I shouldn't."

"Of course you shouldn't, but who else do you have to talk to? And you know I can keep secrets. I'm a good secret keeper." He glanced meaningfully at her.

She looked at him and then away. "He's been contacting her for years, since the first murders."

"You're kidding. She . . . she would have been just a kid."

"Eighteen."

He sipped his beer. "And she has no idea why he picked her?"

"She says not."

"Did she have any connection to the first family murdered?"

"I don't know. I'm going to try to find out. What I really need is some info on Macy. Now that I have a last name, which I hope is her real name, maybe I can look into her background."

"Maybe she doesn't want you to do that," he said. "Maybe that's why she didn't give her real name to begin with."

"Too bad."

He frowned. "That's harsh."

"It's reality. I don't have time to screw around here. This guy is going to kill again and he's going to keep killing until we catch him." She turned in the chair to face him. "She did have one interesting tidbit to offer. She thinks the moon cycles have something to do with the murders. Or at least they did. I'm going to check the records, but Macy says that he always killed on a full moon . . . until the family in Virginia."

"What changed?"

She shook her head. "Macy says she doesn't know. She says he wouldn't say. He contacted her the other night—"

"Since she came to Clare Point?"

"He IM'd her. She asked him why he did it, if someone told him to. He told her, and I quote, 'No one is the boss of me'."

"Ah, Mommy issues."

"You think so?" Fia asked. "I was considering issues with authority."

"Certainly could be."

She rose. "I think I'll go."

"To your mom's?"

"I'm going to stop by the house and then head north." She backed up across the deck, still facing him. "I might just go to the office. Pull an all-nighter. I've got a lot of case files to look through. I'm going to compare the lists of witnesses, people present at the scene. I want to be sure Moon Boy hasn't been at any of the crime scenes."

"*Moon Boy?*"

She shrugged. "Has a better ring to it than *Buried Alive Killer*."

He chuckled. "Does sound like a headline in the tabloids,

doesn't it?" He looked down and then back at her. "You're going to work all night? What about lover boy?"

It was her turn to look away. "Um . . . He had something else going on."

"Ah." Arlan nodded. "I see."

"No you don't. You don't see because there's nothing *to* see. Glen and I have our own lives. We have work, families. We don't feel like we have to be glued to each other's sides." She had stopped at the top of the stairs that lead from the deck into the yard.

He held up both hands, beer still in one. "Hey, your relationship. Who am I to judge?"

"Exactly. Who are you to judge, Mr. Sleep-With-Any-thing-With-A-Vagina?"

"Oh." He cringed. "That's ugly, Fee. Definitely below the belt."

"Good night," she said, her voice without animosity.

She knew what Arlan was. She accepted him. He thought that, on some level, she even understood him. It was just one of the reasons he loved her.

She backed down the steps. "And thanks for tracking Fin down. He doesn't always call me back in a timely fashion, but I knew he'd get back to you."

He waved her away. "Go on, be a workaholic. Let me know if you find anything."

"Sure. In the meantime, can you keep an eye on Macy? She says she'll be here a few days more, at least. I asked her to give me some time."

"No problem."

At the gate, Fia turned around. "Hey, I left you a box of Dolly's popcorn. It's in the living room."

"My favorite," he called after her as she stepped through the gateway and into the dark, disappearing from his view. He could still feel her, though. And even though she was blocking her thoughts, he could feel her pain. Things weren't good between her and lover boy. He wished she felt like she could talk about it with him. After all, he had it all over her as far as disastrous relationships with humans. He wished she would trust him more.

"You sure you won't marry me?" he hollered.

She closed the gate behind her and the lock clicked. Arlan finished his beer, alone in the dark, and waited for Macy.

From half a block away, Macy saw Arlan's silhouette in the darkness of his front porch. What was weird was the way the moonlight and shadows were playing tricks on her tonight. When she first looked up at the dark porch, she could have sworn it was a bear standing there on two legs, rather than a mere mortal man.

Not that Arlan was a mere man. She smiled to herself. He was definitely a cut above most—as well as she ever got to know any of them, that is.

She halted on the sidewalk in front of his house and looked up. He was drinking a beer. She could see the beads of condensation on the cold brown bottle. It was hot tonight. *Close,* as people in this area of the country liked to say when the air was so warm and humid that you felt as if you were walking through hot pudding. Perspiration beaded on her forehead as she looked at the inviting beer.

"You waiting for me?" she asked.

He lifted one broad, muscular shoulder and let it fall. He was wearing a gym T-shirt, the sleeves cut off. It showed his physique well.

She took her time walking up the steps. She was barefoot tonight, wore a T-shirt and gym shorts. No undergarments. No need for them on a hot night like tonight. No need for them in her lover's arms.

"I might not have come, you know." She dragged her

fingertips along the sagging rail of the steps. "Could use a little paint, here, Mr. Handyman."

He watched her from the porch without moving. His stance was relaxed to the point of lazy, but there was something about his muscle-bound biceps and quads that made her think he could spring over the railing in an instant. Catlike, in a ferocious way.

She almost chuckled to herself, wondering where the heck her thoughts came from sometimes. There was nothing special about Arlan. He was a hot guy. She'd known a lot of hot guys over the years. And more importantly, she reminded herself, there was nothing about him that could make her feel special.

At the top of the steps, she leaned against one of the support posts. His gaze searched hers. In his eyes, she saw hunger. A longing for something she couldn't quite put her finger on.

He reached out with his free hand and stroked her cheek.

Without thinking, she covered his hand with hers. There was such depth there. Such longing . . . and pain.

Too personal. She realized it the moment she did it. Too personal was bad. It made it hard to leave. It made regrets. She had to be able to pack up and go without compunction. It was part of the curse she carried. Part of the curse the killer had gifted her. She let her hand fall and crossed the porch, walking into the house. He followed.

Inside the door, she spotted a box of half-eaten caramel popcorn on a chair. Something inside her turned over. Flopped. A lump rose in her throat. Fia had been here.

She walked past the box of popcorn, down the hall toward the bedroom. A part of her wanted to ask him about the popcorn. About Fia. Macy knew there was something between them, something beyond friendship, she just wasn't quite sure what.

Maybe she didn't want to know.

She slipped out of her clothes inside the dark doorway to his bedroom, went to the bed and lay naked on the cool sheets. He had washed them and made the bed. How sweet.

Arlan stood in the doorway, finishing his beer.

She stretched out, enjoying the feel of the crisp, soft sheets and the slight stirring of air against her prickly, hot, damp skin.

"You want to talk about it?" he asked.

"About what?"

"You didn't tell me he's contacted you since the first murders."

She looked up, watching the paddle fan turn. She listened to its *tick . . . tick . . . tick.*

Arlan stood there for a long time until finally, without looking at him, she said, "Are you coming or not?"

His sigh was long and when he spoke, his words were barely a whisper. She heard his shorts and T-shirt hit the floor. "I'm coming."

Teddy paced, counting his strides from one side of the hotel room to the other. Eight. Just eight.

He felt trapped. But lost at the same time.

He did an about-face when he reached the wall and walked in the other direction. He glanced at the desk where he'd left his laptop open. He'd waited for Marceline all evening, but she hadn't come. Where was she? With another man? The thought of her in another man's arms made his stomach twist painfully.

I told you she didn't want you.

Teddy whipped around. "You're not supposed to be here," he said aloud.

I'm just telling you the truth. Someone has to be honest with you, Teddy. You're certainly not honest with yourself.

At the wall, he turned again. His terrycloth slippers made a soft *slap, slap* on the carpet as he paced.

"I have to work tomorrow. I have to go to sleep," he said. He gritted his teeth. "You're not supposed to be here."

Forget about her.

"I can't!" he said, closing one hand into a fist.

You don't need her. You have me.

But I do need her, Teddy thought, not saying it aloud. He sat down on the edge of the bed and covered his ears with his hands. "I need her because of you," he whispered.

Chapter 16

Arlan was carrying wood in through the back door of Eva's house when his cell rang. He could tell by the ring tone that it was Fia. He was glad she had called. He'd waited all weekend to hear from her. He'd wanted to call her, but resisted the temptation. These last few days he'd felt unsettled. Divided. He really cared about Macy. But Fia . . . she was Fia.

He leaned the two-by-fours in the corner of the laundry room. "Hey," he said into the phone.

"Hey, you talk to Regan or Fin?" she asked. No small talk with Fia. There rarely was.

"No. Haven't heard a word from either of them." Arlan walked into Eva's kitchen and took a water bottle from the fridge. It was going to be another scorcher of a day.

"They were supposed to meet yesterday. I would have thought we'd have heard from them by now."

"I wouldn't be too concerned." Arlan leaned against the granite countertop he had installed the year before and twisted the lid off the water bottle. He took a drink. "You know your brothers."

"I suppose you're right," she conceded.

"You sound tired," Arlan said. "You work all weekend?"

"Yup."

"And?"

"And what?"

"I know you found something," he said. "Otherwise you wouldn't be calling me in the middle of the morning to chat."

"I call you to chat sometimes," she defended.

"Not during the workday. Not on FBI time. You're too Type A for that and you know it." He took another long drink of the icy water. "So, what did you find out? Moon Boy leave his name and number with the police at some point?"

"Nothing about Moon Boy, so far. No Teddy, no Ted, no Theodore. I'm sure Macy's right, he doesn't use his real name when communicating with her. As far as the lists of names from all the crime scenes, no duplicates. I got the log of tips called in over the years, but it could take me weeks to get through them. You wouldn't believe how many fruitcakes call in, positive a serial killer lives in the apartment next to them."

"Or an alien," he offered.

"Or a vampire."

They both laughed.

"Okay, so what *did* you find?" he asked.

She exhaled. "I called because I need you to have Macy call me. She's disconnected yet another damned phone. I e-mailed her this morning, but she hasn't responded. "

He walked to the window above the sink and gazed out into Eva's garden. "Probably because she's here."

"Here where? At your house?"

"Eva's. I'm doing some work on her pantry. Macy's taking photographs in the garden." He watched them. "She and Eva are out there looking like best friends. Talking. Laughing."

"That's a bad idea," Fia intoned.

"I know. I told Eva that the other day. And she, basically, told me to mind my own business. She says she likes her. You know Eva, she does what she wants." The women were sitting on a bench under a pear tree. Macy was fiddling with her camera and Eva was talking a mile a minute. "You want to talk to her now? Want me to hand her my phone?"

"I suppose. This is a pain in the ass, her playing secret agent like this."

"You think she has good reason to be hiding out, or is she just a flake?" He walked toward the back door, not sure which choice he was hoping for. If she was hiding, it was because she was A, in cahoots with the killer, or B, being persecuted by him. Neither was promising. So maybe it would be better, at least for Macy, if Fia learned she was a nut job. It wouldn't be the first time he'd fallen for a crazy female.

He entered the garden by way of the back door. "Hang on a minute," he said into the phone; then he lowered it. "Phone's for you, Macy." He held the cell out to her.

"Me?" Macy rose off the bench, leaving her camera beside Eva, but she didn't reach for the phone. "Who is it?" She sounded . . . afraid.

"It's just Fia."

"What does she want?"

He shook the phone. "She needs to talk to you. Something about the investigation, I imagine." He glanced at Eva, who was all ears.

Macy slowly reached for the phone, not entirely sure she wanted to take it. Another conversation with Fia would change things. She knew it. She could feel it. Was this really what she wanted?

She hadn't talked to Teddy in days and it had felt good. She'd had an amazing weekend taking photos and talking with Eva's neighbors. She'd even joined Eva and some of her friends for dinner the previous night at a small restaurant down by the water. Macy had never had friends before, even someone else's. It had felt so good to have someone to talk to. To laugh with.

And then there was Arlan. Each night she went to his bed, they made love, and then she returned to the hotel. He didn't ask anything of her. He made no demands.

If Macy talked to Fia she might have to leave Clare Point and she didn't want to leave. She knew she would have to, eventually, but just a few days more would be heaven.

But he was still out there and he would kill again. Macy knew Teddy would kill again and probably sooner rather than later. If she wanted to help Fia stop him, she really had no choice but to continue on this path.

She slowly drew the phone to her ear as she walked away from Eva and Arlan. "Hello," she said softly.

"Why did you lie to me?" Fia demanded.

Fia caught Macy off guard. She wasn't sure what to say. "Who are you?"

"I . . . I'm Macy Smith," she said carefully. Fia had obviously done some sort of background check on Macy. She knew it would happen if she gave her name. That's why she'd avoided it for the last year. But Macy didn't know how much Fia knew and until she did, she had to stick to her story. "I suppose technically I'm Mary Elizabeth Smith," she continued. "My parents always called me Macy, though." She halted under a red maple tree that was so perfect it should have been in a painting. "What's the problem?"

"The problem," Fia said angrily, "is that you're *not* Mary Elizabeth Smith and the social security number you provided me doesn't belong to you."

Macy thought about just hanging up. She would go back to the hotel, grab her bag, get into her car and drive away. She couldn't help Fia find the killer, but she could help herself. She couldn't save anyone else; that had already been proven, but she could save herself.

That's what Macy had been telling herself all these years. That was her excuse, because she was a coward.

"What do you mean it's not my social security number?" Macy said. "Check with the IRS. *They* think I'm Mary Elizabeth Smith. They take enough taxes out of me."

"Mary Elizabeth Smith is buried in a churchyard outside St. Louis. Where were you born, Macy?"

"Our Lady of Grace Hospital in St. Louis, Missouri."

"What's your birth date?"

"January second. I'll be thirty in January. You do the math." Macy was a little surprised by the sarcasm in her voice. Fia was FBI. Fia could get her into serious trouble over this.

Fia was quiet on the other end for a moment. "That only means that you were careful when you bought this identity. According to my sources, Mary Elizabeth Smith died at birth."

"Obviously *your* sources are wrong." Macy gave a little laugh that didn't sound convincing even in her own ears.

"I can send an agent to the cemetery and take a photograph of the headstone. You want me to do that, Macy?"

It was Macy's turn to be quiet. "Why do you care?" she finally asked, turning her back on Arlan and Eva, who were relaxing on the bench among the magnificent roses.

"Because this is proof that you've been lying to me. And if you're lying to me about who you are, I have to ask what else are you lying about."

Macy plucked a maple leaf from the tree she stood under and held it in her palm, studying its shape. "I changed my name so I could hide. So no one would know who I was."

"Who are you?"

"I'm a woman being stalked by a serial killer." Macy's

voice caught in her throat. "I'm a woman trying to do what's right. Trying to help the police catch a killer."

"What else have you lied to me about?"

"Nothing," Macy said.

"Nothing?" Fia demanded.

"Nothing," Macy repeated. She hesitated. "So did you find anything, looking over the old cases? You know, about Teddy?"

"How did you know I was—" Fia cut her sentence short. "Arlan . . ."

"He just told me that you were going to go over all the lists of witnesses. He explained that killers often appear in the crowd at crime scenes and that you might be able to cross-reference a name."

"Well, I couldn't. I put all the names into an Excel spread sheet and no one is cross-matching. You've got to tell me more about this guy."

"I don't know anything about him." Macy felt her throat constrict as she thought of all the scraps of paper she had saved over the years. The obituaries. The news articles. The cards he sent when she was still in foster care. Was there a clue there that could lead them to the killer? But those *mementos* were personal. Too personal to be shared. "Nothing except that he's been terrifying me . . . for what seems like my whole life," she said, catching herself before she revealed too much. She had to be careful not to kid herself. Fia was not her friend. No one could be her friend.

"Damn it, Macy. He's going to kill again."

"I know," Macy said, a uncharacteristic quaver in her voice . "I *know*. Don't you see? That's why I'm still in Clare Point. It's the only reason."

"You're not there because of Arlan?"

Macy was so surprised by the question that she turned and looked at him, sitting on the bench with Eva. He must have sensed they were speaking about him because he looked up at her at that precise moment.

He did it all the time. So did Eva, she had noticed. Everyone in the town seemed to *sense* things. It was a little weird.

Macy turned her back to Arlan and Eva again. "There's nothing between us, if that's what you're asking," she said. "Is that what you're asking?"

"It's not my business who you sleep with, Macy. You're both consenting adults, but I . . . I guess I just don't want to see Arlan hurt."

"It's just sex." And Macy meant it when she said it. But she didn't feel it with her usual conviction. She wondered if she was going against one of her most important rules of survival: *Don't get attached.* The rule applied to towns, to jobs, and certainly to people.

And she was breaking the rule in every direction possible, wasn't she?

"Tell me what you want me to do." Macy released the leaf and watched it flutter to the ground in the warm breeze. She could smell the ocean from Eva's backyard. She had always thought that if she ever settled down, if she ever could, it would be near the Atlantic Ocean. "To catch him."

"I don't know yet, Macy. I'm going to have to think on this one." Fia was quiet for a second. "But I need you to promise me you're not going to let yourself get spooked and take off. I'm not out to bust you for stealing some-one's identity—"

"I didn't *steal* it, I bought it," Macy interrupted. "It wasn't as if she needed the social security number. She's dead."

"Just so long as you're not doing anything illegal with it," Fia continued. "All I want to do is stop this guy before he kills again. I need you to stay in contact with me be-cause right now, Macy," she said before letting her respond, "you're still the best lead we have on this monster."

"I'll call you later with my new number." Macy heard someone approaching and turned to see Arlan walking toward her.

"Everything okay?" Arlan asked Macy.

"That Arlan? Will you put him back on?" Fia asked.

Macy handed the phone to Arlan.

"Yeah?" Arlan said. He paused. Listened. "Right." He disconnected.

"What did she say?" Macy asked.

"She asked me to keep an eye on you." He wasn't smiling. "There a reason she said that?"

"No reason you could understand," she said. She walked away before he could respond. If she didn't get away from him and those prying eyes of his, she was afraid she might cave and spill her sorry guts on Eva's immaculate lawn.

"Macy."

She was surprised when she felt him tug on her arm. No one had come after her before. Not ever in her life. Her father had certainly not come for her that night. A blessing or a curse?

She halted, unsure of how to respond to Arlan. It was at moments like these in life that bonds were woven or broken. Did she pull away?

"Macy, I don't understand why you won't tell me what's going on. I can help you."

She couldn't look at him. Her eyes stung. No tears, but it was the closest she'd come to them since she was fifteen. She still remembered clearly the last time she had cried, two days before the murders. She had run to her bedroom, slamming the door, tears running down her cheeks because her mother had embarrassed her in front of her boyfriend. Macy had been so angry. So hurt.

And had had no idea at that innocent moment in her life just what pain was.

"What is it about you that makes you think you can

save people?" she whispered, half accusing, half desperate to believe in him.

He was silent.

"Please," Macy whispered, blinking. "Just let me go." She wasn't sure if she meant it literally or emotionally. "There are things about me that you don't know. That you wouldn't like."

She could feel his fingertips burning on the flesh of her arm.

"We all have secrets, Macy," he responded. "We've all done things we're not proud of."

"Not secrets like this."

He let her go this time.

As she walked away, she heard a strange sound that she could have sworn came from Arlan. A growl? It so startled her that she turned around to look at him, to see Eva looking at him.

She walked out through the back gate, leaving her camera behind.

Chapter 17

When Macy arrived at Arlan's just after midnight, he was waiting on the step for her. She took her time approaching the house, watching him. It was a hot, humid night and she could feel sticky tendrils of damp hair clinging to her temples. As she walked up the street, she could hear the hum of the air-conditioning units that protruded from the windows of the old houses. Singly, they would not have made much noise, but together, on such a quiet night, the sounds rose in unison, like the great buzz of a swarm of insects.

Macy sat on the step below Arlan, her back to him, and stared out at the street illuminated by the faint light of a streetlamp.

"You stole a dead woman's identity?" His tone was terse.

"You talked to Fia."

He didn't answer.

"It wasn't Fia's place to tell you." She still didn't look at him. "What is it with the two of you? She in love with you or something?"

He didn't answer right away. She could feel the heat of his body, though they were not touching.

"What would make you say that?" he asked finally.

She lifted one bare shoulder and let it fall. She was wearing a thin, sleeveless white T-shirt and gym shorts. She liked wife-beaters from the men's underwear department because of the way they hugged her body, but were still cool on hot nights.

"I don't know. Something in her voice. Maybe something in yours when you say her name," she said, wondering if it was jealousy she was feeling. She had read about the emotion, seen it in movies, but had never really experienced it. Was she jealous that Fia could have something she could never have?

"Fia and I go back a long way."

"You've said that before." She watched a scrap of paper tumble down the middle of the street, caught on the summer wind. "I don't know what that means."

He closed his hand over her shoulder. An intimate gesture that brought a tightness to her chest.

"It's too complicated to explain, Macy. But she's nothing for you to worry about."

"I'm not worried. Why would I worry?"

"You're avoiding the subject of the stolen identity."

"I didn't steal it. I . . . borrowed it. If Fia told you about the social security number, she should at least have had the decency to tell you the whole story." She rested her palms on her bare thighs. "I bought the social security number years ago. It was assigned to a girl who died at birth. Like I told Fia, it wasn't like she was going to use it."

"It's illegal, Macy."

"So's burying people and then suffocating them. Hasn't stopped him." She rose, turned, and walked up the steps past him. At the door, she hesitated. "You coming or not?"

"Where?"

She heard herself laugh and the unexpected sound lightened her mood. "To bed, silly. Where else?"

He followed her inside, closing the door behind him. "You don't think this is . . . I don't know, odd?"

"What?" She walked toward his bedroom, stepping out of her gym shorts halfway down the hallway. "Two consenting adults having sex without commitment? I don't think it's odd at all. I don't know who ever came up with the idea that people ought to be monogamous." She turned in the doorway to his bedroom and rested her hand on the doorjamb. The white T-shirt rode up, revealing a curly nest of blond hair. "It's not been true in my experience. Has it been in yours?" She looked at him, wide-eyed.

He stepped over her shorts, his dark gaze fixated just below the hemline of her T-shirt. She wondered if this was why she enjoyed sex with strangers so much. Because of the control she had over men. She might not be able to control anything else in her life, but *this* she could. *Here,* she had total power over the situation.

"No," he said. "Yes . . . I suppose."

"So which is it?" she asked, making her voice sultry. She touched his Adam's apple with her finger and drew a line downward over his damp, hot skin.

Perspiration beaded above his upper lip. She spotted the large bulge in his cargo shorts. Macy suspected this conversation would be a short one.

"No, or yes, which is it?" she teased, catching his chin with her hand and guiding his lips to hers.

He took her hungrily, thrusting his tongue into her mouth as she slid her palm downward over the zipper of his shorts. He groaned.

"Macy—" He pulled back, looking down into her eyes. "You know what I'm talking about. You just showing up every night. Having sex and then just . . . leaving. You don't think it's . . . strange?"

She lifted up on her toes and nipped his lower lip playfully with her teeth. "You don't want me to come over any more?"

He stroked her cheek. "No, it's not that, it's just that . . ." His voice was breathy. Already heavy with desire for her.

"How is it so weird?" She gave a little laugh. "I guess the question should be how it could *not* be weird? This whole town is weird. Like M. Night Shyamalan weird."

"What?" He screwed up his face in a most adorable way.

"You know, the director. He does strange stuff in his movies. *Lady in the Water. The Sixth Sense.*"

He nodded, but didn't quite seem to understand what she meant.

"From an outsider looking in, everything about this town is a little peculiar," she explained. "The way you locals talk to each other, the way you seem to know things you shouldn't know. The way you look at us—the tourists, the outsiders. We're drawn to you, drawn here, and we don't know why. You know, I'm not exactly sure how I got here. I definitely don't know why I came."

He broke into a sexy, mischievous grin. "Oh, you know why you came." He grasped her waist with both hands and slowly lowered himself, dragging his mouth downward between her breasts, down to her belly button and then lower. "You came because you couldn't get enough of me," he teased.

Macy closed her eyes and threaded her fingers through his dark hair. Leave it to a man to end a conversation with a blatant sexual boast. Not that she really minded. She herself had used the technique on more than one occasion.

Macy's eyelids fluttered shut and she gripped the door frame for support. She could feel her legs going weak.

From a weird little town or not, the man certainly knew how to use his tongue.

"Arlan," Macy groaned. She clasped his face with both her hands and lifted his head until he was looking up at her. "You wanna move this to the bed, lover boy?" she whispered.

Arlan smiled up at her. The only light in the bedroom, the butter-soft glow of the moon, illuminated her long

blond hair. She looked like an angel. So beautiful. So fragile.

"Come on," she whispered, backing up.

She caught his hand and led him to the bed. She threw
herself onto it and rolled over to look up at him. He was
just lowering himself over her when he saw a flash of light
in the back of his head. He heard a voice and he winced.

"Arlan? You okay?"

Had she seen it, too?

He sat down on the edge of the bed, pressing the heels
of his hands to his temples. Painful light flashed again.
Arlan, I need you.

"Arlan, are you all right?" Macy's gentle voice barely
penetrated his haze.

His eyes were open, but he did not see his bedroom. He
did not see the beautiful, naked woman beside him. He
saw a tree with Spanish moss hanging from it. A stone crypt.

The light flashed again in his head. A painful, blinding
glare. He smelled a foul scent. Mud. Rotting vegetation.
Putrefying flesh . . .

Images burst in his brain. Burial crypts in neat rows.
Iron crosses. A stone statue of an angel hovering over his
head. A tall gate embellished with a simple iron cross. He
smelled the cloying, thick scent of blooming crepe myrtle, so
sweet that it was nauseating.

Arlan, come quick. A bit of trouble.

Regan's voice rang as clear as if he were standing in the
room.

Arlan saw a single flash of Regan's handsome face behind
the black wrought iron gate and the image vanished an instant later. Like that, Arlan was in his room again.

"Arlan?" Macy was standing in front of him, her hands
on his face. She gazed into his eyes. "Arlan, what's wrong?"

His mouth was dry. All Kahill vampires were able to
telecommunicate with one another when in each other's

company, but Regan had the gift of being able to communicate telepathically from great distances. He was also
able to speak telepathically to humans. Right now, Regan
was communicating clearly with Arlan. He was in trouble.

"Are you sick?" Macy murmured, obvious concern in
her voice.

Arlan blinked. His heart was racing, he was hot and
sweaty, and he could feel the hair on his spine bristle—except that he was in human form so he possessed no hair
along his spine at the moment. A small detail that he couldn't
explain, even to himself.

Regan was in trouble. Serious trouble. But where was
he, where was Fin? They were supposed to have met up by
now. They were supposed to be on their way home, together.

"I . . ." Arlan pressed the heel of his hand to his forehead. He had to be careful in Macy's presence. Sometimes,
when he was hit telepathically like this, it was difficult for
him to remain in his human form. He *wanted* to be a lynx
or a wolf. He yearned to become something simpler, more
elemental.

He tightened his fists at his sides, fighting the urge to
morph. He was playing with fire here with Macy; he had
known that from the beginning. He couldn't let her catch
him off guard again. This morning in Eva's garden he knew
she had heard him growl. He just hadn't been able to help
himself. She hadn't said anything, but she had heard him.
Fortunately, like most humans, she didn't trust her own
senses.

But Arlan trusted his.

He could still smell the rot of flesh in his nostrils that
had mixed with the sweet scent of the flowers. An old
cemetery . . .

He had to try to get hold of Fin. Try to find out what
happened. Where the hell were they? "A migraine," he

managed to say to Macy. "I'm sorry. They . . . they just hit me like this sometimes." He squinted and lowered his head, hiding the lie in his eyes, feigning pain.

"Oh, God. Poor thing." Macy sat down beside him on the edge of the bed and stroked his temple. "Can I get you something? Some aspirin? A glass of water?"

"Um . . ." He was trying to think on two levels and not doing so well on either. It had been a long time since he'd been hit so hard telepathically. It had rattled him. Regan had to be in serious trouble to send those kinds of images. "Water would be good," Arlan told Macy.

"I'll be right back." She pressed a kiss to the top of his head and hurried out of his bedroom, bare-bottomed.

Arlan lay back on the bed, his legs still dangling over the end. He lay there for a minute, trying to catch his breath, then sat up again. He slipped his hand into his shorts pocket and drew out his phone. Fin didn't pick up and eventually Arlan got his voice mailbox. He didn't leave a message. He dialed a second number. By the time it was ringing on the other end, he was halfway to the bathroom. Hearing Macy come out of the kitchen, he slipped inside and closed the door behind him.

" 'Lo."

Fia was still awake. He could hear it in her voice.

"Hey," Arlan said, trying to be quiet. "You hear from Regan or Fin?"

"No."

He could hear her tapping on her keyboard. She was still at work, probably. Or working at home. Not with the boyfriend. Her voice was different when she was with a human. Arlan knew it was wrong but he was glad there was trouble in Fia's human boyfriend paradise. The guy was all wrong for her. There were too many secrets between them. It was too hard for her.

"What's up?" Her keyboard grew silent.

"Arlan?" Macy called from the other side of the closed door. "You okay?" She tapped on the door when he didn't answer right away.

"Yeah. Yeah, I'm fine," Arlan called, lowering his cell to his side.

She was quiet for a second, but he could hear her breathing. He could feel her on the other side of the door.

"Why are you in there in the dark?" she asked.

Arlan reached for the light switch and flipped it on. He could hear Fia talking and lifted the phone to his ear again.

"Arlan, who are you talking to?" Fia demanded. "Are you calling me when you've got her in your bed?"

"No. No, listen, Fia." He turned his back to the door and walked toward the shower, trying to get as far from Macy as he could. "Be right out!" he hollered. Then into the phone, "Regan just shot me a bad one. He's in trouble."

"Crap," Fia breathed.

"I know."

"And you can't get hold of Fin?"

"Nope." He put the lid down on the toilet and took a seat. He was sweating hard. He ran his hand through his hair, pushing it back over the crown of his head. "I don't think Fin is with him, though. He needs my help."

"Where is he?"

Arlan propped his forearms on his knees and leaned forward, still a little dizzy. "I don't know. A cemetery. Creepy mausoleums. An iron gate with a cross. Blooming crepe myrtle. I could swear I've been there before." He lifted his head suddenly, snapping his fingers as it hit him. "New Orleans."

"New Orleans?" Fia echoed.

"That's my educated guess."

"But he was supposed to meet Fin in Italy. What the hell is he doing in New Orleans? And where is Fin?"

"I don't know." Arlan got up. "But I gotta go. Tonight. Now."

"I'm going with you."

"Fee—"

"You don't know what kind of trouble he's in. Could be bad. Could be—"

"The Rousseau brothers," he interrupted.

"Shit."

"You sure you're okay?" Macy was at the bathroom door again. She knocked.

"Be out in sec," Arlan called to Macy; then to Fia, "I gotta go."

"Meet you at the airport," Fia said.

"Soon as I can get there." He slipped his phone back in his pocket, took a deep breath and walked out of the bathroom.

Arlan found Macy sitting on his bed. She was now wearing her shorts. She looked up at him, her face sweet and soft. She looked worried. She offered the glass of water, which he accepted. He took a sip and then went to the other side of the bed and lay down, his head on the pillow.

Macy crawled across the bed and peered into his face. "Want me to go or stay here with you?"

He closed his eyes. "I don't know. Usually if I can get to sleep, I can get rid of it."

"I'll go." She kissed him ever so lightly on his lips. "See you around?"

He felt her weight lift from the bed. He kept his eyes closed and smiled, lifting his hand and letting it fall. "See you around."

Macy walked back to the hotel, packed her backpack and her laptop and put on a pair of sneakers. Outside, the air was finally beginning to cool. She got into her car and drove the two blocks to Arlan's house. She didn't know why, just a hunch. Something was going on with him; she had sensed it back at the house, and the feeling was only getting stronger. She didn't know what was going on, but it was something weird. Something M. *Night Shyamalan weird.*

He was just backing out of his driveway in his truck. He didn't notice her. She stayed well behind him all the way through town. Within ten minutes, he was on Route 1, headed north. She wondered where they were going.

Chapter 18

Arlan and Fia caught an early morning flight to New Orleans. Not knowing where to go or what to do, they checked into a quaint hotel on a street off Bourbon. By noon, they were sitting on the lobby's veranda, sharing a muffaletta sandwich and drinking sweet teas.

"You check your phone?" Fia pinched a stray olive that had fallen from the sandwich and popped it in her mouth. "Nothing from Fin?"

Arlan shook his head and used his cloth napkin to wipe his forehead. "Sweet Mary, Mother of God," he said under his breath. "I hate this city. I hate this heat." He tugged on the collar of his John Butler Trio T-shirt. They were one of his favorite bands. Wearing one of his favorite T-shirts should have made him feel better. It didn't.

She frowned, taking a bite of her half of the huge sandwich. "It's not any hotter here than in Delaware in August. Stop being such a pussy." She threw an olive at him. "And be honest, it's not the heat that's got your fur ruffled. It's the Rousseaus."

He pushed back in his chair. He'd been in a foul mood all morning. Mostly just because he was worried. He'd kept his mind open, waiting for word from Regan, but he was getting nothing. *Nothing.*

The possibility that Regan might not contact him again . . . might never contact him again, chilled him to the bone.

And he was worried about Macy back in Clare Point. She'd played along with his migraine story, but he was afraid she hadn't believed him. He had smelled suspicion on her breath. And her comments about Clare Point being weird had him doubly worried. Every summer their town was flooded with humans. No tourists ever noticed that the Kahills were different. After all these centuries, member of the sept did a fine job of blending in, of appearing human. Some of them were so good at the game that they half believed they *were* human. So what was it about Macy that was different than the average human? Was she one of the one in a million who had a pinch of psychic ability? It wasn't unheard of, of course. Just not likely.

"I'm not afraid of the Rousseaus," he grumbled, reaching for his sandwich.

"Didn't say you were. Far as I know, you're the bravest guy on earth. Pedophiles in Athens, serial killers with axes in Brussels." She pointed at him. "And remember those zombies in Amsterdam? Zombies? Ugh. They'd have had me quaking in my stilettos."

If she was trying to make him feel better, it wasn't happening.

She leaned closer, studying him through the dark lenses of her black Ray-Bans. "Look, I don't want to tangle with the Rousseau brothers any more than you do." She shrugged her muscular shoulders. "But they might not even be involved."

"Oh, they're involved, all right." He chewed his sandwich, but he didn't really taste. "If Regan is in trouble in New Orleans, I can guarantee you the Rousseaus are involved. They've hated us for two centuries."

She sat back, flapping her napkin before spreading it on

her lap. She looked like the female tourists seated at the tables near them; khaki capris, a red tank top. But there was an air of sophistication about Fia that few could match. Human males, young or old, gay or straight, couldn't walk within thirty yards of her and not be attracted. She was that hot.

"What do you think we should do now?" she asked. "Just start looking in the cemeteries?"

He stared at her. "I can't believe you just called me a pussy."

"Well, you are sometimes. You're too soft. You're way too *in touch with your feminine side.*"

"It's a good thing I like you," he said quietly. "Otherwise I'd have to turn into a Kodiak bear and eat you *and* your half of the sandwich."

She snatched up the remainder of her lunch.

"I guess we don't have any choice but to start looking for him." He took another bite. "But I don't know if he was actually in the cemetery or if he was just sending me images he thought I would recognize."

"Would have been easier if he'd just telepathed an address," she quipped.

"It's Regan," was his response. He contemplated their options as he chewed. "I'm thinking we wait until dark and hit the French Quarter. Talk to a few of the local freaks. Who do we know?"

She thought for a minute. "The voodoo queens in Vieux Carre. That coven of witches off Dumaine. We can see what the word is on the street. Ask our favorite witch doctors if they know anything. A door to door canvas."

He managed a grin and winked at her. "Shouldn't be much different for you than cruising bars in Philadelphia."

Pussy, she telepathed.

"You keep this up," he threatened aloud, "and we're definitely not touring Anne Rice's neighborhood."

"Now that's cutting below the belt." She rose. "Be right back. Ladies room."

Arlan waved to the waiter and was waiting for him to bring the pitcher of iced tea for refills when he saw Macy stroll through the veranda doors. He was so shocked that he did a double take to be sure it was really her. It was her all right. She was wearing shorts, a T-shirt, and a Saints ball cap and carrying what appeared to be a mimosa in a tall glass.

"This seat taken?" She sat down beside him.

"What the hell—" He looked away. When the waiter had filled the glasses and moved on to the next table, he turned back to Macy. "What are you doing here?"

"Research for a piece on old houses reconstructed since Katrina." She looked at him over the rim of her glass. "What are you doing here?" She glanced at Fia's plate. "You know, you tell me there's nothing between you two and I believe you're not having sex with her, but there's definitely something weird going on here." She motioned, indicating his plate and then Fia's. "Something M. Night—"

"Please," he interrupted, raising both hands. "Don't start that again. I have no idea what you're talking about with that, and frankly, I'm not all that interested."

Macy had taken him so off guard, showing up like this, he didn't know what to say or where to start. She had followed him. Not only had she followed him, but he hadn't *known* she was following him. What was wrong with him? He was better than that. The wrong person following him could get him killed.

"You shouldn't be here, Macy." He leaned toward her. "You can't be here. This is FBI business," he lied.

She set her glass down on the table and dropped her bag over the back of her chair. Apparently, she was intending on staying a while. Fia was going to kill him. She was going to separate his head from his body and hurl his soul into everlasting purgatory.

"So, I'm just trying to figure this out," Macy said conversationally. "Are you an undercover FBI agent, using the handyman thing for a cover, or are you like Fia's Watson? Maybe her Barney Fife?"

"Barney Fife?" He shook his head in confusion.

"You know, on *The Andy Griffith Show,* the sheriff's deputy, Barney." She shrugged. "I watch a lot of TV."

"Macy, I can't talk about this with you." He glanced in the direction of the lobby. "Fia see you?"

"No, but I saw her. Inhumanly nice legs. Is she six foot tall?"

" 'Bout that." He scooted forward in his chair. Fia would be furious when she found out Macy was here. Maybe he could just get her to go. Maybe Fia wouldn't have to know. "You're supposed to be in Clare Point. Fia asked you to stay put. When the FBI asks you to stay put, you stay put."

"I have to make a living. I told you, I just came to New Orleans to—"

"I'm not buying it, Macy. This is not coincidence, you catching a four A.M. flight to New Orleans. The same flight I took."

"I took the six."

"You followed me here," he continued. "You swore you weren't a stalker."

"I'm not a stalker!" She said it loud enough that a husband and wife, cameras around their necks, at the table next to Arlan and Macy glanced in their direction.

This was just what Arlan didn't need—anyone calling attention to his and Fia's presence. If at all possible, he wanted to get into New Orleans, get Regan, and get out before the Rousseaus ever knew he'd set foot on their soggy soil.

"This sure makes you *look* like a stalker," Arlan said under his breath. He was now as perturbed with himself for letting this happen as he was with her.

She glanced away, her face falling.

Arlan was at once contrite. He knew she wasn't a stalker. He just—

"I don't know why I came," she said softly, with that ethereal voice that always tugged at his heartstrings. "I swear, lately, I don't know why I do half the things I do." Her elbow on the glass-top table, she lowered her forehead to the heel of her hand. "I just . . . I feel as if you can keep me safe." She spoke the words like a dreaded confession. "You know, when I asked you yesterday what made you think you could help people, that was about me, not you." Her voice was breathy with emotion. "I guess what I'm saying is that I feel it, too." She ran her hand upward, through her hair, and sat back in the chair. "I feel as if you can help me when no one else has ever—" The words caught in her throat and she couldn't go on.

"Macy . . ." He took her hand. He was no hero. He did what the sept asked of him because he was one of them; it had nothing to do with heroics. But he wanted to be Macy's hero.

"I'm sorry," she said. "I don't mean to put such a heavy responsibility on you. Honestly I don't." She looked up at him. "You think I'm crazy. You think I'm a crazy stalker."

He studied her green eyes, the flecks of gold that seemed to illuminate her very soul. Her good soul. All evidence to the contrary, he *didn't* think she was a stalker. Somehow this was all tied in to the Buried Alive Killer; he sensed it. And he sensed that he would have some part in what was playing out with Macy and this man. He just didn't know where he fit in yet.

He brought her hand to his mouth and kissed her fingers. "I really need you to go back to Clare Point. There are people there who can keep you safe. I think *that's* what brought you to Clare Point." He clasped her hands between both of his. "I think that you know that, on a subconscious level. I think that's why you followed me there."

"You think that's possible?" Her eyes were wild and childlike and Arlan wanted nothing more than to pull her into his arms.

He sensed Fia approaching before he heard her footsteps on the tile flooring. He sat back, releasing Macy's hands. "Warning you now," he said under his breath. "She's going to be pissed."

"Macy." Fia halted at the end of the table. "What are you doing here?" She looked to Arlan, not giving Macy a chance to answer. "What is she doing here?"

"She's going back to Delaware." He shot Macy a look that he hoped might intimidate her. "Aren't you?"

"Just as soon as I see the houses I came to see." None of the vulnerability he had heard in her voice a moment ago was now present. She rose, taking her purse and drink with her. "You two have a good day." She walked away, raising her glass in good cheer. "Good luck on your case."

"I still can't believe you would risk a human's life like this," Fia said. They walked single file in the dark, down a narrow alley. On both sides, the brick walls of the buildings rose high over their heads. The alley smelled of mold, crumbling mortar, rodent feces, and orange jello, of all things.

Arlan led the way. "And I can't believe you don't believe me when I tell you that I didn't invite her. I didn't even tell her we were coming here."

"She just followed you?"

"Yes." He looked over his shoulder. "We've been over this already, Fia. I'm beginning to think she's psychic. She just doesn't know it."

"I think she's a fruitcake." They reached the end of the alley. "Left." She pointed. "That door. The one with the finger bone hanging in the window."

"Charming friends you have."

Fia checked the pistol she wore in a holster at the small of her back, under a loose T-shirt. "They're not my friends."

"More snitches? Witches snitches?"

She brushed past him. "They see you, they won't talk. They don't trust me as it is. So do your thing." She flapped her hand. "Make into a mouse or something."

"A mouse?" He lifted a dark eyebrow, unamused. "I don't *do* mice."

"Whatever." She knocked on the door.

The shop reminded him of a Hansel and Gretel cottage in the Bavarian forest, only the gingerbread was painted purple and a sign hung by the door advertising POTIONS & BREWS.

"Feline or canine?" he asked Fia.

There was a sound on the other side of the door. The curtain in the shop window moved.

"Rodent," she quipped.

As the door opened, Arlan morphed into a lean, leggy mongrel.

Two women answered the door. The best word Arlan could come up with was *hag*. The women were hags. Young for hags, but hags nonetheless. Their hair was long and stringy. Dirty. The four eyes that stared at Fia were white with cataracts. Their faces weathered by harsh living. They smelled of cigarette smoke, gin, and evil.

I hate witches, he telepathed.

Hush, Mousie, Fia shot back. She made eye contact with the closest hag. "Gullveig, long time no see."

"We're closed," the blonde shrieked, catching the door with bony fingers to slam it shut.

"I'm not looking for a love potion." Fia slipped her foot in the doorway before it banged shut. "Want to see my badge or my fangs, ladies?"

The one sister looked at the other and then back at Fia. Her white-eyed gaze would have been unnerving to most, but not to Fia. As far as she was concerned, it was their gimmick and a good one at that. "We got out of the business last year. Nothing but potions for sale here."

"That mean a raid on your house would be a waste of the FBI's time, Gullveig?" She looked to the other sister. "Heid?"

The second sister gave a squeak and stepped back, eyeing Arlan, who had moved up to stand beside Fia.

"Damn strays," Fia remarked, giving Arlan a push with her knee. "You girls ought to call the dog catcher."

Arlan whined and stepped back. *Bitch,* he telepathed.

Pussy, Fia shot back. She looked at the two women in the doorway. "I'm looking for a guy named Regan. He might be in a little trouble. You hear anything about a vampire being in some trouble?"

The sisters looked at each other. Gullveig tried to close the door again.

Fia slammed the heel of her hand into the door and the women fell back. Fia crossed the threshold. Arlan followed her to the door, but remained outside, growling low in his throat. The kind of mood he was in tonight, it wouldn't take much to send him flying at one of the stringy throats. Or making salad of the gray tabby with the green eyes staring at him from the upstairs window.

He hated witches.

"That a yes?" Fia snarled, baring her fangs. "You have heard something."

It was funny how most people didn't notice the Kahill's fangs until they were bared. Filed down by a Kahill dentist, Kahill fangs looked almost normal, but drawn, they frightened humans and witches alike, apparently.

"I don't know nuthin'," Gullveig shrieked, raising her hands as if she could shield herself from Fia's anger. "Just gossip."

"What gossip?"

"Somebody stole some drugs. Ripped them off. A vampire. Nice-looking fellow. Young. A Kahill, I heard."

"You must have heard wrong. Kahills don't mess with that crap."

"I must have heard wrong," Gullveig echoed, her voice high-pitched with terror.

Arlan took a step closer. *Fee,* he telepathed.

She ignored him.

"Stole drugs from who?" she demanded.

"Rousseau brothers, who else?" the witch cackled.

Arlan growled and took another step closer, resting his front paws on the doorsill. Every sinewy muscle in his seventy-pound canine body ached to coil and leap. He wondered what the witches' blood would taste like. Gin and cigarettes? It would probably be so foul he would have to spit it out. He would like to have ripped their throats out, just the same.

The witches yipped in fear as Arlan crept toward them.

Fia shot him a glance. "Get out of here, mutt. Go on."

Arlan acquiesced and stepped back into the street.

"Have they got him? The Rousseaus, do they have the vampire?"

The hags cowered. "Maybe," Gullveig offered when Fia bared her fangs again.

"Where?"

"Could be anywhere in the city."

Arlan growled.

Gullveig eyed the dog in the doorway. "St. Louis, Number One. Corner of St. Louis and Basin."

"I know where it is," Fia snapped. She walked out of the shop, into the dark. "Come on, Fido," she whispered to Arlan, tapping her thigh with her hand. Her anger was gone in a second; now she was just a scared big sister. "Let's go to the cemetery and fetch my brother."

Chapter 19

Macy pressed her back to the brick wall, staying behind a broken drainpipe, and watched Fia disappear down the alley. A dog trotted beside her. Macy watched the animal apprehensively. She wondered where Arlan had gotten to and exactly why Fia was so friendly with the stray. Fia was talking to the mongrel as she walked away.

Macy glanced back at the potion shop. The two ugly women had slammed the door, but she knew they were watching from the darkened window. She could feel their silvery, cataract-eyed gaze.

Despite the trickle of sweat that ran down Macy's spine, she shivered. The alley smelled strongly of something akin to sulfur. New Orleans had always seemed like a perfectly nice city before. Macy liked the French Quarter. She liked the anonymity it provided, and it was always easy to pick up hot guys on Bourbon Street. But the New Orleans Macy was seeing tonight was different. Weird different. Weird like—she stopped herself before the words popped into her head. Arlan was right, she really *did* need a new simile.

Arlan. Everything went back to Arlan these days, didn't it? He and Fia had left the hotel together. Macy had followed them to Café Du Monde, where they had gone around to the back of the building and spoken to a creepy thin man in a greasy apron. She had last seen Arlan one street over from the potion shop. She'd been trying not to follow too closely; after all Fia *was* FBI, maybe Arlan, too. You didn't tail the FBI too closely without getting caught.

Which logically brought one to the question, why was she tailing the FBI at all?

Macy wasn't sure. All she knew was that she wanted to find out what Fia and Arlan were doing in New Orleans. Once again, on some level beyond her understanding, she *needed* to know.

So one minute it seemed as if Arlan had been there and the next he had not. Then the dog had shown up, that weird dog. . . .

Macy waited until Fia turned left at the end of the alley and then she hurried after her. As she walked away from the cover of her drainpipe, she looked back over her shoulder. The women were still watching and Macy self-consciously shrugged her shoulders as if she could shake their sour gazes from her back.

She followed Fia and the dog all the way to a cemetery on the north end of Basin Street, at the corner of St. Louis. She couldn't for the life of her figure out what Fia would be doing in a cemetery. Even sunburned tourists knew the cemeteries weren't safe after dark. Not alone.

Macy halted in the iron gateway that led into the cemetery. She still couldn't believe Fia would go into the cemetery at night, bad ass FBI agent or not. Macy knew enough about the city to steer clear of a dangerous place like this. There were thieves beyond these stone walls, people who would mug you for your Fossil wallet. Druggies who might kill you to get a diamond ring.

Macy glanced up and down the street, lit by golden globes of lamplight. There were a few pedestrians on the sidewalk, but the old graveyard was beyond the boundaries of the French Quarter and foot traffic was light.

She stopped to look at the marker on the gate: ST. LOUIS CEMETERY # 1, it read. THE OLDEST EXTANT CEMETERY IN NEW ORLEANS.

Macy peered into the dark space beyond the gate. She could see shapes in the gloom, tombs, mausoleums. Her mouth went dry. She looked back over her shoulder, then into the cemetery again. Why was Fia here? FBI business? What was wrong with Arlan that he would let her come here alone?

She stepped through the gate and looked behind her again. The street was quiet. She gazed into the shadowed darkness ahead. If she was going in, she needed to go now before Fia got too far ahead of her.

Macy shrugged off her uneasiness and started down the main path, listening for sounds of anyone approaching from behind, or from the stone tombs that towered on both sides of her. As she walked deeper into the cemetery, the mausoleums seemed to close in around her. The quiet made her uneasy. She heard none of the typical night sounds. No car horns. No insect song. Just quiet. *Dead* quiet.

"Christ," Macy muttered under her breath. She was spooking herself.

Gradually, her eyes became accustomed to the dark. The forms that had been shapeless at a distance now transformed into stone people. Angels. All of them weeping.

She thought about where her family was buried. Greenview Memorial Park. It was pretty there, sunny, green. The old-fashioned cemetery sat on a grassy knoll with a white clapboard church in the distance. Pretty idyllic . . . as graveyards went. She hadn't been there in years, but right after they were murdered, she had gone often. In her teenage years, she'd huddled against the large pink granite tombstone and wait for the tears. Eventually she gave up on the tears, and the idea that in order to mourn the loss of her family, she had to go to the place where their bodies were buried.

Macy came to a standstill in the middle of the gravel path and raised her hands to her head, pressing her palms to her ears. What was she doing here? Why did she care what Fia was doing? She knew she ought to be on Bourbon Street right now, drinking a hurricane in a foot-tall plastic cup, checking out the jazz joints, checking out the guys.

Macy was just turning on her heels to head back the way she had come when she heard a voice. . . . She froze and listened. Someone was talking. A woman and a man. Their voices carried on the humid night air, but she was unable to pinpoint the direction. Macy couldn't tell if they were in front of her or behind. She turned slowly in place, the loose gravel crunching under her sneakers. She listened.

She knew the voices. It was Fia and Arlan. How the hell did Arlan get inside without Macy seeing him? Obviously there was another entrance. Was Fia meeting Arlan in the cemetery? Was that why she was here? That theory made more sense than anything else, although Macy still couldn't see where the dog fit in.

She started to walk again, deeper into the cemetery. She now suspected that the voices were coming from her right. She turned off the main path she had followed in, taking a narrower one. Here, the mausoleums were even closer. She smelled the thick, sweet scent of flowers, rotting vegetation and . . . what could only be described as death.

Macy wanted to turn around, but something made her keep going.

"You hear that?" she heard Arlan say.

"Hear what?" Fia said in a loud whisper.

Macy spotted their silhouettes ahead and she ducked left, hoping to hide herself in the shadow of a tomb.

"That," Arlan said.

They halted in the middle of the path. Arlan appeared to be gazing off to his left. There, a giant mausoleum, probably holding multiple family members, loomed.

"I don't hear anything," Fia said impatiently.

Macy couldn't hear a thing either.

Fia suddenly turned around, facing where Macy had been standing a moment before. "Someone's here," she said, her voice quieter.

"Yeah, I think someone's been following us." Arlan's head snapped around. "Regan!" He bolted for the mausoleum.

"Be careful," Fia warned, darting after him. "It could be a trap."

Macy crept forward, crouching low. Regan was the missing brother. Neither Fia nor Arlan had said anything about him, but Eva had told Macy that he had been on a business trip somewhere in Europe and had not returned when he was expected. Macy knew that Arlan and Fia had been worried about him. But what did the missing brother have to do with this cemetery?

Macy rested her hand on a headstone that jutted out of the uneven ground, trying to get closer. She was scared, but not scared enough to run.

In front of the massive mausoleum, Arlan struggled with something upright directly in front of the entrance. She heard stone scrape stone. Was he moving a pillar of marble? This was getting stranger by the second. The thing had to have weighed a thousand pounds, a few hundred at the very least.

"Regan! Regan, we're coming," Arlan called. "Just hang on, buddy."

Macy rose, too shocked to bother to hide any longer, and watched Arlan move aside the massive stone pillar and yank open the mausoleum door.

"Regan!"

"Regan!" Fia echoed.

"Oh my God," Macy breathed, not quite believing what she was seeing. "He's inside?" she whispered.

A figure stumbled out of the open door, into Arlan's arms.

"'Bout damned time you got here," the young man said. "You know it's dark in a tomb. And there're spiders. You know I hate spiders."

"Sweet Mary and Joseph, you're all right. Why didn't you just teleport out?" Fia said.

"Marble was too thick and the pissants knew it," he answered. "Anyone got a fag? This nicotine withdrawal's fierce."

"You're not supposed to be smoking." Fia cuffed her brother on the back of the head, but Macy could clearly hear the relief in Fia's voice. "Let's get the hell out of here."

Macy'd seen enough. She took a step back. She didn't hear anything, but maybe a leaf crackled on the ground or she dislodged a tiny stone underfoot. The three Kahills turned and looked at her.

"Macy?" Fia demanded. "Mary, Mother of God!"

"Ah, Macy, no," Arlan said quietly.

"I'm sorry." Macy held both hands up as if under arrest. No need to run now, she was caught. "I didn't mean—"

An inhuman shriek ripped through the humid night air and the three turned. Three black-caped figures flew out from behind the mausoleum, screeching inhumanly. Macy blinked, wondering if this was all a dream. Was she really back at the hotel, asleep on the bed?

The pale-faced figures flipped and somersaulted, flying through the air as they closed in on Fia, Arlan, and Regan. It was like *Night of the Living Dead* meets *Crouching Tiger, Hidden Dragon*.

This *couldn't* be happening.

Arlan, Fia, and Regan spun around, turning their backs to each other, so quickly, so effortlessly, that Macy knew without a doubt they had done it before. Fia and her brother took a fighting stance, martial arts style, hands raised.

Macy wasn't entirely certain what happened next. One moment her dark, handsome Arlan was standing beside

Fia, the next moment there was a white Bengal tiger in his place.

A white tiger.

In a New Orleans cemetery.

No one else in the crazy scenario seemed to think the appearance of the tiger or the disappearance of Arlan was odd.

No way, Macy thought. This was even too insane for a dream. Maybe her dinner cocktail was to blame. Had someone slipped her a hallucinogenic drug?

Whatever was going on, Macy's sense of self-preservation told her she shouldn't be there.

The white tiger crouched, lowering its head and snarling so viciously that she *felt* its fury, and her knees weakened.

Somewhere in the dark recesses of Macy's mind, she realized she had heard that growl before. Not so loud. Not so ferocious, but she *had* heard it. The other day in Eva's backyard. She had heard Arlan growl.

As Macy stumbled backward, unable to take her eyes off the bizarre scene unfolding in front of her, she told herself she was mistaken. She told herself the enormous white tiger was not her lover.

One of the caped men launched himself toward Regan and the young man spun around to face him head-on. Macy cringed in anticipation of the impending impact. But then he was gone. Regan had vanished . . . only to appear six feet away, his feet planted firmly on an above ground burial vault. Dressed in a tattered sports jacket and dirty, torn jeans, he threw his head back and laughed as if a young schoolmate had just missed him in a game of tag.

The white tiger pounced, claws and teeth bared, and collided in midair with another of the black-cloaked figures. The noise was suddenly unbearable: the shrieks of the men, the growl of the tiger, the renting of fabric, the crunch of bone, Regan's laughter. There were voices, too, human voices, only no one was speaking a language she understood. She heard bursts of thick French Cajun and what sounded to her untrained ear like Gaelic. Fia met the third figure head to head, hand to hand, an equal match to her male adversary.

Still backing away, Macy covered her mouth with both hands to keep from making any sound. Fia and her opponent circled each other, ducking and striking in a dangerous dance. The tiger and his challenger rolled on the ground beside the open door of the mausoleum, the man grunting with exertion, the big cat growling and snarling. Off to one side Regan's adversary scrambled to reach him. Then a fourth cloaked figure appeared out of the darkness, joining the melee. He leaped onto Fia's back and she spun completely around, off-balance, taking a blow to her chin from her first opponent.

The tiger knocked Fia's attacker off her back with one swipe of his massive paw, claws bared. Fia never hesitated, but flung herself forward, attacking the first man. They locked arm and arm and Fia bit him in the neck. Blood spewed as he howled with what seemed like a mixture of pain and glee and fell to his knees, clutching his torn flesh.

Macy stumbled back, almost going to the ground. *Run. Run!* a voice in her head ordered.

Arlan's voice? What was stronger in her mind than the shouted order, though, was the sudden realization that she wanted to live. All these years she had taken chances with her safety, with her very life, telling herself she didn't care if she lived or died. But she wanted to live and she instinctively knew that this moment, this place, was conducive only to pain and death.

Shaking as much from her revelation as her fear, Macy turned and sprinted back down the path she had come, between the towering mausoleums.

She heard the tiger snarl and a man scream in pain.

Then behind her, a sound and the feel of wind rushing toward her. She glanced back to see one of the cloaked figures hurtling through the air straight at her.

She opened her mouth and heard the most inhuman scream.

"You hear that?" Kaleigh asked.

"What?"

The teen lifted her face to the ocean breeze, hesitating. Listening. A bunch of kids had come down to the beach after curfew just to hang out, but everyone had wandered off to the water or down the beach. Somehow she and Rob Hill had ended up alone together, seated in the sand, which was okay. He was kind of quiet, but he was cool. He was definitely cool.

Kaleigh cocked her head. "You didn't hear that? It sounded like . . . I don't know . . . a scream. Like someone was in trouble. "

He glanced down the beach at their friends running in the surf. They were laughing and joking and splashing. He looked back at her, his brow furrowing. "I didn't hear anything."

Light flashed in Kaleigh's head, then an image, startling her. She closed her eyes. This was a new development in the last few months. Her gift of *sight* was beginning to kick in. Another joy of being the sept's wisewoman.

Someone was fighting . A bunch of people. *Shit*. Bad guys. Really bad guys. She knew them. She had encountered them before. The memory was there . . . but just beyond her reach. She groaned in frustration.

"Kaleigh? Are you okay?"

She felt Rob's hand brush her arm. It felt . . . kind of nice.

"I'm okay," she whispered, her eyes still closed. "I just—" She wasn't sure what to say. Rob had only been reborn a few weeks ago. He didn't know everything. Didn't need to know. Like the other teens, he would be given the opportunity to get used to his new skin . . . and his fangs. That was how it worked.

"Just a headache," Kaleigh lied, pressing her thumb and forefinger to her temples.

There were Kahills in trouble. She didn't know who and she didn't know where.

Not here. Not in Clare Point. Not even in Delaware.

There was nothing Kaleigh could do.

She opened her eyes, fighting the frustration that was bringing her close to tears. Everyone told her that this psychic connection between her and the others in the sept would eventually be helpful. Right now it was just a pain in the ass.

And a little scary.

"You sure you're okay?" Rob took her hand between his, gazing into her eyes.

Kaleigh smiled shyly, looking up at him through lowered lashes. He smelled good. Earthy. Distinctly male. "I'm okay."

Okay as long as I'm here with you, she thought.

Chapter 20

The female scream reverberated to the bone, but in his feline state, it took a moment to register in his tiger brain what the sound was. *Who* it was.

Arlan clamped his jaw around the Rousseau's neck, gave him a shake to be sure he was unconscious, and then leapt off him. He crossed the short distance to the human female in an instant, all sinew and muscle coiling and uncoiling. Pouncing, he fell on the vampire that held the female down with his arm around her neck in a choke hold. Sinking his front claws into the flesh of the attacker's back, opening his jaw wide; Arlan closed it over the vampire's shoulder.

The Rousseau howled in pain, arching back, releasing the human female.

She lay face down in the grass in front of a tomb guarded by weeping stone angels.

If the vampire had bitten her, it might be too late to save her.

Arlan wrestled with that thought as he dragged one front paw over the Rousseau's buttocks, his claws tangling in black cape and flesh. *Blood.* He flared his nostrils. The scent of it was heady. And the heavier the red rivulets flowed, the more frenzied Arlan's primitive brain became. A tiger in the wilds of the Indian jungle felt no anger, but the man inside the tiger did. How dare they? How dare the Rousseaus imprison a Kahill? How dare they have the audacity to involve a human in a centuries-old vampire feud?

Arlan sank his teeth into the back of the Rousseau's neck and tore at the soft flesh, blood running from the corners of his mouth and staining his white fur.

"Arlan."

Still pinning the Rousseau to the ground, Arlan bit him again, enjoying the sound of the crunch of small bones.

"Arlan, he's unconscious. That's enough."

Arlan heard the steady voice. Knew the voice. Fia. Fia, his beloved.

"Come on, man, enough already." A male voice this time.

Arlan felt the hand on his rear haunch and snapped his head around. He bared his teeth, dripping with blood, and growled.

The man jerked his hand back to keep from being bitten. "Arlan, it's Regan. Enough."

Regan. Right.

Arlan felt his heart pounding in his chest. He could taste the Rousseau blood in his mouth, feel it wet on his fur. The blood tasted sour. Foul. Like the vampire's twisted soul.

Arlan looked up, watching through his amber eyes as Fia knelt and rolled the unconscious female onto her back.

Macy. Macy was hurt. Dying. Perhaps worse.

Arlan backed up, swishing his tail. *Enough, already.* He closed his cat eyes and morphed back into his human form. He wiped the blood from his lips with the back of his hand, a little unsteady on his feet. Some morphs were harder than others.

"Hey, man, you okay?" Regan laid his hand on Arlan's shoulder again.

Heart still leaping in his chest, Arlan didn't try to bite

Regan, but he did shove his hand away. "Macy." He dropped to the ground beside Fia, peering down on Macy's face. Her skin was pale. Her eyes were closed.

"He bite her?"

Fia pushed Macy's long blond hair off to one side and then the other, searching for telltale puncture marks. "Doesn't look like it."

"Why's she unconscious then?"

"He knocked her down when he flew into her." Fia gently touched Macy's hairline, surprising Arlan with her tenderness. Her fingertips came away stained red with blood. "I think maybe she hit her head when he knocked her down." She touched her fingertips with the tip of her tongue.

"You see the way she fought him?" Regan remarked, standing over them, his hands pushed down casually in his pockets. "She's one tough human bitch. *Hot.*"

"Back off, Regan," Arlan warned. He looked down at Macy again. "So, just a bump on the head, you think?"

Macy moaned and moved.

"I think so." Fia let go of Macy's wrist. "Pulse is good. Respiration seems okay." She looked up at Arlan, hesitating before she spoke. "She saw it all, you know."

He sat back on his heels and clasped his head between his hands. When he morphed back to his human form, it took a few minutes to reacclimate. Sometimes his thought processes were sluggish at first. "I know." He groaned. "I didn't realize she was following us." He frowned, thinking back to a few minutes before, which now seemed like hours. "How did I not know that?"

"Doesn't matter now. What matters is what you're going to do about it." Fia continued to stare at him with her dark, penetrating gaze.

He couldn't bear Fia's scrutiny and gazed down at Macy again. She was definitely coming to.

"You know what you have to do," Fia urged quietly.

Arlan shook his head. He didn't want to do it. He and Macy didn't have that kind of relationship. He . . . he didn't do that anymore. He was beyond the vile, forbidden practice of feeding off humans.

"If you partake, the memory of the last few minutes will be erased from her mind. She might remember following us to the cemetery, but she'll recall nothing of the Rousseaus. Nothing of what she saw."

Arlan hung his head, his hair falling over his face.

"If you don't do it, I will," Fia said.

"Hell, I'll do it." Regan approached them eagerly. "Let me do it. I bet she's sweet as hell."

Macy moaned and rolled her head. She moved her fingers.

"Arlan," Fia pushed.

Arlan leaned over Macy, and Fia moved back to give him a little privacy. He hated to do this. He didn't want to do it, but he knew Fia was right. He didn't have a choice. This would not only keep her safe, but the sept as well, and above all else, Arlan's duty was to protect the sept.

"You have to hurry," Fia whispered.

Arlan drew back his lips and bared his canines. *God forgive me,* he thought. He sank his teeth into the soft flesh of Macy's neck and the first flow of blood hit him like a wave. A wave of sweet ecstasy. *Sweet Mary, Mother of God,* he had forgotten how good they tasted, humans.

He closed his eyes, trying to dwell in the moment. Not since Lizzy had he tasted human female blood. Lizzy had been good, but Macy . . . Macy tasted even better. More illicit, somehow.

The memories he tried so hard to suppress tumbled back as he savored the taste and smell of the woman in his arms.

Lizzy had willingly given her blood to Arlan. One of

those rare humans who understood that the world was more complex, more multidimensional than it appeared, she had embraced who he was. What he was. She had begged him to drink her blood, even begged him to make her a vampire so she could live forever, be with Arlan forever. Then her brother had been caught murdering sick and injured Confederate soldiers. He had been moving from hospital camp to hospital camp, killing his own comrades. *An angel of mercy* he had called himself. But he had suffocated soldiers who were recovering, and he had enjoyed his "work" entirely too much.

Arlan's mistake had been his misconception of his relationship with Lizzy. Naively, despite Fia's warnings, he had thought he and Lizzy were soul mates. He had told Lizzy what the Kahills did. He had told her of her brother's crimes and that he had been condemned by the Kahill High Council to die. Lizzy had gone mad. In an attempt to save her brother, she killed two innocent men. Her brother was eventually executed as planned. Arlan never saw Lizzy again, but had heard she committed suicide, the ultimate, cowardly sin in the eyes of a vampire.

Having taken enough blood, Arlan drew in his fangs and lowered his cheek to Macy's breast for a moment. She had quieted until it seemed as if she were just peacefully sleeping. He felt her chest rise and fall and breathed in her soft, womanly scent. "I'm sorry," he whispered, still tasting her exquisite blood in his mouth. "I'm *so* sorry, Macy. I'll make it up to you, I swear I will."

Then he stood, lifting her in his arms. He cradled her to his body, feeling an intense need to protect her, and not just from the Rousseaus but from the whole world. From that monster out there somewhere stalking her.

"Need some help?" Regan reached out, eyeing Macy's neck where two puncture marks oozed blood.

"Keep your hands off her," Arlan threatened. "You've

caused enough trouble tonight as it is." He walked away, holding Macy tightly in his arms. He needed to get her to the hotel and put her to bed. Within the hour she would wake, hopefully with her memory of the cemetery and the events that unfolded there erased.

"Me? I didn't cause the trouble," Regan defended, following Arlan. "Those assholes were the ones causing trouble." He hooked his thumb in the direction of the three Rousseaus still lying unconscious among the crypts.

"That right? And exactly how did you end up locked in a mausoleum in New Orleans when you were supposed to be on a plane headed home with your brother?"

"Long story, buddy." Regan patted Arlan's shoulder. "Long story."

Arlan jerked out of Regan's reach and shot him a warning glance. Still feeling a burning anger in the pit of his stomach, Arlan could easily have turned it on Regan.

"Boys," Fia warned. "Knock it off. Our Cajun friends won't nap long. We need to get the hell out of here." She hurried to catch up, easing herself between them.

Arlan noticed she limped, but said nothing. They'd all be sore, banged up, and bruised tomorrow.

"Your boyfriend's the one who started it giving me the stink eye." Regan stuffed his hands into his pockets. "Lucifer's balls, I could sure use a cigarette."

Arlan kept walking. "I'll take her back to the hotel. You see if you can get us a flight home in the next few hours. We shouldn't stay in New Orleans any longer than we have to. I imagine the Rousseaus will be looking for us."

"Gonna be pissed when they realize I got away, aren't they?" Regan cackled.

"Keep him the hell away from me," Arlan told Fia quietly. "We haven't even heard his explanation."

They halted at the cemetery gate. Fia looked out, listened, and then waved for the other two when she saw it was safe to proceed.

"I'm not interested in any more of his excuses," Arlan said, his tone flat. "I'm warning you, you deal with him, Fia, or I'm going to."

She exhaled. "Arlan, I don't want you to feel guilty about this." She walked toward him.

"I don't feel guilty," he grunted. *Of course he did. Painfully guilty.* He should never have gone back to Macy's hotel room with her that night. He should never have let her in his house that first time.

They walked single file down the sidewalk, Arlan leading, Regan in the middle, and Fia taking up the rear to keep an eye out for a surprise attack.

"It's what had to be done," she said.

He didn't want to talk. If he kept it short and none-too-sweet, maybe Fia would get the hint. "Yep."

She paused again, watching a couple on the other side of the street. She waited to speak until they had passed. "You need to be careful here."

He said nothing. Macy felt good in his arms. She smelled good. She barely weighed anything; he could have carried her for miles. A part of him wanted to. Could they just walk out of New Orleans, out of this life? Could he and Macy just walk away and leave vampires and murderers behind?

Not hardly.

"I'm talking about Macy. You're falling in love with her," Fia pushed.

He spoke, his teeth gritted. "Nope."

"You *know* it's dangerous. You know it never turns out well."

For the first time since they left the cemetery, Arlan glanced over his shoulder at Fia. "You know that from experience?"

Their gazes locked. Held.

It was Fia who looked away first. "I'm learning."

*   *   *

Macy slowly became aware of the ceiling fan turning, stirring the warm, humid air overhead, and the sounds of traffic outside the window. Beside her, she felt the warmth of a body. Male.

Waking up with a man beside her in bed. Not unfamiliar territory for her.

What was unusual was that she had woken up beside this man before. Arlan.

She took a deep breath. She was getting too attached to him. She knew that. It would be time to move on, soon. It was time, anyway. This was her nemesis's intention, to keep her isolated, emotionally separated from others. In some twisted, lonely way, he wanted her to cleave to him. Macy knew all that, had for years. She just didn't know how to put an end to it.

She opened her eyes and turned her head to look at the clock beside the bed. It was just after six A.M., explaining the bright light filtering around the closed drapes. She turned the other way to look at Arlan, still sleeping beside her. She couldn't resist a little smile. He was already a good-looking guy, but the two-day-old beard and the shaggy bad-boy hair raised him several notches, into the godlike realm.

Seeming to sense she was watching him, he opened his eyes. "Hey," he greeted, the sound of sleep in his voice making him seem younger than his years. Certainly more innocent.

"Hey," she whispered. She glanced around the hotel room. It wasn't hers. "How'd I get here?" She started to sit up and a wave of dizziness forced her to drop her head to the pillow again. "Wow." She raised her hand to her forehead, where she found a tender bump that was forming a scab. She didn't remember falling last night, though obviously she had. "Crazy party night? Beads, boobs, and booze on Bourbon?"

"You don't remember?" He pushed up on his elbow to look down at her.

Feeling slightly nauseous, she closed her eyes, trying to think back to what she *did* remember of the previous night. She ticked through the catalog of memories like flipping through a box of black and white photographs. She'd had dinner alone in that little café on Toulouse, then gone back to the hotel. From there, she had followed Fia and Arlan from the hotel to Café Du Monde. The last thing she vaguely recalled was seeing Fia talking to the ugly women with the cataract eyes. And the dog. She remembered the weird dog. . . .

She frowned. *But then what?* It wasn't like her to have a loss of memory. Not even when she drank too much. And she certainly hadn't had too much to drink at dinner. She'd only had one glass of wine. Had there been more alcohol later? Maybe a couple of those hurricanes she'd been thinking about?

Arlan was waiting for her to say something.

"Exactly how did we hook up last night?" she asked.

"You really don't remember?" A playful smile tugged at one side of his sensual mouth. Such a kissable mouth. And he had the prettiest white teeth. But they all did, the residents of Clare Point. One more tidbit of information to add to the already peculiar status of the resort town.

She touched his rough chin with her fingertips, liking the feel of his scruffy beard. "You're avoiding my question."

"You're avoiding mine," he countered, covering her hand with his.

She glanced around the room, still feeling odd, off-balance somehow. "Why didn't I go back to my room last night?"

"I don't know." He kissed her hand. "Maybe you like me."

"I do like you." She watched him kiss each of her fingertips. "That still doesn't explain why I stayed. I don't stay after sex if I have somewhere else to go."

"Maybe that's the old Macy and this is the new Macy."

She rolled toward him, pressing her hips against his. She gazed into his dark eyes but said nothing.

"If you would just let me in, Macy, you wouldn't have to be alone."

"What if I like being alone?" she asked.

"No one *really* wants to be alone."

She clasped both sides of his face between her palms and guided his mouth to hers. When their lips touched, she slid her hand under the sheet to grasp him, effectively ending the chatter and the psychological mumbo jumbo.

Arlan pushed her onto her back and thrust his tongue into her mouth. She savored the taste of him . . . the feeling of power he seemed to emote. She dragged her fingernails over his hard, muscular buttocks and he groaned with pleasure.

He nuzzled her breast through the thin fabric of her shirt. Then he nibbled on her nipple, making her giggle.

Macy lifted her hips to meet his, annoyed that she was wearing panties. Why on earth had she slept in panties last night? She never put panties back on after sex.

Had she and Arlan not had sex last night? That was a little hard to believe.

God, she wondered. *How much did I have to drink last night?*

The thing was, she didn't feel hungover. Strange, but definitely not hungover.

Arlan kissed her throat, his tongue darting out to take tiny licks. It was the oddest, most erotic feeling. "Mmmm," she moaned.

"You like that?" His breath was warm on her neck.

"I like that," she whispered, thinking it interesting that her neck had never been a particularly erogenous zone before . . . before Arlan.

He slipped his hand inside her panties, and ran his finger along the cleft of her soft, willing flesh. She moaned.

Already hot for him, it didn't take long for her to reach the first orgasm. Then suddenly, she was desperate to feel him inside her.

"Wait," she panted, yanking down her panties. They had thrown aside the sheet. She wiggled out of her thong and then the T-shirt that was now damp and sticking to her skin.

"What's your hurry?" he breathed in her ear, nipping at her earlobe.

She opened her eyes to look into his. "You know, sometimes I like you better when you're quiet."

He laughed, grasping her hips. In one fluid motion, he rolled over, taking her with him.

Macy landed on top, astride him, and needed no further invitation. Using her hand to assist, she slid down over him, moaning as he filled her. She threw her head back and leaned back, weaving her fingers through his. For a moment she sat still, her eyes closed, just enjoying the sensation. But her heart was pounding, her pulse was racing. She leaned forward and her long blond hair partially obscured her face. She began to move over him, slowly at first, but then she picked up the pace. She was close again already.

Arlan was an amazing lover. She had known that from the first night. He knew when to hold back and when to move along. He seemed to know when a woman meant business and right this minute, Macy meant business. As she pushed harder, he pushed harder. He rested his hands on her waist and let her have the control.

At last, Macy was able to set free the last thoughts rattling around in her head. Nothing mattered but her body and these exquisite waves of ecstasy.

Macy came a second time and then a third, and when she had caught her breath, she flattened her body over Arlan's and quickly brought him to climax. Still breathing hard, she rolled off him, onto her back, beside him. She stared up at the ceiling fan as her respiration slowly eased back to something close to normal. Beside her, she could hear Arlan doing the same. Neither spoke. Nothing to say, nothing that needed saying. And she appreciated the fact that Arlan recognized that. He understood her need to keep her emotions in neatly sealed packages.

But then he surprised her by sliding his hand across the bed to take hers. It was a simple gesture, one that might have brought a woman to sentimental tears . . . had she been a woman who still knew how to cry.

Chapter 21

Macy sat at the table in her dark hotel room and stared at the laptop's bright screen. On the very top right corner was her IM icon. It had been taunting her all evening, although she tried hard to ignore it. She had gone for an evening walk. She had attempted to work on the text for her Clare Point cottages layout. She'd even played solitaire.

But he'd been out there the whole time. Waiting for her. Calling to her. She could feel it.

On the flight home the day before from New Orleans, Fia had reminded Macy of their agreement that she would not contact Teddy or put herself in a position, if she could help it, to be contacted by him. Fia wanted him to be eager to speak with Macy and wanted to be there when he contacted her. She hadn't brought up her anger over Macy following them to New Orleans, so Macy saw no reason to introduce the conversation.

It had all sounded well and good at the time, but tonight Macy was having difficultly following through. What if Teddy, frustrated that he couldn't reach Macy, went crazy and shot up people in a mall or tied a bomb to a homeless person in a subway or something bizarre like that? He needed her. He had told her so a hundred times over the years. Occasionally, she thought morosely, he even told her he loved her.

How sick was that?

Macy's hand glanced over the mouse pad. The cursor seemed to have a mind of its own. It found the IM icon. She hesitated, her index finger poised.

Fia was trying to solve this case, she was trying her best. But Fia didn't understand Teddy. Not the way Macy did. Fia didn't understand how fragile he was.

Click-click.

The IM window popped up and a second later, a message from Teddy200. She knew it!

Where have you been? I've been worried about you.

Macy hesitated for a moment before typing. She knew the smart thing to do would be to close the IM box. Wait for Fia. But he was right there . . . Business trip, she typed.

Liar. You've been avoiding me. You can't avoid me, Marceline. You can't do that to me.

He sounded agitated. An agitated Teddy was a dangerous Teddy. She knew that from past experience.

She wasn't sure what to say. She hesitated, her fingertips hovering over the keyboard.

When she didn't respond right away, he sent, What's going on, Marceline? What's wrong, sweetheart?

She hated it when he used endearments. *Bastard. Fucking bastard.*

Her fingers pounded the keyboard. What's wrong with me??? You think maybe the fact that a FUCKING HOMICIDAL MANIAC has been stalking me for fourteen years might be getting me down?

She waited. Nothing appeared on the screen.

Hell, she thought. This *was* a bad idea. Now she was taunting him. She'd never done this before. She was always docile. She always played the game by his rules, reasoning that she had some sort of control over him by going along. How ridiculous was that? He still murdered people, didn't he?

But did he murder fewer people because of her?

God, she was as crazy as he was, wasn't she?

Teddy? Macy typed. Still there?

You hurt my feelings, Marceline. You've upset me.

Teddy . . .

She dropped her hands to her lap. If she wanted to help Fia, if she truly wanted to stop him, Macy knew angering him wasn't the way to do it. It pained her to do so, but she typed, Sorry.

You should be.

She thought for a moment, then wrote, How are you feeling?

Not good. As if you care.

I do care, Teddy. How is the voice?

Loud, he responded. It hurts in my head.

You have to block it out. You can't listen to it. It tells you to do things you don't want to do, she told him.

How do you know what I want to do? Maybe I like it.

No, she answered. You don't, Teddy. You don't want to hurt people.

Hurt, what a bizarre euphemism for cold-blooded torture and murder, she thought miserably.

I don't want to hurt them, he typed. But she makes me do it. She makes me so angry that I have to do it.

Macy leaned back in the hard chair at the table near the window. Lamplight from outside lit her room in a dim glow. This was exactly why Fia had wanted Macy to stay out of Teddy's reach. His mental issues, whatever they were, were escalating. He was becoming less stable. She could see it plainly in his words.

"Boy, you really screwed up this time, Macy," she said aloud. Then she leaned over her keyboard and typed. I have to go now. It's late. I have to get some sleep. Work tomorrow. I'll talk to you again tomorrow night. Promise me you'll try not to listen to her.

You don't understand, Marceline. She's very insistent.

Please, Teddy. The words pained her, but she typed them. For me. Don't listen to her voice, listen to mine.

I can't make any promises.

Macy clicked the IM icon, closing the program. Even though she was no longer connected, Teddy's words remained on her screen.

Macy closed her laptop and glanced at the digital clock, glowing red beside the bed. It was 2 A.M. Arlan was asleep.

He had called her today to check on her and see how she was feeling. He'd offered to have the local doctor take a look at her forehead where the big bump and scab had formed. What was interesting was that he had not told her what happened that night in New Orleans. She still didn't know how she got the bump or how she ended up in Arlan's bed. What was equally interesting was that she hadn't pressed him.

Macy rose from her chair and walked over to the bed and sat on the end of it. She wasn't tired.

She told herself she wasn't going to Arlan's tonight. She hadn't gone last night, either. She was trying to taper off. It would be easier that way when she left town.

She stared at her bare toes on the not-so-nice blue carpet.

But the thing was, she wanted to go. She needed to go. As much as it pained her to admit it, she needed Arlan.

Macy got up and threw on a pair of gym shorts. She tucked her room key in her pocket and walked out the door, still barefoot and braless.

On the way to Arlan's house Macy saw not one but two pedestrians. And she could tell by the way they walked, by the clothes they wore, that they were locals. There was a middle-aged woman who had nodded a greeting to her, strolling past her as if she walked down the street every night at 2:15 A.M. Macy recognized her; she had run into her one morning at the diner. Her name was Mary, she thought. Of course, half the women over the age of forty in this town were Mary. Then Macy spotted an elderly man who made it a point to pretend he didn't see her as he turned the corner almost directly in front of her.

Odd . . . very odd.

Macy let herself into Arlan's house. The door was unlocked, of course. He was expecting her. The thought made her smile.

She was surprised, however, to find that when she reached his bedroom, he wasn't there. He wasn't anywhere in the house.

Macy knew she should go back to the hotel. But she didn't want to. Not there. Not where Teddy was.

She thought of going back to her lonely room, where a killer haunted her. Instead, she stripped and curled up in Arlan's big bed to wait for him.

"I thought you said they'd hunt you down and behead you if you didn't make a council meeting," Arlan said into his cell as he walked down the sidewalk in the dark.

"I said they would hunt you down and behead you if you missed *High* Council," Fia corrected, obviously amused that she had pulled one over on him. Arlan had gone to the boring meeting, but she had skipped it.

"So I didn't have to go?" he asked, incredulously. He opened the bottle of water he'd snatched off the snack table at the museum as he left. "Man, she so set me up."

"Who?"

He took a drink of the bottled water. "Who do you think? Peigi. First she asks me to just stand in temporarily for Johnny at High Council. Then she tells me that means I have to go to General Council, too."

Fia chuckled. "Anything interesting come up?"

"Not really. Same ol', same ol'. Complaints about the

teens breaking curfew, running around at night smoking cigarettes and drinking beer. Oh, and a bunch of kids stole Victor's car in the middle of the night and went joy riding. Funny
thing is, they returned it in the morning with a full tank."

"Hoodlums," she mocked.

"You're just glad they're not into Satan worship this
summer," Arlan quipped. He took another sip of water,
watching Johnny Jr. cut through Mary McCathal's backyard. Word at the pub had it that he was sleeping with her.
The word also was that he was sleeping with her nemesis,
Mary Hill. The previous summer, Mary McCathal's husband, Bobby, had been beheaded. Mary Hill had been his
girlfriend.

"Let's see, what else did they talk about?" Arlan continued. "We're going to dig another pond on the game preserve. Rainfall is still down. Mungo's concerned if there's a
serious drought, the deer will suffer."

"Anything good to eat?"

"Nah, the usual. Zucchini bread, pretzel salad."

"So I didn't miss anything." He heard a hesitation in her
voice. "I don't suppose the subject of Regan was brought
up?"

He frowned. He and Fia had had words at the airport
on the return trip home. Macy had been in the ladies room;
Regan was off buying beer at the bar. Arlan had told Fia
about Regan not showing up for the kill in Athens and
that he had already warned Regan that he wasn't going to
cover for him again. Fia had tried to make excuses for her
little brother, as usual, but Arlan hadn't wanted to hear it.
Regan had refused to say why the Rousseaus had taken
him prisoner, denying he knew anything about the drugs
the witch sisters had mentioned.

Arlan was beginning to suspect that Regan might be involved in drugs, which was strictly forbidden by the sept.
It had happened once before, in the midnineteenth cen-

tury. Opium had been Regan's drug of choice then. He'd gotten involved with some bad-news Mandarin immigrant vampires in the San Francisco Bay area. His brother Fin had bailed him out that time.

"No," Arlan said. "Nobody mentioned Regan. No one knows about Athens but me, Jimmy, and Sean."

"I had a talk with Regan. I told him we weren't going to put up with his irresponsible behavior anymore. I told him that if he wanted to stay on the kill team, he had to start acting like it."

Arlan wanted to say she'd wasted her breath, but he held his tongue. He didn't pretend to understand the connection between siblings; his sister had been beheaded and died early on when the vampire slayer raids had been at their heaviest in the old country. What he did understand was that Fia had a fierce need to protect Regan and he couldn't help but respect her for that, even if she was sometimes misguided.

"So, you working late tonight?" Arlan asked, deciding that the best thing to do was to change the subject.

"No. Folding laundry."

"Two-thirty in the morning? Not in bed with lover boy?" he asked.

"Not your business."

So it wasn't his imagination. Things weren't going well with the human. Fia was spending more and more nights alone, and talking less about him.

"I'm home. Guess I'll say good night. I've got some work to do at Eva's tomorrow. She wants her fence repaired before the big photo shoot." He walked up the sidewalk to the porch. Before he laid his hand on the doorknob, he knew someone was inside. Macy.

"Pleasant dreams," Fia said.

"Bet mine will be better than yours," he teased, walking into the house and closing the door quietly behind him.

"Sweet Mary," Fia groaned in his ear. "Tell me she's not there waiting for you."

"You're just jealous," he whispered. "Because I'm getting more sex than you are."

"Hanging up," Fia declared.

The phone went dead in his ear. Smiling to himself, Arlan walked down the hallway in the dark. She hadn't turned any lights on. A lot of humans were afraid of the dark, but not Macy. She seemed to prefer it.

Arlan halted inside his bedroom door. She lay naked, asleep on her side in the middle of his bed, pillowing her head on her hands.

He set his phone down on the bedside table and slipped out of his clothes. He tried to ease into bed carefully, thinking he wouldn't wake her. It had been kind of nice to wake up next to her yesterday in the hotel.

But the moment the mattress shifted under his weight, Macy stirred.

"Hey," she said sleepily, reaching for him.

He liked her like this, only half awake, her guard down. She was a beautiful woman, but in this state, she seemed more vulnerable, less jaded by life. Even more beautiful. When she looked like this, Arlan had an intense desire to protect her, to take care of her. He even allowed himself to wonder for a moment what it would be like to live with her, to have a relationship with her.

"Hey," he greeted, putting his arm around her.

She glanced at the clock and he waited for her to ask where he'd been. He figured he'd tell her he stayed late at The Hill.

But she didn't ask. She didn't say a word. She just rested her head on his shoulder and snuggled against him.

She didn't ask.

Of course it was better for Arlan if she didn't. Saying nothing was always better than telling a lie, because after a while, there were so many lies that a man couldn't remember the truth. But Arlan couldn't help wondering why Macy didn't ask where he'd been. What if he'd been with some other woman? Didn't she care?

He kissed the top of her head and said nothing, wishing he was the one who didn't care.

"You didn't," Fia said.

"Afraid I did." Macy sat down in the sand and pulled a fried fish sandwich from the brown paper sack. The fish was fresh. Some old geezer caught it this morning, according to the girl at the cash register at the diner. Macy loved fresh fish. She loved lunch out of paper sacks. In the Midwest where she'd grown up, you didn't get fresh fish sandwiches in paper sacks.

"Jesus, Mary, and Joseph," Fia swore. "I don't understand. All you had to do was stay off the Internet."

"I know, I know." Macy held the wrapped sandwich in her hand. "I just couldn't help myself. It was like I knew he was there, waiting for me. He was shook up. He'd been trying to reach me for days."

Fia exhaled. "So what did he have to say?" she asked, still not over it.

"He said *the voice is loud.*"

"Whose voice?"

"I don't know. He just says *her, she.* He would never tell me who she is."

"You think someone is actually talking to him or it's in his head?"

"I don't know for sure," Macy said, "but I would guess it's in his head. He says it gives him a headache sometimes, the voice is so loud."

"He say anything else?"

Macy unwrapped the sandwich on her lap. "Not really." She hesitated. "But he was really worked up. I tried to talk to him about not listening to the voice, about not hurting anyone."

"Jesus H. Christ, Macy!"

"I'm sorry. It's just how the conversation went down."

Fia was quiet on the other end of the line for a minute. "You think he's going to do it again? Soon?"

Macy thought for a second. "Yeah," she heard herself say. "I'm afraid he is. Maybe I can get some more information out of him. I told him I would talk to him tonight. I promised I would be there."

"You shouldn't have said that, Macy."

"I was trying to help. I was trying to keep him from murdering people."

"He use the same screen name?"

"A variation. Like I said before, he switches pretty regularly. This was Teddy 200."

Again, the exasperated sigh. "So far, we've had no luck with any of the others you've given me. He's made it very hard for us to track him down." She was quiet for a minute. "Look, they're talking here about rerouting your IM address and having one of us talk to him."

"Absolutely not," Macy said. "He'll know it's a trick. You piss him off, I don't know what he'll do. The agreement from the beginning was that I would not approach the authorities. Ever."

"And what did he say he would do if you did? He threaten you?"

"No," Macy said quietly.

"So he threatened to hurt others. Who? You said you have no family. No friends."

"He didn't say exactly what he would do." Macy rewrapped her sandwich, not sure she was hungry any longer. "But he used the words *innocent* and *carnage* a lot." She paused. "Fia, I'm scared he's going to do it again. Soon, really soon."

"But it's only been two weeks since the Macphersons." Fia's voice was tightly strung. "That doesn't make any sense."

Macy gestured with one hand. "He's a nut job. Why does it have to make sense?"

When Fia spoke again, it was in her calm FBI agent voice. "The thing is, somehow in his head, Macy, this all makes sense. That's why I need your help. That's why I need you to be more forthcoming with information than you've been."

"What information? I don't have any information." Macy thought about the shoe box in the bottom of her closet in the cottage in Virginia. Was there something there Fia could use? She looked down the beach to see Eva approaching from a distance. She was wearing a crazy black and white caftan and her hair was covered with some sort of turban. "Look, I can't talk anymore. I have a meeting."

It wasn't really a meeting so much as a lunch date. It had been Eva's suggestion that they meet for fish sandwiches after she learned that Macy liked them, too. So this was a lunch date between friends. Macy had never had lunch with a friend.

"What do you want me to do about talking to Teddy tonight?" Macy asked into the phone. She knew that Eva knew she was working with Fia to track down the Buried Alive Killer, but Macy didn't want to involve Eva. She wanted to keep the first friend she had ever made safe.

"Don't talk to him. That's what I want you to do. Did you print out the IM from him last night?"

"Yeah. This morning. Want me to fax it to you when I go back to the hotel?"

"That would be helpful," Fia said.

Macy waved to Eva. "So, I'll call you later."

"What a great day," Eva greeted, opening her arms. The silky fabric of the caftan whipped in the breeze.

Macy hung up her phone and dropped it in her knapsack lying in the sand behind her. "Hungry?" Macy asked, smiling.

Eva grinned, dropping down into the sand. "Famished."

Teddy stared at the blank screen on his new laptop. He bought and sold them regularly off the Internet so if the police did ever try to track his contact with Marceline, it would be difficult. Not that he thought she would ever betray him by going to the police.

The screen was still blank. She wasn't coming. His girl wasn't coming.

"No," Teddy whispered. "Not tonight, Marceline. Tonight is not the night to be petulant."

She's not coming. I don't know why you've been sitting there all night waiting. You know she isn't coming.

He clamped his hands over his ears. "I can't *hear you,*" he sang.

She's not coming because she doesn't care.

"She does care," he said, his voice shaky. "Marceline loves me."

She doesn't love you! What makes you think she loves you? She ever tell you that?

Teddy's lower lip trembled. He stared at the computer screen, trying to will her to log on.

Has she? the voice shouted.

Tears filled Teddy's eyes. "No."

No, no. She's never told you she loves you because she doesn't. She despises you.

"No." He shook his head. Marceline told him to fight her. Not to listen to her. "It's not true," he insisted, tears filling his eyes. "She cares about me. She cares how I am. How I'm feeling."

Lies. Lies you tell yourself, Teddy, the voice screeched. It was now inside his head and outside. But he couldn't see her. He never could. *She doesn't love you and you know why?*

He got up out of the desk chair, shaking all over. He knew the moon wasn't right, but when he got like this, there was only one way to calm himself. One way to get release.

The voice followed him down the steps to the basement. In the basement was where he kept his supplies.

She doesn't love you because no one could ever love you. Not even your mother could love you!

Teddy lowered his hands from his head, knowing it was no use. She wouldn't go away now. Not until it was done.

Say it! she shrieked.

"No one could ever love me," Teddy repeated, taking down the special bag that contained the items he would need to subdue them. "Not even you, Mother."

Chapter 22

Against her better judgment, Macy did as Fia asked and stayed away from the computer that night. But all the next day, she waited in trepidation. She knew in the pit of her stomach that it was only a matter of time before Fia called with the dreaded news. For the first time ever, Macy recharged her cell minutes, keeping the same phone and number.

It was four P.M. when Macy stopped at the hotel's front desk to pick up mail. Mrs. Cahall was chatty, as usual. Today, she was wearing a yellow and pink argyle sweater vest over a white polo. Yellow tennis skirt. Her lipstick was Racy Ruby, she'd told Macy. Cover Girl. Two tubes for seven dollars at Hill's Pharmacy.

When her cell phone rang, Macy knew it was Fia. She was tempted not to answer. She was tempted to drop the phone in the nearest garbage can, go to her room, pack her crap, and move on. She could just skip the Clare Point cottages piece. She didn't really need the job. She certainly didn't need the money. The money her parents had left her in their will was more than enough for a lifetime. It was long past time she moved on, anyway, Macy reasoned, staring at the phone in her hand.

"You gonna answer that?" Mrs. Cahall asked. She was

sipping from a plastic cocktail tumbler. Straight gin, no doubt.

"No."

"Why not?" the old woman asked.

"Because it's bad news."

"Eh?" Mrs. Cahall cupped her hand to her ear.

"I said it's bad news," Macy said loudly.

"You think the bad news will go away if you don't answer the phone?" She peered intently at Macy, clear-eyed, despite the fact that this was probably her second or third cocktail of the afternoon. She shook her head. "Not been my experience. And let me tell you, missy, I've got plenty of experience in the bad news department."

Macy slowly lifted the phone to her ear. She turned her back to Mrs. Cahall and walked away, leaving her mail from the previous day on the counter. "It's Sunday. It's your day off," she said into the phone.

"Apparently our killer doesn't understand weekend hours. Did you know he was going to do it?" Fia asked on the other end of the line. She was pissed. "Don't lie to me, Macy. Did he tell you he was going to kill another family?"

"No." Macy walked out the lobby door, onto the sidewalk. The late afternoon heat and humidity hit her like a wall. "He did *not* tell me he was going to kill anyone. You got the fax. You saw what he said."

"There's no way for me to know if there was another conversation. You could have printed that screen to throw me off."

"Are you accusing me of being a part of this?" Macy demanded. Her heart thumped in her chest. It had been a mistake for her to ever contact Fia. She should have known it would be a waste of time. This was never going to work. Teddy couldn't be stopped. She knew it. He knew it. "Do you really think I have something to do with these

murders?" She was so angry, so upset that her voice qua-
vered.

"No." Fia was calmer now.

"But you *considered* the *possibility?*" Macy pressed.

"I wouldn't be doing my job if I hadn't." Fia's words
were frank, but her tone was not unkind. "This wouldn't
have been the first time a killer or someone intimately involved in the killing tried to get himself or herself
caught."

"*I* called *you* the other night, Fia," Marcy insisted. "I
didn't have to tell you I talked to him after you asked me
not to. Why would I lie about what was said?"

"I don't know. Why would you lie to me at all?"

Macy walked to a tree that partially shaded the hotel
parking lot. She sank to the ground, her knees pulled up,
her back against the rough trunk. She stared at a discarded
Coke can under a car. "I'm not lying to you about the conversation I had with Teddy. I haven't lied to you once since
the day I called you." *Not about anything important,* Macy
thought, wondering if you could burn in hell for lying to
an FBI agent. Jail time, maybe, but *hell?* She was already
in hell.

They were both quiet for a minute. Fia wasn't buying it.
She knew Macy wasn't being entirely forthright with information.

"Not even a full moon," Macy remarked.

"Apparently that didn't stop him last time."

"Who did he kill?" Macy asked, wishing she didn't have
to know.

"The Millers—husband, wife, and six children. The young-
est was an infant."

Macy squeezed her eyes shut. Her chest tightened until
she could barely catch her breath. "Six?" she whispered.
In her mind's eye, she saw the faces of her two little sisters,
imagined them buried, dead. Their arms at their sides. In

those days, Teddy had still been on the learning curve. It wasn't until later that he buried them with their hands above their heads. "Who the hell has six children these days?" She made the comment as much to herself as Fia. "Where?"

"Lancaster. An Amish family. They were found about an hour ago. They didn't show up for church, so after services, a family friend went out to the house to check on them. They're strict old-order so they have no phones. According to the ME, time of death was noon."

Macy hung her head. "I was afraid this was going to happen. He didn't have to tell me, but somehow I knew it." She lifted her head. "How did I know, Fia?"

Fia was quiet on the other end of the line for a moment. "I don't know, Macy. Maybe some kind of psychic connection to him?"

"I don't believe in that crap."

Fia chuckled, but it was without humor. It was as if she was in on some joke that Macy was not privy to. Macy didn't appreciate it much.

"Look, I'm on my way to the crime scene," Fia said. "But we need to have a talk. A serious talk. So far, you're the only lead we have in these cases. You tell me you've told me everything, but you're lying and we both know it. He has a connection to you. What you need to decide, Macy, is if you really want to stop this guy. Do you really want to help stop him? And if you do, you have to be forthcoming with whatever you know. *Everything* you know."

Macy lifted her head. Two teens on skateboards glided by on the sidewalk, laughing and teasing each other. Macy thought about the Miller family. She imagined them dead and buried to their chins, their arms stretched over their heads in some macabre exhibition. How could life go on, how could boys still skate and laugh, she wondered, when the Millers were standing upright in their graves, waiting to be excavated?

"Call me later," Macy said. She hung up.

Arlan was surprised to find Macy sitting on his front step when he got home from work at 5:30. It was early for her. She didn't usually come by until after dark, which he found ironic since *he* was the vampire.

She looked at him, her face childlike. Beautiful, but intensely sad.

"Teddy did it again." Emotion snagged her voice.

Arlan just stood there for a moment, arms hanging at his sides. He didn't know what to say. "This is not your fault," were the first words that came to mind.

She just sat there, arms on her knees, her head hung.

Arlan sat down beside her. "Fia called you?"

She nodded.

"Any details?"

"Not really. Not yet. A family of eight in Lancaster. Old-order Amish." She sat up, pushing away some hair that had fallen free from her ponytail holder and now hung over her face. "Fia's there now."

The thought went through Arlan's head that he should go to Lancaster. That Fia needed him.

He flexed his fingers. *But Macy needed him, too.*

They sat for a moment in silence.

"Come on." Arlan stood, grabbed her hand and pulled her up off the step. Macy tried to resist, but he didn't give in.

"Where we going?"

He half led, half dragged her down the sidewalk. "To the Dairy Queen."

"Eight people were murdered today by someone stalking me, and you want ice cream?" Macy stared at him.

"A Reese's Pieces Blizzard will do us both some good

right now." He put his arm around her shoulders. "And there's someone there I'd like you to meet."

"You've got to be kidding." Kaleigh stood at a deep fat fryer, filling paper envelopes with French fries. "I'm not talking to her."

"Please, Kaleigh. She's in a bad place right now. She needs . . ." Arlan tried to find the right words. "She needs some wisdom."

The teen cut a sideways glance at Arlan. She wore a red smock and a paper food services cap with the Dairy Queen emblem on the side. *And you think I have words of wisdom?* She rolled her eyes.

"Kaleigh, she can help with the case. I know she can. She's just scared. Confused."

Kaleigh dumped a bag of frozen fries into a basket and lowered it into the hot oil. It spit and sputtered. *"And that never works, does it?"* she mused aloud. "You can't run from who you are," she added to no one in particular.

"See that." Arlan patted her on the shoulder. "That's what I'm talking about. Words of wisdom." He took his sunglasses off his head. "Come on. For me. I'll leave my keys in the ignition and you and your friends can steal my truck for a couple of hours. I just need it back by morning so I can go to work."

"I was not part of that." She pointed at a group of teenagers congregated in the parking lot. "I told them not to take that old codger's car. I told them he'd squeal on them."

Arlan grinned as he lowered his sunglasses over his eyes. "We're outside at one of the picnic tables." He headed out the kitchen's back door. "And we'll take two Blizzards, too."

"I'm not giving away free ice cream," Kaleigh called after him.

Ten minutes later, Kaleigh walked out the front door of the ice cream shop, carrying three cups. She strolled over to Arlan and Macy's table and set down the cups. "My break is ten minutes." She handed Arlan his. "Reese's Pieces with chocolate ice cream. Take a hike. Oh, and you owe six dollars and sixty-six cents," she said. "Pay up."

Arlan walked away, not giving his human girlfriend a real chance to protest against being stuck with a teenager wearing a stupid paper hat and smelling like chocolate syrup. Kaleigh sat down at the table opposite Macy and pushed one of the cups across the table toward her.

"I don't know what Arlan told you about me," Macy said, looking at the ice cream. "But frankly, this isn't any of your business."

Kaleigh tugged her hat off her head and tossed it on the table. She pulled the long plastic spoon out of the cup of ice cream and licked it. Oreo Cookie Blizzard. Her favorite. "Well, I don't know what he told you about me, but I have a way of, I don't know"—she shrugged—"*getting* things. You know what I mean? Lot's of people talk to me. You'd be surprised."

Macy found herself mesmerized by the teen's steady gaze. There was something in those young eyes that appeared to . . . be not so young, and Macy had the strange feeling that she did understand what Kaleigh meant by *getting* things.

Macy definitely had to get out of this town. It was just too M. Night Shyamalan weird to be safe. And she still needed a new phrase.

Kaleigh looked down at her cup and stuck her spoon in it. She pulled the spoon out, observing the way the vanilla ice cream and little bits of chocolate cookie mounded on the red plastic. She saw a flash of light as she touched the spoon to her tongue. A picture. Like a photograph, which was kind of strange because she didn't usually see things that way.

Macy. Only younger. Standing alone in a cemetery, wearing a jean skirt.

Kaleigh felt the younger Macy's overwhelming grief and fought to keep the sadness out of her own heart. That was hard for Kaleigh, sometimes. People told her she needed to insulate herself from others' emotions, but that was easy to say, not so easy to do.

As the plastic spoon scraped her teeth, Kaleigh saw another flash. Another photograph. One small white casket beside another. Two little blond-haired girls, dressed in yellow sundresses, lying in the caskets. Dead.

Against her will, tears filled Kaleigh's eyes. The cool, sweet ice cream in her mouth suddenly tasted like mud. It was hard to swallow.

"Kaleigh? Are you all right?"

Macy's words seem to start from far away and then come from some place closer.

Kaleigh blinked. "They were wearing yellow sundresses. Your sisters. The dead ones."

Macy stared at Kaleigh as if she had seen a ghost. It was just like one read in books. All of a sudden she was white as the napkin that fluttered on the table.

"How did you know that? I've never told anyone. Arlan—"

"Arlan didn't tell me anything." Kaleigh frowned. She probably should have just kept her mouth shut, but it was too late now. "I just know stuff."

Macy sat there, hands on the table, looking like she was going to bolt.

"It's okay," Kaleigh said quietly. "I don't tell things."

Macy stared like a skittish doe.

"What I was thinking was that you can't keep running," Kaleigh said. "That's what I'm getting. That no matter how scared you are, you can't outrun it." She set her cup of ice cream down. "Sometimes, the only way to put out the fire is to turn around and run right into it. You know?"

"What are you talking about?" Macy asked.

Kaleigh got up from the picnic table. She took her paper hat, but she left the ice cream. "I have no idea. But I think you do. See ya around."

Flabbergasted and scared at the same time, if that was possible, Macy watched the teen walk away. How could that girl have known about Mariah and Minnie? How was it possible?

She watched as Arlan spoke to Kaleigh before she went back into the ice cream shop. He approached the table where Macy still sat.

"What did you tell her about me?" Macy accused as Arlan sat down.

Having finished his ice cream, he picked up what Kaleigh had left behind and began to eat it. "What do you mean? Nothing. What could I have told her? I don't know about you. You won't tell me anything."

"My sisters died. They were buried in yellow dresses," Macy murmured. Her hands trembled.

"I'm so sorry, Macy." He looked up from his ice cream, spoon poised.

"You're missing the point here, Arlan. *How did she know?*"

"I told you. Kaleigh knows things." He shrugged, going back to his ice cream. "Around here, we call it a *gift*."

Macy's head reeled. None of this made any sense, but did anything in her life? "Kaleigh doesn't know about Teddy, does she? About him stalking me?"

"She knows Fia's working on the Buried Alive Killer, but I haven't said anything to her about you helping out with the case. Fia certainly wouldn't say anything. Neither would Eva—I mean, *if* you've mentioned anything to her."

Thinking, Macy slid the DQ cup in front of her closer. The paper was wet and cool. She pulled the spoon up and plunged it into the ice cream. It was melting. Vanilla ice cream with real strawberry bits in it. How the hell had Kaleigh known Macy liked strawberry ice cream? She had never told Arlan. She'd never told anyone. She took a tentative taste.

The cold, sweet ice cream was shockingly good. "Kaleigh told me I can't keep running. She said the only way to end it was to meet it head on. Something about fire." Macy looked up at him. "She was talking about Teddy. She knows he's connected to my sisters' deaths."

Arlan watched her through his dark sunglasses. His face was not just handsome, it was sweet. She liked the way he looked at her—like he really did care.

Macy took another tentative taste of the strawberry ice cream, still pensive. "I think I need to talk to Fia."

He reached across the table, taking her hand in his. He squeezed it. "I was hoping you would."

While preparing for a presentation the next day, Teddy waited for Marceline. He checked his laptop. It was early still, but he kept his IM program on, just in case she couldn't resist.

And he knew she wouldn't be able to resist.

She never could.

Chapter 23

Macy sat in the booth at the diner, the Nike shoe box beside her. She'd driven all the way to Charlotte last night to retrieve it. Then back to Clare Point. Oddly enough, she wasn't tired. Adrenaline, she supposed. And a strange feeling that this was all coming to an end.

Macy wasn't like Kaleigh, she didn't *know* things, but she sensed an impending conclusion. She didn't know if Teddy was going to kill her or if Fia was going to catch him. And Macy wanted to live. For some reason, she'd come back from New Orleans knowing that, and the realization had brought on the seed of an emotion she hadn't known she could still experience. Fear. Years ago, she had resigned herself to the idea that Teddy would kill her one day. She knew that eventually he would tire of his sick cat and mouse game and he would murder her. She was afraid because she didn't want to die. But her new desire to live had also planted another seed and that was the will to fight back. She wanted to fight to live.

Fia walked into the diner wearing a fitted suit, her signature dark sunglasses, and a bad ass attitude. On the phone last night, while she'd seemed interested to see the box, she'd wanted Macy to come to the FBI offices in Philadelphia.

Macy didn't do FBI offices. And she didn't do Philadelphia. She wasn't sure why. She just didn't like the city.

"Up all night?" Macy asked as Fia slid into the booth across the table from her.

"Left the crime scene to come straight here. I don't usually drink caffeine, but I'm having it this morning." She pointed to her coffee cup and a waitress came to fill it. "Rye toast, dry."

"Anything for you, Miss?"

Macy shook her head and waited for the waitress to walk away. "Thanks for coming."

"You've got the stuff?"

"As I said on the phone, there's not much here that is going to help you."

"And as I said on the phone"—Fia sipped her black coffee—"that will be up to the bureau to decide." She took off her sunglasses to scrutinize Macy. "Why didn't you tell me he sent you things in the mail?"

"It was a long time ago. And he only did it for a few years. Once I graduated from college, I started moving around to steer clear of him. And the Internet had become more readily available. He definitely likes the Internet."

"That still doesn't explain why you didn't tell me what you had."

Macy thought about it before she answered, trying to be honest not just with Fia, but herself. She had decided it *was* time to be honest. She was tired of running and she was tired of living with the idea of dying. She was determined she was going to do what Kaleigh had suggested, turn around and run into the fire. Even if it destroyed her. "I think I didn't want to tell you about the things he sent because you'd want them. You'd want to, you know, keep them."

"And you want to keep them . . . *why?* You like mementos from sick fucks?"

Macy tucked a lock of hair behind her ear. She'd washed her hair this morning and not yet pulled it back in a ponytail. Fia had a point. Why *did* she want the stuff? But she knew why. She had always known why. She'd kept the clippings Teddy sent her because, as sick as it sounded, he was her only connection to her dead family. The mementos also reminded her, lest she ever forget, the part *she* played in their deaths.

Her whole life was really about that, wasn't it? All of it, her lack of ability to form relationships with anyone, her promiscuous behavior. Her nonstop travel. The way she had alienated herself from the world.

Fia put her hand out. "Let me see what you have."

Macy looked down at the old shoe box beside her. She'd driven all the way to Charlotte and back and not opened it. In fact, she couldn't remember the last time she *had* opened it. Not in the year since she'd moved to the cottage, she knew. Her fingers found the box and she grasped it, lifting it slowly to the table. "I don't think anything is going to make sense in here. I used to ask Teddy why he sent this stuff, but he would never say."

Fia took the box, sliding it across the table in front of her. She removed the lid and then, glancing inside, pulled a pair of latex gloves out of her pocket and put them on.

"Aren't you going to look at it back at your office?"

"I am. But I'm curious now. I'd just like to get a first impression."

"It's almost all bizarre clippings from magazines. A couple of notes he sent me early on."

"How early?" Fia glanced up, tearing her eyes away from a clipping of a little boy riding in a wagon, a mother-figure pulling him.

"For fourteen years," Macy said softly.

"Fourteen years?" Fia repeated. "You've got to be kidding me. You said he'd only been contacting you for *a couple* of years. Just since the Smiths."

"I know what I told you."

Fia thumbed through glossy magazine clippings that were growing faded with time. "You save the envelopes?"

"No. No return addresses. Postmarks from all over the U.S. I think he travels for work."

"Good guess. Our profile indicates the same thing." Fia pulled out a newspaper clipping. "He sent you this?"

Macy leaned over the table to get a better look. It was an article from the *Chicago Tribune* reporting the murder of a family. The Patels, 2001. "The very earliest clippings he sent. I saved the others."

"Jesus, Mary, and Joseph," Fia swore under her breath. "They all here? A clipping from each of the deaths?"

"Nothing in there for the Macphersons . . . or the Millers," Macy heard herself say. "Eleven in the box."

"Eleven?" Fia tossed a picture of a boy seated at a table grinning as his mother served him cereal. "The Millers make twelve, Macy. If the Macphersons and the Millers aren't in the box, there should be ten."

"Eleven in the box," Macy repeated.

"More coffee?" The waitress walked by the table with a carafe.

"No thanks," Macy and Fia said in unison.

"There's one I don't know about?" Fia sounded angry but perhaps a little hurt, too.

Fia was disappointed in her. Of course she was. Disappointment was all Macy could offer anyone. And death.

Macy glanced out the window and watched as a family biked by. This was her chance. She could stand up and just walk away. There would be nothing Fia could do about it. Sure, maybe she could arrest her, but there wasn't enough evidence to link Macy to the crimes. The box was nothing but a collection of old clippings and obituaries. Weird thing for her to have in her possession, but not illegal because it wasn't really evidence.

"The other family. Who else did he kill?" Fia pressed.

The diner was bright and loud. Patrons were laughing and talking. Dishes clinked as waitresses cleared them away. The smoky smell of bacon frying hung in the air. A child near the cash register cried.

But the diner didn't seem bright and loud to Macy. Suddenly it seemed dark. Small. It was just Fia and Macy and the darkness that loomed at the edges of Macy's mind. "Nineteen ninety-four," she said flatly. "Lawrenceville, Missouri."

"Macy. The first time the Buried Alive Killer appears on the FBI radar is nineteen ninety-seven." She watched Macy carefully. "Chattanooga. The Downing family. Mom, Dad, two children."

"It's there inside a condolence card." Macy felt as if she were speaking in slow motion. She pointed to the box. "In the bottom."

Fia began to leaf through the items. "Lot of cutouts of smiley boys and their mommies, huh?" she remarked.

"Definitely mommy issues," Macy commented, feeling slightly detached from what was happening.

Fia pulled a faded white greeting card decorated with pastel flowers from the Nike box. She opened it up, catching the newspaper clipping before it hit the Formica table. She quickly scanned the article. "They were strangled in the house and then laid in shallow graves. Not the same MO." She looked up at Macy.

Macy felt her lower lip tremble. Her voice came out in a croak. "It was his first time, I think."

Fia watched her intently with those dark eyes that seemed to Macy to be able to see to a person's very soul. "Who were they, Macy?"

"Husband and wife Alice and John Carpenter, and their daughters Minerva and Mariah, ages four and ten, respectively." Macy shifted her gaze to look at a clock on the far wall. She focused on the numbers and the black second hand, *tick, tick, ticking* as she spoke. "He strangled them in their beds and then carried them outside to the family farm orchard, where he dug shallow graves and laid them to rest." Her voice caught in her throat. "He didn't cover them up. In the morning, the teenage daughter found them there. All lying side by side under a cherry tree."

Macy was surprised to feel Fia's hand cover hers on the table. Fia had never struck Macy as the emotional type. Macy hadn't been entirely sure the woman felt anything at all.

"*You* were the teenage daughter," Fia said gently. It was a statement, not a question.

Macy intended to answer, but the words wouldn't form in her mouth. She thought she could handle this, but she realized she was wrong. She got up from the table.

"Macy."

Macy walked out of the diner, down the street. She'd walk into the fire, but it was going to have to be in baby steps.

Fia's first impulse was to follow Macy. To demand answers. She usually let her first impulse pass. It was often wrong, and more than once she'd learned that the hard way.

She removed the latex gloves she had donned in case, on the outside chance, there were fingerprints or DNA evidence on any of the clippings or cards. She then put the lid back on the shoe box and finished her coffee. She left the toast untouched. She had to get back to Philadelphia. First, everything had to be checked by Evidence. Then it might take days to go over everything in the box and try to make sense of it. But the first thing she would do was track down information on the Carpenter murder. She'd contact the Missouri State Police as soon as she got on the road.

Fia's cold-blooded vampire heart ached for Macy. For the girl she had been. For the woman she was now. Tears came to her eyes when she thought of Macy standing under a cherry tree looking down at her dead family.

Saints in hell, life was hard for humans.

Fia massaged her temples. She didn't have time for emotion. It wasn't her place to feel for the victims. If she was going to catch this monster, for the sept, for the world, she had to get her head in the right place. She had to think logically.

Of course Macy had known some of the Buried Alive victims. Fia had suspected that from the beginning. She should have guessed from Macy's behavior that this was personal. But how could she have guessed that Macy's family had *been* victims?

Which led Fia to the next logical question, the question she would have asked had Macy not taken off.

If Teddy killed Macy's family, why hadn't he killed her along with them? And why didn't he go after her when he realized there had been a Carpenter missing that night? Why the years of stalking her?

After paying at the register, Fia went outside into the bright sunlight. She called Arlan as she walked across the parking lot to her car. "I need you," she said when he picked up.

"Any time, any place, sweet cheeks."

"How long has she been here?" Arlan asked Eva.

They stood side by side in the sunroom, looking out on Eva's rose garden. Macy sat on the stone bench, a camera propped on her knee as she studied the garden fence and took notes. If she knew Eva and Arlan were watching her, she gave no indication.

"Not long. Half an hour, maybe. She's taking the photos herself for the magazine article. She said she wanted to get some preliminary shots, get an idea of what she was looking for." Eva turned to him. "What's up?"

"Looks like the shit might be hitting the serial killer fan." He watched Macy, unsure of the best way to approach her. Fia had been concerned when she called him, not so much about the case, but her emotional state.

Seated on the bench in the midst of the roses, Macy seemed very fragile to him. All humans seemed fragile, but she more so. Fia said she'd walked out of the diner. Fia had been afraid she might leave town. Arlan, who'd been changing the locks on Victor Simpson's doors, had gone straight to the hotel when Fia called him. They had agreed that it would be better for Fia to back off a little, that if Macy was going to talk to anyone, it would be him right now.

Macy's car had been at the hotel. Mrs. Cahall said she'd come in, gotten a camera bag from her room and left through the lobby at 9:37 A.M., headed east. Arlan wondered if the FBI had room for Mrs. Cahall at the bureau; the old lady was more observant than half the bozos Fia worked with.

Arlan had guessed that Macy had left the hotel, headed for Eva's. He knew she'd decided to take the photographs herself and had wanted to start today. He hoped she followed through with her plan, despite her meeting with Fia. Fortunately, she had and she was here, safe, at least for the time being. Fia hadn't given him any details, but she had told him that Macy's family had been murdered by the Buried Alive Killer when she was a teenager. A case the FBI had been unaware of.

Arlan had asked how that was possible, but he knew very well that often serial killers murder off the radar, especially early in their "careers." He'd once tracked a man in Bordeaux who admitted at the hour of his death that authorities had only known of half of the thirty-seven men and women he'd tortured and murdered.

The thought of Dauncy left a sour taste in his mouth; he wiped it with the back of his hand.

"What can I do to help?" Eva asked.

"Right now, probably just tell her you're leaving, and go on to work." He eyed the clean black apron thrown over a chair. "She knows where to find you if she wants to. I think she just needs some time alone."

"You think she'll take off before we catch this bastard?"

"Hard to say." Arlan watched Macy squat down on one knee and peer through her camera's viewfinder. "She's made a life for herself by never staying long in one place. That kind of pattern is hard to change."

Eva watched him. "You really have a thing for her, don't you?" she said, wonder in her voice. "Arlan Kahill, have you fallen in love with a human?"

He glanced at Eva and then away, trying to harden his heart. "Nah, I know better than that."

She swatted him on the behind as she walked away. "You better."

Teddy gazed out the small window of the airplane, wishing he didn't have to travel today. He would rather have stayed at home and cut out all the articles they had written about him in the newspapers. He was flying south today. Atlanta. Macy sometimes worked in the Atlanta area but she wasn't there now.

No. She was much closer to home. She hadn't said so, but at night, when he sat on his front porch, looking up at the moon, he could feel her near him. They were growing closer each day. And despite what his mother said, he knew she was falling in love with him.

Teddy had been waiting his whole life for this. He'd hoped. He'd prayed. He'd been patient. And now, it was time to make plans.

Chapter 24

Kaleigh sat with her friends around the bonfire they'd built on the beach, laughing at something stupid one of the guys had said. Fourth of July was always one of her favorite holidays because the whole town threw a big Independence Day block party. It was also one of the few times each year that a bonfire permit for the beach was issued. There had been a parade today and with traffic rerouted, booths had been set up on the street that ran along the beach, featuring food for sale and carnival games to play. A block off the water, a strip mall parking lot had been turned into a mini midway featuring kiddy rides. Of course there were no "kiddies" in the sept, but the tourists seemed to enjoy the carnival. There was also a bandstand and dance area at the end of one of the streets along the waterfront. A goofy country and western group was playing now, but later tonight, an awesome local rock band would play. The whole day would have been better without the human tourists who seem to come in flocks, but Kaleigh understood the sept needed them, at least financially. The yearly block party also made Clare Point seem ordinary, despite its extraordinary townspeople.

Someone joined the circle of vampires-only teens around the bonfire and Rob Hill scooted closer to Kaleigh to make room. His arm brushed hers, but she didn't pull away. She kind of liked him close like this. She'd been seeing Rob a couple of times a week. They weren't *dating,* but they were definitely making the effort to hang out with the same people, do the same things. Yesterday he'd stopped by the DQ just to say hi. His timid attention was nice as long as Kaleigh didn't dwell on what Rob had looked like a couple of weeks ago at his wake. She knew that was how the circle of life worked in the sept; she just didn't want to think about it too hard.

"Let's play a game." Katy, one of Kaleigh's good friends, stood and clapped her hands, something she did whenever she was giving the group an order. She had to speak above the music blaring from a boom box someone had brought with them.

"Yeah, let's play a game," someone piped in.

"Like spin the bottle?" one of the guys chimed in. "Or truth or dare!"

All the girls groaned. Someone threw an empty Coke can.

"We're not kissing your lame vampire asses," one of the girls on the other side of the campfire called.

"No, I know what we can play." Katy eyed Kaleigh.

Kaleigh shook her head. *Don't you dare,* she telepathed, blocking the message to anyone but Katy. She knew very well where Katy, who was *supposed* to be her best friend, was going with this. They had played the game the other night at a sleepover—Kaleigh, Katy, and Maria. It had been fun, but that was different. It had been private. Here, she was in front of everyone, in front of all the guys. What if it didn't work? How lame would that be?

"Come on," Katy pushed. "It'll be fun. It's sort of a guessing game," she told the group.

"It will *not* be fun," Kaleigh said between clenched teeth.

"Come on, it will," Maria chimed in.

Kaleigh groaned.

"Look, you don't have to if you don't want to," Rob said quietly in her ear.

She looked at him. That was so sweet of him. "Nah, it's okay," she said. "It's kind of like having a dog that can do tricks, for Katy. She likes to show me off." She rolled her eyes. "Go ahead, Katy," she called.

"Okay." Katy got up on her knees. She was wearing jeans shorts and a bikini top that was little more than two triangles of pink fabric. "Johnny, hold up some fingers behind your back," she called to one of the guys on the opposite side of the bonfire.

Kaleigh could barely see his face because of the bright flames licking the driftwood between them.

"Got it," he called.

"How many?" Katy shot at Kaleigh.

She frowned. Boring. "Four."

"What about me?" one of the other guys hollered.

"Three."

"Me?"

"Six," she said. This was stupid. She'd been able to do this for almost a year. It was the new development that was really freaking her out, and fascinating her friends, apparently.

"Me?"

"One, Wills," Kaleigh said. "You're giving me the finger behind your back, guaranteeing you get your ice cream after its melted next time I serve you."

Red-faced, he shot her the bird for all to see.

She didn't give him the satisfaction of returning the favor.

The teens howled with glee. Some chimed in with how impressed they were. How, if they had that ability, they would use it.

"Wait, wait, it gets better," Katy said, up on her knees

in the sand again. She liked being the ringleader and she liked ordering people around. Kaleigh told her all the time that she should go to law school and become a judge. It was time the Kahills got someone on the Supreme Court, anyway. "Somebody, anybody, I want you to go over to the cooler and get a soda. And block your thoughts. Don't let her read what you're thinking."

"I'll go." Joe shot up out of the sand.

Katy turned to Kaleigh. "Kaleigh's going to tell the rest of us what he's going to get. *Before* he gets it. Go ahead, Joe." She shooed him with her hand. "Keep your back to us."

Everyone watched Joe, shirtless, saunter off into the dark. They'd dragged a cooler from one of the girls' houses nearby to the beach and it sat about thirty feet from the bonfire. Inside were dozens of sodas mounded over with ice.

"Tell us when you're there," Katy hollered. "But don't open the cooler yet."

"I'm here," he called back.

Everyone turned to look at Kaleigh. A couple of teens on the far side of the bonfire stood up to get a better view.

"What kind of soda is he going to get?"

Kaleigh hesitated. She really didn't like being the evening's entertainment. But these were her friends . . . and she supposed it was harmless enough.

"He's not going to get a soda," she said dryly, folding her arms over her chest. "He's going to dig around and realize that Pete hid a six-pack of beer under the sodas." She eyed Pete, sitting to her right, beside Katy. "Your dad's going to figure out tomorrow that you snitched them and you're going to be on restriction this week so you can't go to the Coheed and Cambria concert with Rob and Joe."

Everyone stared at her, eyes wide with amazement.

"You gotta be shittin' me," Pete groaned. "If I'm going to get busted, I ought to at least get to drink the beer."

"Go ahead," Katy hollered. "Pick a soda and then come back and show us what you have."

Joe sauntered toward them across the sand, one hand behind his back. He halted just behind Kaleigh and to her left. She didn't look at him.

"What kind of soda you get?" someone shouted.

With great fanfare, he produced a sweaty can of beer.

People started clapping and hooting and hollering. Kaleigh stood up. Everyone was congratulating her. Joe was protesting, saying she must have cheated. Kaleigh just walked away. It was hard being sixteen and the sept wisewoman. Hard because she wanted to be a teen like all the others and she knew she couldn't. When she reached the water's edge, she turned north toward the bright lights strung between the booths, thinking she'd get something to eat. As she walked, she could feel someone following her. She knew who it was and he made her smile.

Rob.

She halted and waited for him to catch up.

"Hey," she said.

"Hey." He fell into step beside her and they walked up the beach.

"I'm hungry," she said. "You hungry?"

He walked with one hand in his pocket, the hand closest to her kind of dangling at his side. "I'm always hungry."

"I was like that the first few weeks, too. It's nice to have decent teeth again."

They walked in silence, their hands bumping once in a while. "So, what'd you think about my trick?" she asked. "You really didn't say anything."

"It's cool and all." He shrugged. "But I don't like everyone making a big deal about it. They all know who you are, what you'll be someday. I mean, I'm just starting to remember, but it's a pretty big deal. Pretty big responsibility. I don't like joking around about it. It's your powers that have kept us safe all these years."

She was, again, touched by his understanding. Pretty cool for a seventeen-year-old, gangly boy. "That's a bit of an exaggeration. We all keep each other safe." She glanced at him, feeling shy, but warm inside. Maybe a little bit safe, here with Rob.

"I still think you're pretty cool." He flashed her a reticent grin and surprised her by catching her hand in his. "You want oyster fritters or a crab cake?" he asked. "My dad gave me money so I'm buying."

They cut across the softer sand, headed toward the street and all the vendors. "Hard decision. Can we have both? Like, share?"

He squeezed her hand. "Whatever you want, Kaleigh, that's what I want."

"So fine. Don't come." Fia perched on the bumper of a car that was illegally parked on the street at the north end of the food and game booths. It was dark here, and she was out of the foot traffic, giving her a little privacy. Still, the music coming from the bandstand was so loud that she had to plug up her other ear with her finger to hear Glen.

"I'm sorry. I thought I could get out of here sooner," he said on the other end of the line.

And he truly did sound sorry, although it might have been guilt fueling his sorrow. Feeling sorry for himself, the sorry ass. He was in Baltimore again, with another lame-ass excuse. Fia wanted to just come out and ask him if he was seeing his ex, Stacy-the-hygienist, again. But she wasn't sure she wanted to know. At least, not yet.

"Look, I have to go." She lowered her head to the heel of her hand, her hair falling over her face. She'd worn her hair down tonight, despite the heat, so she'd look sexy for

Glen. Now she was wishing she'd brought a hair tie. "We'll talk tomorrow night? Dinner?"

"Sure." He sounded as if he was trying to be enthusiastic, but she wasn't quite feeling it.

She hung up without saying good-bye. When she lifted her head, Arlan was standing in front of her. He was wearing faded, knee-length swim trunks, a T-shirt from a surf shop, and flip-flops. His sunglasses were up on his head, pushing his hair off his face. He looked suntanned, relaxed, and damned good.

"Hey, surfer boy. Where's your HF?"

"Where's your HM?" He sat on the car bumper beside her.

"Not coming." She held up her phone and then slid it into the pocket of her capris. "Just wish he'd told me before I shaved."

"Sorry."

"Don't be. He didn't want to come, anyway. He thinks I'm from a weird town. He thinks you're all strange."

"He's right."

She leaned back against the hood. "I just wanted him to walk around with me, have something to eat, maybe take a stroll on the beach. Talk about something *other than work*. Make love in the sand, maybe." She looked at Arlan, feeling oddly close to tears. "Am I being unreasonable? Greedy? Am I looking for too much in a relationship with a man?"

"With a human? Probably," he joked. But then he grew more serious. "No. No, of course you aren't. You deserve to be happy, Fia." He rested his hand over hers. "So you think it's over?"

She stared at the string of bright white lights that ran between the funnel cake booth and the Italian ice booth. The funnel cakes smelled good. Fattening, but good. "I think so. Stupid thing is, I'm not even sure why. Too many secrets. Not enough in common. Him being mortal, me being a bloodsucking *immortal*."

Arlan chuckled, but he understood. She knew he understood. His hand felt good on hers.

She glanced at him and then away. "So where's Macy?"

"She walked back to the hotel to drop off her camera and get a sweatshirt. She should be back any minute." He squeezed her hand. "I needed to talk to you alone."

"She come clean with anything else? Because so far, I'm not getting any information out of that box of crap, except that our guy may be even nuttier that we guessed, if that's possible. And I'm still waiting on info from the Missouri police. Seems their inactive records room was water damaged when a contractor accidentally set off the sprinkler system. The files were moved to another room, only whoever logged them out didn't exactly keep accurate records." She looked at him, gesturing with open arms. "How the hell does that kind of thing happen?" She dropped her arms to her sides. "Anyway, they swear the file wasn't destroyed, just *misplaced,* and they'll have everything to me by Monday, Tuesday at the latest."

"And no new evidence has come out of the Miller case?"

She shook her head. "No, there are no loose ends. No fibers, no footprints." She chuckled without humor. "The lab did say that a hair collected appeared to come from an animal of the *Canis lupus* family."

"A wolf in Pennsylvania?"

"They've sent the hair to another lab. There were several dogs on the property. I'm sure it belonged to one of them." She shook her head. "I swear, I think he's getting better." She clenched her fist. "This is such a frustrating case. I just wish Macy could help me more. I've talked to her a couple of times, but she's all but shut down on me. Which is certainly understandable, now that we know her connection," she reasoned aloud. "But she doesn't want to talk about the details of her family's death right now, which leaves me with not knowing any more than what I could get from newspapers and news magazines." She looked at Arlan. "Macy tell you why she wasn't murdered along with her family?"

"I didn't ask." He put his hands together in his lap.

"I didn't ask, either." Fia stared at the bright lights again. "I wanted to have all the facts in front of me before we talked about it. I'm scared to death she's going to take off. Just disappear. And I'll never hear from her again if she does. I'm sure of it."

"Yeah," he admitted thoughtfully. "I've been thinking the same thing. She's done photographing Eva's rose garden. Finishing up the two other cottages on the block. In her mind, she won't have a reason to stay much longer."

Fia looked up at him. She always liked being with Arlan; at six-four, he was considerably taller than she was. "She won't stay for you?"

"Me?" He looked at her, giving her one of those bad boy grins of his. "Nah."

She sensed he was more disappointed than he was letting on, but she didn't say anything more. She understood what he was going through, being with a human. She just wished she had been as practical as he was about it a year ago. "So what did you need to talk to me about?" she asked.

The squawk from the country and western band had finally ended, but Fia didn't have much hope for the next group. One of the musicians had walked by wearing a Korn T-shirt.

"It's about Regan, Fia."

"He's fine."

"He's *not* fine. He's doing cocaine."

She whipped her head around to look at him. "He is not!"

"You know what was stolen from the Rousseau brothers? I made a few phone calls. Talked to a zombie in Baton

Rouge. A shipment of cocaine was stolen. That's what they had their capes in a dither about."

"You shouldn't be making accusations like that, Arlan. You have any idea—"

"It's not an accusation," he said quietly. He cracked his knuckles. "It's a fact." He looked at her. "I'm hurt that you would suggest I would lie about this. I would never try to hurt you or hurt someone you care about. You know that, Fia."

"You never liked Regan," was all she could think of to say. Regan doing coke? He wouldn't jeopardize his position in the sept that way. *Of course he would,* the small dark voice inside her said. He's done it before. The truth was that Fia was often suspicious of Regan's actions. They didn't get along particularly well, except when Regan wanted something. Was that why he'd been nice to her the last few months? Because he was into drugs again and knew that if he got into trouble, he would need an ally?

"I'd have to have proof," she said after a moment of silence between them. A musician with hair dyed blacker than any vampire she knew was tuning his electric guitar and making quite a racket.

"Ask him," Arlan said.

"He'll just lie to me."

Arlan was quiet again for a minute. "So you believe me?"

Fia looked toward the funnel cake booth. She really wanted one. She needed some fat and sugar and excess calories. "I believe you," she said miserably, launching herself off the car's bumper. "You want a funnel cake and a beer?"

He grinned. "Sure."

They started walking toward the bright lights and commotion and Fia caught a glimpse of a shadow near the rear of the end booth. Two young people in a lip-lock. She squinted. Having superhuman vision in the dark came in handy sometimes. "I'll be damned," she said, realizing who it was.

"What?"

Fia pointed. "Isn't that Kaleigh and Rob Hill?"

Macy looked both ways and crossed the street, slipping into her hoody sweatshirt. It had been a hot day, but the ocean breeze was cool now that the sun had gone down. She had run back to the hotel to leave her camera and get the sweatshirt while Arlan stayed at the block party. He had said something about catching up with Fia and her boyfriend.

Macy walked down the street, passing families pushing tired kids in strollers, pulling them in wagons. Red, white, and blue helium balloons floated over their heads, dancing in the breeze. The people who walked by her—moms, dads, children—looked tired but happy.

Macy remembered the county fair she and her family had gone to each summer. She remembered the rides, the cotton candy, the smiles on her parents' faces.

As she walked, hands in her sweatshirt pockets, she wondered if this wasn't a good time to just load her car and go. Wouldn't this day, this moment, be a fine note to end her visit to Clare Point?

She knew Fia would be disappointed, angry, if she took off now. And Arlan would be hurt. Sweet, handsome, hot Arlan. But she had no intentions of saying good-bye to him whenever she did go. She never said good-bye.

At the corner, Macy spotted a crowd of people. Sunburned tourists, kids perched on their shoulders, were trying to get a better look at whatever was going on. Macy skirted the crowd. There were several news cameras. Someone was interviewing Senator Malley, a U.S. senator who hailed from Clare Point.

News cameras. Cameras flashing.

As much as Macy enjoyed taking photographs, she was weird about having her own photograph taken, even accidentally. Years of hiding did that to a girl. She hurried past the commotion and cut down a side street toward the bright lights of the food booths. She'd left her cell phone in her bag back at the hotel, but she doubted Arlan would be hard to find. When there was food and beer, he wouldn't be far.

Chapter 25

"There you are." Arlan looked up as Macy approached. He and Fia were sitting on the curb, eating funnel cakes and drinking ale from plastic cups. Tavia had set up shop for the day in a booth between the fried oyster fritters and clam boats and was doing a banging business selling her microbrews. "I was beginning to worry."

"That I got lost?" Macy nodded in Fia's direction as she sat on the other side of Arlan, leaving him in the middle.

Fia acknowledged Macy with a return nod.

"No, I didn't think you *got lost*." Arlan offered the paper plate he balanced on his lap. "I just—"

"He's afraid I'm going to take off," Macy told Fia as she tore off a piece of the funnel cake on his plate.

"So am I," Fia admitted. "That mean you don't intend to?"

"I don't intend to," Macy said. "I intend to see this through."

Arlan took note that she did not say she *wouldn't* flee, only that she didn't *intend* to. She was clever, his Macy. Clever with words.

"You stag tonight, Fia?"

The sweet confection had left powdered sugar on Macy's upper lip and Arlan wanted to lick it off.

"I thought I was going to get to meet your hot FBI beefcake," Macy continued, reaching for another piece.

"Not a good subject," Arlan said.

Macy leaned forward to speak around him. "I'm sorry to hear that. Short term issue or permanent?"

"Headed for permanent, I'm afraid."

Arlan was surprised that Fia was willing to speak about her personal life with Macy. She was usually pretty tight-lipped about that sort of thing. He admired Fia for having the guts to cross her own comfort zone to reach out to Macy. At this point, it could only help the case. Both women could certainly use some female companionship.

"Bound to happen in my line of work. Relationships don't seem to last long," Fia said.

She had powdered sugar on her lip, too.

Arlan licked his own lips, trying not to think of Fia's. He didn't know what was wrong with him. He really was a monogamous kind of guy. For the most part. But all bets were off when it came to Fia, and always had been. It wasn't that he was happy that her relationship with her human was falling apart. But he had known from the beginning it was a bad idea. He had known it would never work. He just didn't want to see her hurt, and emotional upset seemed to be the only thing she was getting out of the relationship anymore.

Fia wiped her mouth with a paper napkin. "I should have the police report on your family by Monday or Tuesday," she told Macy, keeping her tone professional. "I'd like to read it over and then talk with you."

Macy reached for Arlan's beer.

"I bought you one," he said. "But you took so long, I drank it."

She smiled at him as she lifted the cup to her lips. When she took a sip she made a face, wiping her mouth with the back of her hand. "Yuck. That's awful. Beer and sugar."

Arlan laughed. "Everything goes with beer."

Fia stood. "I'm out of here. You want the rest?"

"Sure." Arlan accepted the plate.

Fia licked her sticky fingers and wiped them with her napkin. "We'll talk Tuesday or Wednesday, Macy? Same number?"

"Same number."

Fia seemed ready to go, but she hesitated. "You talk to him?"

They all knew who *him* was.

Macy tore another piece of funnel cake. "Two nights ago. He didn't bring up the Millers and I didn't either. I think he was away on business. I can usually tell. He's better when he's away. He says he can't hear her as *loudly*." She looked up. "I can send you a copy of the conversation, but we really didn't talk about anything."

"Send it anyway." Fia turned to Arlan and tapped her foot against his. "I'll look into that other matter, okay?" She glanced at Macy. "Talk to you later."

Macy watched Fia walk away. "What was that about?"

"What?" Arlan bit off a big piece of funnel cake. He loved hot, fresh funnel cake, deep fried and covered in powdered sugar. Sometimes, at council meetings, they all sat around and talked about the good old days; peat fires to warm the house, horses for transportation, Sunday mass in a roofless stone building. Arlan liked the present. He liked fast cars, he liked cell phones, and he *adored* deep fried funnel cake.

"The *matter* she was talking about," Macy pushed. "That about me?"

"Nah." He turned to look at her and her face was only inches from his. "You've got some sugar here." He touched the corner of her mouth with his finger.

"Here?" Looking into his eyes, she dragged her tongue along her upper lip.

"Here." He licked the side of her mouth and then kissed her. He pulled back. "We finish this, you want to go for a walk? I snitched a beach towel from one of my niece's friends. We could sit and watch the tide come in."

She cut her green human eyes at him. "Or we could do something else."

Arlan laughed, thinking how sad he would be when Macy was gone from his life.

They finished the beer and the funnel cakes and tossed the trash into a can before cutting across the sand, down to the water's edge, leaving behind the noise and bright lights of the Independence Day block party. Beach towel flung over his shoulder, Arlan held Macy's hand as they walked. At the water's edge, they turned north. They passed a bonfire where all the local kids were gathered. The *vamp camp*, the teens liked to call it. Arlan had good memories of the vamp camp when he was a teenager.

"Bonfires are allowed on a public beach?" Macy asked.

He lifted one shoulder and let it fall. "With a permit. It's usually just local kids. A once or twice a year thing. They do it on All Hallows' Eve, too." He spotted Kaleigh as he and Macy walked by and he raised a hand in salute.

Kaleigh was snuggled up to Rob Hill. She waved back, a silly grin on her face.

Arlan had to smile. He was happy for Kaleigh. She'd been waiting for more than a year for Rob to die and be reborn. She was ready for a boyfriend. Rob Hill had been her original mate more than a thousand years ago and would be her only mate for the rest of eternity.

Arlan and Macy walked past the bonfire. They kept walking until they were alone, beyond the city limits, at a section of beach that backed up to the wildlife preserve.

"How about here?" Arlan asked, standing back far

enough from the water that the incoming tide wouldn't wet the towel.

Macy turned slowly in a circle, taking in the dark night. Pale sand stretched to her left and right as far as she could see. Behind them were dunes, in front of them, the Delaware Bay, stretching into the vast Atlantic Ocean.

"This is perfect," she said softly. She sat down on the brightly colored beach towel, making room for Arlan. It was a warm night, but the breeze coming off the ocean was cool. She was glad she had gone back for her sweatshirt. She peered into the sky. There would be a full moon again in a couple of days. "You think he's looking at the moon right now?" she asked, turning toward Arlan. "I think he is."

"Macy . . ."

She knew Arlan wanted to comfort her, he just didn't know what to say. What was there *to* say?

She put her hands behind her and leaned back on her elbows, so that she could look up at the moon hanging low on the horizon. A rising moon. "You didn't ask me why he didn't kill me. I divulged my dirty secret more than a week ago and no one has asked."

"I was trying to respect your privacy." He lay back beside her, tucking his arm under his head. "I thought you would tell me when you were ready. If you wanted to."

She turned her head to scrutinize him. "Are you human?"

He seemed so startled by her question that he took a moment to respond. "Excuse me?"

"Are you human or are you some kind of creature from another planet? A creature created merely for the pleasure of women?"

He laughed.

"Because you just don't act like guys do. You're way too good a listener. And frankly, you're way too nice."

"Well, thank you." He looked up at the sky again, frowning. "I think."

She lay back beside him. "And what about Fia? Why hasn't she asked me why I didn't end up in a grave under that tree?"

"You know Fia. I think she wanted to read the official report first."

"Ah. To be sure I hadn't made the whole thing up to look like the poor, terrorized victim."

"She's a good person, Macy." Macy could hear the smile in his voice. "She just likes to be thorough," he explained.

Macy stared at the dark sky, trying not to think about the moon on the horizon. Trying not to think about Teddy, who she knew was thinking about her. She had told Fia she didn't believe in psychic abilities, but she had lied. It was a phenomenon she had been trying to deny for years. What else could this be, this bizarre connection she had with him, this tie she couldn't break?

"That night I had a fight with my mom at dinner," Macy started slowly. "I wanted to go with my new boyfriend to hear some garage band in the next town over. It was a school night and Mom said no. She was concerned about the friends I was hanging with, and with good reason. They weren't bad kids, but they were drinking, smoking pot, driving too fast. You know, kids-headed-for-trouble stuff." She exhaled. "Anyway. Mom said no. She didn't like the guy I was dating. He was older than I was. Seventeen. She was afraid we were having sex, which we were, but I resented being accused. I went to my dad to ask if I could go, but he checked with my mom, so I was really in trouble then."

Arlan was quiet as he listened.

"I was so angry with them that I sulked through dinner. She made pork chops and homemade macaroni and cheese," Macy recalled. When she closed her eyes, she could still smell her mother's farmhouse kitchen. "They made me sit at the dinner table with the family, even though I refused to eat." Her voice caught in her throat as the images flashed in her head like pages in a photo album. "I was mean to my two little sisters. I said ugly things."

Arlan rolled onto his side, propping his head up with his elbow on the towel. When he spoke, his voice was husky with emotion and she loved him for that.

"You were only fifteen years old," he said.

She kept staring at the sky. She couldn't look him in the face, she was so ashamed. "After dinner, I was sent to my room. I played my music loud until my dad threatened to ground me for a week. After they went to sleep, I sneaked out the window. I walked down our lane, through the orchard that ran on both sides of the road. Most of the trees had been planted by my granddad. My dad was so proud of that orchard. There were lots of people with big orchards in the area and ours was small, but he loved it."

She was quiet for a moment. It had been a while since she'd allowed these memories. "I met my boyfriend at the end of the lane, got in his car and we drove away. I went to hear the band. I stayed out all night, just to"—again, her voice cracked—"get back at my parents."

This was so hard, harder than she thought it would be. She hadn't spoken of these events since she was interviewed by the police. The day they carried the bodies of her mother, father, and two sisters away in ambulances.

Ambulances. It had seemed silly as Macy had watched them drive down the lane. What was the point? Her folks and her sisters had been dead for hours. She remembered thinking at the time, *don't you call a hearse for dead people?*

"Apparently, Teddy went to the farmhouse sometime around midnight. I was probably sitting in that garage, listening to that stupid band when he let himself in with the key under the stone in the front flower bed. He killed them all in their beds. Strangled them. Then he carried them one by one to the orchard. He didn't actually bury them, he just dug up some ground and laid them in it. They were posed." Without thinking, she crossed her arms over her chest.

Realizing what she'd done, she let her arms fall to her sides. "So, my family died and I lived because I sneaked out of the house to party with my boyfriend."

"Ah, Macy." Arlan rubbed her arm, covered in goose bumps.

"I should have been there," she whispered.

"No."

Although she did not cry, something close to a sob rose in her throat. "I should have died with them. They were my family. I should have been with them."

"No, no you shouldn't have." He leaned over her, pressing his hand against her cheek, forcing her to turn her head and look at him. His dark eyes penetrated the film of sorrow on hers. "Listen to me. It *wasn't meant to be*," he said. "You weren't meant to die that night."

"That's ridiculous." She couldn't seem to catch her breath and she suddenly felt dizzy. "I would have, had I been there."

"So *you* weren't meant to be there."

He was still so close that she could feel his breath on her face and for a moment, it seemed as if she let him breathe for her.

"You don't understand." She squeezed her eyes shut.

"No, I don't. But you don't either. There are some things we can't understand, Macy. Maybe we aren't meant to."

"He sent me a condolence card with the obituary in it. Then, over the next three years, while I bounced around in foster care, he sent me clippings from newspapers. Those ridiculous pictures of the little boys. Three years after he killed my family, he killed another. And the asshole had the nerve to send me that obituary, too."

"We'll get him, Macy."

"Why me?" she asked. "Why couldn't he just leave me alone?"

"I don't know. But Fia—"

"Fia's not going to find him. It's not going to end." Her jaw trembled. "It's never going to end until he chooses to end it."

He looked into her eyes, smoothing back her hair. "You don't know that."

Macy lifted her head until her lips met his. She kissed him hard, silencing him. She didn't want to talk about this anymore. She didn't want to feel this way.

She wrapped her arms around Arlan, pushing him onto his back. She climbed on top of him, flattening her body over his. They kissed deeply, tongues entwining.

She just wanted the agony to go away.

Macy sat up, panting, and unzipped her sweatshirt. The T-shirt came off next. The cool ocean breeze and the erection growing in Arlan's shorts made her nipples pucker. She yanked his T-shirt over his head, knocking his glasses into the sand.

They kissed again and she ended up on her back, him on top this time. They lay halfway on the towel, halfway in the sand. He kissed her mouth and then he did that amazing thing he did with his mouth on her neck. She moaned softly, dragging her fingers through his salty hair.

"It's all right, Macy," he whispered in her ear.

She didn't want to hear soft words of encouragement. She just wanted to feel him inside her.

Macy slid her hand downward, between them, over the bulge in Arlan's shorts. He groaned and she massaged him roughly.

He kissed her face, her neck, and then her breasts. She dug her nails into the flesh of his back, mad for him.

"Take them off. Take them off," she panted, struggling to get her shorts off.

"Shhh," he hushed in her ear. He pushed her hands aside, raised up and sat on his heels between her legs, and smoothly unbuttoned her jeans shorts. In the semidarkness, he made eye contact with her as slid her shorts down, over her thighs, over her knees and then her feet.

"Yours, too." She closed her eyes, unable to stand the scrutiny of his gaze. He didn't understand what a bad person she was. He didn't understand. They died and she didn't. What right did she have to live?

Arlan stood up in the sand to take off his shorts and she opened her eyes to watch. She had always loved men's bodies. Loved the hard, planed muscles, the anatomy that was different than her own. She put her arms out to him, parting her legs, brushing her fingers across her blond tuft of hair. She was already wet for him. Pulsing with need.

He knelt and then climbed over her. "Me on top, you on top?" he asked huskily, straightening the towel so that her head didn't rest in the sand.

"You on top." She lifted her hips, needing to feel him hot and hard inside her.

He smoothed her hair, kissing her temple. His gesture was tender, but tenderness wasn't what she needed. Tenderness didn't make her feel alive. Passion did.

Macy clasped Arlan's narrow hips and lifted off the towel, opening herself up to him. She moaned with satisfaction as he drove deep. This was the one part of her that Arlan did understand. He pushed hard into her and she welcomed his thrusts again and again.

Macy wrapped her arms around his neck and held tightly as she rode the waves of building pleasure. A part of her wanted to make these few minutes last for hours, but the need for release was greater than the need for lingering gratification. She rocked beneath him, moaning.

Arlan whispered her name in her ear.

Macy had once read that simultaneous orgasm was rarely possible with a couple. Certainly not common. Did that mean Arlan was the perfect lover, or were they just perfect together?

All too soon, the pressure inside Macy swelled until it burst. Every muscle in her body seemed to contract and release as the orgasm rippled through her. She clung to Arlan and he grunted and pushed hard into her one last time. He collapsed over her, cradling her in his arms as he rolled onto his side. Macy nestled her head on Arlan's shoulder, pressing her face into his damp, musky skin. The air smelled thick with the salt of the ocean and the scent of lovemaking and Macy breathed deep, wishing this could be the end of her life, instead of what was coming.

In clean boxers and a T-shirt, Teddy sat down with a cup of chamomile tea to watch the eleven o'clock news. His mother had often given him chamomile tea to help him sleep. He hated the taste, no matter how much honey he put in it, but if Mother said it was good for him, it had to be.

He picked up the remote and turned the channel to the local Philadelphia station. It was nice to be home. While he had a teenaged neighbor check on his house and water his flowers when he was gone, Teddy never liked to be away from home too long.

The first piece that ran on the nightly news was a report on the Liberty Bell and how many U. S. citizens visited it each year. Then a piece on the rising crime rate in the city. Homicides were down, but assaults and robberies were up. Good thing he lived in the country, away from the crime and pollution. The next piece featured a schoolgirl collecting used eyeglasses for poor, elderly citizens on her block in downtown Philly. When the station flashed a Post Office box number where donations could be made, Teddy jotted it down. He liked the smile on the little girl's face and he liked the idea that a young person was trying to help the less fortunate. He would send a donation.

Teddy was sipping his hot tea when Senator Malley's handsome face flashed on the screen. Apparently he was the grand marshal in his Independence Day hometown parade today. How nice. Teddy smiled at the sight of the children with their cotton candy and red, white, and blue balloons. As the senator said something about our founding fathers, the camera panned the crowd. A face caught his attention. A face he recognized.

Teddy nearly spilled his tea setting his cup down. A woman passed behind the crowd in the camera shot. She was only on the TV screen for a split second, but it was long enough. It was Marceline! It was Teddy's Marceline, and she was in Clare Point, Delaware.

He sat back in his recliner, flabbergasted. It had been years since he had known exactly where she was. She always kept moving. She was smart, his Marceline. Even though he'd been worshipping her from afar for a very long time, he could not have necessarily found her if he wanted to. But now he knew where she was.

Was this divine intervention?

Was it time for them to be together?

It was. Teddy was sure of it.

Chapter 26

"It's all true," Fia stated incredulously.

Arlan shifted his cell phone to his other ear and opened the barbeque grill on his back deck. He was surprised to hear the animation in her voice. When he'd talked to her this morning, she had sounded plain worn out from pulling another all-nighter. "What's true?"

"Everything she said about her family being murdered in Missouri. It happened just the way she said it did."

"You thought she made the whole thing up?" He checked the heat coming off the grill with the palm of his hand. He was hoping to get dinner made before the skies opened up. He could smell the rain thick and heavy on the night air.

"It's not as if she has a history of being truthful and forthright with me."

"I knew it was the truth," he said. Satisfied the grill was hot enough, he placed two steaks on it, leaving the skewered shrimp on the plate on the table. "It was too bizarre, too . . . tragic a story to make up. That tragedy was the profound sadness I saw in her face that first night."

"Please don't get sappy on me, Arlan. I'm hanging here by an emotional thread."

"You're upset about this? A case, Special Agent Kahill?" he mocked, only half joking. A part of him was just a little annoyed that she hadn't had more faith in Macy. Maybe in him. "That's not like you."

"It's not just the case. It's . . ."

He turned his back to the grill. It was after eight and growing dark. Insects chirped in an overgrown flower bed off the end of the deck. It was hot and humid and the atmospheric pressure was dropping. A thunderstorm was building. He could smell it in the air. "He broke up with you."

"We broke up. It was a mutual agreement and I don't want to talk about it right now."

"Okay," Arlan said. "Later?"

"Sure. Later, after I've arrested this Teddy bastard." She hesitated. "It was a bad day all around. I also talked to Regan."

"And?" He poked at a steak with a fork.

She exhaled.

"He confessed to being involved in coke," he said for her. "Fee, I know how hard this is for you—"

"He didn't exactly admit to anything," she interrupted. "He did say he had *some problems*. I've got a call in to the rehab place in London and he's agreed to go."

"That's great news, Fee."

"Okay, back to the problem at hand," she said, sounding like Special Agent Kahill again. "Here's what I've got. None of the names connected to any of Teddy's murders have cross-matched, but now I have a list of all the people the police talked to at the time of Macy's family's murder. I have lists of neighbors, teachers, repairmen, business associates, you name it. Macy's the only one who's ever survived; he's obsessed with her. Her family was the first he killed. The connection is Macy. Our man has got to be on this list," she said emphatically. "I've been running everyone through the system. I stayed up all night."

Arlan was tempted to push Fia back toward the conversation concerning Glen, but he thought better of it. Work was how she always got through her personal pain.

So he would talk about what she wanted to talk about. He'd help her any way he could. "Any possibilities, so far, on this list of names?"

"Maybe. There's one guy who's just fallen off the face of the earth. Someone who worked with Macy's father. I talked to his ex-wife last night. She says she hasn't seen him in fourteen years."

"So he fell off the radar about the time of the murders?" Arlan sat down in one of the chairs on the deck. Macy had said she was coming for dinner. She was late. More than half an hour late, which wasn't like her. He couldn't help wondering if this was it. Had she flown?

"Anybody else?" Arlan reached for the bottle of beer at his feet.

"Let's see." Fia sounded as if she was scanning the list. "Got a traveling salesman. Unmarried. Lives with his elderly mother. "

"Good possibility."

"Definitely. He lives in New Jersey, has for years. The software company he works for operates mostly on the East Coast."

"Sounding better all the time."

"Who knows? But I have a call in to his employer."

"Sounds like you've got a good start." He hesitated. "Fia, you're going to get him. I know you are."

"Going through these names is going to take days. My boss actually gave the okay to bring in another agent from our office to help me rather than waiting on those guys from the Baltimore field office to arrive, or have me join them in Baltimore. But I was thinking that I'd like Macy to look at the list. See if there's anyone in particular she thinks we should check into."

"I imagine the Missouri police did that at the time of her family's death."

"Sure, but she was fifteen and in shock. And things look different from a distance. Maybe she's far enough from the murders now that she can be more objective. She there with you?"

"No, but she should be on her way."

"I called her cell. It's still connected, but she didn't answer." Fia sounded annoyed. "She swore to me she'd answer if I called."

"She's running late. Maybe she was in the shower." His words sounded perfectly logical, but rang hollow in his own ears. Arlan wasn't the paranoid type, but with every passing moment, he was growing concerned.

"Why don't you fax me the list?" he said. "I'll have her look it over after dinner and then call you."

"I don't know."

He could hear the hesitation in her voice.

"The FBI doesn't take kindly to agents faxing sensitive stuff like this to civilians."

"Fia, do you hear yourself? You're talking about faxing it to *me*. You've known me forever." And as if she could have forgotten, he added, "And that's *eternal* forever. You know I'm not going to let the information fall into the wrong hands."

"I don't know. I guess I kind of wanted to be there to see her reaction when she read over the list."

"Fine, then." Arlan tried not to be perturbed. He knew that sometimes Fia had to follow conventional rules. She had to, in order to remain the most effective in her job. He knew it wasn't easy living and working among mortals. "Come tomorrow. You know she's not coming to you. Hell, come tonight if you want." He tipped back the beer bottle, finishing it off while she thought about it.

"No," she said. "You're right. I need to stay here where I have access to the bureau computers."

Realizing that the steaks had been on for five minutes, Arlan bolted out of his chair. If steak wasn't bloody rare, it was ruined. "I'll go make sure the fax machine is on. Give me five minutes. We'll call you after dinner."

"Okay. Okay, thanks, Arlan," Fia said. "For everything."

He dropped his cell into his pocket and reached for the tongs. Damn it. He hated to waste perfectly good bloody steaks.

When Macy stepped out of the bathroom, towel wrapped around her, her hair bundled on her head in another towel, she wasn't surprised by the man sitting on the end of her bed. Adrenaline shot through her body, but the fact remained that, in a way, she was almost relieved he was here. This was it. Live or die, she knew her nightmare was finally coming to an end.

"Marceline," he said as he picked up the remote and turned on the TV, cranking up the volume.

"Teddy." She just stood there in the bathroom doorway, naked except for the towel.

"It's a full moon," he said. "You just can't see it. The rain."

She always wondered if she would recognize him if she saw him. She did not. He looked entirely ordinary and nothing like she thought he would. He was at least forty-five, though he seemed fit. Receding hairline. Soft jaw. He was wearing a polo shirt and madras shorts. Madras shorts, for God's sake. Who expected a serial killer whose kill numbers were so high to wear blue madras? And black Velcro sandals.

Had she spotted him before, the sandals would have been a giveaway, she joked to herself. Only a killer could have taste that bad.

"The full moon," she repeated numbly. "I should have guessed."

"Please don't scream," he said quietly. "Or try to run." His voice was gentle. Calm. He tried to avert his gaze as he spoke. "Others will only . . . get hurt."

"So you're going to play that card again?" she asked, tucking the edge of the wet towel under her armpit. "That's getting a little old."

"You know I'll do it. And you know it will be *your* fault."

He slipped his hand inside a white fast food bag that she hadn't noticed on the bed beside him. He withdrew a gun. A very expensive-looking gun, with a silencer.

How the hell did a man like Crazy Teddy, Moon Boy, the Buried Alive Killer manage to buy a gun like that? It wasn't for hunting, or target practice; it was a gun meant to kill—kill people.

"It was purchased perfectly legally," he said, seeming to know exactly what she was thinking. "The silencer." He looked apologetic. "Not so legal." He turned it in his hand, admiring it. "You'd be amazed what can be bought over the Internet."

Macy shivered. She'd turned the air-conditioning up before stepping into the shower because she'd gotten hot, walking around town. Sort of saying good-bye, she saw in retrospect.

But she'd thought leaving would involve a couple of good-byes, a farewell wave, one more Oreo Cookie Blizzard for the road, not a handgun with a silencer.

Macy was late for Arlan's surf and turf dinner. She'd be even later now.

In the back of her mind, she wondered if he would come looking for her. But she knew he wouldn't. He would follow the rules they had laid down from the beginning, rules she had set in place, and that would mean not coming to look for her. Not at least for many hours, maybe a day, maybe two.

Her gaze shifted to the phone beside the bed. Next to it had been her cell phone. She looked back at him.

"Of course you can't make calls. Who are you going to call, your mommy?" He chuckled at his stupid, cruel joke.

Macy walked to the dresser and opened the top drawer. She let her towel fall.

Teddy surprised her by jumping off the bed and turning away, both hands up in defense. He still held the pistol. "Please . . . please don't do that. I won't tolerate that kind of licentious behavior from you, any longer, young lady."

She ignored him. First she stepped into a pair of gym shorts. Then a faded blue T-shirt. *What did one wear to one's death?*

She pulled the towel off her head and let her wet hair fall over her back.

"You going to do it here, or somewhere else?" She picked her brush up off the dresser, feeling oddly detached from the whole situation.

"Going to do what?"

She turned to face him, giving him a look as if what she spoke of was obvious.

He gasped. "Oh! No, no, Marceline, dearest. I don't want to *kill* you." He took a step toward her, lowering the gun to his side. "I've come for you. It's time."

She held the brush at her side, looking at the madman who didn't appear all that mad, except for the pistol with the silencer at his side. And the Velcro sandals. "It's time for what?"

"My love, for us to be together, of course." The expression on his face softened. "Forever," he breathed.

She turned around to face the mirror and run the brush through her wet, tangled hair. "You have got to be shitting me," she muttered under her breath.

"Hey, hey, turn around."

She could see his reflection in the mirror. He was waving the pistol at her. "We have no time for grooming. We have to go. I'll allow you to pack your bag if you hurry. But we have to go. It's a long ride and the storm is rolling in fast. The roads will be slick and dangerous."

Macy had always assumed that when he came for her, he would just kill her. It had never occurred to her that he might kidnap her. She tried not to think about why he would take her or what he was going to do. She just needed to figure how she was going to get away from him without putting anyone else in danger. "Where are we going?" she asked.

He lifted her knapsack off the floor and tentatively offered it to her, a glowing smile on his face. "Home, of course, darling."

"I'll take Marvin Gardens." Kaleigh, lying on her stomach on the carpet in her parents' basement, handed over the paper money. Her mom had been annoyed that her friends hadn't even arrived until nine and Monopoly games could go on for hours. But Kaleigh's dad had convinced his wife it was perfectly safe to go to bed and leave the "young folks" to play a board game in the basement on a rainy night.

"Stay in the house and don't wreck anything", her dad had warned.

"No problem, Dad," had been Kaleigh's response. Where had he thought she was going to go in the rain?

"You can't buy Marvin Gardens. I've got Ventnor and Atlantic," Pete, Katy's on-again, off-again boyfriend, protested.

Like Kaleigh and Rob, Pete and Katy were life mates. But sept rules didn't require that they date exclusively while teenagers, only that they pair off as adults. Katy broke up with Pete at least once a month, just to show she could, but they always ended up back together again after a few days of drama.

"Too bad for you, Petey." Kaleigh plucked the card from Rob. Rob was serving as the banker because everyone agreed he was least likely to steal money from the till.

"I hate it when she calls me Petey," Pete told Katy.

"Too bad for you, Petey," Katy mimicked Kaleigh. But then, to appease him, she leaned over and nipped at his ear.

"Hey, you're not supposed to be drawing blood," Pete complained, but then his tone turned daring. "Not unless it's right here." He exposed his neck and he and Katy giggled.

"My turn." Rob scooped up the dice, obviously uncomfortable with the exchange.

Rob knew he was a vampire and had been told what it entailed, but Kaleigh sensed that he didn't entirely understand the innate craving for blood that he would develop over time. That, she knew, would come whether the desire was wanted or not.

"Come on, Pennsylvania Railroad." Rob blew on the dice before rolling them.

"Anyone want something to drink?" Kaleigh got up to go to the mini refrigerator her parents kept in the basement.

"I'll take a vodka and cranberry," Pete snickered.

Ignoring him, Kaleigh opened the door. "We've got water, Coke, and Gatorade."

"Okay, Gatorade," Pete called. "Red, if you've got it."

"Water, please," Katy ordered.

"Rob?" Kaleigh leaned down and reached into the refrigerator, intending to grab the bottles.

Just as she bent forward, she grew light-headed. At the same instance, thunder cracked outside and she saw a flash of light through one of the basement's uncovered windows.

"Whoa." She tried to straighten, but another flash blinded her. This time it was not lightning; it was in the room. Behind the light she saw the silhouettes of two people, people who *were not* in the room with her.

"No," Kaleigh groaned, pressing her hand to the wall to steady herself. These *flash forwards,* as Katy had started calling them, were getting annoying. Kaleigh wasn't in the mood for this. She didn't want to be the town's wisewoman tonight. She just wanted to play Monopoly with her friends and make out with Rob on the couch after Kaleigh and Pete went home.

"You okay?" she heard Rob's voice from what seemed a good distance off, though she knew he was only a few feet away.

Kaleigh still felt dizzy. The room spun. She saw the silhouettes again, from the back. They were in a car, these two people. It was like Kaleigh was in the backseat. She smelled the rain, heard the slap of windshield wipers.

She also felt the fear. Cold, shivering fear.

"Macy?" she whispered.

"Kaleigh." Rob grabbed her arm and she clung to him for support. But she couldn't look at Rob, only at the car seat and the people in front of her.

It was Arlan's human friend, Macy . . . she had entered the car against her will.

Kaleigh slowly turned her head, as if she could somehow get a better look at the person behind the wheel. Suddenly she smelled a stench that startled her so badly that she pulled back.

"Kaleigh?" Rob's voice again. Almost frantic now. "Katy! Katy get over here."

Kaleigh smelled wet fur and something like dog urine. She squeezed her eyes shut, more than just a little freaked out.

But the images didn't dissolve.

She saw Macy's wet hair and her pale skin as she turned to look at the driver. He was holding a gun on her. Macy was trying to be brave, but she was scared. Scared she was going to die. Kaleigh looked up into the rearview mirror in her mind's eye and caught a glimpse of the man in the driver's seat.

"Oh, my God," she breathed. Her eyes flew open. The images vanished. Rob stood on one side of her and Katy on the other, each holding one of her arms, staring at her with big, startled eyes.

"Another vision?" Katy asked.

Kaleigh pressed her lips together and nodded as she fought to prevent Macy's emotions from becoming her own. "I . . . I have to find Arlan," she said in a half whisper. *"Now."* She looked at Pete. "Can you take me in my parents' minivan? To Arlan?"

"You can't just call him?" Katy asked.

Kaleigh shook her head. She had to go. She didn't know why, but she had to.

"Kaleigh?" Rob gazed into her eyes.

"It's okay," she murmured, trying to smile so he wouldn't be scared. She freed her hand from Katy's grasp and turned and smoothed his cheek with her fingertips. He needed a shave. Stray whiskers were sprouting here and there, as they first did in early puberty. She remembered far in the recesses of her mind that she enjoyed Rob's face a little scratchy against her skin. "Don't worry. You'll get used to this," she told Rob gently.

He swallowed and his Adam's apple bobbed. "You need to go see Arlan?"

She nodded.

Rob glanced over his shoulder at Pete and then at Kaleigh again. "Okay, but I'm going, too."

"Me, too!" Katy cried, acting as if this was some great adventure.

Still unsteady on her feet, Kaleigh allowed Rob to lead her up the stairs. The four teens were quiet in the dark kitchen. Kaleigh snatched her mother's key chain, the one with the blue rubber Smurf on it, and they slipped out the back door, one after the other.

A hard rain pelted and thunder rumbled. Lightning streaked the sky a few miles in the distance.

They piled into the minivan. Pete was the only one of them who could legally drive unchaperoned. Not that that was going to help if her parents found out they had "borrowed" the car.

"Arlan's?" Pete asked, backing cautiously down the driveway. He didn't turn on the headlights until they were half a block away from the house. In the front passenger seat, Kaleigh turned to peer back, but saw no light in the upstairs window. With any luck at all, they'd be back in twenty minutes and her parents would be none-the-wiser. "Yeah. Arlan's," she told Pete as she faced forward again.

But halfway there, speeding down the wet street, Kaleigh got the strangest feeling. A voice in her head, but not a voice. A command so strong, she had to obey it. "No, no turn here," she ordered Pete.

Pete squealed wheels, making the sharp left.

"You're going to get us in trouble." Katy slapped Pete's arm from the backseat. "Slow down."

"The Lighthouse Hotel," Kaleigh told him. She didn't know why, but she had to go to the hotel.

Speeding only a little, Pete had her there in less than five minutes. The instant they pulled up in front of the hotel, Kaleigh knew why she had been sent here. *The voice had been right. The voice was a good thing.*

Arlan's truck was pulled catty-corner into a parking space at the end of the parking lot. Kaleigh jumped out of the van and ran down the sidewalk. Before she reached the parking lot, she saw Arlan standing in the rain. He was on his cell phone.

Kaleigh rushed toward him. Her hair was getting wetter by the second. Soon, it would be plastered to her face, which was really annoying because she'd spent an hour straightening it before Rob arrived tonight.

"Macy's in trouble," she yelled, running across the parking lot toward Arlan. Her lavender flip-flops made a *slip-slapping* sound on the wet pavement.

"Hold on," Arlan said into the phone. "It's Kaleigh." He lowered the phone, listening. "You know something about Macy?"

"I saw her. She's in trouble. She's in a car with this . . . this—" Kaleigh didn't know what to say because she didn't know who or what the thing was.

"You *saw* her?" Arlan asked. He was wetter than she was. It was odd, but with his T-shirt plastered to his chest and transparent and his wet hair curling in tendrils at his chin, he didn't look any older to Kaleigh than Rob did. "I didn't *see* her, see her," Kaleigh explained, trying to calm down. "It was a vision. I haven't really been telling people, but I'm getting the visions," she confessed, suddenly close to tears.

"Kaleigh had a vision," Arlan said into the phone. "Macy's in a car with someone. It has to be him."

"It has to be who?" Kaleigh asked. Her heart was pounding and the rain was beating on her face. "Arlan, this was the weirdest thing—"

But Arlan wasn't listening to her, he was listening to . . . Fia. It was Fia on the other end of the line. Of course it was. When he spoke with that tone, it was always Fia. Had been for centuries.

"Her car's not here. They took it. I'm sure they took it. Mrs. Cahall's nephew saw them leave around eight forty-five," he said into the phone. "He must have made her get into the car, which means . . ." He spun around, glancing around the parking lot. "He must have left his car here. The car has to be here somewhere, Fee!"

He paused, listening to Fia. "Okay, okay, I'll start getting license plates. I'll talk to Kaleigh and then call you back." He snapped the phone shut. Having parked the minivan on the street, Pete, Rob, and Katy ran across the parking lot toward them.

"You have to tell me what you saw. Where were they going?" Arlan asked.

Kaleigh shook her head, fighting the fear creeping under her skin again. That thing in the front seat had spooked her. What was it? She wanted to ask Arlan, but was afraid to. What if her imagination had been playing tricks on her? That was possible, wasn't it? If it was possible in life, wasn't it possible in visions? After all, it was still just her interpretation of a scene, or whatever.

"Kaleigh, this is important." Arlan clasped her arm, looking into her eyes. "Macy's in serious trouble. I think she was kidnapped by the Buried Alive Killer."

"The Buried Alive Killer?" Kaleigh looked at him, trying to mesh what she had seen with what her uncle was saying. That didn't make sense. The Buried Alive Killer was a human, flesh and blood and bone. "You sure?"

The three teens came to a splashing halt beside Kaleigh.

"What's going on?" Katy demanded.

"Arlan thinks Macy, you know, the human photographer who's been taking pictures all over town, that she's been kidnapped by the Buried Alive Killer. That's who I saw in my vision. It was Macy."

"Holy hell," Pete swore.

Kaleigh felt Rob's warm touch on her wet, cold, bare arm. He didn't respond immediately, but he didn't need to.

"Tell me exactly what you saw," Arlan said. "She was in a car?"

Macy nodded.

"Her car? A blue Honda."

"I don't know." Kaleigh wiped rain from her eyes. It was pelting so hard that it hurt. "But he was driving. This . . . guy. Macy was scared. I think he had a gun." As she spoke, more truths came to her. "She couldn't get away from him. She was afraid he would hurt someone else if she tried to run."

"You know where they were going?"

Kaleigh shook her head.

"You think you can help me find her?"

Kaleigh meant to say no, but before the word came out of her mouth, she realized, somewhere in the back of her mind, she felt a string. A thread really . . . connecting her to this human she barely knew. It hadn't been there when she went to the refrigerator for the drinks, but now it was. "Maybe," she whispered, looking up earnestly into her uncle's eyes. "But I'm scared. I don't like this."

"It's okay to be scared." He reached out and touched her cheek with the palm of his hand. His touch only lasted a second, but it was reassuring. It made her feel strong, maybe even a little confident. He believed in her, even if she didn't believe in herself.

"You want to help?" Arlan asked the other teens.

"Sure. Yeah," they chimed in.

"No. They have to take my parents' van back," Kaleigh insisted, panic fluttering in her chest again. "I'll be grounded until I'm dead again if they catch me."

"Kaleigh, they'll understand," Arlan said.

"No, they won't. I'm already in trouble. I don't want to get grounded."

He looked at her, his wet face illuminated by the neon lights of the hotel's sign. "You think they haven't been through this before, hon?" he asked gently.

That thought had never occurred to her until this very

moment. She'd been a wisewoman and their daughter for fifteen hundred years. Of course Michael and Cassie had dealt with her visions before. And probably all the crazy behavior that went along with them.

Arlan turned to the teens. "Kaleigh and I have to go, but I need you guys to start writing down license plates of any vehicle you don't recognize. Start in this parking lot and then down the streets in a two-block perimeter around the hotel. Work your way out." He glanced at Kaleigh. "If they took her car, he must have left his here. There's no other way to get into town except by car." He turned back to her friends. "Somebody got a cell?"

"I do!" Katy was practically bouncing with excitement as she held up her phone.

Arlan turned to Kaleigh. "You've got her number, right?" She nodded.

"Okay, Katy, someone from the FBI will be calling you for plate numbers."

"The FBI? Cool."

"It might be Fia, but maybe someone else. You give them the plate numbers. They need the state and the plate."

Kaleigh felt Rob's hand on her shoulder. "You going to be okay with this?" he whispered, his mouth close to her ear.

She pressed her lips together, afraid she might start to cry. She was scared, but she knew this was her destiny. Aiding the sept in this way. Always had been, always would be. She didn't understand what this human had to do with her people, but there had to be a reason why she was being called. "I'll be fine," she assured Rob, sounding like she meant it.

"You want me to come with you?"

She smiled, squeezing his forearm. "I have to do this myself," she told him.

Arlan grabbed Kaleigh's hand. "Come on, we need to get on the road."

She hurried after him, letting him lead the way. As they ran, water sprayed from under their feet, soaking them further. "But how are we going to know which direction to go?" she shouted.

Over his shoulder, above the sound of the drumming rain, she heard Arlan's voice. "You're going to tell me."

Chapter 27

"Please take your hand off the door handle, Marceline," Teddy said calmly. "Surely you don't intend to jump from the car. You're going sixty-three miles an hour." He glanced at the steering wheel. "Hands at ten and two, please."

Macy lifted her cold fingers off the door handle. The stupid thing was that Teddy was right. Jumping *would* mean suicide, and while Macy knew she was in pretty serious trouble, she wasn't ready to choose that option. "You're making me nervous with the gun," she said, trying to sound as if she was scared. Which of course she was, but she had assessed pretty quickly that Teddy wanted to be the alpha male in this screwed up relationship. He wanted to protect her. He wanted her to be frightened so he could come to her rescue. He wanted her to be complacent so he could manipulate her. Macy could pretend to be whatever he wanted, if it might save her life.

He had forced her into the driver's seat and ordered her to take Route ! North from Clare Point. Two hours later, they were now going around the southeastern end of Philadelphia on 495. The rain had let up as the storm passed, but the pavement was still wet and motorists drove cautiously. She had thought of trying to get the attention of someone in a passing car, but decided against it. It probably wouldn't be easy to do, anyway. People in cars were behind glass, locked in their own worlds. They didn't see the passing scenery or the serial killer driving next to them. And if she did attempt to get someone's attention, Teddy would realize what she was doing, and then she'd be putting an innocent person's life in jeopardy.

"I'm sorry, dear. I only kept it out to remind you that you have to behave."

"But I am behaving." She looked up at him through lowered lashes, the submissive words practically sticking in her craw. Streetlamps zipping by cast fleeting arcs of yellow light across his face, making him look pretty creepy. "In the hotel lobby and in the parking lot, I did just what you told me to." Her words were as close to a simper as she could manage.

"Tsk, tsk. No fibbing, Marceline. You did as you were told because you were afraid I would shoot that nice grandma behind the front desk in the face. Then you were concerned about the kids on the skateboards in the parking lot."

Teddy was right. Again. She'd allowed him to march her right out the front door of the hotel lobby with half a dozen people within shouting distance. He'd threatened to kill someone else should she attempt to flee. She'd hoped for a chance to get away in the parking lot, but there had been boys there, hoodies up, skateboarding in the rain. Teddy said he would shoot them, and then he would shoot her. Then himself, if necessary. He said he had decided a long time ago that he would never allow himself to be taken into custody. He had been quite chatty. He had also told her that he was a good shot. She hoped he was lying, but she wasn't in a position to test him.

"Please, Teddy. Could you put it away?" Macy asked, turning off the windshield wipers. "I was resting my arm on the door, trying to stay away from the gun, is all. I told you I would go with you and I am, right? I'm going with you."

"You promise you'll behave?"

"I swear it on my mother's grave, Teddy."

He looked at her shyly. "You . . . want to come with me, don't you? You've wanted me to come for you for a long time. You understand we're meant to be together?"

Pretending to concentrate on the road, she chose her words carefully. "I'm with you, right? That's what's important, isn't it? That I'm with you and that no one gets hurt."

"No one gets hurt if you're with me," he repeated. He lowered the gun to the floor of the car, under his feet. "That better?"

He'd moved it even further out of her reach. "Better," she said, glancing quickly at him, then ahead again.

Macy stared longingly out the windshield as they passed Philadelphia airport. She remembered the flight home from New Orleans, sitting next to Arlan, her head on his shoulder as she dozed. That had been a flicker of happiness in her life. She never thought she was ever happy, but she was wrong. There had been other moments, too. Making love to Arlan on the beach on the Fourth of July. Sharing a cold beer with him on his back step. Watching kids fly kites in Clare Point's park. Eating cookies with Eva in her cozy kitchen.

Macy'd had more happy moments, especially in the last few weeks, than she had ever cared to admit to herself. So maybe this was okay, dying at Teddy's hands now. She'd been happy for a few fleeting moments. Maybe that was as much as she could expect out of life. As much as anyone could expect.

But then she looked at him, at the pathetic man who had murdered her family. Who had murdered all those innocent, unsuspecting families. And she decided it wasn't okay to die today. And it wasn't okay for him to kill her. Macy didn't know what life had in store for her, but she knew those few fleeting moments of happiness weren't enough. They just weren't.

She looked at him again, this time for a second longer before returning her attention to the road. "Do I know you?" she asked, trying to stir some memory from the far recesses of her mind. She *should* recognize him. She had always suspected she might have known him, although neither she nor the police had been able to come up with any viable suspects at the time of her family's death.

"Eyes on the road," he instructed. "Of course you know me, darling. I'm Teddy."

She shook her head. "No, I mean, I recognize you," she lied. "How do I recognize you? Did you know me—when I was a kid?"

She noticed he tightened his hands into fists at his sides. "No," he said.

"Come on, Teddy," she plied softly. "It's me"—she made herself say the next words because it was about surviving—"your Marceline."

"You . . . you didn't know me. You never would have noticed me. You were so young and pretty." He flushed. "I . . . I had to wait for you to grow up. I'm not a pervert, you know."

"But *you* know me," she suggested, ignoring the possible sexual inference. She could only handle one issue at a time, and fortunately, her virginity wasn't at stake. "You *knew* me."

He nodded, glancing apprehensively at her, then straight ahead.

Still, she tried to wrack her brain. The weird guy at the grocery story where her family had shopped? The one her mother always told Macy and her sisters to stay away from? Or maybe the colleague of her father's who had always been friendlier to a gawky teenager than Macy had thought appropriate. No. Teddy wasn't either of those men. She was still coming up blank. "How did you know me, Teddy?" she pushed, in the sickeningly sweet voice he seemed to like.

He lowered his head, childlike. "I was your neighbor in Lawrenceville. Sort of."

"Our neighbor?" Macy frowned, tightening her grip on the steering wheel. They had lived on a rural road outside town. On one side of her family had lived an elderly couple, the Johnstons. On the other side, there had been a divorced woman and her two young daughters. They had often come to play with Macy's little sisters.

"Down the road from you." He stole another glance.

Macy still had no recollection of him. Fifteen years ago he would have been what, twenty-five, maybe? He was definitely around forty now.

"Lazy Orchards. Remember it? We . . . we sold apples and peaches alongside the road. My mother and I." He stared straight ahead. "Until she died."

"She died?" Macy still couldn't remember Teddy, but she did remember the fruit stand where she and her mother had stopped sometimes for produce. It had to have been at least three miles from her house. Not exactly neighbors. "I'm so sorry," she said, trying to keep up the conversation. "You must miss her."

"I don't." Another glance her way. "The thing is, Marceline, I killed her. I told everyone she married and moved away, but actually I buried her in our orchard."

He said it as if he were telling Macy she *had* just moved away. No regret. Absolutely no sorrow. *Certainly explained the mommy issue.*

The weird thing was that the more she got to know Teddy, the more fascinated she was. It was a repulsed fascination, but a fascination nonetheless, and for the first time, she thought maybe she understood why Fia did what she did.

"Look, dearest." Teddy pointed, smiling. "Our exit."

Arlan drove north on Route 1 through Delaware as fast as his old truck could take and still remain on the road. At least the rain had slowed to a drizzle. As he picked up his ringing cell phone, he glanced at Kaleigh seat-belted in the passenger's side. "Keep going this way?" he said.

"Keep going," Kaleigh repeated, continuing to stare straight ahead.

The teen looked pale and he wondered if he had made a mistake in bringing her along. But when they left Clare Point, it had been his belief that Kaleigh might be his only chance to save Macy. He also wondered if he should have at least called her parents, but Mike and Cassie had been through this many times before and they trusted Arlan and Fia. They knew that the sept came before the immediate family. And right now, even more important than saving Macy, was catching Teddy before he killed another family.

Arlan put the phone to his ear. "Yeah?"

"Nothing so far. None of the cars parked in the area of the hotel are owned by anyone in our Buried Alive database."

"Damn it!" Arlan swore. "What about the rentals?"

"We're running those, but that's going to take longer. I had the kids go back to the rental cars and tell me which companies they came from to speed up the process."

"It makes sense that Teddy would have driven a rental. He could just leave it in Clare Point. Tell the rental company it broke down and to have it towed. It would cost him, but he wouldn't have to show his face in Clare Point again."

"That's what I was thinking," Fia said. She sounded

tired. Maybe a little disheartened. "So what's going on on the Kaleigh front?"

Arlan glanced at the teen. She was still staring straight ahead, hands tucked under her thighs. "She's scared, but she's doing a great job. She says we have to get off this road onto the one near the mall and go north. I'm guessing that's Ninety-five North."

"She know where you're going?" Fia asked.

"Not exactly, but she seems pretty confident of the direction. She says there's a thread between her and Macy. That the thread will lead us to both Macy and the guy who took her."

"Sounds like a hell of a lot more efficient way to nail Teddy's ass than running all these license plates," she said dryly.

Arlan laughed. The situation wasn't all that funny, but he liked the way Fia looked at the world.

"Okay," Fia said, FBI serious again. "I think we let these guys keep running plates, but we go with Kaleigh's lead. I need to meet you. Follow you."

"Okay." He ran his hand through his hair, which was mostly dry, but now clumpy from the rain. "Problem is, we don't know where we're going. Kaleigh says turn on the big road, I turn."

"But you're on Ninety-five North."

"Am now."

"How about I head toward the Philly airport? We can meet there. If you end up turning off before that, give me a ring. I'll catch up."

"Sounds like a plan, but let me check with Kaleigh. She's the one running the show." He lowered his cell. "Fia wants to meet us at the Philadelphia airport."

"I don't think he took her to an airport." Kaleigh narrowed her eyes in thought.

"It's just a good place to meet—on this road, north of

here. If it doesn't work out, if we have to turn before that"—he shrugged—"she can catch up."

She glanced at Arlan, looking very young to him in the dark, with her damp hair hanging in her face. "Think we could stop long enough for me to run in and pee?" she asked hopefully.

"Definitely." He offered a reassuring smile.

She smiled back.

"That's a go, Fia," Arlan said into the phone. "We'll meet you at arrivals. Kaleigh needs to hop out for a sec. You want to join us? It'll be pretty cozy in the cab of the truck."

"I better take a bureau car. I've spoken with the head honchos on the case in the Baltimore field office and they'll wait to hear from me. I've two guys here on call to back us up, should we find anything."

"So we meet at arrivals. Half an hour?"

"Will do."

When Arlan set his cell phone beside him on the truck seat, he saw that Kaleigh was watching him. "What is it? What's wrong?"

"This guy who's got Macy," she said, her voice breathy. "He's a monster."

"Yeah, no kiddin'. His body count is up over thirty, and that's what the FBI knows about."

The teen nibbled her lower lip nervously. "No, Arlan. I mean, he's really a monster. He's *not* a human."

Chapter 28

Macy carefully assessed her surroundings as she drove up the long, unlit driveway toward *home*. They were only an hour from the Philly airport, but in a rural area, near a ski resort whose name she recognized from billboards. She'd passed very close to this house at least once in the past couple of years. She had driven right by him and never known he was so close.

Macy saw lights in the distance, but the property was isolated. On foot, she guessed it was at least half a mile to the nearest porch light and the terrain was both hilly and rocky.

"I sold the orchard after you went to college, Marceline. Just too many good memories," he said nostalgically.

Macy wondered if the *good memories* included killing and burying his mother in the orchard, but she knew better than to ask.

"You knew when, where I went to college?"

"Of course I did." He sounded hurt.

A Cape Cod–style house loomed ahead; she could make out a front porch and shutters. It looked nice from what she could see of it in the dark.

"Teddy, can I ask you something?"

"Certainly, dearest."

"When you . . ."—it took her a second to find her voice—"when you killed my family, did you already . . . like me?"

He looked at her. "Of course I liked you, Marceline. You were pretty, though distant, I must say. You never even said hello when I handed you a bag of apples. Pull up there in front of the garage." He pointed. "But if you're asking me if I spared you that night on purpose, I have to be honest with you, dear. I did not. It wasn't until later that I realized that we were meant to be together."

"You realized?" she asked. It was all she could do not to scream at him. She stopped the car in front of the door, as instructed, and put it into park.

"It was fate. It was meant to be, you and I. That's why you were gone that night. At a sleepover on a school night. You weren't meant to be there when I arrived."

She wondered where he'd gotten the sleepover crap, but then remembered that that's what had been printed in the papers. Someone's idea of protecting her.

"When I got there to do what had to be done and saw you weren't there, I knew that I had been set on a path. You and I had been set on a path together. Ending here, I suppose." He opened his window, looking out. "I wish I could see the moon, but it's too cloudy," he worried. "It would be better if I could see the moon."

"Wait a minute. Go back." Macy tried to keep her voice even, but she had to understand. If she died tonight, she wanted to die knowing. "You said when you got there to do what had to be done, you meant killing them. Why did it *have to be done*, Teddy?"

"Mother." He picked the gun up off the floorboards. He unscrewed the silencer from it.

"What does your mother have to do with killing my family?"

"I did it to shut her up. Sit tight." He jumped out of the

car, taking the pistol with him, and went to the side of the garage and punched keys on a key pad.

Macy just sat there, hands on the steering wheel, staring at the garage door as it went up. She supposed she should have considered making a run for it, but he had the pistol and they were so close. She'd never get away.

Teddy waved the pistol at her, signaling for her to pull in.

Macy eased her car into the spotless, empty garage. Lights overhead illuminated a row of shiny shovels, hung precisely. There had to be a dozen of them, all nearly identical.

Macy tried not to think about his shovel collection or what he did with it. What was interesting was that, to her knowledge, he always used tools available to him at the crime scene. Was he keeping some kind of score?

He walked around and opened the door for her. "Let's go inside, Marceline; it's been a long evening and we're both weary. Now, no funny business." He didn't exactly point the pistol at her, but he made it clear what he meant.

At the steps to the house, he hit the button on the wall that closed the garage door and then used a key from his pocket to unlock the door. He pushed it open, allowing her to enter the dark laundry room first. Inside the laundry room, he closed the door, turned the dead bolt knob, and flipped on the light.

"Mother! We're home!" He pushed open a door off the laundry room. "The powder room, if you need it."

There had been a fatal accident on Route 1 and they'd had to sit nearly an hour while no traffic moved northbound. Macy had to pee badly. She'd asked Teddy to stop at a rest stop, but he'd refused, suggesting it wasn't safe.

She stepped inside, turned on the light and closed the door.

"I'll wait here for you," he said. "Don't worry, I won't listen to you tinkle."

His eerie, juvenile giggle made her want to vomit.

She pulled down her shorts and sat on the john.

"Mother, we're home?" What the hell was that all about? Didn't he just get finished telling her he'd murdered his mother and planted her in the orchard back in Missouri?

Macy rested her forearms on her thighs, leaning forward. There was no window in the bathroom. No way to escape. Only a place to catch a breather. Figure out what she was going to do.

For a fleeting moment she thought of Arlan. It was after midnight. Surely he was concerned that she hadn't shown up for dinner. Or was he lying in bed right now, watching the ceiling fan spin, waiting for the late night visit she often paid him?

That was a better guess. And it was her own fault he was at home in bed. Not out looking for her. Not calling Fia to tell her something was wrong. Not even worried. Arlan was only following Macy's rules. She had wanted a relationship with no emotional strings attached and people with no emotional strings died alone, with no one looking for them.

There was a light tap on the bathroom door. "Marceline, are you all right?"

She reached for the toilet paper; its end had been folded in a point like maids sometimes did in hotel bathrooms. "Just a second," she called. She finished and stepped out of the bathroom.

"Hot tea? A cold drink? What can I offer you?"

They entered the kitchen and he flipped on the light. It was a country kitchen with yellow walls and oak cabinets. An oak table with four chairs occupied one end of the room. No knickknacks on the counters. No mail tossed on the table. The room looked like a staged showroom in a furniture store.

"How about something to eat? I don't know about you, but I'm famished." His expression grew worrisome. "Unless, of course, you're tired. I've prepared your room for you. I know you won't like the bars on the windows or the locks on the door, but other than that, it's a nice room. I painted it purple for you, just like your bedroom in Missouri."

She'd been thirteen when she and her mother painted her bedroom purple. She wanted to ask him if he'd put up Metallica posters on the walls, but she kept that thought to herself. "Something to eat would be great. I'm hungry, too." She wanted to stall being locked in the purple cage for as long as possible. At least here she might find the opportunity to escape or knock his block off. Something.

"Why not sit on a stool at the breakfast bar?" He waved the pistol, indicating she should move to the other side of the kitchen island, which was higher than the countertop. He set the pistol down, again out of her reach, but within his own. "Let's see." He opened the refrigerator. It may have had more stuff in it than the garage, but each item was arranged equally as neatly. Condiment jars lined up in straight rows, labels facing forward. Milk and juice cartons placed just so. "How about grilled cheese sandwiches and tomato soup?" He leaned on the door of the refrigerator to look over his shoulder at her. "I know that's kind of a winter meal, but it's quick and I make an excellent grilled cheese sandwich with just the right amount of butter and cheese to be ooey gooey without being greasy."

The man was a total freak. She forced a smile. "Grilled cheese would be great."

Macy glanced around the kitchen, noting the cordless phone on the wall near the archway that led into the living room. If she could get to the phone, she could dial 911. "So you live here with your mother?"

He set a pack of cheese slices and a covered butter dish on the counter in front of her. "Marceline, weren't you listening, dearest? Mother's dead. I smothered her with a blue bath towel and I buried her in the orchard under the Bartlett pear tree. She always liked Bartlett pears."

"But when we arrived, you called into the house, 'Mother, we're home.'"

He exhaled, leaning over to take a loaf of white bread out of a cabinet. Macy hated squishy white bread.

"Do we have to talk about this?" he asked tersely.

"We don't have to, Teddy." She did the looking through her eyelashes thing again. "But I'd like to. If you and I . . . if we're going to be together," she said, "I want to know everything there is to know about you."

"That's nice." He took a small saucepan and a frying pan from the cupboard. Then a can of soup. She noted that the other cans of soup on the shelf were lined up perfectly, labels facing forward.

"So . . . does she live somewhere else or will I have to share you with her?"

He giggled as he removed a wooden spoon and spatula from a drawer.

Macy waited.

"It's just you and me, Marceline, I swear to you."

"So she's not here?"

He hesitated. "Actually, I'm not sure."

"You're not sure?"

He placed both hands on the countertop, leaning toward her as if they were great confidantes. "You're going to think this is crazy, but . . .

Not any crazier than any of the rest, she thought. "No, I'm not."

"I think Mother's a ghost," he whispered.

She lifted her eyebrows. She couldn't help herself. "A ghost? Really?"

"I hear her," he whispered.

She thought she noticed him twitch but it was so quick, she couldn't be sure.

"Can *I* hear her?" she said, speaking equally soft.

"I don't think so. She haunts me because she hates me." He removed four slices of bread from the bag and then took his time in twisting the plastic bag just right before putting the tie back on to secure it. "She hates me, you know."

No surprise there, since you murdered her, Macy thought. It was strange, but she couldn't keep wild thoughts from popping up, even in this dire situation. It was just all so . . . surreal. As if it was a dream, but of course it wasn't.

"Why do you say that?" Macy asked. "What makes you think she hates you?"

"She always hated me. Since I was born. *Rape bastard,* that's what she called me." Again, the twitch, this time more obvious. He put the frying pan on the stove, then the saucepan. "She was attacked while sleeping in her bed when she was twenty years old. She was somewhere in Europe on a trip through her college. Her parents never believed she was raped. They thought she had *ruined* herself with one of the boys she was traveling with."

Against her will, Macy felt a pang of empathy for him. A child of rape, despised by his mother? No wonder he turned into a homicidal maniac. But that was unfair. Some children of rape became doctors, lawyers, truck drivers. It was no excuse.

"I'm so sorry, Teddy. It must have been hard for you, growing up."

He smiled, shy again, not making eye contact as he opened the soup can. "Not always. Sometimes she was nice. Sometimes, she called me her Teddy Bear." He looked up at her, grinning proudly.

"So Teddy's not your real name?"

He shook his head. "Marvin. Marvin Clacker. She didn't give me a middle name."

"You were raised alone? No brothers or sisters?"

He shook his head. "Just me and Mother and the grandparents, when I was young. We kept to ourselves. Mother was . . . embarrassed by the situation. The orchard was her parents' before they passed. She buried them in the orchard, too. Only not under the Bartlett pear." He looked at her. "Water or milk?"

Macy was the one who twitched this time. She was having a hard time following Teddy's bizarre story while choosing from the late night dinner menu. Had Teddy really just confessed that his mother had murdered his grandparents and buried them in the orchard? Was there an entire graveyard there?

"Marceline, do you like your tomato soup made with milk or water?"

"Water, please," Macy managed. She stared at her hands on the countertop. In a sick way, everything he was telling her made sense. It made sense why he did what he did. He was burying family after family, trying to rebury his mother. Trying to get rid of her. But why the grotesque disposal of the bodies? Why bury them with their arms over their heads? She had to ask. "Teddy? Could I ask you something . . . about the families that . . . you did what had to be done. Why did you bury them with their hands in the air?"

He struck a macabre pose, arms over his head, fingers splayed. "An orchard," he said sweetly. "I always bury them in an orchard like Mother and the grandparents, but orchards are hard to find, so I make my own."

"You make your own?" For a moment she thought she really would vomit.

He struck the pose again. "Don't I look like a sapling if I stand like this?" Before Macy could respond, Teddy turned his head sharply, letting his hands fall to his sides. "Hush, Mother. Please."

She watched him carefully. "Is . . . is your mother here, now?"

"She says I shouldn't have brought you here. She says you don't love me. That you could never love me. She says I'll have to kill you." He glanced at the dark window. "Good thing you can't see the moon tonight. I love it, but it makes it hard for me to think sometimes, the moon."

The way he said it made her skin crawl. She had to get out of here. She wouldn't survive until morning, she knew it in her bones. "Teddy, please don't listen to her," Macy said softly. "Listen to me." Again, the forced smile. "Your Marceline. We've waited a long time to be together."

"A long time to be together," he repeated, filling the empty can with water from the faucet.

She watched him go through the simple preparations, thinking that she had to keep Teddy talking. He was so crazy, so starved for attention, for love, maybe there was a chance she could talk her way out of this.

Teddy set the saucepan down hard, so hard that red water splashed over the side, onto the immaculate stove top. "I'm not listening." He covered his ears with his hands and spoke loudly. "I'm not listening, Mother. You're dead with worms crawling in and out of your eyes," he said petulantly. "You're dead, and I'm alive."

"That's right." Macy rose off the stool and walked around the counter, into the kitchen. "You're alive, Teddy." She couldn't bring herself to touch him, but she stood there beside him. "Look at me," she said. "You're alive."

His lower lip trembled. "She hurt me. She hit me." He pulled up one leg of his long shorts. "She burned me."

Macy couldn't help but stare at what appeared to be small round scars on his overly hairy leg. Cigarette burns?

"I'm so sorry," she whispered, surprised by the emotion she felt for him. She still hated him, but now she also pitied him. She found herself looking into his face. He had grown a serious five o'clock shadow in the last few hours; she wasn't sure how she hadn't noticed it until now. In fact, under the bright light of the fluorescent kitchen lamp, she took note that Teddy was a particularly hairy man.

And he smelled funny. Strong and musky. She hadn't smelled him in the car.

She took a step back from him. "That was wrong of her, Teddy, to hurt you like that." She glanced quickly at the pistol on the counter. It was still just out of her reach, but if she could distract him . . .

Macy had never handled a gun in her life. But she'd seen enough cops and bad guys on TV fire them to guess what to do with it if she managed to get to it.

Teddy squeezed his eyes shut. "Shut up!" he shouted. "Shut up!"

"Me, Teddy?" Macy whispered, inching her way closer to the counter. He was so distracted by the voice he heard. Maybe too distracted to realize what she was doing until it was too late. "Do you want *me* to be quiet?"

"No! No, I want to talk to you. It's her. She won't shut up." He covered his ears with his hands again, squeezing his eyes shut. "She says I can't trust you. She says—"

Macy never made the conscious decision to go for the pistol. One second she was standing in front of Teddy, the next, she was lunging for the gun on the counter.

Teddy's eyes flew open. His hands fell from his ears. "You promised," he screamed at her. "You swore on your mother's grave!"

As Macy sprung for the pistol, she knocked into Teddy, pushing him backward. Her hand closed over the handle of the gun and wrenched around, grappling to get a proper grip on it.

"You promised," he shouted, his voice suddenly deep and gravely. "You promised on your dead mother's grave."

She whipped around, pointing the pistol at the tearful Teddy. She wrapped her finger around the trigger. "I lied."

Macy didn't know what happened next. Maybe she jumped from the present to some dream world. Maybe she'd been dreaming all along. One instant she was staring at forty-something, balding Marvin Clacker in his madras shorts, the next instant, a hairy half-man, half-wolf creature loomed over her, fangs bared.

Macy screamed and pulled the trigger.

Chapter 29

"Did you hear that? Turn here! Turn here," Kaleigh shouted, pointing repeatedly.

They were traveling fifty miles an hour down a country road on wet blacktop. "Here?" Arlan hit his brakes hard.

"Hurry!" she insisted.

He made a sharp left and swung the truck onto a gravel driveway. "Sorry," he muttered, glancing up in the rearview mirror at Fia, who was driving a bureau car. He couldn't see her face because of her headlights, but he could imagine Fia was cussing a blue streak, using several variations of her favorite, *Mary, Mother of God.*

"Is she here?" Arlan hit the gas, speeding down the bumpy road.

"Did you hear that? Did you hear it?" Kaleigh's face was pale. "A gunshot. A . . . a scream. Growling. He's growling at her!"

Kaleigh sounded close to hysterical. The girl was scared out of her pants. She wasn't making sense.

"Growling?" Arlan asked.

She held on to the armrest on the truck door to keep from being thrown too hard in the confines of her seat belt. "It doesn't make any sense," she cried. "I kept thinking it didn't make any sense."

"What didn't make any sense?" Arlan hit a pothole and the truck bounced violently.

"In my vision. The man who kidnapped Macy, he wasn't . . . he wasn't a man."

Arlan suddenly got a bad feeling. It had never occurred to him or Fia that Teddy was anything but an evil human. If they were dealing with something else, the two of them and a teenager might not have a big enough arsenal to fight it. "What *was* he?"

"I don't know. It was like . . . a wolf driving the car." She covered her face with her hands. "I'm sorry." She shook her head. "That sounds crazy. That's why I didn't tell you."

"A wolf? Anything else you can tell me?" The bad feeling was getting worse.

"It wasn't exactly a wolf, but like . . . a wolf man. All hairy with a snout. And . . . and he smelled bad, like . . . dog pee."

Arlan swore under his breath as he speed-dialed Fia. Spotting a house in the distance ahead, he cut his headlights. Fia, behind him in the Crown Vic, immediately did the same thing.

"What? Are we four-wheeling, here?" Fia demanded when she picked up the phone.

"Something's happened in the house. We have to get there fast. Kaleigh thinks she heard a gunshot."

"I didn't hear a gunshot."

"Fee, we don't have time to argue," Arlan said tersely.

"You're right." She sounded breathy. Pumped up. She had to be thinking they might finally be so close to stopping this bastard.

"I'm sorry," she said in a rare apology. "She get anything else besides a gunshot?"

Arlan glanced at Kaleigh on the seat beside him. He wasn't sure how much to say in front of the teen, especially when he wasn't clear on what, exactly, they were about to encounter. "Just be ready," he said into the cell phone. "This is going to get ugly."

The gun exploded with a bone-rattling bang and the smell of burning black powder. It jolted Macy's arm all the way to her shoulder and she stumbled to stay on her feet. The monster that had been Teddy a moment before howled with pain and staggered back.

And she still didn't wake up from the dream.

Run. It was the only thing Macy knew to do. But where? Which way? Deeper into the house, there might be doors she could lock herself behind, but her instinct was to get away, get as far away as possible.

Macy sprinted for the garage door, the way she'd come. She knew Teddy had the car keys and the creature wasn't wearing pants; she wouldn't be able to take her car and she had seen no other car.

She raced through the laundry room, slamming into the door to the garage. The dead bolt. She fumbled with it, one handed, still gripping the pistol, and unlocked it. He . . . *It* was getting up off the floor. She heard its nails scraping on the tile. The thing was howling like . . . like nothing she'd ever heard, human or otherwise. Her blood ran cold. She thought she'd hit it with the single shot she'd pulled off, but if she had, obviously the gunshot had not been fatal.

It was coming after her.

She smelled his hot breath on the back of her neck as she heard the dead bolt slide free and she jerked the door open. She bounded down the steps, having the sense to punch the automatic door button.

The creature howled with fury. It barked and growled as it lurched after her.

Terror-stricken, Macy kept running, the gun still in her

hand. The garage door was rising, but too slowly. Too slowly! He would catch her before she made it outside.

In a split-second decision, Macy threw herself on the immaculate cement floor behind her car. As she fell, she hit her head so hard that it bounced and she saw stars. The beast fell to all fours and swiped at her with his paw. White-hot pain ripped through her calf.

Macy rolled under the door, trying to take aim and squeezing the trigger as she went.

Arlan slammed hard on the brakes of the pickup as the garage door went up. The truck fishtailed and he heard Fia's tires slide on the gravel.

"Here it comes!" Kaleigh screamed. Before Arlan could get the truck into park, she was out of her seat belt and throwing open the passenger side door.

"Kaleigh!" Arlan flung his door open. "You have to stay in the truck!" But his words were lost to the night as the teenager raced up the driveway.

At that moment, someone—Macy—rolled out from under the garage door that was only one quarter of the way up. A gun fired.

"Fee!" Arlan shouted, running after Kaleigh.

"Behind you," Fia called. He heard her footsteps.

Macy rolled into the driveway and bounced up with startling agility. It was at that moment that Arlan realized she had a gun. He could barely see it in her hand in the dim light, but he could smell its discharge.

"Kaleigh, get back here! Macy! It's Arlan! Don't shoot."

The predator crawled out from under the door and staggered to its feet. Blood oozed from a wound in the left shoulder, matting the long fur. It was pissed off as Arlan had ever seen one.

Kaleigh screamed, still moving forward with the momentum she had built up, scrambling to stop.

"Arlan!" Macy screamed. "It's him! Get the bastard! It's him."

"Holy shit!" Fia shouted. "Arlan, I don't have the right ammo."

"Shoot! Shoot!" Arlan hollered.

Macy passed Kaleigh and suddenly the teen was looking up at the creature. She was so stunned, she couldn't move. She had never seen a werewolf. Never smelled one. At least that she could recall. But there was no doubt in her mind what it was or that it was real.

"Down, Kaleigh," Fia ordered.

The kid had the good sense to drop to the ground. Fia hit the beast with her first shot, but it kept coming at Kaleigh. Fia fired again. The werewolf howled in pain, staggering backward, but remaining upright on its hind paws.

"Jesus!" Macy kept saying. "Jesus, what is it?"

Arlan put out his hand. "Give me the gun!"

Fia fired again. Third shot. She had four more. A silver bullet wasn't necessary to kill a werewolf, but it took plenty of firepower. If Arlan had had an Uzi right now, he'd have been kissing the barrel.

Four.

"Macy, get Kaleigh!" Arlan shouted.

He wasn't at all surprised when Macy turned and ran right at the werewolf. Sweet God, her balls were as big as Fia's.

Fia fired again. Five.

Now the werewolf was seriously pissed. It dropped on all fours and lunged at Fia.

Six.

Thankful that Kaleigh and Macy were out of the line of fire, Arlan took aim and pulled the trigger on the pistol he'd snatched out of Macy's hands.

Fia fired her last bullet. Fur and blood and bits of flesh exploded in the air. And still, it kept coming.

Macy dropped to the ground on top of Kaleigh to protect the teen as the werewolf and Fia collided.

Sweet Jesus, how was Arlan going to get a shot in now? A bullet wound wouldn't kill Fia, but it would injure her and the thought of putting her in further danger was more than Arlan could stand.

"Take the gun!" Arlan flipped the safety on and hurled it at Macy. She caught it and spun it around, aiming in the direction of Fia and the werewolf grappling on the ground.

Arlan flexed his jaw, concentrating on the beast attacking his Fia. He felt the muscles and sinew in his body tighten like bands and his vision grew hazy as the transformation took place. The moment Arlan's front paw hit the ground, he leapt into the air. He landed on the werewolf's back, taking it completely by surprise.

Fia rolled out from under him as Arlan sank his teeth into the back of its neck, clenching his jaw. The werewolf howled with pain and struggled to escape Arlan's grip. *Gun. Macy,* Arlan tried to telepath. In an animal state, the messages were harder to form, harder to send. *Fia!*

Fia sprang to her feet and ran limping toward Macy.

The werewolf managed to knock Arlan off balance and the two rolled, biting and snarling and snapping. Pain ripped through Arlan's back as the creature sank his claws into him. Then, somehow, the werewolf managed to pin him. It bit again and again. Arlan howled, as much from anger as pain. Out of the corner of his yellow eyes, he saw Fia running toward them. She was limping, blood gushing down her leg. A neck wound, too.

Gunshots exploded over and over and the werewolf fell backward, as if hit by a truck. Arlan rolled over, crouching on all fours, tongue lolling, panting hard. He hurt everywhere.

He watched Fia fall to one knee, then eyed the werewolf, which lay quiet on its side. Before his eyes, it morphed into a human.

"He's down," Fia breathed.

Arlan lowered his head and felt his muscles relax. A moment later, in human form again, he got shakily to his feet and walked over to Fia. She was resting her hands on one knee, her head bowed.

"You okay?" he asked.

She nodded, not looking up at him. "Just give me a minute. I've got to get my service weapon. Dropped it in the grass. Check Kaleigh and Macy."

By the light from the garage, Arlan saw Macy sitting in the driveway, cradling Kaleigh in her arms. Kaleigh sobbed, holding tightly to the young woman she barely knew.

"It's all right. It's all right," Macy soothed, rocking the girl as if she were a babe in arms.

Arlan went down on one knee in front of them. "You two okay?" He pushed the hair away from Macy's face so he could get a better look at her. "Macy?"

"We're okay," she whispered. "What . . . what happened? How did you—" She was dazed, her eyes glassy with shock. He knew she was trying to ask him about his metamorphosis, but she couldn't find the right words. The strange thing was, she didn't seem to be afraid of him, or worse, repulsed. "Is he . . . it . . . dead?"

"He's dead." He ran his hand over Kaleigh's back, trying to soothe her.

Macy looked up at Arlan, her own eyes filled with tears. It was the first time he had ever seen her cry. "Good," she said.

Twenty minutes later, Arlan sat in the truck with Macy. Fia was getting ready to call in the shooting. He and Kaleigh would have to hightail it out of here before the swarm of cops arrived. Macy would have to stay to help with the pieces of the puzzle; only he and Fia had already agreed she wouldn't remember anything of the last hour to tell the police.

Marvin Clacker, aka Teddy, a class-one ninth-century Ukrainian werewolf, lay dead in the grass beside his driveway. Fia would have some explaining to do with the FBI, but she'd been in more compromising situations before and survived with her job intact. The fact that she had brought down the Buried Alive Killer would be what mattered most to law enforcement and citizens alike. There would be inquiries, of course, but all would work out in Fia's favor in the end. It always did.

"You sure you're okay?" Arlan repeated, putting his arm around Macy's shoulders, trying to make eye contact with her. He had used gauze from his first-aid kit to wrap her leg wound. She had a bump on the back of the head and a bloody spot marred her beautiful blond hair, but she showed no signs of a concussion. He was bloody and covered with scratches and bites, too, but by morning, they would be barely visible. Another plus to being one of the living dead.

It was dark inside the cab of the truck and she moved her face close to his to look into his eyes. "What was he?" she whispered.

"A werewolf." No sense in lying.

"A werewolf?" she repeated. "But . . . but he looked like a man."

"Didn't you tell Fia he told you he was a child of rape?" After Teddy was dead, Fia had quickly gotten Macy to fill her in on whatever she knew about the killer, so she could get her story straight.

"That's what he said," Macy told him. "He said that his mother hated him because he was a rape bastard."

"She was probably raped by a werewolf, so he was a half-breed. It's easier to fit into everyday life if you're half, but they usually end up being nut jobs," he explained. The fact that he was only half werewolf also explained why they were able to kill him relatively easily.

"Half-breed werewolf?" she questioned.

He nodded. "Probably Ukrainian heritage—on the sire's side. They're rare but nasty. I haven't seen one in centuries."

She looked away, staring out the windshield of his truck, dazed by not just what she had seen, but by what she was hearing now. "And you . . . you turned into a wolf and you fought it and you saved Fia."

"You think that's what you saw?"

"I know that's what I saw."

"And you're all right with that?"

"I guess. No." Her eyes widened. "How could . . ."

He exhaled, smoothing her hair, kissing the top of her head. "It's complex, Macy, but the best explanation I can give you is that God's world is far more complex that you know. Than any of us knows."

Her brow furrowed. "Am I dreaming?" she asked.

"You want to be?" He kissed her cheek, tenderly. She'd been through so much. He was so glad it was over for her. Of course it would never be completely over—he of all people knew that. But maybe now, with Teddy dead, she could start recovering from the loss of her family all those years ago and the guilt for not dying with them.

She closed her eyes. "I think I *would* like it to be a dream. There's no way any of this makes any sense." She opened her eyes for a second. "But I still want him dead."

He nuzzled her neck.

"Arlan," she murmured, clinging to him. "He really is dead? The . . . whatever it . . . he was that killed my family. Am I free?"

"The monster that killed your family is now dead, Macy." He kissed her sweet, soft neck and then took a tentative, practice nip. "He'll never harm anyone again." He kissed her neck once more. "You're free." And then, before she could speak again, Arlan sank his canines into her.

The taste of her hot blood made him dizzy. Greedy for more. She relaxed in his arms and fell unconscious.

Pleasure stabbed his body. She was so sweet, so— That was probably enough blood, but—

"Arlan." Fia leaned in the passenger's side truck window. "You just want to erase her memory of what happened here, not make her one of us," she chastised softly.

Embarrassed to have been caught in his selfishness, Arlan lifted his head, wiped his mouth, and then her neck, where two tiny trickles of blood oozed from his bite marks. Still holding her in his arms, he slid toward the passenger's door. "Let me out. Where you want her?"

"Right there in the driveway near the door. I called it in, so you and Kaleigh need to hit the road." She followed him up the dark driveway toward the garage where Kaleigh waited.

"You going to be all right, here?"

"Got everything under control. Local cops"—she stopped long enough to listen to the sirens—"will be here momentarily. FBI as soon as they can. An hour and fifteen, hour and a half, they estimated."

Arlan kneeled in the driveway and gently laid the unconscious Macy on the gravel. "You'll bring her back to Clare Point?"

"Initial questioning shouldn't last long. I doubt she'll remember even arriving here. That bump on her head gives us an easy explanation. But she'll have to go to the hospital. They'll keep her overnight. We should be back in Clare Point tomorrow."

Hating to leave Macy, but knowing he had to, Arlan stood up. "You sure this is going to work out?" He searched Fia's dark eyes, trying not to look worried. "With the FBI and all?"

"I'll take care of it." She rubbed his forearm and he closed his eyes for a moment, comforted by her touch.

Then he turned away. "Kaleigh?"

The teen loped toward him, seeming none worse for the wear after her first experience, at least of this life cycle, with a werewolf. "Ready." She walked past him. "You think we could stop at an all-night McDonald's? I'm starved."

Fia's and Arlan's gazes met and they both smiled.

Later, he telepathed Fia.

Later.

Chapter 30

Naked, Macy lay on her side in bed beside Arlan, propped up on her elbow. In his sleep, there was a half smile on his sensuous lips, his dark hair pushed behind his ears, curling enticingly at his neck. The strong brow, the high forehead and broad jaw. She couldn't be certain, but he may have been the most attractive man she had ever slept with. What she *was* sure of was that he was the kindest, the most good-hearted, the most selfless.

And she would hate to leave him.

But leave him she would. They had both known that inevitable fact since the first night they had made love in that hotel room in Virginia.

She brushed her fingertips over his bare chest, taking care not to wake him. This was the way she wanted to remember him. Relaxed, smiling. She dragged her gaze over his nude body, trying to put to memory every hard plane and muscle.

Macy had made it through the initial FBI interviews. She told the police what she remembered about the night Marvin Clacker kidnapped her, but at some point in trying to escape she had apparently fallen and hit her head, causing a mild concussion. She still couldn't remember anything beyond passing the Philadelphia airport.

Apparently, when Arlan had realized she was missing and called Fia, Fia had followed a hunch. Marvin Clacker had been listed as a neighbor on the original police list of people interviewed after her family's death. She had already tracked him down to the address where he had taken Macy. Lucky hunch, Fia had told Macy with a chuckle in that first interview. Her ex-boyfriend, Special Agent Duncan, had told Macy that *Fia gets all the big breaks.*

Thinking about Fia made Macy smile. Fia had believed in Macy. She'd followed her hunch and tracked Teddy down, rescuing Macy. Now Teddy was dead and he would never torture and murder another family. Her parents and Minnie and Mariah could truly be laid to rest in Macy's mind.

Taking care not to jostle Arlan and wake him, Macy eased out of the bed. She dressed slowly, standing in a puddle of moonlight on the floor. Perhaps moonlight should have had a bad connotation for her, but it didn't. In a way, moonlight now represented survival to her.

Dressed in shorts and a T-shirt, Macy padded barefoot to the other side of the bed. Taking one long, last look at Arlan's handsome face, she leaned down to kiss him. She had wanted to feel his lips on hers one last time, but the way his head was turned, she was afraid she might wake him. Instead, she kissed his neck.

Macy didn't say good-bye.

She walked out of the bedroom, down the dark hall to the front door. Her car was packed and parked at the hotel. She didn't know where she was headed. Maine, maybe. She knew the FBI would look for her, but she hoped they wouldn't look too hard. She'd have to have a new ID made. Maybe change her name.

Macy rested her hand on the doorknob, feeling a little sad. For a fleeting moment when she woke up in that driveway and saw that Teddy was dead, she had thought maybe she was done running. Done roaming. But the truth, she realized, was this was still who she was. A drifter. A woman who didn't lock her car doors and left windows unlatched at night.

Macy opened the front door. As she stepped out, she saw Fia sitting on the step. Macy should have been surprised that Fia was there at one o'clock in the morning, but she wasn't. Macy still wouldn't say she believed in psychic ability, but she would no longer say she disbelieved it. She and Fia had some kind of connection Macy could not explain.

"You're leaving," Fia said, her voice unnaturally soft.

Macy sat down beside her. "Yes."

"We're not finished interviewing you."

"I know." Macy stared out at the darkness, listening to the night sounds, peepers and crickets. Somewhere in the distance, she heard the hoot of an owl.

"We'll have to come looking for you," Fia said.

"I know." She turned to meet Fia's gaze. "But don't expect to find me."

Fia stared straight ahead again, clasping her hands in her lap. She was dressed uncharacteristically in shorts, a T-shirt, and flip-flops, her hair falling across her cheeks in a sleek sheet of dark red. "You didn't tell him you were leaving, did you?"

Fia saw tears in Macy's eyes.

"I'm sorry," Macy said, sniffing and wiping her eyes. "I spent the last fourteen years of my life trying to let myself cry, and now it seems like I can't stop." She lowered her hands from her lovely face. "The thing is, Fee, I'm no good at good-byes."

"He'll be sad you're gone. Hurt you didn't tell him you were going."

"He knew I was going, just not when." Macy rose off

the step, her cheeks damp with tears. "And you'll be here for him, won't you? You'll love him in a way I never can."

Macy followed the sidewalk to the street. She didn't look back and she didn't say good-bye to Fia.

Fia watched Macy walk away until she could no longer see her shining blond hair in the dark. Then she rose, crossed the porch and stepped inside the house.

Fia entered the dark bedroom to see Arlan asleep on his stomach in the middle of his bed. He was naked, his arms stretched out to each side, his cheek pressed into a pillow.

Gazing down at him, Fia slipped out of her flip-flops, wondering how long she had been coming to this. A few weeks? A few decades? The last century or two? Arlan had been telling her for the last thousand years that they were meant to be together.

Maybe he wasn't as wrong as she thought he was.

She pulled her T-shirt over her head and stepped out of her shorts. Lastly, she dropped her lacy black bra and matching panties on the pile. Naked, she slipped into bed beside him and wrapped her arm around his narrow waist, curling up against him, feeling the heat and strength of his body against hers.

Arlan stirred and nuzzled her hair. Then he opened his eyes. "Fee?"

Fia smiled, feeling a heavy sadness in the pit of her stomach. She and Arlan would both miss Macy. "Arlan," she said softly, smoothing his dark hair, which she still thought was too long to be respectable.

He searched her gaze and for a moment they were both lost in the past . . . perhaps a little in the future, where hope still gleamed for the Kahill sept, where redemption by God might still be possible.

"She's gone, isn't she?" he finally asked.

Fia nodded, not trusting herself to speak, closer to tears than she wanted to be.

He rolled onto his side so that they were facing each other. "But you're here."

"I'm here." She looked into his eyes, for once willing to be vulnerable. "And I want you to love me, Arlan," she whispered, her chest so tight she could barely breathe.

He kissed her lips, his attention slow and deliberate.

"Love me," she repeated.

"Ah, darlin'," he breathed huskily, smoothing her hair off her face so that he could gaze into her eyes. "Don't you see that's what I've been trying to do all along?"